STEALING SHIVA

A NOVEL

KATHLEEN ORTNER

STEALING SHIVA
P.O. Box 444
Woodbourne, NY 12788

Stealing Shiva is a work of fiction. All names,
characters, places, and artwork are either invented
or used fictitiously. The incidents described are
make-believe, arising from the author's
imagination. Any similarity to real
persons, living or dead, events, locales,
or organizations is coincidental
and not intended by the author.

Designed by Gerhard Ortner

Edited by Carol Gaskin

First edition published 2015

Manufactured in the United States of America

ISBN: 978-0-986-35261-4

for all the humans on earth who strive to elevate their state of consciousness

Chapter 1

Jessabelle Knox stood with her broken-in white leather tennis shoes planted on a dried-out patch of brown grass. From this withered spot of earth, bumped against the curb bordering an edge of the parking lot at Wally's SUPERCENTER, she searched for her next buyer.

Bright sunlight blared into her theatrical colored contact lenses that rendered her eyes angel blue. Squinting hard, she cupped a hand over her orbs of faked innocence, transforming the hand into her visor, a convenient accessory that traveled well. There was never a need to find space for it in the suitcase she lived out of.

The consumer corral she saw before her contained herds of those four-wheeled mechanical beasts called automobiles. Light sparkled off their painted bodies as the mounts tarried in rows, awaiting the return of their riders from shopping. A Florida state license plate pierced each metal ass pointed in her direction.

It didn't take a glance at a thermometer to know the heat raged here in the Sunshine State. The sweat pooling beneath the stretch cap of her wig with long blonde braids told her that.

Exactly where in Florida she stood, she didn't know, and to tell the truth, it didn't really matter. With its cheap steel roof, gray stucco walls, and "We Sell for Less" motto posted in navy letters on a gray sign, this Wally's looked like the last one she'd visited, and the one before that, and the one before that, and…

She hadn't seen all 5,003 Wally's in America, only about 1,000, or was it more like 1,500? Long ago she'd lost count. But whatever the number, it was enough to know that every automotive/retail/grocery store in the chain looked exactly like the others.

Okay. Maybe not exactly. Wally's of Wolf Whistle, Alaska, shivered inside a thick-walled tomb of ice and snow. In Lei, Hawaii, Wally's frolicked in a storm of tropical breezes, while this Wally's languished under a blazing sun. According to geography and time of year, Wally's externals changed; but whether freezing, sunbathing, or dancing in the wind, the store itself remained the same, from head to toe and from Wolf Whistle to here. When, oh when, would it change?

She'd grown so tired of Wally's one-fits-all store design, it made her absolutely positively sure of one thing: If she wasn't working Wally's, she would never ever gaze upon another Wally's. But work she must, so gaze she did.

Her eyes roved the familiar scene, stopping on a prospect in the form of a man whose tanned and buff arms hung loosely from a ribbed white cotton muscle shirt. He snorted, cleared his throat, and spat a gob so putrid in color, the mere sight of it turned Jessabelle's stomach.

She decided not to approach The Gobber, and not because he grossed her out, but because of the boy in the baseball cap who trailed him. With their unpretentiousness, kids often made her feel like a liar, and that wasn't how she wanted to feel.

Shopping for a better prospect, her eyes traveled a faded canvas of blacktop where sticky impressions of spilled soft drinks shone more brightly than the yellow lines of parking spaces. Splattering its surface were cigarette butts, a clear plastic Pizza Palace cup, the paper covering from a Pizza Palace straw, a crumpled personal-sized Pizza Palace box, and the top half of a broken and chewed yellow wood pencil.

The top half of a broken and chewed yellow wood pencil? Who sits in their car and decides, Gee, I think I'll chew on this pencil awhile, bite it in two, and throw half out the window? But she had no more time to consider the disparate and incomprehensible nature of the garbage in this parking lot. Work was calling. A Neon in the not-neon color of black with hundreds of bugs plastered to its grille zoomed into the lot and parked in Row #3. Out of the car sprang a wiry woman with a head of hair so blonde it looked as if it had been soaked in a tub of industrial-strength bleach. Blondo embarked on her course to Wally's sliding front doors.

Jessabelle clasped the canvas strap of the grass-colored "GoGreen" shopping bag she carried and hefted it higher on her shoulder. She strode across the parking lot toward Blondo, maneuvering around uncollected shopping carts. Luckily she caught her just before the woman advanced into range of Wally's security cameras. "Excuse me, ma'am."

Blondo stopped and turned her chiseled features in Jessabelle's direction. Judging by the fine lines on her forehead, she was older than Jessabelle had first thought.

Jessabelle positioned herself before Blondo so as not to

invade her space or step on the bright orange wad of bubble-gum melted on the blacktop between them. "There's been a terrible accident," Jessabelle said. "It's Grampa! He was hit by a Mack truck!"

"Oh honey," Blondo said. "I'm sorry it wasn't a moped."

Jessabelle blinked, then stared at Blondo in disbelief. Had the woman really just said she was sorry Grampa didn't get hit by a moped?

"That must have sounded terribly unfeeling," Blondo admitted. "I just meant that if you've got to get hit by some-thing, a Mack truck is about the worst you can do."

"Oh," Jessabelle said. "I see what you're saying. Finding yourself flattened to the grill of a Mack truck is definitely high on the scale of disasters. It nearly killed Grampa." She swiped at an imaginary tear.

"I'm so sorry." Blondo nodded.

"They rushed him to the hospital," Jessabelle continued in a shaky voice, loaded with artificial grief. "He needs an operation, but the hospital won't operate until they have their money."

"Damn hospitals!" Blondo uttered in sympathy. "Won't his insurance cover it?"

Jessabelle took a deep breath, blew it out. "He doesn't have any. He's just a poor farmer, a humble man with no cash in the bank. But once, he saved a woman's life, and her hus-band rewarded him with three twenty-four-karat gold bars." Jessabelle opened her GoGreen canvas bag and showed Blondo three metal bars inside. They gleamed in the sun.

"Wow!" Blondo exclaimed. "That husband must have been really grateful."

"He did own a gold mine. And Grampa wasn't the spend-ing type. All these years, he kept the bars under his mattress for a rainy day." Jessabelle paused for dramatic effect before going on. "Today thunder cracks. Lightning fills the sky. And rain falls heavily upon the earth."

Confusion spread over Blondo's face as she gazed up toward the bright and sunny sky. "But it's a beautiful day."

Oh boy, thought Jessabelle. *This one's got the brains of an amoeba.*

"For you, it might be," Jessabelle said. "But for Grampa, it's a very dark day. He's crushed in a million pieces, near death, just waiting for the doctors to save his life. I'm selling his gold bars to pay his medical expenses." Jessabelle brought up one of the bars from the bottom of her bag and held it before Blondo. Sunlight illuminated "24k" etched onto it front and center. "Please buy this, and help me save Grampa," she pleaded. "It's worth twenty thousand dollars."

Blondo gaped at the thought. "I'm sorry about your grampa, but I don't have twenty thousand dollars."

"I'll take whatever you can give me."

"If it's worth that much, why don't you take it to the bank and sell it there?"

Jessabelle sighed. "I wish I could. But here in America, I can't just go into a bank and sell gold. Back in the old country where Grampa immigrated from, I could just walk into a bank and they'd give me twenty thousand dollars cash for this block. But here it takes time, and right now that's one thing Grampa doesn't have. Time. He only has one, maybe two hours at the most, and then I'll lose him." Jessabelle sniffled, scrunched her face, and choked back a sob.

Uncle Trix approached wearing an Armani suit and tie, carrying a Prada briefcase. "Sorry to butt in, miss," he said. "But I couldn't help overhearing your plight. Mind if I have a look at the gold?"

"No sir." She passed him the bar.

Blondo watched Uncle Trix weigh it in his palm and examine it closely. "I'll give you ten thousand dollars for it," he said, handing the block back to Jessabelle. He pointed to a glass office complex across the road. "See that building over there?"

"Umm hmm."

"That's where my office is. I'll go there now and get the cash."

"Okay, but Grampa doesn't have much time, so could you hurry?"

"I'll be fast," he said and rushed off.

"Hope your grampa gets well soon," said Blondo, making a move to leave.

Jessabelle grabbed at Blondo's arms, hyperventilating and collapsing to the pavement for effect. Blondo reeled, then knelt beside her, placing a hand on her elbow.

"Are you okay?"

"How can I be okay when I'm soooo worried about Grampa?" Jessabelle wailed. "He's the only family I have in this world."

"You look terrible. I think you could use an ambulance." Blondo pulled a cell phone from the red fake leather sling she wore over her shoulder.

"No!" Jessabelle pushed the phone back toward Blondo's purse. "Put that away. One ambulance in a day is enough. I'll be okay." She sat up, striving to appear perkier. "The fear of losing Grampa, it just overwhelmed me. Please just stay with me until that man comes back, and I'll be fine."

Blondo fanned Jessabelle's face with her hand.

Uncle Trix returned carrying an envelope stuffed full of cash. "Here's twenty thousand dollars," he said and gave her the envelope.

Jessabelle frowned as if confused. "But I only asked for ten thousand."

"I'm giving you ten from me and ten from my partner. He knows a good deal when he sees it and wanted to get in on the action."

Jessabelle watched Blondo watch her as she deliberately counted the money, slowly enough for Blondo to get a good look at the faces of the presidents. "Yep, that's twenty thousand all right." She handed Uncle Trix two metal blocks. He slipped one into each of the side pockets on his suit jacket. "Thanks so so much, sir. I'll be sure to tell Grampa about the saint who saved his life."

Uncle Trix looked straight into Blondo's eyes. "If I were you," he said, "I wouldn't miss this opportunity." Then he walked away.

"I don't have ten thousand dollars," Blondo said, looking crestfallen.

"Thanks to that kind man," Jessabelle said, "I've already got twenty thousand. The hospital wants twenty-two thousand to save Grampa's life. I'll give you this block for two thousand."

Blondo took a deep breath. "You mean, if I give you two thousand, I'll get twenty thousand in return?"

"Yes, ma'am," Jessabelle said. "That is correct."

"So I'll make"—she paused to do the arithmetic— "eighteen thousand, and at the same time do a good deed."

"Yes," Jessabelle said again, carefully enunciating the word. "Yes."

Slowly, Blondo began to nod, and kept on nodding until that nod turned into a smile. "Okay," she said. "I'll do it. Only one problem."

"What's that?" Jessabelle asked.

"I don't have the money on me. I have to get it from the bank."

"That's not a problem."

"Okay. Let's go." Blondo hooked her arm in Jessabelle's, spun her around, and did a skip-step in the opposite direction, propelling Jessabelle along with her. Together, they tramped back to the black Neon. "Here are the keys." Blondo lifted

Jessabelle's arm and slapped a ring of keys with a pink plastic heart dangling from it into Jessabelle's palm.

"You want me to drive?" Jessabelle asked. "I don't even know where we're going."

"I give good directions," Blondo said with a wink.

"What if I crack your car?"

"If that happens, it's okay." Blondo darted over to the passenger side of the car and hopped in. Just before she slammed shut the door, she called out, "I'm getting rid of this old car. As soon as I get that eighteen grand, I'll buy a new one."

Jessabelle trudged around to the driver's side and climbed in behind the wheel of the car, its dash weathered and dull. Foam oozed from a tear at the edge of the white bucket seat on which Jessabelle established her rump. She fidgeted with a knob on the side of the seat, adjusting it to accommodate her long, lean legs.

"For so long," Blondo said, "I've wanted a new car."

Jessabelle locked the seatbelt around her waist and shoulders, then tried a couple of keys until one of them fit the ignition. She started the engine, threw the car in reverse, and stamped her foot on the gas. The Neon promptly sailed back into the metal poles marking the shopping cart cage.

"Hey," Blondo said. "We're not in a shopping cart. We won't fit in there." She threw her head back, stretching her adam's apple, opening her mouth. A laugh like a cartoon hyena poured forth.

"Sorry," Jessabelle said.

"It's okay. In fact, anything that happens today is okay, because I've won the lottery!"

Jessabelle slammed the gearshift into drive and headed for the road.

Out on the road, Blondo tuned into an oldies station on the radio and belted out the song "Don't Worry Be Happy."

At the bank, Jessabelle refused to go inside with Blondo

for practical reasons involving security cameras. Parked at the back of the tan brick bank building with about a dozen different industrial-style ventilation ducts on its roof, she waited in the Neon for Blondo.

She'd made a sale, no doubt about that. All signs were present. She and Blondo were at Bank U.S.A. Blondo already knew how she'd spend the eighteen thousand dollars. So why didn't Jessabelle feel like singing? She knew she should feel happy, and at this point, she usually did. So why didn't she now?

Instead she felt a strong desire—not the desire for two thousand dollars, but a longing so deep it practically brought tears to her eyes. It was to get out of this car. Right now! March over to that metal dumpster, throw away this life she led, and run as far as her tennis shoes would take her, away from lies.

She remembered planning her career at the age of ten. Sitting in this car under these circumstances was nowhere in those plans. She wanted to be a legitimate special-effects makeup artist, creating characters for movies and plays that made people feel good to be members of the human race, inspiring them toward noble actions.

She wanted to be good, to do the right thing.

The car door opened, and Blondo hopped in beside her. She handed Jessabelle a bank envelope. Jessabelle dumped the cash from inside it, then counted twenty $100 bills. She pronounced, "Yep, it's all here." But she just couldn't bring herself to give Blondo the block in exchange for the money. "I have something to tell you," Jessabelle said.

"What is it?" Blondo asked.

In search of the right words, Jessabelle began, "Umm, umm—"

"You want to back out of the deal, don't you?"

"Yeah. That's it. While you were in the bank, I got a

call from the hospital. They'll do the operation for twenty thousand dollars. I have enough money. I don't need yours."

Jessabelle set the money on the cracked console between them. Blondo snapped it up. "But we had a deal."

"I know, but it turns out I don't need your money. So the deal's off."

"Well, I need that eighteen thousand dollars for my new car."

"No you don't," Jessabelle said. "You didn't have it this morning, and I'm sure this car was fine then."

"Little Sister, you are not talking your way out of this deal. You will take this money."

"I can't."

"I went through all this trouble to get it for you. You'll take it!" Blondo set the cash back on the console. "And give me that gold block!"

"Don't Worry Be Happy" had given way to "Money— That's What I Want." And the cartoon hyena had become a flesh and blood animal deprived of its favorite food: Gold. Blondo raised her hands, her fingers bent like claws. She bared her teeth. Jessabelle thought she heard her growl.

Blondo lunged toward Jessabelle. Jessabelle shrank back, bumping her head on the driver's side window.

Blondo bent right over Jessabelle's knees, grappling for the bag at her feet. She sunk a hand in the bag until she latched onto a gold block.

With a karate chop to Blondo's wrist, Jessabelle knocked the block out of her hand. Then she splayed her hand against Blondo's chest and pushed. "Hold on," she said, muscling Blondo back into her own seat. Shock and fear vibrated in Blondo's eyes, and in their intensity, Jessabelle's resolve to do the right thing crumbled. "If you insist, I'll give it to you." She heard Blondo breathe a sigh of relief. "Let's just be civilized."

"Yes, civilized," Blondo agreed.

Jessabelle collected the cash envelope from the console, stashed it in her bag, and grasped a metal block. In the light through the windshield, it shone more like a penny than a gold dollar, but it didn't matter. Jessabelle knew Blondo was so busy imagining it to be what she wanted, she couldn't really see it. She handed Blondo the block.

"Thank you," Blondo said.

"Sure thing," answered Jessabelle. "Now can we go back to Wally's? I need to get my car and get to the hospital."

"Okay. Do you mind if I drive?"

"No." Jessabelle got out and crossed the front of the car to get to the other side, moving like a semi-deflated party balloon caught in a slow breeze. Maybe if she'd told Blondo the whole truth, the situation would've turned out differently.

But how could she? How could she say, "I've conned you into buying a brass bar that cost five dollars for two thousand dollars?" Blondo would've been mad. She could've called the cops, and instead of cruising out of town a few grand richer, as planned, she and Uncle Trix would be running from the law.

Through the front windshield, Jessabelle saw Blondo climb right over the console, positioning herself behind the steering wheel. Jessabelle rounded the front corner of the vehicle to get to the passenger side, grazing its hood with her fingertips. Suddenly the metal slipped out from underneath her fingers. Her hand dropped through air. Tires screeched.

The Neon plunged backward, skidding to a stop. Its window dropped about three inches. Into that space, Blondo thrust her mouth and yelled, "I'm so sorry, honey. Really I am. But I'm afraid you might change your mind again." She threw the car in drive and streaked out of the parking lot, leaving Jessabelle and a fresh pair of skid marks behind.

Jessabelle exhaled her last bit of breath, then sucked in

another deep breath filled with the poison from the Neon's exhaust. She coughed, and coughed again. She coughed again and again, and when she'd finally coughed all the poison out of her lungs, she felt relieved.

Jessabelle saw the truth in Uncle Trix's words: Scamming is easy, because people are greedy.

She used to think people were stupid. She couldn't understand why they believed one iota of what she said. She wouldn't if she were them. But truth be told, they weren't stupid. They just wanted something, and that wanting made them blind, or in Blondo's case, just plain crazy.

Jessabelle reached into the back pocket of her faded and slightly loose blue jeans and slid out her smartphone to call the only person listed in her contacts.

Chapter 2

Uncle Trix parked their Chevy step van with the ten-foot bed in the vacant spot left by Blondo. Jessabelle slid open the door, climbed up, and dropped into a large bucket seat. She handed him the bank envelope plump with cash.

"Another sale!" He eagerly counted the money and gave her a thumb's up. She returned the gesture with a half-hearted smile.

"I got lunch to celebrate." He indicated a Burger Barn bag on the floor at Jessabelle's feet. "There's a burger for you in that bag."

"Great, but can we go somewhere else to eat?"

"Where'd you have in mind?"

"Someplace pretty."

Uncle Trix glanced in the rearview mirror. "I've got the

perfect spot." He backed up the step van, then swiveled it in the opposite direction, and drove to the other side of the parking lot where he parked in a corner space.

"This is the perfect spot?"

"You asked for someplace pretty."

Through the tall front windshield, Jessabelle saw a fence painted green and rooted in a narrow plot of grass separating the bank parking lot from the red brick side of a small professional building, offices for three attorneys-at-law and a psychologist.

Uncle Trix waved a hand toward the scene laid out before them. "Take a look at all that greenery. It makes this place quite picturesque, don't you think?"

Jessabelle studied the scene further for anything she may have missed.

Uncle Trix nudged her, impatient for a response. "Don't you think, Little Darling?"

"That vine climbing the side of the fence. It's pretty. But the Arizona Green Tea can tangled in its stems, that's pretty ugly."

"At least it's a green can." Uncle Trix smirked.

Jessabelle rolled her eyes. "When I said 'someplace pretty,' I meant the beach or…someplace like that."

"Well then, Little Darling, why didn't you just say the beach?"

"Because it didn't have to be the beach. I just thought you understood that someplace pretty did *not* mean the other side of the parking lot."

"Right now, we don't got time to find Shangri-la-di-da. The coast is still fifty miles away. Eventually we'll get there, and when we do, we can go to the beach. Okay?"

"O-kay." She'd gotten used to eating lunch like this. Why should today be any different?

She extracted two burgers and a bunch of plain white

napkins from the Burger Barn bag. One she handed to Uncle Trix; the other she positioned on her lap.

She removed her false buck teeth, gently wiggling them downward. These she balanced on the dashboard. Then she used the napkin to dab the sweat seeping through the make-up she'd applied on her face that morning to appear fresh and natural, and not fake. The napkin turned a fair skin color.

"It's too hot for this," he declared, jerking a thumb toward the short hair and deeply wrinkled face with flat nose disguise he wore on his head. "Besides, I'm way too sexy for a pug nose."

Jessabelle unwrapped her burger, spreading its waxy covering over her legs. She bit into it and slowly chewed, gazing out the window in aimless fashion.

She noticed three pine trees crowded into an area of sod meant only for two. Her heart went out to the one that obviously didn't belong. It had a trunk and branches like the others, but a trunk made of thick cracked bark, and branches so frail and bare, it bore not one single pine needle. Next to the two trees with full bodies of smooth brown bark, adorned in thick clusters of sharp green needles and rich cones, it struck Jessabelle as a fleshless skeleton. Unable to move itself to the open space of a forest, was starvation-by-death its only way out of a cramped situation?

The fear that she and that tree were very much alike needled her. Oh sure, flesh padded her bones and she breathed in and out, but she felt dead inside.

Unlike the tree, she had two legs and could move herself. So why did she stay with Uncle Trix when it felt all wrong?

He gulped the last bite of his burger, then swigged Cola through a straw, swishing it around his mouth to rinse his teeth before swallowing.

He lifted a cheek to grope the right side of his butt for the Italian pocketknife he kept in the back pocket of his trousers.

With a push of its tab and a flick of his wrist, he flipped its metal blade out. That blade may have only been four inches long, but he'd sharpened it to a point so fine, the mere sight of it pierced holes in Jessabelle's heart and brain and guts.

Uncle Trix manipulated the honed point of the knife in his mouth, chiseling out a piece of burger from between two of his premolars.

Jessabelle breathed in deep, and when she breathed out, she heard herself say, "Maybe it's time for us to do something different."

"If it's something different you want, we could find investors for a gold mine," he uttered with the right side of his mouth twisted up so it wouldn't get cut by the knife, currently in use as a dental hygiene tool.

"And that could turn out exactly like it did the last time we found investors for a gold mine." Jessabelle rinsed her own mouth by running her tongue over the front and back surfaces of all her teeth. "Maybe it's time for us to do something *completely* different." She eased her real teeth into the clay she'd sculpted her fake teeth with the previous evening.

"How 'bout we give up gold and rob a bank?"

"How 'bout we give up thievery, get normal jobs, and live like real people?"

Uncle Trix spat the piece of burger he extricated with his pocketknife out the window. "At my age, what kind of job am I going to get?" He refolded the pocketknife and tucked it in his back pocket.

"Maybe you can become a doctor or lawyer."

Uncle Trix scoffed at the suggestion.

"They make good money."

"And what're you going to do? Work the knife and gun counter at Wally's? I tell you, Jessie, it'll be rough, going from two to four thousand dollars a day to $8.50 an hour."

Jessabelle sunk further in her seat. While the means to

two to four thousand a day was draining her insides, $8.50 an hour sounded like a ferocious challenge.

He rested a hand on her shoulder. "Just so you don't lose heart, I'll tell you what."

"What?"

"If our current racket continues to go as well as it has, we'll have two million dollars when we reach the northern tip of Maine. Then you can do whatever you want."

"Why can't we do what we want now?"

"We don't have two million dollars."

"But we've got money."

"We've made money, but our expenses are killing us."

She knew that was probably true. Between food and hotels, there were days when it seemed they spent as much as they made. Something requiring money always sprang up. Brake and transmission repair, new tires, the everyday expense of the diesel it took to drive the truck.

"When we get to Maine," he said, "we'll have the money we need to retire."

She sighed. She'd been a thief for so long. What was a few more months? If she could stand lying for just a few more months, she'd be free from lying forever. "I just hope we're not arrested before we get to Maine," she said.

"Now why would you say a thing like that?"

Because of the terrible dream that had made her bolt upright from sleep that morning. In it, she was standing before a huge crowd when she suddenly realized she was naked. She tried to cover up, but then looked down at her hands and saw there was nothing there she could hide behind. When she glanced up again, everybody in the crowd wore judge's robes. All those examining eyes glared at her naked body!

She couldn't tell Uncle Trix about the dream. He would only make fun of her, call her Worry-Wart. She shook her head. "I just have this terrible feeling something bad is about to happen."

Uncle Trix snorted. "Save the drama for our clients."

She curled her lips upward in an attempted smile, battling to appear as if she didn't feel terrible. But try as she might, she couldn't shake the emotions stirred by the pictures that came in her sleep.

Fear of being exposed as an impostor swam just below the surface of her daily awareness. Its companion, dread, did the backstroke alongside, spreading waves of imaginings of a lifetime in jail. Fertilized by this fear and dread, panic as yucky as a water weed grew inside her. No doubt, exposure would soon come to pass. She only hoped that when it did, the judges would go easy on her. After all, she wasn't as bad as she looked, was she? Deep down inside, she really was a good person, wasn't she?

After her morning with Blondo followed by the-lunch-in-the-parking-lot-behind-the-bank that Uncle Trix deemed scenic, at yet another Wally's in the next town south, Jessabelle searched the parking lot in desperation, rolling the same thought over and over: She'd be set free in Maine. There was light at the end of the tunnel, and that light glowed brighter than the hot sun beating down upon her.

In this great wide beam of new hope, she chased a guy who couldn't have been more than twenty-five as he crossed the parking lot on his way to Wally's sliding front doors. In his black T-shirt, camouflage pants, and work boots, he looked like a real country boy.

She got Country Boy's attention and started her spiel. It rolled along without incident until she got to the part, "I'm selling Grampa's gold bars to pay his medical expenses." As she did with all prospects, she opened her GoGreen bag and tilted it so Country Boy could get a good view of the three metal bars glinting inside. She paraded one bar on her open flat hand, a float she passed before his eyes. "Please buy this," she said, bringing the bar to a standstill, "and help me save Grampa. It's worth twenty thousand dollars."

He ran a hand over his head of short, oily blond hair, and with that same hand, clasped the edge of the bar, smudging it with his fingertips. "Can I see it a second?"

"Sure." Jessabelle handed him the bar.

He studied it for about thirty seconds. "Who said this is worth twenty thousand dollars?"

"Grampa."

"This ain't worth no twenty thousand dollars."

Jessabelle gulped. Her stomach tightened. "Huh?" she said, in her best dumb tone.

"This here is pure twenty-four karat gold. It's worth at least forty thousand."

Jessabelle's eyebrows shot up so abruptly, she almost dislodged her wig. "It is?"

Country Boy peered at Jessabelle's sneakers. Then his squinty eyes traveled up her legs, hips, and torso, and came to rest on her breasts. "I really want what you got."

You can't have that.

"I'll take it," he said, and Jessabelle opened her mouth to protest, but before she got a word out, he held up the bar. "This," he said. "I'll take it, and the other two bars. Give you ninety thousand dollars for all three."

Jessabelle was dumbstruck, for real this time. She'd never had an offer that good. But was it legitimate? His squinty eyes screamed untrustworthy. And the Timberlands on his feet were honest-to-goodness work boots; they had dried dirt caked around their edges.

With his bulging biceps, he appeared the type who did strong physical labor, somebody who repaired heavy machines in a muddy field with no tools but his bare hands and the edges of his teeth, and all for only ten dollars an hour. He did not look like somebody with $90,000 to invest in gold.

But Jessabelle knew from experience how looks could deceive. She briefly recalled the time she tried to get $2,000 from a guy who drove a Porsche and wore a Rolex; it turned out he had nothing in the bank and a long line of maxed-out credit. That same day she almost passed over an old woman wearing polyester pants and a tattered shawl, because she looked as if she had nothing; in fact, she had eight million dollars in the bank. Just to help Jessabelle, the woman gave her $3,000, and did not even care for a gold block in return.

Jessabelle reminded herself of one of the things she'd learned in her three years of conning: *It's impossible to tell who's got money just by looking at people.*

She knew she had to play the game with Country Boy, bide some time until she knew the truth about his economic status. She'd been surprised before; maybe Country Boy would surprise her again.

"Well, what'll it be?" Country Boy asked. "We have a deal or not?"

"Okay," Jessabelle said. "It's a deal." She slowly extended a hand toward Country Boy for a shake, but not really wanting to touch him, quickly retracted the hand, shoving her fingers in her back pocket. "What's your name?"

"Friends call me Wrench. You can too."

"Wrench. What a charming name." Jessabelle cleared her throat. "Nice to meet you, Wrench. I'm…" She searched her internal data bank for a name similar to Wrench. Uncle Trix had taught her if a person actually introduced themself to her and they had a common name, hers should be common. If they had a sophisticated name, hers should be sophisticated, and so on. His logic was that similarity breeds familiarity, making prospects feel right at home, and therefore more prone to trust her. "Hammer," she blurted to the man whose name suggested he lived in a tool chest.

"Really?" he asked.

Jessabelle nodded. "Really." Ironically, she was sort-of telling the truth. According to family legend, a clever woman in her mother's cell block once broke out of prison using simple diversionary tactics. "Hey, look over there!" she told three different guards at varying checkpoints. When they looked, the woman clubbed them over the head with her fist, knocking them unconscious.

That one who got away became a celebrity in prison circles. Admired by inmates everywhere, she earned the nickname The Human Hammer or just Hammer for short. Jessabelle's mother wanted her daughter to be Hammer's namesake, hoping it would act as a kind of good luck charm, not only helping her daughter one day break out of jail, but keeping her daughter out of jail altogether.

Mrs. Macadoo, Jessabelle's second mother and good friend to her first mother, wouldn't agree to a name like Hammer. "Can you imagine how that child will feel when she gets to kindergarten with girls with names like Daisy and Violet? You can't underestimate the power of a name. We need to give our girl a strong pretty one."

Thanks to Mrs. Macadoo, Jessabelle never knew what it was like to be called Hammer until Wrench said, "Hey, Hammer." It tasted like metal, made her feel steely. "Here's the thing," he continued. "I don't have the money with me."

"Of course not. Who brings ninety thousand dollars to Wally's?"

"Somebody who wants to buy one hundred and eighty thousand Jupiter Bars," he said and started to laugh, exposing a set of teeth as yellow as daffodils on a smoker's wallpaper, the kind of yellow that wasn't really a color at all, but a hueless buildup of rotting bacteria leading to tooth decay.

"Math must have been your strong subject," she said in

attempted flattery, and to take her mind off the pathogens lurking in his mouth.

"No. I'm just in love with those candy bars." He laughed some more. "At fifty cents each, they are the best bargain around." After a slight pause, he asked, "What was your strong subject?"

"I was strong in all subjects. After all, I am a VSP."

"What's that?"

"Very smart person." She winked.

"So what was your favorite subject?" he asked.

"Art."

"Art? You said the magic word. That's me, Mr. Art."

"Mr. Art? What does that mean?"

"I'm a prominent art dealer."

"Really?" Jessabelle stifled the laughter straining to break forth. Prominent art dealer? C'mon, in those camouflage pants?

Time to bring it back to the money. "I hate to change the subject," she said, "but Grampa doesn't have much time. Do we have to go to the bank to get that ninety thousand dollars?"

"Actually," he said, raising an eyebrow, "the money is at my house. Wanna take a ride?"

Who keeps $90,000 cash at their house? She didn't want money from a drug dealer, if that's what he was.

His eyes weren't glazed or bloodshot; nor were his pupils dilated. So if he was dealing drugs, it didn't look like he was doing them too.

He didn't seem smart enough to be a counterfeiter.

Over a big muddy pit of confusion, common sense played tug-o-war with wishful thinking, and both teams held tight to the rope. Common sense told her Country Boy was lying. But wishful thinking said that if he wasn't, $90,000 would be a huge step toward her and Uncle Trix's goal. But if he was lying, what was his game?

"I can show you the art on my walls," he said.

Stalling, Jessabelle asked, "What if Grampa dies while I'm looking at it?"

"Don't worry. We won't be gone that long."

The walls of Wrench's house were more likely to exhibit the stuffed heads of moose, elk, and deer than the works of Picasso, Gauguin, or Chagall. She felt stupid for even considering his proposition. "Sorry, I can't." She stepped back. Her brain sent a command to her feet to turn, so she could go on her way.

Before her body carried out the order, he pointed. "C'mon. My car's right over there."

Jessabelle's eyes widened as she followed the direction of his finger. He looked like a guy who'd drive a John Deere tractor—not that car. It stood all the way at the end of the parking lot, alone in the shade of a tree so small its shadow barely covered the rearview mirror. There were no other cars around it, so Jessabelle was sure he was pointing to that one. But just to be double sure she asked, "That tan Mercedes, it's yours?"

"Yep."

Hmm, maybe he really was who he said he was. She'd follow him to that car, and if he had the key for it, she'd get in and go. But on the way over she gave Uncle Trix a cautionary hand signal behind her back—just in case.

Chapter 3

Jessabelle sat in the tan Mercedes, traveling along a country road en route to Wrench's house. She glanced over at him, and he glanced back. Then his lips moved, but she couldn't hear a word he said over the country rock music blaring from the Mercedes' speakers.

"I can't hear you," she yelled.

He lowered the volume. "What?"

"Forget it," she said.

"How you like the way this baby rides?" he asked with a proud smile.

"Smooth."

"Yeah," he said. "Real smooth."

She wondered where he'd gotten the money to afford a car like this. Did it all come from selling art? "Mind if I ask you a question?"

"Those eyes give you permission to ask me anything you want." He stared into her blue-colored contacts as the car careened across the white line, bumped over a gravel-filled shoulder, and rolled across a flat grassy field. He slammed on the brake, and the car skidded to a halt just before it hit the only tree in the field—an oak with a base so large, it was spacious enough to live in.

Jessabelle shrieked as she was jolted forward, then flung back into the Mercedes' cushy creamy leather seat. She breathed in deeply to regain her equilibrium, and as she breathed out, she rested her left hand on the console.

"Don't you worry." Wrench laid his hand upon hers. He started to rub the back of her palm. "I got everything under control."

The feel of his hand against hers startled Jessabelle even more than the near collision with the tree. She yanked her hand away from Wrench, back toward her body, pressing it tight against her stomach in a fist. "Please don't touch me, okay?"

He remained silent. She repeated "Okay?" and waited for an agreement.

But he didn't agree. "Not used to having men touch you?"

"Actually, no."

"C'mon, a woman as hot as you?"

Her "creep alarm" began screaming, but she kept her answer casual. "You must like buck teeth if you think I'm hot."

"Don't be so hard on yourself, sugar. You're a good-lookin' country girl. I myself can be quite sexy in a slick shirt and nice pair of cowboy boots. Even sexier when I take them off."

"I'll keep that in mind. Now can we get back on the road so we can get to your place before the end of the century?"

Wrench smiled. "Alrighty, if you insist." He directed the

car back to the road, and soon they were rolling again. They whizzed past a field populated by wildflowers and a lone red barn. Further along the road, a group of horses grazed on a vast fenced-in pasture.

"Do you want to go to the demolition derby with me?" he asked.

Jessabelle's face must have said, *What? Are you kidding?*

"If you don't like the derby," he said, "we can build a bonfire and drink beer."

"Like on a date?"

"Yeah."

Was this really happening? He almost just cracked-up the Mercedes, and he was trying to pick her up? "Please, just one thing at a time. Right now, I have to save Grampa. After the kind of accident he's had, he may need intensive care. All that nursing won't leave much time for dating."

How long was this trip going to take?

In the rearview mirror she caught sight of a white step van and breathed half-a-sigh of relief. Was Uncle Trix following them? She hoped so, but couldn't be sure. She'd never realized how many boxy-shaped white trucks with high rooftops there were on the road until she and Uncle Trix drove theirs.

After they bought it, Jessabelle wanted to paint it purple and add some zingy artwork to its sides. Uncle Trix squelched the idea. "No flashy, eye-catching, or colorful stuff!" He said anything that drew attention to him and Jessabelle or made them stick out could blow their cover, and therefore was out of the question. She agreed, settling for the bland color of white for their common vehicle.

Oh, how she cursed him now. If the step van was the way she wanted, and not how he wanted, she'd know for sure he was behind them now, and not a courier, ice cream, or mail truck, or somebody running a mobile store or some other business on wheels. Then she could relax more fully—because she was in a car with a creep, going who knows where, and with each turn of the odometer, he made her more nervous.

The road turned to gravel. Along with that change, her view became dense woods on both sides. Occasionally she saw the beginning of a stone driveway leading to property shrouded by trees.

"We're almost there," he said and reached out to pat her hand, but she jerked it away before he could.

"Jumpy jumpy," he said.

"I told you not to touch me."

"Okey dokey, artichokee, I won't touch you." He hit the brakes, and finally they slowed to turn up one of those private drives.

Just before they made a left, Jessabelle glanced in the rearview mirror, but could no longer see the white van. Her nerves on edge, she bit her lower lip as she and Wrench traveled a quarter mile up a dirt drive with wild forest on each side. Jessabelle gazed at soft evergreens with dusty blue-green needles, six-inch pinecones, and rounded crowns that rose a hundred or more feet in the air. They held court with sixty-foot oaks with smooth diamond-shaped leaves.

When Wrench shut off the engine and Jessabelle stepped out of the Mercedes, the sweet aroma of the trees met her nose, and the sight of a large circular home her eyes. She scanned the clearing, but saw no other houses beside this mansion-in-the-round.

Two gothic angels, sculpted out of stone, greeted her from each side of the entry. She studied both for a long moment and smiled, enjoying the contrast of beings as ethereal as angels sculpted from such an earthly substance as stone.

The smile disappeared when she remembered her reason for coming. "Can you get the money quick, so I can get to the hospital?"

"Sure, the money's in here," he said and waved her along. She followed him through a hall that opened into a kitchen. The kitchen opened into a dining room. Each room had glass walls and doors that displayed a central courtyard with lush vines, foliage, flowers, and trees. Everything was so beautiful—unlike Wrench.

He led her into the living room, with ceilings so high, they soared like birds. Its warm and simple décor featured wood floors. A cozy caramel-colored leather couch lazed against one wall, adorned with plump silk pillows, handsown with decorative gold thread.

Jessabelle gazed at a painting on the sand-colored wall above the couch, of an enchanting goddess of lustrous complexion, seated on a white lotus, plucking a stringed instrument with a long neck and a gourdlike chamber.

"Do you specialize in religious art?" she asked.

"Uh, yeah. Matter of fact, I do."

"It looks ancient. Is it from a certain period?"

"Uh, yeah. The medial period."

Wrench must have meant the medieval period, since there was no such thing as the medial period—surely a mistake the owner of this house would not make. *Wrench is lying*, she heard from inside. No way was this his house.

She felt the urge to run like hell. Or should she wait for Uncle Trix? What if he didn't show up? What if, for some freak reason, Wrench actually had $90,000?

A framed photograph on the wall behind a grand piano beckoned Jessabelle. Afraid, not sure what to do, with so many questions racing through her, she moved toward it for a closer look. Six people wearing sailing hats and boat shoes gazed back at her from the sidedeck of a yacht. "Who are they?" she asked.

"My family."

Indeed, the group gave the impression of being a family.

A patriarch and matriarch stood with two grown boys, and beside one of them, a woman holding a baby.

Jessabelle studied the faces of the grown boys to see if she recognized Wrench in either of them. "But you're nowhere in the picture."

"I took it."

"Oh."

"On our caribou sailing vacation."

Her confusion deepened. The elements large deer + Atlantic Ocean didn't add up to a logical picture, which was absolutely fine in a work of abstract art, but not when it came to figuring out if Wrench had $90,000. *Wrench is lying*, she heard again from inside. "What did your family do on that vacation?" she asked. "Hunt caribou off the side of a yacht?"

Now he was the bewildered one. "Huh? No. We visited the islands."

"I see," she said, realizing he meant to say Caribbean sailing vacation. Okay, maybe he was just plain stupid. In her experience, dullness of mind certainly didn't preclude a person from having lots of money. "About that ninety thousand dollars—" she began, testing, turning away from the photograph. She stopped when she came face-to-face with Wrench. If she took another step forward, she'd wind up on his toes.

"What's your hurry?" He slid the GoGreen bag from her shoulder. "Why don't you stay a while?" He dropped her bag on the floor and reached a hand toward her hair.

She nabbed his wrist and held it mid-air. "You seem like a nice person, really you do, but right now, I've got to think about Grampa. Can I just give you the gold and get the money so I can get back to him?"

"I'll give you the money, but first I get to touch your hair."

"You can't touch my hair."

"Yes! I can." He wrung his wrist free.

She thrust her hands into his chest and shoved hard. He staggered back.

He regained his footing. "I like a girl who knows how to fight," he said. His face morphed into a sinister mask. Then he charged toward her.

Jessabelle swung her fist. It connected with a steel wall of pectoral muscles. She shook out her hand.

"This is the most fun I've had all day." He hurled a right punch. She ducked and felt his knuckles swish over the top of her wig.

She leapt, throwing the weight of her whole body, right shoulder first, into him. The crash drove him back, but not far enough.

She spiraled and started to run. He caught her in a bear hug. She tried to break his hold with her elbows, but couldn't.

She stomped on his feet with both of hers. He grunted and released her.

Bent on escape, she attempted another mad dash away from him.

He swiveled her by the elbow and hurled her like an empty metal pie tin. Unfortunately, at 125 pounds, she was incapable of wafting like one. She sailed down fast, nearly smashing her head on a glass-topped coffee table, landing on the woven area rug beneath it instead. She rolled over the earthy fibers of the rug, onto her back, adrenaline pouring through her.

He came toward her.

She anchored her palms on the floor at her sides and spread her fingers wide, bracing her body. Then she threw up a right kick. He snagged that foot with both hands, clinching them around her ankle.

While he held her right ankle, she delivered a wicked left

kick to his testicles.

"Oof!" Howling, he undid his handlock and doubled over. "Bitch! You got my balls!"

"Bull's eye!" She scrambled to her feet. Breathing hard, she got a hand on the GoGreen bag and swung it like a lasso. Then she brought it down with all her force. Three brass bars clonked the back of Wrench's head.

His hunched form teetered. Again she slammed him with the bars. He tottered and collapsed.

He lay on his side with his knees to his chest, holding his balls in one hand and his head in the other. The blood went out of his face. He issued a long low groan, emanating from deep in his bowels.

Seeing him in pain made her feel kind of sorry for him. She almost had the urge to ask him, Are you okay? Almost, but not quite.

"Sugar," he blathered in a muddled way, "you got the nicest hair…of any girl I ever laid my eyes on…I just wanted to see it out of braids…and touch it."

His eyes fluttered closed. Then he lay as inanimate as a rock.

She heard a voice from behind her. "You certainly know how to knock 'em out." She whipped her head around. Uncle Trix stood in the doorway, cleaning his fingernails with his Italian pocketknife. "Is he dead?"

Chapter 4

Uncle Trix's Italian pocketknife was the means by which Jessabelle had reconnected with her uncle three years before their visit to the mansion-in-the-round.

At the time, she'd been working the knife and gun counter at Wally's, the only place in Rolling Rivers, Washington, that would hire her. Rolling Rivers was home to Creativo, one of the best art colleges in the country, and owing to its pristine beauty, a popular place to hunt and fish.

She'd planned on working at Wally's only long enough to make the $33,000 she needed to return to Creativo and finish her formal education in Special Makeup Effects. But after two years of making $8 an hour, $64 a day, $384 for a six-day work week, and paying $600 rent plus living and makeup expenses, she hadn't gotten one step closer to her goal. The total balance of her savings still only amounted to about $250.

Then one day, as part of her duties, she was cleaning a shotgun on top of a glass showcase filled with hunting knives. She wore Carhartt brown cotton bib overalls with a red flannel shirt underneath, and men's hunting boots.

With the help of the costume and prosthetic makeup, she'd made herself up to look like an outdoorsman, wanting to appear as an expert in the field of knives and guns, or at least like somebody who'd actually use a knife or gun. She got an extra five dollars for every knife or gun she sold and hoped the new look would boost her sales, reaping her greater bonus money.

She glanced up to see a man making his way toward the showcase, wearing a gray suit that fit so well, it appeared custom made. The wave of his hair looked familiar.

"I'm looking for a lightweight knife," he said, resting his hands on the counter. "Something easy to handle." His voice sounded familiar too.

"I have just the thing for you," Jessabelle said in the man's voice she put on to go with her makeup and clothes. She chose the Italian pocketknife from among the showcase weaponry and clapped it on the counter.

In the amount of time it took him to snatch it up, it came to her: Uncle Trix. It had been so long since she'd seen him! Forgetting any formality and all appearances, she ran out from behind the counter. She draped her arms around his neck and planted a big kiss on his cheek. "I can't believe it's you!"

He disentangled himself from her with the urgency and speed of a man freeing himself from a monster, capable of swallowing him whole. "Are you crazy? I don't want any lumberjacks getting sweet on me, you hear?" He glared at her, wielding the knife.

That scowl reminded her she had on a bright orange

woolen cap with its earflaps tied up over its visor, part of her costume. "Oh no no," she said in her own voice. "I'm not really a lumberjack."

"Then who the hell are you?"

"Jessabelle."

Uncle Trix paused for a long count. "You sound like Jessie, but you don't look like Jessie."

"I'm wearing a wig and green-colored contacts."

He stepped back, his eyes grazing the length of her body. "If you really are Jessie, you've been eating way too many Ding Dongs and Twinkies."

"I'm wearing a fat suit to give the impression of a big man."

"Take it off."

"I can't right here!"

Anger spilled out his eyes. "What are you trying to do to me?" He slammed her against the showcase, holding the knife against her throat. "I'm going to ask you a series of questions that only Jessie would know the answer to. Mess one up, and I'll cut your throat. Got it?"

Would he really do that in the back of Wally's? She was too afraid to ask, or to cry out for help. So she just nodded, confident in her ability to pass the test, and waited for him to fire the first question.

"What was the name of your foster parents?"

Shoot. Which ones? Her first or second? It had been so long since she'd seen Uncle Trix, she was sure he didn't even know about her second ones, so she said the name of her first. "Mr. and Mrs. Macadoo."

Just saying their names warmed her heart. She loved them as if they were her real parents, and in a sense they were, having adopted her the way they did when she was three. To her, they were Mom and Pops.

"An easy question," Uncle Trix said. "Something any

undercover cop could find out if they wanted to trick me."

He asked more questions, getting progressively more specific. She answered them all, virtually telling her whole life story: She was born seven months after her mother, his sister, had been sentenced to nine years in prison for armed robbery. A prison board told her mother she could not keep her baby in jail.

Her mother refused to farm out her baby to just any foster parents and talked the board into allowing her friends, Mr. and Mrs. Macadoo, to take care of the baby until she got out of jail. But she never got out of jail. She died there of pneumonia.

On and on the story went, until a Wally's manager spied the two. He pried Uncle Trix away from Jessabelle. "You crazy, man? Trying to hurt Jessabelle?"

Uncle Trix relaxed when he heard her name from somebody else's lips.

"It's okay," Jessabelle told the manager. "He's my uncle."

"Sorry for the disturbance," Uncle Trix said. "I was just trying to get a feel for the knife." He straightened up. "I think I like it."

The manager continued on his way. Once he was out of sight, Uncle Trix slipped that knife in the back pocket of his trousers. Then he shook his head in disbelief, saying, "My own flesh and blood, and I didn't even recognize you. Jessie, we need to talk."

And talk they did. Over lunch at the Pizza Palace adjoining Wally's, Uncle Trix's treat, she told him everything that had happened in the years since she'd last seen him. How Mom and Pops had gotten thrown in jail for robbing a sneaker store, how she then had to go live with Mr. and Mrs. Cozie, her evil foster parents. How she couldn't go visit Mom and Pops because the Cozies wouldn't give her the money to take the bus. How she ran away from home and hitchhiked all the way to where Mom and Pops were locked up only to find out they'd been released from jail. How she'd looked, but couldn't find them. How she managed to get into Creativo. How her time there was cut short when her scholarship money ran out.

He listened to her whole saga with rapt attention and then told her he was a business proprietor. As fate would have it, he'd just lost his partner and was looking for a replacement. He said Jessabelle had skills, exactly the kind that could bring innovation to his business. If she came to work for him, she could make $2,000 a day, more than she made in a whole month at Wally's. Was she interested? Definitely. She'd have to be crazy not to be. What was the job?

"You'll see," he said.

Jessabelle followed Uncle Trix through the doors of Wally's and out into the parking lot. Discomfort flooded her when she saw the shape of the folded Italian pocketknife resting inside Uncle Trix's back pocket. She wanted to tell him, Go back and pay for that! But she choked back her anxiety and kept on following, quiet, hoping for a new life.

Right there in the parking lot, he showed her his profession. It shouldn't have surprised her, but it did. "I can't believe you steal from people," she said.

He'd looked at her with such innocent eyes. "What are you talking about? I take nothing from anybody. People give me their money, and I give them the opportunity to feel really good about that. You want to make people feel good?"

"I'm not sure."

"Suit yourself." He offered her a lift home. Happy not to have to take the bus, she accepted.

Parked in front of the slum that was her home, he handed her $2,500 and said, "Here, take this."

"It's okay."

"Take it," he insisted. "It looks like you can use it. I'll

make it again tomorrow."

"Really I'm fine," she said at the same time her fingers fastened around the money. She'd never held that much money at one time. It made her feel rich all over. "You make this kind of money every day?"

"Some days I make about five times that."

She produced a small wirebound pad of drawing paper and a pencil from a pocket on the bib of her overalls and flipped through the pictures she'd sketched of people she'd seen until she came to a blank page. Scratching the numbers, she divided 33,000 by 2,500 to come up with 13.5. Thirteen and a half days. If she did this job, that's how long it would take to make the tuition and room + board to return to Creativo.

"You can try scamming just once."

"I don't think I can," she said, not wanting to let go of the $2,500.

She thought about all the stuff in her apartment. Shelves of carefully categorized containers of liquids, gels, and powders. Drawings, sculptures, and molds. Anatomy and physiology charts. Ninety-seven different noses, seventy kinds of ears, and fifty-seven sets of teeth. A full-sized mechanical bear cub.

Fear struck her when she thought about leaving it all behind. "If I go with you, what will I do with all my stuff?"

"What stuff we talking about?"

She described her stuff, which inspired him to put on a thinking face. After a moment, he snapped his fingers and said, "We'll take it with us."

He'd bought the step van used from a couple who ran a laundry service. She called it her workshop on wheels; he called it his business on wheels.

In it, they traveled what felt like a million miles. Along the way she pretended to be countless different people: a red-headed mom trying to save her baby from leukemia, a gray-haired widow wanting to get on a plane to visit her sister on her deathbed, a poor boy needing a special tutor to pass twelth-grade math so he could graduate high school.

The list of characters she'd been and fake causes she championed went on and on like a roll of paper towels unraveling, each frame a new persona. Thirteen and a half days began stretching into what seemed like forever.

By the arrival of the day when Jessabelle and Uncle Trix's paths crossed Wrench's, she'd developed her skills to the point where she could turn herself into anyone. But in the process, she'd lost herself, wasn't even sure who that was anymore. And she couldn't get rid of the sneaking suspicion that in the past three years she'd gone virtually nowhere—only from inside Wally's to outside Wally's.

Jessabelle kneeled beside Wrench's inanimate body, sprawled on the wood floor of the living room in the mansion-in-the-round. She extended an index finger under Wrench's nose, and while it turned her stomach, it soothed her conscience to feel his breath on it. "He's alive," she told Uncle Trix.

"Disable him." Uncle Trix straightened his Armani suit jacket, then curled his fingers around the black handle of the knife. "I'm going to search the rest of the house."

Wrench wasn't her favorite person, and she had no idea what his story was, but she hardly wanted anyone in this house, perhaps some unwitting napper upstairs, to get hurt. She had to stop Uncle Trix from doing something stupid with that knife. "You don't need that," she told him.

He waved the knife in an arc. "Take a look at this house."

"I've seen it."

"Well, in case you haven't noticed, it ain't no shack. There's something here to get, and I aim to get it." He left, holding the handle of the knife so tightly, blood rushed to his fingertips. "Scream if you need help."

Jessabelle started after him, then remembered Country Boy on the floor. Fear of Wrench waking up and coming after her bolted through her like a sheet of lightning. Uncle Trix was right; she needed to fully incapacitate the creep.

Chapter 5

Jessabelle was studying the photo on the wall near the grand piano in the living room of the mansion-in-the-round. Her gaze traveled from one face in the family to the next, the picture rekindling her yearning to be reunited with Mom and Pops.

Uncle Trix re-entered. The tip of his knife drooped, dangling from loose and disappointed fingers. "I've been through this whole house, and you know what I found?"

"What?"

"A big fat goose egg." He folded the knife and replaced it in his pocket. "No safe, no cash, no jewels, no credit cards. No nothing. Nobody home either, except this fool." His gaze dropped to Wrench.

"And this fool is not exactly home right now."

Wrench lay straight out on the floor like a stone cold statue of Wrench. Using a quarter roll of packing tape, Jessabelle had wrapped the Country Boy's body in heavy gray plastic from the tips of his toes all the way to the top of his neck.

Wrench groaned.

"Oh wait," Jessabelle said, cupping a hand to her ear. "I think I hear something."

Wrench opened his eyes and rotated his neck to one side, releasing a crack at the top of his spine. He turned his neck the other way and rested his ear on the floor. "What the hell is this?" He glowered at the two bowls on the floor beside his head. Water filled one; Fruit Loops overflowed the other.

"I wanted you to have them," Jessabelle said, "in case you got hungry or thirsty before the police find you."

"The police?"

"I'll give them an anonymous call once we cross the town limits."

Wrench struggled against the plastic and tape that bound him. "I'm not a dog! Get me out of this…this…" He craned his neck forward to see his synthetic captor. "This garbage bag!"

"It happens to be special plastic used to ship statues. You had a huge roll of it in your storage room."

"I'm not a statue! Un-tape me," Wrench ordered. "Now!"

"I will," Uncle Trix said, "when you give her the ninety thousand dollars you promised."

"Who the hell is he?" Wrench demanded at the sound of Uncle Trix's voice. "Whoever you are, I don't have the money here in my little plastic bag. Un-tape me and I'll get it for you."

"Tell me where it is," Uncle Trix said. "Once I have it in my hand, I'll un-tape you."

"I can't tell you where it is," Wrench said.

"I bet you could if I applied enough pressure." Uncle Trix

again drew the knife, snapped it open toward Wrench, and held it taut against Wrench's throat. As if his hand had developed a sudden spasm, he jounced the knife. A crimson thread appeared on the skin of Wrench's neck, where a drop of blood oozed out, trickling down until it hit the floor. "Next time it'll be deep enough to bleed you dry."

"I don't have it!" Wrench screamed. "I swear I don't have it!"

"I knew it!" Jessabelle told Uncle Trix. "Can we please go now?"

"Okay," Uncle Trix said, a little too easily. That told Jessabelle he had something up his sleeve. "Let's go. But no phone call, and no food and water." Uncle Trix whisked up the bowls of water and Fruit Loops. "Good luck busting out of that plastic," he told Wrench, beginning an exit. "It looks like the durable, no-tear kind."

"No!" Wrench yelled. "Don't leave me like this. Please don't leave me like this!" He tried to break through the mummy wrappings. "I don't want Mr. Halloway to find me like this!"

Uncle Trix stopped.

"Who?" Jessabelle asked.

"The owner of the house," Wrench said.

"By any chance, is he a prominent art dealer?" Jessabelle asked.

"Yeah. I'm just staying here until him and the old lady get back from France."

"May be good for him to find you like this," Uncle Trix said. "Let him know who he's got watchin' the house."

"He doesn't know I'm here."

"A squatter," Uncle Trix said.

"Hey man," Wrench told Uncle Trix. "I'm just like you."

"I doubt that." Uncle Trix again started toward the exit.

"Please," Wrench pleaded. "If you free me, I'll give you

something so good, you won't have to pedal brass in front of Wally's anymore."

"You knew it was brass?" Jessabelle exclaimed, indignant.

"Tell us where this thing is," Uncle Trix said. "We'll get it and then un-tape you."

"It's not exactly a thing. It's a tip."

Uncle Trix shrugged. "I've gotten hundreds of tips. I've lost enough weight already. I want money."

"How 'bout three million dollars? That enough money for you?"

"You don't even have ninety thousand," Jessabelle said.

"The three million ain't mine, but I can tell you where it is."

"Tell us now," Uncle Trix said.

"It's something I have to show you."

Exasperated, Uncle Trix handed the bowls of water and Fruit Loops to Jessabelle. "Hold these." Now only the knife remained in his hand.

Uncle Trix rushed toward Wrench and thrust the knife toward his chest.

Jessabelle gasped. Water and Fruit Loops spilled onto the floor. With her mouth agape, she watched Uncle Trix slash a long hole through the casing of plastic and tape, freeing Wrench from the knees down.

Wrench sat up.

Relief washed over Jessabelle.

"I don't want any trouble," Uncle Trix said, raising Wrench by the mummified elbow, holding the knife at his throat.

"You won't be disappointed," Wrench said.

Hopping, Wrench led them out a glass door and into the lushness of the central courtyard. Did he really have a secret worth three million to her and Uncle Trix? Or was this just a trick to save his own butt?

As if it was the thing that would assuage all doubts about

him, he jutted his chin toward a statue that sat in the heart of the courtyard—at the very center of the whole house, really. "I know where you can get one of these," he said.

Jessabelle gazed at the statue to see if she could make any sense of Wrench's "secret." The painted concrete image of a crosslegged young man returned her gaze from his stone platform. He wore a tiger loincloth around his waist and held one hand up, palm toward her, with the thumb and index finger joined in a circle. The other hand rested in his lap, palm up. He seemed to be immersed in meditation.

But his eyes stayed open, and oh what beautiful eyes he had! Two perfectly rounded jewels of black onyx shone from his eye sockets, their beauty matched by his long shining locks of jet black hair, drawn up at the sides and spiraled into a bun that sat on the crown of his head. Gold rings hung from his ears, and in the space between his eyebrows, a red jewel shone. A serpent adorned his neck and two more his biceps.

"Why in the hell would I want one of these?" Uncle Trix asked.

"You would if it was made of twenty-four-karat gold, wouldn't you?"

"Of course," Uncle Trix said.

"Mr. Halloway has a guru," Wrench told them.

Jessabelle had never heard the word guru uttered by anybody she actually knew. "A guru?" she asked.

"Yes, some saint from India who lives over in Lalliville."

"In a house like a normal person?" Jessabelle asked.

"Whoa, wait," Uncle Trix told Jessabelle. "Don't get carried away." He brandished the knife at Wrench and asked him, "What's all this got to do with three million dollars?"

"One time Mr. Halloway gave his guru this same statue, but made of twenty-four-karat gold. The thing weighs a hundred and forty-four pounds, and it's somewhere in Lalliville now. He says it's some god named Shiva."

"How do we know you're not making this up?" Uncle Trix asked.

"I come here to clean the pool," Wrench said. "One day I heard Mr. Halloway talking."

Jessabelle stopped listening to the two flesh and blood men, and shifted her gaze back to the one made of cement. Wrench and Uncle Trix's voices whirred into a blur, melding with the buzz of a bee as she studied the figure.

A carved wooden stick rose before the god's body, its top forked like a wide U or the broad smile on the face of a giant. The crook of the U cradled the man's right forearm, supporting the entire weight of his arm. Between his thumb and ring finger, he held a beaded bracelet.

Three strands of the same beads decorated his bare chest. Two were molded as part of the statue; the third was a live version of the others that somebody, maybe Mr. Halloway, had draped over the young man's neck.

Tiny clefts covered the dark brown surfaces of the bracelet and necklace's beads. Jessabelle had seen blue plastic beads, yellow glass beads, copper beads that twisted and twinkled in the sun, but never beads like that! They struck her as the most interesting and pretty of all beads. She couldn't take her eyes off them.

A longing arose to touch one, hold it in her hand, know how it felt.

She stepped through the foliage that surrounded the statue and reached beyond a large quartz crystal and metal bell on its platform. She extended her hand upward past the serpents, then gingerly placed her thumb and forefinger on one of those beads.

She gently squeezed what felt like the pit of a tiny fruit, and a longing for truth and beauty surged through her. It was so strong the whole world went out of focus.

She gulped hard, regained her bearing, and released the bead. But she didn't want to let go of the serenity she felt.

She saw two hands—her hands—lift the necklace off the statue and lower it around her own neck.

"You can't take that," Wrench protested.

"Sure I can. Look." She traced the necklace's line as it fell down her chest and looped over the top of her stomach.

Grimacing, Wrench lumbered toward Jessabelle. Uncle Trix grabbed his plastic casing and jerked him back. "Whoa! Easy, boy. If the lady wants the necklace, she can have it."

"Fine," Wrench spat. "Take it."

As Jessabelle looked into the black onyx eyes of Shiva, remorse surged through her. He seemed so real, she felt as if she'd just stolen something from a man with the most beautiful eyes in the world. She lifted the beads off her neck and replaced them around his. "I changed my mind," she told Uncle Trix. "I don't like them as much as I thought I did."

"Suit yourself," Uncle Trix said. Then he turned to Wrench. "C'mon, Tool. Let's get back to the house."

Uncle Trix escorted Wrench back the way they came. Jessabelle stayed behind, counting the beads on the necklace, 108 in all, waiting until the two men disappeared inside. Then, gripped by the spirit of exploration, she was off to wander the house, where she found many more painted and sculpted forms, of Eastern origin, exuding compassion and beauty, both human and divine. This included the woman who stood in an alcove in the hallway, her waist narrow, hips wide, and breasts full and round. She wore a tall conical crown on her head, rich jewelry, and a long sheer dress that accented her sensuous curves. A raised hand synchronized with a swung-out hip produced the impression that she was swaying.

As with all the rooms, the master bedroom had windows that let in lots of light. Seated at the end of a simple, king-sized platform bed flanked by plain end tables, she encountered a three-foot-tall elephant man, carved in sandstone, displayed on a cubed maplewood pedestal. He had a head with a curved trunk and big ears atop a human body with a huge pot-belly. She stretched out her arms and threw herself back on the bed. Oh, what it must be like to live amid such beauty and simplicity.

By the time she made her way back out to the step van, Uncle Trix was settled at the kitchen table with Wrench, sharing a bottle of wine with the creep. Jessabelle stood outside the window, looking in. Uncle Trix had cut Wrench some plastic on the top right side of his casing, freeing one arm. With his liberated hand, Wrench held an ice-filled hand towel atop his head. He balanced the makeshift icepack there a moment, so he could swig a sip of wine from a hand-blown wine glass.

With his butt occupying one chair, Uncle Trix rested his legs and feet on another, scratching the side of his nose with the tip of his pocketknife. He may have been demonstrating signs of relaxation, but his lips moved at high speed. By the hyped-up manner of his voice vibrating through the glass pane of window, she knew he was excited. While she couldn't make out everything he said, she clearly heard the word "Shiva" thrown into his colloquy. Plans fired in his eyes.

Suddenly she didn't feel so good. Together, the two did not make a pretty sight. Whatever they were cooking up, it had to mean trouble. She grimaced at Uncle Trix. Then she walked out to the step van, climbed into the driver's seat, and wailed on the horn.

Uncle Trix exploded out the front door. He marched right up to the driver's side window, dragging Wrench behind him. "What the fuck you doing?"

"It's time to go," Jessabelle said.

"I'll decide when it's time to go," he pronounced, and receded back into the house with Wrench.

Finally, about an hour later, he came out of the house again and climbed into the passenger seat. In the meantime, Wrench crossed in front of the truck carrying a tangle of plastic and tape loaded in his arms. He stuffed the bundle inside a silver trash can with a plastic green bag for a liner.

"I can't believe you freed him," she said. "Have you forgotten he tried to rape me?"

"Rape is a strong word. He said he just wanted to touch your hair, but you got mad. It started a fight."

"Who do you believe?"

"You. No doubt, he's a weird guy. But I'm not worried. You proved you can take care of him."

Jessabelle shook her head and heaved a desperate sigh.

Chapter 6

Bright sun beamed through the step van's open back door, warming the metal floor Jessabelle had slept on the night before. The step van's one-ton rear end was parked in front of the Good Night's Sleep motel where Uncle Trix had spent the night.

She could have joined him in the room. As usual, he got a suite with two beds in case she wanted to sleep in one, and as usual she preferred to sleep in the van, feeling more at home surrounded by the tools of her craft than the room of any motel, hotel, or motor inn. And as usual she'd arisen at five a.m. to take on her character of the day.

Now she stood in front of the mirror, examining her latest masterpiece. Her gaze shifted to an elephant in a picture she held, one she'd clipped from the travel magazine that was her life. She'd taken the picture with a telephoto lens during a visit to an elephant sanctuary on her and Uncle Trix's way through California.

She noted the similarities between her reflection and the creature in the photo with a deep sense of satisfaction. "Not bad," she murmured, but critiqued what she could have done to make it perfect.

After the review she decided it was time to get Uncle Trix out of bed. The quicker they got on the road, the quicker they'd make it to Maine, where she'd have one million dollars, and along with it, freedom. Oh, how she liked that word: Freedom.

She pinned the elephant photo on her vista of inspiration, a wall that overflowed with images of all kinds of people and animals, with close-ups of eyes, ears, noses, lips, teeth, wrinkles, scars, scabs, and a multitude of other human and animal features.

She sniffled through the trunk, two inches round and six inches long, that hung from her face in place of her nose. It arched up over an upper lip elongated for effect, then came down again, ending in nostrils that lightly touched the top of her chest.

The prosthetic skin on her arms moved like tough gray Jell-O as she stepped toward the back of the truck. She dropped to a seated position, curling plump and padded hands with enlarged fingernails around the truck-bed ledge. She turned for one last look at the contents of the step van: shelves of feet, hands, fingers, ears, and other body parts she'd created; lifecasts and molds she'd made of herself and Uncle Trix; her rotating sculpture stand and corner laptop for designing 3-D makeup effects. She glanced at the many sets of original teeth, short and long, rotten and buck, that stood beside dental and tooth trays atop a small refrigerator. "Good-bye," she said to it all, her voice filled with intimacy and sweetness. "See you later."

The bottom of her tennis shoes smacked the pavement as she hopped out of the van.

"Jessie," Uncle Trix called as he came around the back of it with a naked chest and bare feet, wearing nothing but a pair of navy cotton lounge pants tied at the waist. "Wait until you hear—" He gasped as he came face to face with her. "Ugh! You look like an elephant!"

Receiving the jab as a compliment, Jessabelle smiled, spreading the narrow, two-inch-long ivory-colored tusks she wore over her own canines to opposite sides of her animal face. "That's the point!"

"Of what?"

"Our new act." Jessabelle clasped both hands over her heart. "I was born half human, half creature. All my life other kids made fun of me, called me Elephant Girl. Threw rocks at me. One day a mob of bullies attacked me, beat me bad, left me for dead."

Jessabelle sent a blast of air out her nose and through her trunk. Then she hummed out a rumbling growl and opened her mouth to amplify the growl, transmuting it into a full-fledged bellow. She sank to the pavement, pretending to fall flat on her back. Her arms became limp. Her head fell to one side.

"Dear Old Dad found me this way," she said in a raspy whisper. "He took me to the hospital, but the hospital wouldn't accept me without insurance. I need medical attention. I'll die without it! Of course, you'll have to do all the talking because I'm unconscious, lying on the side of Wally's parking lot."

Jessabelle sat up, smiling big and proud. "Pretty good, huh?"

"Pretty gross is what it is."

"The effect has to be slightly disturbing to elicit sympathy from our clients."

"It's so disturbing they'll throw up."

"Throw up?" Now that hurt. She scratched the cap of gray fuzz that covered her scalp. "Don't you think I'm cute?" she asked. A small breeze blew, and she felt her enormous elephant ears flap forward. She inched them back with the tips of her fingers.

"Yeah," Uncle Trix said. "You're cute. But the fact that you were born that way makes it seem like your mother slept with an elephant and gave birth to you nine months later."

"Gross."

"That's what our clients will say when they hear your story."

"They will not. Their hearts went out to the Elephant Man. So much so they even made a movie about him."

"The Elephant Man didn't have an elephant's trunk and ears. He was just a guy with thick and lumpy skin and enlarged hands and feet. Can you see the difference?"

"Yes. My trunk and ears are a modern twist on an old disease."

"What disease? Elephantiasis?"

"Yes."

"Okay, Jessie. You win. We'll do Elephant Girl."

Happy, Jessabelle hopped on her toes, venting an elephant cry of excitement.

She was a little surprised that Uncle Trix had agreed. She had to admit, Elephant Girl may have been a little out there, but she'd grown so tired of playing humans she was dying to give it a try, having been oddly inspired by the elephant man she'd seen inside the mansion-in-the-round. Elephant Girl felt new and exciting, and when it came right down to it, no more far-fetched than any of the other stories they propagated for profit.

The half human and half beast could be a hit, and who knew? With all the sympathy Elephant Girl would accrue,

maybe they'd even sell out of brass bars before they reached
Maine!

"Someday," Uncle Trix said.

That word hit Jessabelle's excitement like the bottom of a
25,000-pound flip-flop, squashing it completely. "Not someday," she protested. "Today!"

Uncle Trix massaged his forehead with his fingers as if he
were tired, very very tired. "This is all a moot point," he said,
"because we're not going out today."

What was he talking about now?

"I've come up with a plan to make three million dollars,"
he said.

"But we've already got a plan to make two million dollars.
Sell this brass." Jessabelle waved a hand indicating cardboard
boxes, stacked floor to ceiling in a corner of the step van bed,
each filled with 150 brass blocks, the one on top half empty.

"Did you hear me? This is a plan to make *three* million
dollars."

"This got anything to do with that statue?"

"You bet. Last evening me and Wrench, we went to
Lalliville."

He and Wrench. Were they best friends now? "Why
didn't you tell me?"

"You were too busy figuring out how to slather goop
on your face." He brushed his gray-speckled hair back with
his fingers, launching into a brief explanation of what he
had discovered the previous night: Lalliville was a spiritual
community. Its residents practiced the teachings of a guru,
teachings that represented a spiritual path, or Way of Truth.
"Turns out," Uncle Trix said, "Lalliville isn't for visitors. If you
want to stay there, you got to apply and be accepted as one
of the guru's students." Excitement bubbled into his voice.
"Didn't you say just the other day that you wanted to be a
student?"

"I said I wanted to go to art college."

"Now's your chance."

"But this isn't art college."

"I saw a bunch of kids there who looked like they could be in college."

"What do you want me to do there, anyhow? Steal Shiva?"

"For now, I want you to go there and see if Shiva exists. If so, then we can steal him." He rubbed his hands together.

"Stealing a statue from a guru. It sounds so grubby."

"A guy who tried to beat you up because you wouldn't let him touch your hair called the guru a saint."

"Well, what if he really is? And we steal all that gold from him? That's like stealing from Mother Teresa. What if he plans to feed a village of starving kids with it?"

Uncle Trix roared with laughter. "Don't be so damn gullible. We're talking about a guru. Everybody knows gurus are the biggest con artists around. He conned a rich man into giving him the statue in the first place. He's not going to feed starving kids with it. He's going to use it to line his own pockets."

Jessabelle frowned. What if the guru really was just a con man? Half of three million dollars was a lot better than half of two. With 1.5 million dollars, she'd really be free. Never have to tell another lie, if she didn't want to. But how did Wrench factor into this whole deal? She asked Uncle Trix what percentage he'd promised Wrench.

Uncle Trix said, "Don't worry about Wrench. I'll take care of Wrench."

Even if Uncle Trix gave Wrench a third, it still came out to a million for her, a chunk of money she could make without having to stalk Wally's shoppers. Visiting the town of a guru was definitely different than their usual fare.

"I'll do it on two conditions," she said.

"What's that?" He scratched the dark stubble on his chin.

"One, you keep me safe from Wrench."

"Of course."

"Two, we get to eat breakfast at the Scramble Damble."
Jessabelle pointed to the family restaurant across the way and
up the road, knowing that for Uncle Trix a proper breakfast
had to be worth a crack at three million. "And the makeup
stays. I got up at five in the morning to be Elephant Girl. I
don't want all that hard work going straight down the drain."
She rolled the back door of the step van shut, waved to Uncle
Trix, and bounded for the road. "Meet you there."

"I'll bring your application," he called.

Jessabelle romped across the road and up a sidewalk toward
the Scramble Damble family restaurant. She passed a park,
a place that issued bail bonds, a police station, and a small
library that stood next to an elementary school.

A flaming swatch of fabric flashed in the corner of her
vision. She whipped her head sideways to see a boy no taller
than four feet, dressed in a long-sleeved silk shirt that hung
all the way to his knees. It glowed bright orange and had small
red and yellow vertical stripes running through it. Sequins,
beads, and embroidery embellished the neckline and cuffs.

Her rumbling stomach reminded her of how much she
wanted a big egg breakfast. But in that second, her desire to
fully absorb all those vibrant colors, golden threads, and brilliant beads was even stronger than her need to eat. She hid
behind a bush to get a really good look at the boy when he
passed.

From her hiding place she further examined his garb, noticing that with his shirt, he wore matching bottoms and a
pair of flat slip-on style shoes made of yellow, blue, and red

leather, long shoes with a pointed toe that curled upward.

She might have looked like an elephant, but in that get-up, he looked as if he should be riding bareback on one, over a river and along a forest trail, to get to some village school in a remote corner of India. She wondered, *What school play is he in? Aladdin? Is there a costume shop nearby?*

Suddenly, boy twins, two heads taller than the Short Kid, converged on him. Each wore skinny jeans, belted beneath a two-inch strip of exposed black and white plaid boxers. The single word—TROUBLE—emblazoned their gray T-shirts in bold black letters. Black baseball caps were turned to one side of their heads.

They towered over the Short Kid, standing so he could not pass on the sidewalk. "Hey," Trouble #1 said. "Did you just roll out of bed?"

"No," answered the Short Kid. He moved onto the grass in an attempt to walk around them, but Trouble #2 side-stepped to block him.

"Then how come you got your pajamas on?"

"These aren't pajamas," the Short Kid said. "This is a kur-ta."

"Is that Wimp language for dress?" Trouble #1 asked, or did Trouble #2 say that? Jessabelle could hardly tell the difference between the two.

"It's real pretty," said Trouble #2. "All you need now is a purse, earrings, and a necklace."

Both Troubles laughed.

"We're gonna mess up your dress," said Trouble #1. His sneer said he meant it.

"No," the Short Kid stated. "You're not."

"Oh yeah, whatcha gonna do about it?"

"Invoke protection."

What did he just say?

"Invoke protection," one Trouble mimicked, and both

Troubles laughed.

The Short Kid sat right there on the sidewalk. He crossed his legs and rested his hands on his thighs. He took a short shallow breath and blew it out.

He took another breath so deep, his chest rose. Then he began to chant foreign words as if he were singing to the beat of a silent drum.

Jessabelle could hardly believe her elephant eyes and considered removing her gray-colored contacts just to be sure they weren't clouding her vision. Did the Short Kid really just sit down in the face of a fight and start singing?

"You sound like a singing cow." Trouble #1 mooed, then cackled a mean laugh.

But the Short Kid didn't respond, just kept chanting.

"Did you hear me?" Trouble #1 asked.

"He said you sound like a singing cow!" Trouble #2 said. "Mooo, mooo!"

The Short Kid kept up his steadfast chanting.

"Time to give the cow a bath!" yelled Trouble #1. He seized the Short Kid's arms. Trouble #2 undid the cross of his legs and grabbed hold of his feet.

They hauled him off, his body dangling a foot above the grass. The Short Kid squirmed to free himself, but the two Troubles firmly gripped his limbs, their hands obdurate as iron manacles. Realizing the impossibility of wiggling his way out of his predicament, the Short Kid surrendered to it, relaxing his body and increasing the volume of his chant.

Jessabelle's heart went out to him. Just because he had an unusual fighting style and wore a colorful costume, he didn't deserve to be punished. She stepped out from behind the bush and followed the three.

Trouble and Trouble lugged the Short Kid through a field stretched out behind the schoolyard. At the edge of a pond heavily coated with slime, Trouble and Trouble swung the Short Kid back and forth by the arms and legs. Over the Short Kid's song, they counted in unison. "One, two…"

Jessabelle rushed forward, grabbed Trouble #2 around the waist, and slung him. The Short Kid's special leather shoes slipped out of his grasp as Trouble #2 stumbled back.

As Trouble #1 gaped at her, she pried his hands loose and pushed his chest. He tripped, falling to the ground.

Jessabelle watched the Short Kid scurry from the water's edge. He sat blinking at her.

She shifted her focus, eyeing the two Troubles. They stared back at her.

"Who are you?" Trouble #1 gasped, scooting back on his rear end.

"Elephant Girl."

The two Troubles uttered a unified cry of shock, then sat motionless and panting until they again caught their breath.

"You're the ugliest girl I ever saw," Trouble #2 said, his skill at hurtling insults returning.

"That's 'cause you never met my mama. She's thirteen feet tall and weighs seven tons."

"That's fat," Trouble #1 said. "She must eat a lot." He rose to his feet and set his hands on his hips.

"Three hundred green salads a day," Jessabelle said.

"Yecchh," said Trouble #2. "Disgusting." He stood next to his brother, doubling their menace.

"She's killed many boys just by sitting on them," Jessabelle told him. "If you're not careful, I'm going to call her. Your head could be her next La-Z-Boy recliner."

"Oh yeah? She's not here now," said Trouble #2.

"Yeah," added Trouble #1. "Right now it's two against one. And you're not *that* big."

"We're gonna get you, Freak-Face—"

"And pound you down to his size." Trouble #1 pointed at the Short Kid.

Trouble #2 charged toward her. She grabbed his wrist, twirled him around, and let go. He tumbled into the watery green pit.

She spun back just in time to see Trouble #1 rushing toward her. She took two steps to the right. As he whizzed past, she gave him an extra push. It sent him crashing into the water.

She stepped toward the water's edge. Two baseball hats floated on its surface. Between them, one Trouble came up for air, and then the other. "Go away!" she yelled, then trumpeted like an elephant.

The Trouble Twins climbed out of the water. Green algae glistened in their hair and on their clothes. They shook themselves like dogs. One hissed and the other huffed, but they both moved off.

The Short Kid kneeled on the grass before her and bowed his head, staring at her tennis shoes, studying the two purple smiley faces handpainted on the outside edge of each. She'd added the smiles to her sneaks the night before, while the pieces of her elephant face dried, and sealed them for durability. If they didn't last forever, they'd at least hold up until she obtained the million or so dollars that would paint a smile on her own face.

"Thank you for coming," the Short Kid said and handed her a bunch of dandelions he'd arranged like a small bouquet. She squinted, dubious. "You don't like 'em?" he asked.

"Sure I do," she said. "I just never had anybody give me a bouquet of dandelions."

"It's the best I could do on such short notice." After a slight pause, he said, "Can you pretend they're gardenias?"

"Sure." Jessabelle accepted the dandelions. "Thanks for the gardenias." She held them under her elephant nose and breathed in deep. "They smell bee-oo-tiful." Her gaze fell on his outfit. "Is there a costume shop nearby?"

He shrugged. "Not that I know of."

"Where'd you get the duds?"

"My outfit," he said, running a proud hand over his shirt. "My friend gave it to me."

"Oh," Jessabelle said, realizing this was no costume, but his real clothes.

"Will you come live with me?"

"I'm too old to be your girlfriend."

"I don't want you to be. You can sleep in my bedroom. I'll sleep on the couch in the living room. I'll make you breakfast, fix your…hair…" The Short Kid examined the gray fuzz that covered Jessabelle's head. "Your hair is un-bun-able, but I'll find something for it, maybe a ribbon or a bow, if you'll stay with me and walk me to school and back." He aimed a finger in the direction of dense forest adjacent to the field where they stood, a forest full of trees flush with bright green foliage. "I come on a path through the woods."

He sounded so sincere, she realized he wasn't kidding. "You really want me to stay at your house?"

"It doesn't have to be forever, just until the end of school this year."

"I bet your parents would love that."

"They'd be happy to have Ganesh as a guest."

"Who?"

"The Elephant God."

"Call me what you want, but I ain't no God."

"You are! I prayed for protection, and you showed up. Please stay and protect me some more."

She'd love to stay, walk him to school every morning, and return in the afternoon to walk him home again. Eat dinner with him, his mom, and his dad. How nice it sounded to be part of a real family again! But she couldn't stay here. There was still work to do. Once she accrued her million dollars, maybe then she'd settle down and have a family of her own.

"Protect yourself," she said.

"How? They're twice my size."

"No offense, but how about changing your clothes? In that getup, you're begging to be picked on."

The boy pulled himself to his full-short-height. "I'll have you know, these clothes saved my privates."

"How?"

"Trouble and Trouble told me they'd hang me on the school sign by my underwear. Today!"

"That's impossible. They can't do that."

"You don't know them. Yesterday they gave me a wedgie, yanking up the band of my Fruit of the Looms so hard it tore a big hole in my underwear. But today they didn't hang me by my underwear. You know why?"

"Why?"

"They were too focused on my clothes."

"But then you almost got thrown into a pond."

"You see? With them, I can't win. That's why I need protection."

"Sorry, kid. I can't protect you. I've got a business meeting to attend, and then I must be on my way to other places. Good luck."

Chapter 7

Heads turned as Jessabelle entered the Scramble Damble family restaurant. She found Uncle Trix at a booth, gazing at the screen of her laptop. The corner of his genuine crocodile leather bifold wallet protruded from a side pocket of his navy lounge pants. A plain cotton burgundy T-shirt now covered his chest and $459 Italian calf-leather shoes his feet. The stylish cap-toed, lace-up shoes were the same ones he wore with his ensembles of designer suits and imported silk ties. He didn't own a pair of sneakers.

"Hey, Dumbo," he said. "What took you so long?"

Jessabelle didn't answer, glaring instead at Wrench, who sat across from Uncle Trix. "What's he doing here?"

"He came to help us," Uncle Trix said.

"Help us?" Jessabelle could hardly believe her elephant

ears. Wrench stared at them, and then her elephant face. She
scratched her big gray stomach, busting out from under a soft
pink T-shirt, and he gawked at that too.

"Are you the same girl I met yesterday?" he asked.

"Yes." Jessabelle glided in beside Uncle Trix, where a glass
of ice water and menu awaited her. "But yesterday I was in
disguise. This is the real me."

Uncle Trix slid the laptop across the table until it rested
in front of Jessabelle. "Here it is," he said. The top of the open
page read "Lalliville Application."

"I called him for help filling it out," he said about Wrench.
"He brought some information."

"What is it?"

Wrench pulled a piece of white paper from the breast
pocket of a button-down camouflage shirt without a single
button buttoned. Jessabelle glanced at the pancake syrup in
the condiment caddy; Aunt Jemima's face seemed a more de-
cent place to rest her eyes than Wrench's bare chest.

In her peripheral vision, she saw Wrench slide the paper
across the table. She took it and asked, "Couldn't you afford
buttons?"

Wrench looked down at his shirt, running his hand along
a row of clear green buttons. "This shirt has buttons."

"Then why don't you use them?"

"It's a free country. I can use 'em or not."

"This is the Scramble Damble. There're kids here."
Jessabelle motioned to the next booth, where a woman sat
with two small girls, probably her daughters. Actually, they
were ogling Jessabelle, not Wrench, and one of the girls was
cupping her hand over the other's ear, whispering.

"My mom was an elephant," Jessabelle told them both.
"What can I do?"

They sucked in their breath. "You talk!" exclaimed one.
The other shrugged, raising her eyebrows along with her small

shoulders. "Elephants are nice," she said in a high-pitched voice.

"I know." Jessabelle gave them both an elephantine grin, one that really showed her elephant teeth. Shifting her gaze back to Wrench, her smile ran away. "I don't want to look at your chest, so can you button it?"

Uncle Trix motioned to Wrench, who obeyed.

"What can I get y'all?" A waitress in a white shirt and black pants had stepped to the edge of the table, pad poised, ready for their orders.

"I'll have a bottle of Budweiser and double order of T-bone steak," Wrench said.

Uncle Trix's face registered alarm.

Jessabelle consulted the clock on the wall. It wasn't even nine in the morning.

"I said I'd buy you breakfast," Uncle Trix grumped in Wrench's direction. "I didn't say find the most expensive thing on the damn menu and make it a double."

Wrench scowled. "Make that T-bone a single," he corrected. "And don't forget the beer."

Uncle Trix ordered an omelet and black coffee before the waitress turned to Jessabelle. "And what can I bring you, hon? A hay bale and water trough?" She beamed at her own joke.

"No need. If you have them out back, I'll just get my breakfast there."

Uncle Trix tapped his fingers impatiently while Wrench practically drooled over the waitress's ample cleavage. Jessabelle could clearly see what that perv wanted with his T-bone steak.

"Hey hon, your features are so real. How'd you get yourself to look like that?"

Jessabelle narrowed her elephant eyes. "Like what?"

"You know, an elephant."

Jessabelle drooped her head. "This isn't a costume. I was

born this way, half human and half beast."

The waitress twisted her face, unsure how to react. "Oh," she said after a moment, turning serious and polite. "Do you really eat hay bales?"

"Yes. But today, since I'm feeling more human than beastly, I'll have the big egg breakfast and an orange juice."

"Sure thing." The waitress scribbled Jessabelle's order on her pad, collected their menus, and headed off to the kitchen.

Jessabelle unfolded the paper Wrench had given her, spreading it out on the table. Scratched across it in pencil was the word "Lalliji."

"Lalliji," she said aloud. "What's that?"

"That's the name of Mr. Halloway's guru," Wrench said. "I copied it from one of his papers."

"Lalliji. Lalliville. Does the guru own the town?"

Wrench shrugged. "I guess."

"Do you have a picture of the guru?"

He shook his head.

"Can you tell me what he looks like?"

"I ain't ever seen him."

Jessabelle frowned, wondering why Uncle Trix had invited Wrench. He wasn't really supplying any groundbreaking knowledge in guruology, or even something to help her get through the application. She shifted her gaze to all those daunting lines on the first page, deciding to give it a go on her own. She found herself stumped by what for most people was the easy stuff: name and address. "What's my name?" she asked Uncle Trix.

"Bitch," Wrench interjected.

Jessabelle gave him the finger with a leathery elephant hand.

"Make something up," Uncle Trix said. "And I'll get the paperwork."

"How about a name that sounds smart?"

"Alberta Einstein," Uncle Trix suggested.

"Maybe something more subtly smart." Jessabelle typed the name Isa Newton on the application. "What address should I put?"

Wrench smirked. "Cage number three, the kennels on Manning Road."

"No. That one is already occupied by your brother. You sure you don't want to join him for dinner? I hear they're serving Purina."

"Make one up," Uncle Trix said.

Jessabelle typed a make-believe address, her real phone number and email address, makeupFX@cybermail.com, and then concocted answers to several questions about her education and job experience.

She filled in a questionnaire about her health, stating that she was fit and strong, capable of full participation in life at Lalliville.

Then she came to the essay: Why do you want to visit Lalliville? She stared at that question. Twenty-five blank lines stared back, waiting to be filled. With a whole page devoted to it, she knew it was important. The instructions said she could use extra sheets of paper if needed, but she felt it would be a feat just to make it through those first twenty-five lines.

She read the question to Uncle Trix and Wrench: "Why do you want to visit Lalliville?"

"To steal the solid gold Shiva," Wrench said.

"I'm not sure that'll get me in." She knew she had to think up a good lie. She turned to Uncle Trix for help. "What do you think I should write?"

"To become enlightened," he said.

She silently repeated the word "enlightened." What did it mean? To be free from stealing? Free from Uncle Trix and Wrench? To not be so confused all the time? If it meant that, she wanted it. "To be enlightened," she said. "That doesn't sound so bad."

"It's perfect," Uncle Trix said, "because gurus always promise enlightenment as part of a trick to take control of people's minds, inherit their possessions, and in the end, satisfy nothing but their own vanity."

Her confusion thickened. Jessabelle considered herself to be open and nonjudgmental, but knew she couldn't trust gurus from India for the reason Uncle Trix had just mentioned.

She didn't know this for sure because she'd never had one single experience with an Indian guru, or any other guru, for that matter. Come to think of it, she couldn't name one person she knew who'd ever had an experience with a guru, but Uncle Trix had just spoken as if he had. So she asked him, "When did you visit a guru?"

"Me? Visit a guru?" Uncle Trix laughed. "I ain't no sucker."

Jessabelle continued to think about the guru. She couldn't even remember where her mistrust of gurus came from. It didn't seem like something Uncle Trix had implanted in her. No. It had been around for a while, floating like a superstition in the muddled mass of undistinguished ideas she'd spent her life collecting. Suddenly she felt this muddled mass like a cloud that blocked the sun.

She longed to see the light, and from out of this desire, she furiously typed a sentence, filling the first line with: Reason #1) To end my confusion, and become enlightened.

Jessabelle started to think of another reason, but Wrench interrupted. "I can't believe you're the same girl I met yesterday."

"Shh. I need to concentrate."

"Are you really a blonde? Or was that a disguise too?"

"I'm really a blonde," Jessabelle lied, and typed again:

#2) I want to learn how to be truthful. She followed on the third line with: #3) I want to see what Lalliji is really like.

None of that was even made up.

While it amounted to less than an essay, she couldn't think of anything else to say. And with an answer supposed to take up twenty-five lines that only took up three, she didn't expect to get accepted into Lalliville.

A month after her now-forgotten breakfast at the Scramble Damble family restaurant, Jessabelle was at a Wally's in a small town in Georgia, in a region devoted to peach farming. Things had not been going her way that day.

In the morning she'd emerged from the step van with velvet-soft skin the color of a pastel palette of pale orange, autumn red, and deep plum. Petals of a pink flower formed around her left eye. A stem and leaf with carefully crafted veins grew out the top of her head, and in the space over her heart, a football-sized brown pit bulged from her skin, made visible by a small slit cut into her white T-shirt.

"I have peachitis," she told Uncle Trix with a squishy sweet accent. "It's a rare disease a person gets when they have a certain gene and eat way too many peaches. As a kid I loved peaches, ate them all the time. Unfortunately, nobody knew I had the gene until it was too late and my heart turned to peach pit. I quit peaches, but the change didn't stop. Is in fact accelerating. If I don't get help soon, the transfiguration will complete itself, and before long, I'll be one hundred percent Sweet Georgia Peach."

Uncle Trix nixed the idea, telling her she could keep the squishy sweet voice, but must lose everything else. "No disguises that'll land you in the newspapers," he reminded her.

Soon she was back in her blonde country girl disguise, headed for the neighborhood Wally's. She and Uncle Trix pitched a brass bar to three different people. They all said no. The last one threatened to call the cops shortly before the men in black showed up, rolling toward her like a tornado.

She took off running. The brass blocks clacked and smacked her hips. She dropped the bag and sprinted, urging her sneakers to move faster. She hopped over the edge of a landscaped island curbed with cement, full of stones and pink flowering bushes dotted with discarded gray plastic shopping bags.

She ducked into a tire-changing bay at the automotive center. When her phone jangled to the tune of the theme song of the fantasy film *Metamorphosers*, her chosen ringtone, she answered it. An accented voice said, "I'm Pierre Dubois from Lalliville. You've been approved for a two-month stay." He gave her the details, which he had to repeat three times over the sound of an electric drill unwinding lug nuts.

"Thank you," she said after she finally heard. "You won't be sorry. I'm a good student, a good woman…an all-round exemplary person."

She clicked off her phone, tucked it back in her pocket, and waited for the cop car to whiz past, the sound of its siren cutting a hole in her heart. When its flashing lights faded, she came out of hiding. She ran across the blacktop, climbed over a fence, zigzagged through trees, and whizzed out to the highway.

The step van cruised toward her with its door open, slowing so she could hop up on the step to its passenger door. She climbed inside, took her seat beside Uncle Trix, and suddenly everything seemed to be going her way. It didn't matter that she'd just been chased by the cops or that she'd lost out on two grand three times over. Opportunity for three million was knocking; hopefully she had the ability to open that golden door.

Chapter 8

On the day Uncle Trix drove her to Lalliville to begin her stay there, Jessabelle awoke in the back of the step van at her usual time of five a.m., wearing what served as her pajamas, comfy blue-and-white-striped lounge pants and the soft cotton light yellow T-shirt with the name of the art college she'd dropped from, CREATIVO, arched over the school's logo, a red ladybug, paintbrush in its hand, facing her canvas of a half-painted human.

More than anything, she wanted to fit in once she got to Lalliville, but had no idea how the average female visitor to Lalliville actually looked and dressed or what she was like.

She'd gone through many possibilities, finally settling on Seriously Smart Nerd, something to go with a name like Isa Newton. Everybody admired brilliant people.

As for Uncle Trix, a few days earlier, he'd asked her for a new disguise to wear to Lalliville. His fear of a security guard he'd seen the first time he went there convinced him he needed one. He didn't want the same guy to see him again and get suspicious. "I don't care what it is," Uncle Trix had said. "Just make me look normal."

Normal to her was anything from a grain of sand to the moon, from a baby to a president, from a blade of grass to a mountain. An ant looked just as normal to her as Uncle Trix did any day of the week, but when she suggested, "How about ant-like?" he insisted normal meant no bugs, no animals, no fruit. "Just a person."

"How about a celebrity look-alike?"

"Who'd you have in mind? Brad Pitt?"

"No, Twinkie Winkie."

"Hah hah."

"If you don't like Twinkie Winkie, how about Beyoncé?"

"Double hah hah. Maybe you can talk like a man, but I can't talk like a woman."

"Then you're just going to have to describe exactly how you want to look."

"Thick dark hair, deep brown eyes, no wrinkles around them, smooth olive skin."

From what she could tell, he had described himself, only younger. She'd made the face he wanted, and for clothes bought a Nutty Professor costume, something to complement her own disguise.

With those costumes hanging on hooks above her and pieces of faces waiting to be donned, there was no need to bounce right out of bed. So she lingered on her air mattress, her sheet stripped off and kicked aside while her small space heater huddled alone in a corner, on vacation since her and Uncle Trix's return to Florida.

When she finally did rise, she sat behind her laptop and

dove into some last-minute homework, which amounted to surfing the internet, as she'd already done once, looking for information to elucidate her understanding of Lalliville. Three searches—Lalliville, Way of Truth, Lalliji—produced a bunch of hits that shuttled her onto a tract of barren land, void of any real connections to Lalliville, a spiritual community; Lalliji, an Indian guru; or Way of Truth as a spiritual path with Eastern origins. After perusing a few websites in this no man's land, she typed "SFX character creation" and immersed herself in reading for several hours about the latest techniques special makeup effects artists used in materializing their character visions.

Somewhere about mid-morning Uncle Trix appeared in the doorway between the cab and the cargo area with an announcement. "Brunch awaits you, madame." He smiled, a crooked smile full of charm, one he used so much it seemed a permanent facial feature, like his nose or eyes.

Jessabelle followed him out of the step van and toward his room at the Good Night's Sleep motel. In the room, twin double beds sagged in line with each other, one made up perfectly with a plain brown spread, the other's sheet and cover tossed up and twisted, spun together, and thrown aside, as if Uncle Trix performed gymnastics in his sleep, a testament to his high ranking as a restless dozer. The beds' dark imitation mahogany headboards matched the nightstand between them, its top supporting a red-digited clock radio, a small lamp apexed by a cream-colored shade, and a single-line, push button phone with a red message light, currently unlit. The room contained no couch, no plants, and dull brown curtains—a fitting setting for a photo essay on the depressing effects of pure utilitarianism, but for the single piece of art, a cheaply framed poster of Van Gogh's "Vase with Fifteen Sunflowers."

"Go ahead, sit down." Uncle Trix guided her toward a

laminated particleboard table with a black cast-iron base, where she chose one of two metal chairs, depositing herself on a seat cushion covered in solid burgundy fabric, happy this stopping spot was just temporary. From the center of the table, black letters etched into a small tented rectangle of silver-toned plastic told her, "Thank You for Not Smoking." Around that sign, a spread of food rambled: Three six-inch shrink-wrapped subs with packets of mustard, ketchup, and mayo; two salads consisting of spinach, oranges, and walnuts in black-bottom-and-clear-top plastic containers; a bag of fifteen cheese bars, individually packaged in foil; a one-pound container of crab salad; naval oranges, kiwis, and starfruits; a frapuccino coffee drink in a can; a bottle of orange juice; a few bottles of spring water. She recognized the food as the kind sold in a small commissary at the Good Night's Sleep.

Uncle Trix slid the bottle of orange juice across the table to her. "What's your fancy? Roast beef, turkey, or ham?" He swept a hand, drawing her attention to the subs like a pretty-boy game show model past his prime, showcasing the illusion that her choice of sandwich was a prize she'd just won.

While that prize didn't amount to the fulfillment of all her desires, it would appease the thing that never shut up for long, and was in fact screaming for something right now—her stomach. She raked the turkey sub over to her side of the table. "Why're you being so nice?"

Uncle Trix snapped up the roast beef sub. "I'm just a nice guy." He uncovered his sub, removing the plastic wrap.

While eating their sandwiches, he described what he planned to do while Jessabelle was in Lalliville and he was camped out at the Good Night's Sleep. Since they'd passed through these parts the last time, people were on the lookout for the brass dealers, so he wouldn't be working their usual gig. Instead he'd concentrate on figuring out how to fence the gold statue once they stole it.

She told him that seemed like a waste of time, since they didn't know for sure there even was a golden Shiva in Lalliville.

"It's there," he said, breaking open the bag of cheese bars. "I can just feel it."

After Jessabelle polished off her sub, one of the spinach salads, and three cheese bars, Uncle Trix casually related how he'd stolen their brunch from a pantry that stocked the small commissary at the Good Night's Sleep. He firmly believed he was entitled to a free breakfast, since he'd opted out of using the motel's complimentary shampoo and conditioner. When he couldn't get the motel manager to agree with him, he'd sneaked into the pantry and taken what he felt rightfully belonged to him.

Jessabelle knew she was supposed to feel guilty about having just eaten a stolen meal, but she didn't. After all, she'd already eaten the food. How was she supposed to know he'd stolen it? And was there really any difference between eating stolen food and eating food purchased with stolen money?

She did, however, attempt to point out to him, "It's not a fair trade. This food is worth a lot more than trial-size bottles of shampoo and conditioner. We're talking—" She paused to garner a rough estimate. "—maybe twenty-five dollars compared to sixty-six cents.

He eyed her over his frapuccino in a can. "Whose side are you on? Mine or theirs?"

She plucked up a wad of carpet fiber at her feet. "What you really should've taken are a couple of these."

"Yeah, and what am I going to do with carpet fibers?"

"Make a necklace out of them."

"Hah hah."

A moment later, she said, "Let me ask you a question."

"Shoot."

"How would you feel if you ended up in jail for stealing

food from a pantry?"

"It'll never happen. The justice system doesn't have time to throw me in jail for stealing fruit. That's like throwing somebody in jail for stealing shampoo and conditioner from a motel room."

A few hours after Uncle Trix's stolen brunch, Jessabelle and her misfit relative left the Good Night's Sleep motel in a silver Civic, rented especially for the occasion of driving Jessabelle to Lalliville. They traveled eastbound along route 54, a two-lane road.

Jessabelle's hands rested in the lap of the red plaid skirt with suspenders she wore with a long sleeve white cotton shirt. A plastic protector crammed with nine multicolored fine-point markers filled its breast pocket.

They quickly passed the Scramble Damble family restaurant and the other establishments in town, a supermarket and a hospital, an ice cream parlor, auto repair place, and a used car lot.

They followed 54 through the country, past Country Flowers and a farm market, before entering another small town, Orangetown, which seemed to contain the staples the last town didn't: Burger Barn, Dippin' Donuts, a funeral home, and a hardware store.

Just outside Orangetown the Civic came up behind a slow-moving farm truck. Uncle Trix executed a pass of the farm truck, smashing the accelerator and crossing over a double yellow line. That's when Jessabelle saw the blue Jetta coming in the opposite direction. "Look out!" she screamed.

Uncle Trix swerved into the right lane, missing the front bumper of the Jetta by the length of a shoebox. Okay. It might have been a shoebox belonging to a giant; nonetheless he'd brought them damn close to a crackup.

Clearly Uncle Trix had missed his calling as a racecar driver. With his heavy foot, quick reflexes, and composure in the face of a potential accident, he had all the makings of one. Add to that his slim figure that fit easily behind the wheel of a car, his stamina to drive several hundred miles a day, and his showmanship skills, and the man could've been a professional—a NASCAR driver with a nickname like Turbo Trix.

Just because he was too old to begin a NASCAR career didn't stop him from acting as if the Civic was a high-tech racecar. Rather than slowing behind a grey SUV, with a white SUV in the oncoming lane, he passed the grey SUV on the shoulder of the road. For somebody on semi-vacation, he sure was in a hurry. What had gotten into him, anyway? Was it the excitement of getting his hands on three million dollars worth of gold? Jessabelle reminded him of his own advice about flying under the radar, of not attracting attention.

He conceded her point and slowed down, probably because it was his point. Then he claimed that in going from the step van to the Civic, he'd lost about half a ton. "That'll make anybody more agile."

Jessabelle lowered the sun visor and unfolded the vanity mirror to take another look at her face. The coke bottle glasses made her already large brown eyes, like those of a cottontail rabbit, appear extra large, and the wig of shoulder-length red hair moved every which way but down toward her shoulders. Her hair frizzed so much that each strand seemed charged with 100,000 volts of electricity. It just didn't look natural. She'd intended disheveled, not electric, but she didn't dare complain.

Uncle Trix had often asked why she didn't just buy wigs. The few times she'd done just that, the wigs had arrived a little bit off, not exactly what she wanted. Making them ensured they matched her own specifications. If she lamented now about the unwanted voltaic quality of the handsewn hair on her head, he'd only start in again about how she should buy premade, save herself the trouble of handmade. So she kept her mouth closed while staring in the mirror, silently noting her recent mistakes in wigmaking.

"Never met a woman who wasn't obsessed with her appearance," Uncle Trix mused.

No longer sure if Seriously Smart Nerd was such a smart idea, she worried the others might somehow discover she was nothing but an art school dropout. She ran a hand over one side of her wig, trying to smooth her hair. The wig may have been a mistake, but there was no time to modify it. The green sign was right over there! Its reflective white lettering heralded the coming of Lalliville, only one mile from the next left.

Uncle Trix made the left, turning onto Way of Truth, a winding dirt road. Its bumps jostled Jessabelle in her seat while she turned her head right, left, and straight, scouting for the entrance to Lalliville. It wasn't hard to find, since it was the only human-made thing in sight and the road dead-ended at its entrance.

The Civic paused before a gate. From each of its side posts, the gate sloped up to arc around a mysterious gold wavy-lined symbol painted at its center. Rays of light shone in all directions, to all edges of the gate, giving the appearance that the symbol was nestling in the middle of a giant sun. A gold marquee over the gate read "Welcome to Lalliville: Gateway of OM," lettered in red pigment.

The gate automatically opened, swinging wide. They drove through it and arrived at an intersection. At the same time Uncle Trix gave the car gas, moving it straight forward, Jessabelle yelled, "Go right!"

Uncle Trix stomped on the brake. "Listen—" he began.

"Why do we always have to do what you want?"

An apple-red Cherokee trundled toward them, stopping on the road just before the Civic. The bar of amber warning lights straddling its roof wasn't flashing. Jessabelle breathed some relief about that.

A young man stepped out of the Cherokee, followed by a five-pound snowball that rolled out of the car. Wait! A five-pound snowball? It was summertime in Florida. She looked again and realized the snowball was a puppy with a coat of long, fluffy straight white hair.

The little guy took a few clumsy steps on wobbly legs, then caught up to the big guy. The big guy wore a pair of red sneakers with green stripes, blue jeans, and a short-sleeved heather green cotton twill shirt with two breast pockets. A small memo pad and pen stuck out of one of the pockets.

When he discovered the puppy at his heels, he said, "You stay here." He snapped his fingers and pointed back to the truck. The puppy gazed up at him with sad eyes. "Oh all right, if you insist. But you'll have to let me hold you." The man lifted the puppy in his arms, cradling him close to his body. "I don't want you accidentally getting run over."

While the man and his dog negotiated, Uncle Trix tried to make peace with Jessabelle. He said, "Let's not fight. We're partners. Remember?"

"Yes, partners," she said through gritted teeth—crooked horse teeth with a large chunk of the upper right central incisor chipped off.

Uncle Trix rolled down his window. They both smiled at the young man as if he was about to take their picture and had just told them to "Say cheese."

The young man rested a right forearm on the window ledge. On his head he wore a straw hat with a gold badge shaped like a seven-point star pinned to its front. The words SECURITY OFFICER hopped off the badge. Dangling from his neck was a strand of the same pretty beads she'd seen around the Shiva statue's neck. The puppy curled in his left arm gave a few tiny barks in greeting.

"You seem lost," the man said. "Can I help you?"

"I'm Professor Newton." Uncle Trix pushed his black-rimmed glasses, taped at their bridge with half a Band-Aid, higher on his nose.

"That's my uncle." Jessabelle smiled, although she was hardly beaming.

Looking at Uncle Trix in his young Uncle Trix face, black polyester pants, and green plaid cotton shirt topped with a white lab coat, embarrassment nudged her. The bow tie, fake mustache, and black rimmed glasses hardly labeled him a work of art.

His Italian shoes remained on his feet. Before they'd left the hotel, she'd tried to get him to change into the steel-toed, black lace-up shoes with thick rubber soles she'd scraped to-gether as part of his costume. He refused to put them on, saying a man had to have some dignity. She insisted the styl-ish Italian shoes were incongruous to his costume, might send up a red flag. He agreed, took them off, and carried them out behind the Good Night's Sleep, where he rolled them in a snippet of dusty earth, "dulling them down," as he said. Later, when he was back at home in his motel room, he planned on reversing the effects of the dust by re-spiffening the shoes with polish.

Jessabelle wondered if the security guard, the one with his eyes on them right now, was the security guard Uncle Trix had seen the first time he came. If so, she had to laugh. With his soft features, he appeared very unthreatening. Were there real law enforcement officers in this town, or was this security guard and his K-9 companion it?

"I'm dropping her off," Uncle Trix told the man.

The guard glanced through the driver's window at Jessabelle. "And who are you?"

"Only one of the smartest girls in the world," Uncle Trix said. "She graduated Summa Cum Laude."

"Impressive," the guard said. Jessabelle wasn't sure whether he meant it or was just humoring Uncle Trix.

"Intelligence runs in the genes," Uncle Trix said, "and I'm not talking Levis or Wranglers."

The guard snickered. Again, Jessabelle wasn't sure if he really thought Uncle Trix's lame joke was funny, or if he laughed just to be polite. He asked Jessabelle, "What's your name?"

"Isa Newton," she said. "I've been approved for a two-month stay." She didn't know if she'd be here that long; it all depended on how things went.

"Nice to meet you, Isa," said the guard with a bright smile, not the kind that made her feel as though the sun shone in her face, but the kind that made her feel as if she were gazing at a single star on a cloudy night. She had the strangest feeling she'd seen him somewhere before, but could not place where.

"The Welcome Center is the first building on the right," he said, pointing up the street in the direction she originally wanted to go.

She didn't know if it was the guard's smile or something in the air, but this place gave her good vibes. The puppy barked again, and she reached across Uncle Trix's chest to stroke the top of his head. A cooing sound followed, and for a second Jessabelle wasn't sure if it was arising from her or the puppy. There was just something about this place, maybe the exotic music she heard from far off, that soothed her.

Uncle Trix and Jessabelle cruised a short way up Main Street, a narrow dirt road called Liberation. Lalliville reminded Jessabelle of any of the very small towns popped up in the middle of nowhere that she'd visited in America. She wasn't particularly fond of small towns but for some reason, she did not know why, she felt as if she loved this one.

Uncle Trix parked the Civic in a space reserved for visitors in front of the Welcome Center, a one-story building with a roof of rounded, desert-red clay tiles and stucco walls the shade of white dromedary camel hair.

Jessabelle buttoned her plain white shirt all the way to the top and tucked it into the skirt. She noticed the fake teeth she had custom-made for Uncle Trix resting on the console. "Uncle Trix! You forgot to put your teeth in!"

She handed him his teeth. He anchored them in his mouth and smiled at himself in the rearview mirror. "Big and perfect. Just the way I like teeth."

Jessabelle pulled up her white knee socks and stepped out of the car in low heeled, lace-up black shoes that clumped as she walked toward the entrance.

Uncle Trix unloaded Jessabelle's khaki fabric rolling trunk from the backseat of the car and dropped it. "You got a dead body in there?"

"Just a few body parts. A professional can't be too prepared."

He tipped up the trunk, slid out its handle, set it on its wheels, and reached to retrieve her other piece of luggage, an orange tackle box he perched atop her suitcase, resting it against the trunk's metal handle.

Inside the Welcome Center, a young Indian woman with a cheerful expression greeted them from behind the registration desk. A small diamond pierced the side of her nose. "Welcome," she said with a smile. "I just got a call that Isa Newton is here. You must be her."

"I am," Jessabelle said.

The woman came out from behind the desk, allowing Jessabelle a full view of her. She wore a tunic-length shirt, hitting mid-thigh, designed with gold flowers woven into emerald green fabric. A long shawl draped her shoulders, settling on her back, where one end looped over the other. Matching pants fit tightly around well-toned calves and petite ankles. Gold bands adorned her toes, red paint her toenails, and flat gold thongs her feet.

Jessabelle took in the woman's dark eyes, umber-colored skin, and shining black hair. "I'm Vishva," the woman said.

The sound of crashing metal smashed against Jessabelle's ears, jolting her eyes to the floor where her orange tackle box had fallen from its precarious position.

"What an interesting travel bag you have," Vishva said.

"It's from Louis Vuitton's latest line of travelware," Jessabelle said, scurrying to restore the tackle box to its former position.

"I bet you could buy the same thing at a bait and tackle shop for a fraction of what you probably paid for a Louis Vuitton."

Jessabelle was sure she could, since that was where she had actually bought this piece of luggage. "This is my uncle, Professor Newton," she said, diverting attention from her "travel bag."

Vishva smiled warmly. "Pleased to meet you."

Uncle Trix again pushed the black-rimmed glasses higher on his nose. "The pleasure is all mine," he said, extending a hand. His lips slid open, each corner spreading high and wide to form a smile that fully showed off his huge fake teeth.

Vishva shook his hand. Long after the handshake ended, he grinned from ear to ear, displaying his extra-large set of white chompers.

Jessabelle glared at him, wishing he'd stop. She cleared her throat and apologetically told Vishva, "He just came to drop me off."

"I'll get your key," Vishva said, "and take you to your room."

The second Vishva turned her back, Jessabelle snapped at Uncle Trix at whisper pitch, "Stop smiling!"

"I can't. It feels so good to be my virile young self again. Can't wait to get out of this labcoat and into my purple silk shirt and black leather pants, and head out on the town."

"If you can find a town to head out on."

Vishva returned with a key, and to Jessabelle's chagrin, Uncle Trix smiled, and smiled, and smiled.

He grinned out the doors and up Liberation Street, past a café, an education center, and a gymnasium positioned between dirt sidestreets named Compassion, Fearlessness, and Unity. They rounded a corner onto Strength Street, then trotted by simple houses, each painted a different pastel color. Mauve, aqua, fruity orange, lime green. They arrived at one of the houses, two stories, the color of purple lilacs, with a walkway but no driveway, and a lush green lawn. They followed steps running up along its side to the second-story entrance.

They walked through the front door on the top floor, and down a wooden hallway with rooms spurting off it. Jessabelle saw a living room on the right, and across from that, a kitchen. Farther down the hall, Vishva pointed out her own room. "We're roommates," she said, then escorted Jessabelle to a room across the hall, furnished with a single bed, dresser, and simple desk with wooden chair. It also had a small closet and a private bathroom, just as Jessabelle had requested.

Uncle Trix smirked as he laid Jessabelle's travel bags near the foot of the bed, and speaking with the barest movement of his lips, he said, "I didn't see any discos, bars, miniature golf courses, bowling alleys, or swimming pools."

"This isn't a resort," Vishva said.

"What do people do here?" he asked.

"Chant, meditate, and offer service," Vishva replied.

Uncle Trix snickered and told Jessabelle, "If you get bored, give me a call."

"There's no chance of Isa getting bored," Vishva told Uncle Trix. "This is a really fun place." She paused and added, "After all, you just arrived and haven't stopped smiling since."

"It's true," Jessabelle said. "I've never seen him so happy."

"C'mon," Vishva said. "I'll give you a tour of the place." And Uncle Trix went on smiling.

Outside, Vishva pointed off in the distance to the woods surrounding Lalliville. "First off, if you like nature, the facilities include 111 acres of hills, fields, and forests to meander. There's even a river back there."

Next Vishva took them inside the gymnasium. "Sometimes people play basketball here. But mainly this gym is used for hatha yoga classes held early mornings and evenings."

In the education building, Vishva showed them a large multipurpose room. "This is where chants are held," she said, "and on weekends, special events."

"What kind of special events?" Jessabelle asked.

Vishva informed her: "Seminars, dances, plays, musical performances, talent shows, painting and ceramic exhibits, storytelling events—you name it."

When they got to a café called Krishna's Corner, Vishva told them, "Here's a place to purchase food and snacks." The café offered chairs and tables inside, and a deck stretched along the outside with more chairs and tables. Attached to the café was a library with tall shelves of books to browse, all related to yoga philosophy.

"Well, my little scholar," Uncle Trix tittered. "I bet you'll feel right at home here in this corner with all these books."

Vishva ended the tour in a spacious dining hall with picture windows that overlooked the park. "This is where you'll come for breakfast, lunch, and dinner."

"What kind of food do they serve?"

"Cereal and fruit at breakfast," Vishva said. "Lunch and dinner buffets. Always vegetarian."

"Sounds delicious," Uncle Trix said, grinning. "Wish I could stay for dinner."

"Too bad you can't," Jessabelle said. In her opinion, he'd smiled enough for one day. "Isn't there someplace you have to be?"

Uncle Trix nodded. "Walk me to the car," he told her. Then he glanced at Vishva. "Thank you for the tour."

At the Civic, Jessabelle and Uncle Trix traded good-byes. She hugged him, and in place of a hug, he offered a bit of advice. "Don't forget why you're here. Keep your eye on the prize." Then he left her with these words: "Look for the statue in all the places she didn't show us. And don't get fat."

Chapter 9

Two hours after Uncle Trix dropped Jessabelle in Lalliville, she went to the dining hall for dinner.

She got on line at the buffet, a hot food table on casters, picked up a cafeteria-style tray, and set a simple white porcelain plate and bowl and stainless steel utensils on it. Then she moved along, ladling and scooping out portions of rice, grilled veggies, and a soup labeled Dal from rectangular wells protected by an acrylic sneeze guard.

She filled a mug with mint tea from one of the stainless steel beverage urns accented with brass handles at the end of the line. Glancing up, she spotted Vishva in the crowd.

Vishva sat at a round table with four other people in her and Jessabelle's age group, dressed in varying ways. Three were guys. One wore pressed slacks with a lime green business shirt, matching tie, and sassy eyeglasses with tortoise frames. The second had on a chef's uniform, a half-sleeve white coat with black and white checkered pants and sturdy black leather clogs. The third was the security guard Jessabelle and Uncle Trix had encountered earlier. He held the puppy on his lap, feeding his furry friend dry puppy kibble drawn from the stock of it he kept in the front pockets of his blue jeans; the puppy ate the kibble right out of the guard's cupped hand.

The fourth person with Vishva was a slender young woman with a head of wild and loose blonde curls. She had on a yellow T-shirt with a huge black smiley face, and a long billowy skirt so brightly colored that just seeing it made Jessabelle feel like dancing. But geeks didn't break loose and dance, she remembered.

The minute Vishva saw Jessabelle standing there with what must have been an "I can't dance 'cause I'm a geek" expression on her face, Vishva smiled and waved. "Come sit with us," she called, motioning Jessabelle in their direction.

As Jessabelle plodded toward the table, she heard Vishva direct the others to make room for Isa. Vishva slid an empty chair from a nearby table over to the cleared spot.

Jessabelle plopped down in the chair, a molded blue-stained wood chair with chrome legs. Thankfully it had a cushion strapped to its seat. As the sixth person to arrive at a table built for five, she needed comfort where she could get it.

Her elbow butted against Vishva's arm as she set her tray of food on the finished plywood tabletop. A red napkin dispenser stood in its center, flanked by a set of clear glass salt-and-pepper shakers and a plastic vase with a sprig of wildflowers spouting out its top.

"Everybody," Vishva said, scooting further to give Jessabelle more room. "I want you to meet Isa Newton."

"Is it your first time here?" the blonde asked.

88

KATHLEEN ORTNER

All eyes rocked in Jessabelle's direction. She didn't want to be singled out as a newcomer. She'd planned to slip into this place, blend in so she was hardly noticed, search for and find Shiva, and move on to the next phase of the heist. That plan had just been incinerated.

"No, I've been here before," Jessabelle said, trying on humor to veil her discomfort over the fact that the blonde had just announced her as a newbie. "It's just that I've been out of the country building railroads in China so I haven't been here in a while." She burst out in laughter, as if to say "Just kidding."

The others laughed with her.

"Oh yeah," the blonde said with a mischievous wink. "Now I remember." She squinted into Jessabelle's face. "I heard you got the bubonic plague while you were in China."

"Actually," Jessabelle said, "it was a mix of the black plague, tuberculosis, and consumption with a dash of the measles thrown in."

The guy in the chef uniform feigned vomiting his dinner. "Not exactly what I'd call appetizing."

"You're right," Jessabelle said. "Let's not talk about it anymore."

"Let's not," the blonde said. "But just in case your illness left you with amnesia, I'm Madeline." She smiled. "Do you remember these other people, or should I introduce them too?"

"Please do. My memory could use some jogging."

Madeline went around the table naming the people. The one in the stylish eyeglasses was Johann, a German MBA; he had come to offer his service in the Finance Department. Chet was the one in the chef uniform. He had recently graduated from the C.I.A. That was C.I.A. as in Culinary Institute of America and not Central Intelligence Agency, Jessabelle discovered.

"And this is Doc." Madeline pointed to the security guard.

"We've sort of already met," Jessabelle said.

Doc's eyes, the shade of maple syrup, leveled with hers. She was sure she'd gazed upon those same eyes before she arrived in Lalliville. Names came and went like hotel guests, but faces lodged inside her forever. Doc's gentle visage was there, somewhere. She turned on her internal search engine, browsing her memory for the connection. Maybe if he took off the straw hat with the security badge pinned to its front, she could see more of his hair, making the link easier.

"If you've met Doc, then I'm sure you know Fuzz." Madeline motioned toward the fur ball on Doc's lap, drawing Jessabelle's attention back to the table.

Jessabelle nodded.

"I'm from Arkansas," Madeline told Jessabelle. "I'm here for a year before I begin my hospital internship."

"Are you a doctor?"

"Pediatrician."

A pediatrician, a chef, an MBA, and Vishva with her PhD in Sanskrit, whatever that was. They seemed like smart people.

Jessabelle's hand traveled to her artificial face. She ran her fingers over its edges bordering her jawline, ensuring its seams were still smooth, hence invisible. Then she inserted a slice of grilled zucchini squash into her mouth. "This is really good."

"Thanks," Chet said, punctuating the word with the clinking of the knife and fork he set to rest on his now empty plate. "We buy vegetables from local farmers. I think it makes a difference in taste." He leaned back in his chair, interlacing his fingers behind his head. "Where are you from, Isa?"

"Boston," she said.

"A Massachusetts girl," said Chet.

"An M.I.T. girl, actually. I was there on a science scholarship."

"Hmm," Johann murmured, after a sip of mint tea.

"I don't like to toot my own horn," Jessabelle said. "But others call me a wizard at invention. I developed my first masterpiece at eight."

"What was that?" Doc asked.

"A substance to unstick bubble gum."

"From what?"

"Hair, walls, driveways, or anything else it can get stuck to. De-Gum was a hit with the mothers in my neighborhood. They threw me a party. From there I progressed to bigger and better things."

"Like what?"

"An automatic leaf-raker."

"Are you talking about the leaf blower?" Madeline asked.

"No," Jessabelle said. "I'm talking about a robot that rakes leaves." She shook out an embroidered handkerchief, so her co-diners could see the letters MIT embroidered in the corner. With it, she polished smudge marks off the lenses of her eyeglasses.

"You working on anything now?" Doc asked.

Jessabelle nodded. "I'm nearly finished with something that will enable a human to fly." In an ostentacious display, she held her eyeglasses up toward the overhead fluorescents, ensuring they were clean. She deposited them back on the bridge of her artificial nose.

"They already have something like that," Madeline said. "It's called an airplane."

"One can fly in an airplane, but all that metal makes a plane quite bulky as a flying instrument. I'm working on something lighter and more practical, a wingsuit that will allow a person to fly totally unencumbered—free as a bird." The faces of her new friends told Jessabelle she'd reached the crescendo in this movement of BS; they were impressed.

"Cool," Doc said. "Really cool."

"You're kidding, right?" Madeline asked.

"No."

Madeline crossed her arms over her chest, looking serious. "This isn't a joke?"

"No," Jessabelle said.

"But a wingsuit that will enable me to fly like a bird?" Madeline persisted. "That sounds impossible."

"My great-great-grampa died in 1875," Jessabelle said. "He'd have told you it's impossible to hear the voice of somebody on the other side of the world. But today we know that's easy because we all have these." Jessabelle held her cell phone high for the others to see. "From right where I sit, I can use this instrument, no bigger than my hand, to call Johann's mother in Europe."

"But can you talk to her?" Johann said. "Do you speak German too?"

"Ein wenig," Jessabelle said, and smiled, thinking about the time she and Uncle Trix paused from their usual gig of selling gold to play two German immigrants who couldn't find a job, and in their despair became drug addicts. From town to town, they worked parks. They lived in the park (or so they said) of each city, appearing like dirty beggars, playing junkies, petitioning park-goers for the money to go to rehab.

They spoke a combination of English and gibberish made up on the spot to sound like a foreign language. At one park, an actual German immigrant, the CEO of a banking dynasty, had threatened to call the cops if they didn't get out of his face. To add a touch of authenticity to their next performance, she had learned a little bit of German, including "ein wenig," "a little bit" in German.

Now she sat grinning, satisfied that learning was paying off here. She hoped someone would ask about her front tooth, so she could share her ready-to-tell story about how one day, after flying around for several hours, she'd come down a little hard, falling on the rock that chipped her tooth.

She continued grinning. C'mon, for sure they noticed a chip like that, one screaming out from center stage of her mouth.

Chet took a breath. *Here comes the question*, she hoped.

"What are all those for?" he asked, his eyes on the colored pens crammed into Jessabelle's breast pocket.

Jessabelle closed her mouth, sighed in disappointment. Polite people were great for conning, but took all the fun out of pretending by the way they refrained from asking about the obvious, which usually involved exactly what they wanted to know. She didn't believe they found her colored pens more interesting than the missing third of her front tooth. But who knew? She'd been wrong before.

"I use them to plan my inventions," Jessabelle said of her colored pens.

Madeline faced Jessabelle. "Isa, do you feel like we're drilling you with questions? We can stop."

"It's okay," she said. "Ask whatever you want." Once again, she smiled her chipped-horse-tooth smile, when a bell rang.

"I have to go," Madeline said, rising from the table.

"Me too," said Johann.

"I need to change."

"Where's everybody going?" Jessabelle asked.

"The chant," Doc told her. "It starts at seven-thirty."

"Go!" Vishva practically commanded as she rushed off.

Chet headed to the dishroom, carting a stack of every-body's trays, loaded with more stacks of bowls and cups, and a heap of silverware piled on top.

That left Jessabelle with Doc and Fuzz.

Chapter 10

With his small, furry shadow in tow, Doc escorted Jessabelle up the sidewalk on Liberation toward the evening chant. "I'm looking for a Shiva statue," she told him. "Have you seen one of those?"

"I've seen plenty, especially around here. What kind do you want? One to give as a gift? One to set on a desk? One to put in a garden?"

"I don't want to buy one. It's just…I'm a lover of Shiva. To see him in his purest form—his golden form—would mean so much to me."

Fuzz dashed up the street, klutzy as a baby who had just learned to walk, sniffing everything along the way. Suddenly he seated himself on the grass next to the sidewalk. His body trembled with excitement as he stared into the dusky light.

An Indian woman with long and straight luscious black hair appeared wearing a solid white sari. Fuzz greeted her with a tiny bark, his tail low and wagging.

"Good evening," she said to him in a soft, resonant voice. She bent on one knee, gently laid a hand on his head and caressed the length of his body, all the way to the tip of his tail. She repeated the motion. In three strokes time, the little guy had become so relaxed, he appeared half asleep.

The woman rose to her feet, cradling Fuzz against her chest. She wore a serene expression and possessed eyes mirroring the unforgettable black onyx eyes Jessabelle had seen on Shiva during her visit to the mansion-in-the-round.

"Lalleshwari," Doc said. "I want you to meet Isa Newton. She arrived five hours ago."

"Welcome," said Lalleshwari. "Where did you come from?"

"Massachusetts."

Lalleshwari smiled, resting her eyes on Jessabelle, fully taking her in. Her penetrating gaze derailed Jessabelle's mind, making her thoughts run off track and collapse to a complete standstill. Deflected from her purpose, Jessabelle forgot all about the Shiva statue.

An impulse to hand this stranger something of value jolted Jessabelle. She surveyed her own body. She had nothing to give. No money, no jewels. The most valuable items she carried were her colored pens, the wig on her head, and her prosthetic face, the nose of which she saw when she crossed her eyes. She was pretty sure this stranger would not consider these items as valuable as she herself did.

The irrational desire to give something to Lalleshwari grew so strong that Jessabelle wanted to strip right down to her skivvies, handing over everything she owned, and in the process, becoming nothing but herself. Was she losing her mind?

"Isa is a lover of Shiva," Doc told Lalleshwari.

"Good!" Lalleshwari exclaimed. "Here we encourage love of absolute Truth."

How had the conversation jumped from Shiva to absolute Truth? Had she missed something? A heavy fog of confusion rolled in.

"Make it your goal," Lalleshwari said.

Make what her goal? "Absolute Truth?" Jessabelle asked.

But Lalleshwari didn't answer. Her eyes glinted with sparks of light. That told Jessabelle she was correct. She said the words again, silently. *Absolute Truth.*

She didn't understand how Absolute Truth differed from just plain old truth. Was it like a sculpture and an unpainted sculpture? Or was the contrast more profound? Jessabelle wanted to ask Lalleshwari but the woman with the strange effect on her was already moving on, handing Fuzz to Doc and wishing them all a good evening.

Jessabelle and Doc, with Fuzz in his arms, wended their way up the street. Remembering her purpose for coming to this place, an air of righteousness lifted her. Truth already was her goal, at least plain old ordinary truth, and the reason she needed the statue. A million or so dollars would give her the freedom to quit her current job and never have to lie again.

"You can leave your shoes here," Doc said once they entered the coat room inside the education building. He in-dicated a column of shelves built into the wall, containing pairs of everything from patent leather stilettos and silver mules to Converse high-tops and flip-flops.

He sat on a fabric bench, untied his red and green sneak-ers, stepped out of one and then the other. With his index and middle fingers, he hooked both and carried them to one of the shelves. He rested his straw hat over the sneakers.

Instead of studying his hair and the exact shape of his skull to help figure out where she'd seen him before, she found herself absorbed in the shape of his feet, veneered in thin cotton crew socks. It seemed the width at the ball of one was slightly wider than the width at the ball of the other. It was such a small difference, she couldn't determine if his feet actually were different, or if the difference in his two feet was an optical illusion produced by her extra thick fake glasses. Wearing them was like seeing the world through an unwashed double pane window. They distorted the appearance of things, a frustration for a woman interested in the exact details of human anatomy.

She kicked off her black lace-up clompers and left them in the shoe room before proceeding on Doc's trail. He walked with a barely perceptible limp. Or was that just her glasses playing tricks again? As one attuned to the rhythms of human movement, she was sure she saw something, even through the glasses, although she couldn't exactly define it.

The lights were low in the multipurpose room when Jessabelle entered. Her eyes moved through the haziness in search of the Indian guru, but she didn't see him.

What she did see was about fifty average-looking men and women ranging in age from about twenty to ninety, mixed in their wardrobe choices, which included everything from Indian to country western. Some of the women wore brightly patterned bohemian-style maxi dresses or skirts like Madeline's, while others wore chic business attire. Like Johann, some of the guys wore stylish pants, slacks, and ties while others leaned toward Doc's style of casual. He still had on the blue jeans and short-sleeved heather green cotton twill shirt Jessabelle had met him in. Another young man sported a T-shirt and knee-length lime-green beach shorts. Jessabelle matched him to the flip-flops she'd seen earlier in the shoe room. The beach bum sat next to Chet in his chef uniform.

Some people sat crosslegged on large rectangular cushions near the front of the room. Many had their eyes shut, maybe meditating. Jessabelle wasn't sure how to tell.

An alternative to the floor existed in the form of five rows of chairs with foam-padded seats lined up behind the floor cushions. Jessabelle chose the floor, making herself comfortable beside Doc and Fuzz.

Once situated, she studied another chair, one-of-a-kind in this room, positioned at front and center. The armless chair had simple wooden legs and a seat and back upholstered in fabric with emerald-green paisleys against a sapphire-blue background. At two-and-a-half feet wide, it was more expansive than most. Jessabelle had never seen another chair quite like it.

To the right of the chair an oil lamp shimmered on an end table, and on the floor at each side of its front feet, the open faces of a dozen yellow roses ascended from hand-blown glass vases.

An Indian man sitting crosslegged on a sheepskin gazed out of a life-sized photograph displayed on the the wall behind the chair. His hair was a blend of black and gray. Along with a simple loincloth, he wore a blissful smile and a red dot between his eyebrows.

Jessabelle glanced at her watch, a high-tech digital thing with a face the size of a plum and a black PVC strap. It had a barometer, a digital thermometer, a weather trend indicator, and a dozen other features she'd likely never use. She wore it because of the nice touch a computer on her wrist added to her desired image of smart. It also came in handy when she needed to know the time, which was now 7:27. She wiggled her foot, wishing the Indian guru would hurry up and get here.

She tried to imagine how he would be dressed. Could that be him in the photo? Loincloth man? And would he just walk into the room when he arrived? Or would he enter in grand style, seated on a gold platform carried by four strapping young men?

Maybe he wouldn't enter through the door. Maybe, just maybe, a ball of fire staged by a couple of well-trained pyrotechnicians would explode in a corner, and like magic, he'd be standing there when the last plume of smoke faded out.

Then he'd jet into the midst of the people and proclaim, "There is a newcomer among us." Everybody would ooh and ah as he beamed right at Jessabelle. Then he'd explain the purpose and meaning of life in one profound sentence. Again, everybody would ooh and ah.

Jessabelle scrutinized the crowd for potential stagehands (people in black bodysuits), but didn't see any. She glanced back at the doorway for any signs of guru entry, but no, nothing yet.

What if she and Uncle Trix were all wrong about the guru and he proved to be totally legitimate, somebody who could indeed communicate the purpose and meaning of life? Doc, Johann, Vishva and Madeline seemed smart. Would they let themselves be deceived by a false guru? Maybe. They'd been fooled by her.

A young woman entered the room. She made small steps toward that front and center chair, kneeled, and bowed before it. *Hmm, weird.*

A guy entered and did something else weird. Approaching the chair, he stretched his entire body face down on the floor before it, extending his hands overhead in prayer position. The gesture made no sense to Jessabelle; it seemed like total submission to an empty chair, some kind of weakness on his part.

She reminded herself that she'd come to get the statue. She didn't have to make sense of what people did here.

At the front of the room, Johann took his place behind a standing microphone positioned to the far left of the Chair.

An overhead lamp came to life, shining from the ceiling, placing him in the spotlight. "I'm happy to host tonight's kirtan." Smiling, he introduced himself, and continued, "I want to welcome everyone, especially anyone who is here for the first time."

A few people smiled in Jessabelle's direction. She'd seen so many smiles that day: kind smiles, friendly smiles, welcoming smiles, sweet smiles. Not to mention that one long humungous smile from Uncle Trix. She'd grown so tired of smiles that her own fake smile turned to a grimace.

It had to be for her benefit that Johann went on to explain, "Tonight is our evening kirtan, in which we honor our inner divinity that has been shown to us by Lalleshwari."

Johann indicated the Chair. And Jessabelle realized it was the guru's chair, that the guru was not even a he, but a she—the very she Jessabelle and Doc had met on the road. Lalleshwari. Lalliji must be a nickname.

Johann explained that the man in the photo above the chair was Lalleshwari's guru. Johann said his Indian name, and one single second after he did, Jessabelle couldn't remember it. With about ten foreign syllables, it challenged her memory far more than Uncle Trix and the other one-, two-, or three-syllable names to which she was accustomed. Johann added, "In the west, he has come to be known as the Free & Blissful Yogi."

After a brief pause, Johann continued, "In order to experience our inner divinity, we will chant. The practice of chanting stills the mind, opens the heart, and makes us more susceptible to meditation. Tonight we will chant 'Om something something' for forty-five minutes in a call and response fashion."

He didn't really say "Om something something," but Jessabelle couldn't understand the words she heard after Om, so her mind just substituted "something something."

Johann explained that "call and response" meant people would take turns singing those mysterious words beginning with Om. The musicians who sat on the floor up front would sing them and then be quiet while everybody else sang them.

Forty-five minutes seemed like a long time to say a couple of indecipherable words over and over. That could get boring. Would Doc notice if she got up and left? Jessabelle turned her head, glancing at him. His eyes locked with hers, and he smiled. If tomorrow he asked about her quick departure, she could give headache or stomachache as a reason.

No, no. She couldn't leave. She had to make a good impression. That meant staying.

The fingers of one musician fluttered across the keys of a harmonium. Another musician pounded a two-headed drum; a third clinked a pair of hand cymbals. An exotic melody gushed into the air.

Soon everybody, except for Jessabelle, chanted with great enthusiasm. Even Fuzz, sitting on the floor before Doc, yelped and howled. Despite not being in sync with either call or response, his little voice brimmed with devotion.

The song that sounded so foreign to Jessabelle, everyone else knew by heart. While everybody sang "Om something something" over and over, a repetition of a different kind played in her head: "I don't belong here, I don't belong here, I just don't belong here."

She fell into a terrible state. She wanted to leave but couldn't, didn't want to sing but would've sworn everybody was staring at her because she was a newcomer. To those scrutinizers, it would look weird if she continued sitting there doing nothing. For the sake of appearances, she had to make some kind of effort. So she closed her eyes and when her turn came to chant, she moved her lips to make it look like she was chanting.

The chant progressed with a constant acceleration of the music's rhythm. The faster the music moved, the more animated her lip-syncing became.

Suddenly Jessabelle no longer heard where one word ended and the next began. She could only feel the rhythm of the words like a slow-moving mass of whirling energy. She felt the energy first in her feet, then her chest and head.

Moving within and without, this energy lifted her like a bird in a thermal, raising her to an altitude of two thousand feet. With great momentum, her spirit soared through a warm and sunny sky. The experience was exhilarating! And then it ended.

After the evening chant Jessabelle strolled to Krishna's Corner with the other young people. The lingering effects of the chant made her want to let loose and do jumping jacks.

While she kept herself in check, it was hard to subdue the playful energy that had risen inside. She found herself skipping through the door to the café Vishva held open for her.

"Do you want a burfi?" Vishva asked.

"Okay," Jessabelle said without knowing what she'd said "Okay" to.

On a dessert cart, clear glass covers shielded porcelain plates containing a variety of crisp, powdered, and cinnamony-looking sweets. At the sight of them, and loitering baking smells, Jessabelle's mouth watered.

Small white cardboard cutouts displayed the name and price of each dessert in black calligraphy. Australian Anzacs $1, Mexican Wedding Cakes 75 cents, Spanish Sand Cookies 50 cents, Swedish Dream Cookies $1.

Vishva lifted one of the glass lids, uncovering a pyramid built from sweets cut in two-inch squares and sprinkled with sliced pistachios. Using silver tongs, she placed one of the squares on a small paper plate and slid the plate to Jessabelle.

Jessabelle studied the dessert.

"You act like you've never seen a burfi."

"I've seen plenty of burfis in my day," Jessabelle lied, and without even getting a cue from the printed identification card, she guessed, "It's an Indian dessert, right?"

Vishva nodded.

With a name like burfi, how could it not be?

Vishva and Jessabelle took seats at the end of a long table, its edges populated by Johann, Madeline, Chet, and other young people.

Following introductions to those people at the table she hadn't met, Jessabelle sunk her teeth into the burfi. The tastes of cardamom and toasted almond melted over her tongue. "Mmm," she murmured. In her uplifted state, the dessert seemed especially delectable.

The "Om something something" chant had effected her mood so dramatically she wanted to know what it meant. "Oh hey," she said in a voice that didn't sound smart, but that she couldn't help. "You know that chant we just chanted for forty-five minutes? I can't remember the words to it, but could you tell me what they mean?"

Vishva said the words of the chant. Jessabelle still didn't understand. She tried to hide her confusion, but Vishva must have gleaned it, because she eased a napkin from the dispenser on the table and spread it open on the tabletop. "Mind if I borrow a pen?"

"No." Jessabelle glanced down at the bright collection of pens stuffed in her breast pocket. "What color do you want?"

"Green."

Jessabelle pulled Vishva's color of choice, clicked it open, and passed it to her. Vishva wrote on the tissue-thin paper and handed it to Jessabelle.

Jessabelle read the words "Om Namo Bhagavate Shivanandaya," written in neat letters along an invisible straight line. Seeing the words, it now seemed obvious they were the words to the chant. Jessabelle continued studying them as Vishva spoke them aloud, enunciating each word in a slow manner so Jessabelle could comprehend them. "It's a chant that praises Shiva," Vishva added, "the bliss of the truth."

When she heard "The bliss of the truth," the hair on Jessabelle's arms stood up and she thought she felt the earth move. In a far-off place a chorus of high-flying birds began to sing, and she smiled. This smile was not something she felt on her lips but somewhere deep inside.

Jessabelle entered her bedroom and locked the door behind her, more than ready to get her mask, glasses, teeth, and wig off, and let her real hair down. After nine hours in her emblems of nerdship, her scalp and face needed to breathe again.

She stripped down, one level at a time, beginning by casting the glasses onto the dresser and moving along to her red plaid skirt with suspenders and long sleeve white cotton shirt, which she hung neatly in the closet. She shed her wig, capped the head of a foam bust with it, then went into the bathroom, extracted her fake teeth with a tender rocking motion, and rinsed them with cold water. While her fake teeth dried on a copy of her real teeth, she brushed her real teeth.

She stood before the sink in her white cotton bra and underwear, and vinyl bald-cap. The torso of a woman, a slender five feet seven inches, peered out of the mirror. The bald-cap's edge ran the way Jessabelle had conformed it to move, protruding and receding like the contour of a ragged coast as it followed her hairline along its natural peaks and valleys and up over her ears before disappearing around the back of her head.

She unlatched her bait-and-tackle box, felt past the Pros-Gum for the Pros-Gum Remover, uncapped it, and then went back into her tackle box, routing for a paintbrush. An impression of Lalli came to her, Lalli all dressed in white, standing on Liberation earlier that evening.

Jessabelle lingered over the impression as she dipped the brush into the adhesive remover and painted it on an edge of her face piece, at her forehead, just underneath her hairline. Soon a crevice began forming between her skin and the mask. She inserted the bristles of the paintbrush into this crevice, and gently wriggling the brush, widened the gap, prying the top of the mask loose. Echoes of the evening's chant, Om Namo Bhagavate Shivanandaya, resonated inside. Continuously applying adhesive remover, she gently peeled the mask from the top of her forehead to the bottom of her chin, working it free of her face bit-by-bit, careful not to get any remover in her mouth or eyes. Along the way she found herself mouthing the words Om Namo Bhagavate Shivanandaya in tempo with the music she heard in her head.

She temporarily set her mask on the counter while she gave her skin some tender loving care by cleansing, toning, and moisturizing her face, a face with a white hue, clean and even, free from freckles and moles, a face with a slender upturned nose and full lips. She rinsed away all residue of stickiness and then did the same for her mask, washing it and dissolving inside glue blemishes with a small cotton pad saturated with more adhesive remover. She patiently picked bits of glue from the mask's edge with tweezers. Only when it was completely clean did she place the mask on a cold foam copy of her real face.

She plucked off her bald-cap, snapped off bobby pins,

and shook out her fine, soft brown hair. Chopped to a length just below her ears, it didn't fall far. Naturally straight, it now kinked and swirled, loosely retaining the shape Jessabelle had pinned and molded it while damp, guaranteeing that it would lie flat and stay that way, safely hidden all throughout her work day.

When she came out of the bathroom, with the chant playing inside, she felt full of energy, lifted all over again. She turned on the ceiling fan, then slipped between the white sheets of her bed in her underwear and Creativo T-shirt.

The sound of the chant circled round inside. She couldn't get it out of her head! With it as background music to her thoughts, she pondered Doc and Fuzz. She searched her mind for where she'd seen Doc before arriving in this town, by dropping his form into her memories of the spaces she'd occupied in past years. He couldn't be found in any Wally's parking lot, her college or high school.

The fan's humming prevented her from sleep. She got up, turned it off, and went back to bed. She fell asleep and dreamed she lay sprawled on a platter inside an oven set at 400 degrees Farenheit. She woke with a start, turned on the fan. Again the humming kept her awake. Instead of rising a second time to turn it off, she lay for hours in open-eyed sleep, Om Namo Bhagavate Shivanandaya moving inside, better than being baked alive.

She shut off her alarm just before it went off at five-thirty a.m. and plodded into the bathroom for the ninety-minute makeup/costuming job that would transform her from Jessabelle to Seriously Smart Girl, Isa Newton.

In her bra, underwear, and short dark hair vanished under a bald-cap, she stood before her sink and cleaned her forehead, cheeks, nose, and mouth with a sudsy gel, ensuring the canvas on which her art was made—her face—was clean and oil free. She dried her face on the institutional white towel doubled over the towel rack.

She reached inside her bait-and-tackle box, this time feeling past the cream foundations and Pros-Gum Remover until she found the Pros-Gum and a brush.

She spread on a thin layer of the clear adhesive, covering every surface of her face. Then she lifted her pliant mask from its repose on the cold foam copy of her real face, propped on the counter.

Slowly, carefully, holding her breath, using two hands, she set the mask gently upon her face, into the stickiness. She pressed it on her forehead and cheeks, under her eyes and nose, on her lips and chin, nudging it where necessary to get it into correct position as it settled into the adhesive. With her nerd face properly aligned, she could breathe and simply relax a moment, resting in the pleasure of having once again diverted the job of having to correct a misaligned piece and the folds and wrinkles that resulted from it.

Her nerd face glued in place, she undertook blending the edges, a most important step toward securing believability in her artistic design. After that she applied creams, powders, and tints, further concealing the edge between her skin and the mask, and matching the mask's color to the color of her own fair skin.

After she put on her wig, she opened her mouth wide, and pressed on her teeth, chomping down a few times to en-sure their proper placement. She leaned into the mirror for a better look at her creation, the face with the hooked nose and thin lips. The woman in the mirror pitched a big, chipped horse-tooth smile Jessabelle's way. It was always amazing—even to Jessabelle and even close up—how real prosthetic alterations appeared.

With face and hair done, she came out of the bathroom and donned an outfit she found in her closet, the second in the series of three she planned to wear in rotation. She began with the white knee socks. Then came a Neptune-blue plaid skirt, white shirt buttoned all the way to the top, and finally a vest and bowtie made from the same material as the skirt. Working to connect the bowtie's hook and closure, it was suddenly there, just as the singing of the cardinal in the oak outside her bathroom window was there—the memory of where she'd seen Doc before she arrived in Lalliville.

Chapter 11

On Jessabelle's first morning in Lalliville, she enjoyed two bowls of mung sprouts and puffed rice, alone in a corner of the dining hall. Following this simple breakfast, she sauntered over to the pale orange administration building. At four stories, it was the tallest in Lalliville.

She stepped off the elevator on the third floor, into a large and open office without dividers or cubicles, just five desks and enough plants to fill a jungle. At the first desk she told a woman, "I'm here to see Pierre Dubois about my service assignment." That woman led her to the door of an office on the periphery of the room. A gray-haired figure in a solid yellow dress shirt with a green striped tie jumped up from behind an L-shaped desk, so Jessabelle could see his white linen slacks and beige loafers. He shook her hand. Entering his office, the first thing Jessabelle noticed was a photo on the wall of Lalli standing on a dirt path, surrounded by lush woods.

Pierre offered Jessabelle her choice of seats, either the wheat-colored leather sofa or the office chair. She chose the office chair because it put one length of L between them. Although she took meticulous care with her disguises, the less anybody saw of her, the better.

After a bit of small talk conducted over the cherry wood top of the L, Pierre gave her a three-minute interview that had her shaking her head for three minutes. The head shimmy began after he asked, "Do you have any business skills?"

Unless selling a five-dollar brass bar for $2,000 counted as business skill, she had none.

"Any skills in the legal field?"

No. And if she didn't play her cards just right, she might soon need somebody with skill in the criminal defense area of the legal field.

No, no construction skills either, unless building elaborate lies out of thin air constituted experience in that field. Tree surgery? What exactly did that involve? Did tree surgeons perform root canals on Weeping Willows? Hee hee. She had no idea. Better shake her head.

"What computer programs do you know?"

3D, she thought, and wondered if Pierre knew 3D was a graphic design program for modeling and animating three-dimensional characters. Just in case he knew, she didn't want him putting two and two together. "I don't have computer skills," she said while shaking her head again.

"We have the perfect assignment for you," Pierre said at the conclusion of the interview.

A perfect assignment based on three minutes of head shaking? "What is it?" she asked.

He opened a small top drawer of his desk, filled with pens, sticky notes, erasers, paper clips, and rubber bands, from what Jessabelle could see. In the jumble of office supplies, he found two keys on a ring, then hopped to his feet. "The Purity Project."

"What's that?"

"It's designed to beautify this town," he said. She imagined herself planting flowers or putting a fresh coat of paint on one of the buildings in Lalliville.

Eagerly she followed Pierre out of the administration building and down Liberation past the gym, auditorium, Krishna's Corner, welcome center, and bookstore. They came to the end of the street, to the intersection near the front gate, hung a right, and walked up Peace Street. They swung left off Peace and tromped across a field, to what seemed the edge of the earth, arriving at a structure part shed, part barn.

Pierre put a key in the door and fought with it until it opened. He led her inside. She couldn't see much in the windowless room, lit now only by a rectangle of sunlight that stretched from the open door, partway across the floor. Pierre's crisp linen and bright dress shirt seemed especially beamy in the dank atmosphere.

He unlocked the door of another room and led Jessabelle inside this second room. Darkness enveloped her. The smell of mildew made her skin prick. Pierre clicked a switch, rousing a single incandescent forty-watt bulb to shine as best it could.

In its dim light, Jessabelle made out metal shelves filled with pictures stacked sideways. *What are they pictures of?* she couldn't help but wonder. She reached for one, but quickly retracted her hand and covered her mouth to stifle a gag. "Yuck," she said from under her hand when she saw what she almost touched: Mold.

The mold on the picture was so thick and furry it obscured the image, making it look like a topical map, not of green grass, blue lakes, and high mountains, but of a black and desolate land, a country from which no traveler returned. "Yuck," she repeated.

Pierre laughed. "You can say that again."

"Okay, yuck."

"We want you to clean these pictures, along with the room," he said. He then explained that there'd been a leak in the roof. Rainstorms left about two inches of water on the floor. All that dampness combined with the onset of summer made conditions ripe for the mold to flourish.

"How I am supposed to clean this place? I can't even see in here."

"Once the electrical position is filled, we'll repair the connection." He pointed to three non-working lightbulbs. "Until then, do the best you can. You can start by cleaning the room out there." He pointed to the external room. "Then move the pictures out there, clean this room, and then clean the pictures out there and move them back in here." After a brief pause, he asked, "Did you get all that?"

Did she get all that?

She could make and properly arrange artificial teeth. She knew how to create a head of hair, eyebrows, mustache, or beard, and how to trim those wigs, eyebrows, mustaches, and beards for a more natural appearance. She had the ability to use tints and pigments to render silicone, foam latex, or gelatin any shade on the entire spectrum of human skin color. Her detailed knowledge of anthropometry and biomechanics gave her the capability to engineer a living body. What was she doing here?

The way she kept shaking her head during her skills interview must have given Pierre the impression she was a humdrum kind of person, capable of only one thing, cleaning. That's something everybody could do, right? Wrong. Given her aversion to mold, she could not clean this place. She had the sudden urge to blurt "I'm so much cooler than I look!"

and tell him about her real skills.

But if she did, Pierre would want to know the meaning of the sudden outburst. One question would follow another until she was uncovered for the fraud she was. Better to look like a bore than get locked up for being a criminal. Besides, she doubted there was any work to be done in Lalliville for a person who could produce special character effects.

"Isn't there something else I can do? Like teach arts and crafts to kids? Or help them put on a play?"

"No."

"Why do I have to clean this place?"

"It needs to be cleaned."

"Yeah, but why do I have to do it?"

"Somebody has to do it. Why not you?"

"I don't have cleaning skills."

"Perhaps you can develop some here and now. Can you at least give it a try?"

"Sure," she said, with about as much enthusiasm as a cup of double fudge rocky road ice cream could be expected to muster when asked to marry a bowl of unflavored white yogurt.

"The cleaning supplies are there." Pierre pointed to a corner of the external room, filled by the dusky silhouettes of white buckets, a mop, sponges, and a gallon of bleach.

To attack this mold, she needed a disposable set of coveralls, protection against toxic substances. Surely this mold would only find her Neptune-blue plaid skirt, matching vest, and bowtie funny.

Pierre jangled the ring of two keys he held. He lifted Jessabelle's hand and slapped the keys in her palm. "The keys are in your hands now." Then he left her alone in that dark place.

Jessabelle tucked the keys in her skirt pocket and snatched the glasses off her face. She was probably the only glass-wearing nerd in the world whose vision functioned better without glasses than with. She glared around the room in the hope of seeing something different, anything she hadn't seen before. But everywhere she looked, she saw more of exactly the same thing, moldy metal shelves stacked with moldy pictures.

"Mold mold everywhere," she muttered under her breath, noticing mold on the walls and floors too. Blah! She returned to the external room.

Mentally, she attempted to repeat the instructions Pierre had given her. Start by cleaning the room out here. Or was that start by cleaning the room in there? The smell of this place distracted her. Gazing into the gloom all around her, the most unpleasant memories began to surface.

Suddenly she was fourteen again, and standing in the spare room of her house, the one Mom planned to turn into a nursery. The day before, Mom had told Jessabelle, "You can help me pick out a crib and changing table, and buy newborn jumpsuits, pantsets and beanies for the baby."

Jessabelle had wanted to help take care of the baby, had her own plans of painting a Winnie the Pooh and Friends mural on one of the walls. Or maybe she'd make a rubber Tigger or Eeyore for the baby to play with.

She couldn't wait to share her plans with Mom and Pops, see what they thought. Where was Mom? She was always home by six o'clock.

When the phone rang, Jessabelle answered, thinking it would be Mom telling her she had stopped to grocery shop or pick up a pizza. And it was Mom, only she delivered terrible news. She and Pops had been arrested breaking and entering a sneakers store a few towns over.

Jessabelle almost laughed when she found out why. They planned to sell stolen Nikes, Pumas, and Adidas on eBay, garnering a little more money, because these sneakers were the real thing, not knockoffs. It had seemed like such a stupid idea. Did they really think they could break the law like that and not get caught?

Jessabelle could ask herself the same question now. Oh, how her understanding had grown. She knew now what she didn't back then: Sometimes being good wasn't easy. She had no right to be so mad at Mom and Pops the last time she saw them. Mom had tried to explain. "From time-to-time, everybody needs a boost, and we needed one for the baby." She had reached out to caress the side of Jessabelle's face, and Jessabelle swatted her hand away.

Now she felt ashamed over the way she'd behaved. They were headed to jail and all she could think was, What will happen to me now? The way Mom's hand had shaken and the anxious look in her eyes took on meaning Jessabelle didn't understand back then. Mom was afraid. Well, so was Jessabelle! She'd known her separation from Mom and Pops was coming, and that scared her as badly as knowing the whole earth would soon be incinerated by aliens. Mom, Pops, and her baby sibling still in the womb were all about to be taken away. They were her world.

Jessabelle remembered waiting in the Department of Children and Families to meet her new parents, Mr. and Mrs. Cozie. Hah! What a joke! They turned out to be anything but cozy. What they should've been called was Mr. and Mrs. Torture-Jessabelle-for-No-Reason-at-All.

Why? Why couldn't they have been more like Mom and Pops?

Pops had always let her stay up and watch *Frankenstein*, *Dracula*, *The Mummy*, and all those other late-night flics with him. Her whole life seemed to start the time they took in the film about the making of *Frankenstein*. So mesmerized by the special effects artists, she must have looked like a bunny staring at a carrot as she viewed them on TV. Pops smiled when she made the determining statement, "I want to make characters."

"Well then," he said, "guess you'll have to learn to draw and sculpt."

He took her for lessons; she turned out to be pretty good. Mom let her experiment with her cosmetics to materialize the characters she sketched. Then Mom started to give Jessabelle money to send away for theatrical makeup from Characters R Us, a specialty store in California, and not because she was tired of Jessabelle playing with her makeup, but because there was only so much she could do with it. Mom wanted her to expand her abilities.

Jessabelle wanted that too, and went after it so whole-heartedly, it was as if her life depended on knowing all there was to know about Special Makeup Effects. She collected books, magazines, and internet articles that she scoured all hours of the day and night for tips and instructions on how to make characters. She learned different kinds of makeup, including basic and corrective. They were okay, but her absolute favorite, the kind she loved the very most, was character makeup. Making creatures. Transforming a person from one thing to another. The art of illusion. She just couldn't get enough of that.

Pops got a kick out of what he called her hobby. As the ever-willing guinea pig, he let her make face and body casts of him, and from those molds, she practiced creating prosthetic devices to fit his face and body. She experimented so much on Pops, she could make him look like anything. She took pictures of him as different characters, including a Chinese man, an African-American man, a very old Caucasian man, Rabbit Man, Alien, Monster, Zombie, and a Giant Fairy-man with wings.

Mom and Pops let her have the whole garage as a work-shop. Pops even built shelves in there for her to store all the feet, hands, fingers, ears, and wigs she produced.

Why? Why couldn't the Cozies have done stuff like that?

The Cozies' basement had mold in it, but it was the only place in their house not filled with some item of theirs. So Jessabelle asked if she could keep a few things of hers there. Mrs. Cozie said yes.

In a corner under a high window Jessabelle had begun to unpack her stuff, first lining up plastic containers of liquids, gels, and powders. Mrs. Cozie entered, and when she read the neat labels on the containers, she wrinkled her nose. "I never dreamed your things were called plastiline and nitrile. For all I know, you'll blow us all up."

"I won't," Jessabelle protested. "I never did before."

Mrs. Cozie gasped when she peered inside Jessabelle's open suitcase and spotted body parts, tooth trays, a bag of dental stone, and seven two-pound bags of alginate. "What's all this?" she asked.

"Materials," Jessabelle said.

"Can't imagine what a girl like you would do with all this—"

"With this stuff, I can make—"

"Junk!" Mrs. Cozie declared before Jessabelle could complete her sentence.

Jessabelle had wanted to tell Mrs. Cozie, "With this stuff, I can make anybody or anything!" She wanted to get out all the feet, hands, fingers, ears, and wigs she'd created and spread them before Mrs. Cozie so she could see them, but Mrs. Cozie's sneer invited no further discussion.

The day Mrs. Cozie sold Jessabelle's tooth trays without her consent, to a dentist in town, Jessabelle felt as if she'd been held down and kicked in the stomach. She couldn't move or breathe, wondering, Who sells another person's pride and joy? Even if that pride and joy is tooth trays, something they just don't understand?

Mrs. Cozie said it was to pay for Jessabelle's upkeep, which Jessabelle didn't understand since the state of Wisconsin did that.

Then Mrs. Cozie sold Jessabelle's jiffy mixer and used the money to buy socks and underwear for her husband.

When Jessabelle saw Mr. Cozie wiggling his toes under the weave of a gold-threaded toe cap, she lost it. After a long fight, Mr. Cozie grabbed her, forced her to the top of the basement stairs, and flung her down. "If you love your stuff so much, sleep with it!"

Hurled by the force of his anger, one leg rolled over the other until she lost her balance and collapsed at the bottom of the stairs. The door closed. She heard the click of the lock. Darkness enveloped her. Shock prevented her from moving.

"How long you gonna leave her down there?" she heard Mrs. Cozie ask her husband.

"Until she learns her lesson."

"Shouldn't we at least bring her some supper?"

"Let her go hungry. Starvation will teach her who is boss."

The next morning, Jessabelle sat slumped with her back against a wall, arms wrapped around her knees. Mr. Cozie opened the door at the top of the stairs and poked his head in. "Have you learned your lesson?" he asked.

"What lesson is that? Socks and underwear are more important than a jiffy mixer?"

"In this house you don't question the shots we call. That's the lesson. Have you learned it?"

She sat without speaking until Mr. Cozie closed the door.

All day she sat smelling mold, growing hungrier and more terrified. At night, when it grew dark again, she heard Mrs. Cozie say, "We can't leave her down there forever."

"Yes we can," Mr. Cozie grumbled.

That confirmed Jessabelle's fear that she could be in the basement for a very long time, until she turned from a flesh-and-blood woman into the skeletal remains of a flesh-and-blood woman. Not the thing she wanted when her whole life lay before her. There were still so many characters to invent. She couldn't die. She had to fight!

She plotted her escape. She planned to make a three-dimensional copy of herself with a cut and a bruise on her face and lay her distressed double under the window. Then she'd mix the liquids in those two bottles she always kept separate to create an explosion.

Once the Cozies heard it, they'd have to come downstairs. Seeing the Jessabelle replica, Mrs. Cozie's eyes would grow big. "Oh my," she'd say. "Do you think she's dead?"

"Only one way to find out," Mr. Cozie would say. He'd advance toward the replica with his wife on his heels.

From her hiding place under the stairs, Jessabelle would see Mr. Cozie bend over the silicone body and extend two fingers to the decoy's throat for a pulse check, just before Jessabelle bolted from her hiding place and raced up the stairs.

With heart pounding, she'd slam the basement door and lock it. "It's not her," Mr. Cozie would say once he realized. "It's a fake."

Then the banging on the basement door would begin. "Young lady," Mr. Cozie would say. "Open this door right this second!" But she would ignore him.

To the sounds of Mr. Cozie's repeated banging, she'd take a bowl from the cabinet, ladle out beef stew (or whatever else Mrs. Cozie made for dinner that night), and sit down to eat. Mrs. Cozie's cooking would never taste so good.

Even now, as she sat with her back against the outside of the Lalliville shed, it was a satisfying fantasy. "Let's see how you like being locked in the basement," she uttered aloud.

But the fantasy never materialized. Mrs. Cozie had already depleted her makeup FX supplies to such critical levels, she hadn't been able to build her replica. She needed a jiffy mixer to do it. In the end, she'd gone on fantasizing until her thoughts became disconnected, and all the pictures in her head dulled into a blur.

She couldn't say how many days the Cozies left her in the basement, but it was until she got so ravenous, she thought about scraping mold off the wall and eating it to relieve the hunger that gnawed at her.

She had lain on the basement floor with both hands on her stomach to ease that pain. The feet, hands, fingers, ears, and wigs piled on and around her body had provided some warmth when the chills set in, and for a time she'd been doing okay. At least she'd been able to convince herself of that.

Then she'd felt her blood slow. Her breathing became shallow, her heart thumping a few irregular beats. She feared that if she didn't starve to death, she might have a heart attack!

She had no choice. All she could think about was donuts and pizza, water and orange juice. She knew if she didn't get food and beverage soon, she would die, and the people upstairs wouldn't even care.

Too weak to stand, she raised her head, and with a voice nearly gone, called out to Mr. Cozie. The door opened and his face appeared in the crack of it. "You can have all my stuff," she said. "Can I just get something to eat?"

From then on, all she had to do to keep on eating was be nice to them, to not protest about them selling all her stuff. Not an easy feat, but she managed to get through her days in this way, until she turned sixteen and ran away from their home.

She wasn't one to dwell on the past, didn't really like

dredging up all those bad memories. Let bygones be bygones, she told herself. Keep your life moving forward. Erase the past by creating a bright new future.

Jessabelle felt her pocket and reminded herself the keys were in her hands. She wasn't trapped now, and once she found that statue she'd never again have to live with anybody who'd starve her in a locked basement.

She jumped to her feet and thundered off in search of the golden Shiva.

Chapter 12

The Cozies were the very last people in the world Jessabelle wanted to think about. Unfortunately, from the moment she stormed away from that moldy shed, they occupied her mind as if they were the only people in the world.

She reached the bottom of Liberation, then started up past the dining hall where the aroma of hot and spicy food filled her nose. *Mmm*, she thought, *I will eat in an hour*. For a second this thought comforted her. Never again would she go hungry.

Then the pain of being starved in a locked basement rose with a vengeance, sucking all her attention to it.

Was it possible that if she'd gone back to the Department of Children and Families and told them her story, everything would have turned out differently?

Who in Child Services would have believed that these people sold off a fourteen-year-old's stuff and locked her in a basement to starve?

The case workers would have accused her of making up stories. If she hadn't lived through it, she'd accuse herself of making up stories, thinking, *Nobody is really that crazy.* "Yes, Isa, or whoever you are," she muttered now, "people really are that crazy."

But if the social workers believed her, she may have gotten a new foster family. She may have been notified when Mom and Pops were released from jail and wouldn't be separated from them now.

If only she'd done something different, she wouldn't be in the strange predicament she was in at this moment: tasked with cleaning a moldy shed, dressed as a geek, in the town of a saint where she'd come to steal a statue.

Jessabelle felt superior to the Cozies. At least she could admit she was a thief. They couldn't. She might hurt people's pocketbook, but she caused them no physical harm.

Okay. Occasionally, she'd had to defend herself against people like Wrench. But she'd never lock a teenager, or anybody else for that matter, in a basement to starve! That was just plain cruel. The Cozies deserved punishment.

She took pride in the fact that she'd stolen $800 from them, a justified act considering it was money they made from selling her laptop, the one she used for digital designs. Stealing their money was getting even, a minor act of retribution.

She needed that money to escape, and flee she did. With the money she stole from them, she rented a room over a garage, the perfect place to practice her craft. She immediately looked for jobs to support her new life. But soon her new life didn't feel fresh at all. Years of living underground had changed her; lying to survive had become a way of life. She couldn't help but drop little white lies everywhere she went.

To get a neighbor to hire her for help with gardening, she said "I helped my mom plant flowers" and then said the job took five hours when it really only took four. "I babysat my little brother" was the line she used to get a babysitting job. She stole a bag of grapes out of a refrigerator in a mansion she cleaned. "They have so much," she told herself. "They won't miss it."

These weren't criminal acts. She'd just done what she needed to do in order to endure in jobs she didn't love but was happy to have for the freedom from the Cozies they afforded. Isn't that what she was doing now, for crying out loud? Doing what she needed to do to survive? To get back to art college? To succeed in life?

Her head ached from not understanding what was normal or regular anymore.

She passed the welcome center, café/library, education building, gym, and administration building, rotating her head this way and that, desperate to spy a gleam of gold.

Panic snared her and held tight as she neared the top of Liberation. She'd been inside all of those places, except the gym, and she hadn't seen the statue. Would anybody put a three-million-dollar statue in a gym? Probably not. She was running out of areas to search. What if she never became rich, remaining always as a scrimper and fibber?

Gold flashed at the edges of her vision, and this new possibility for success soothed her. Drawn toward that wink of fortune, she followed its shining trail, arriving at an elephant—a real elephant. Slipped over her body, trunk, and ears was an elaborate silk covering with an intricate design of lilies embroidered in gold. Around her neck she wore a long necklace strung with sandalwood beads.

Jessabelle moved closer to her. She reached out to touch one of those giant beads. A dark hand came out of nowhere, catching her wrist. She sucked in her breath and spun, coming face-to-face with an Indian man. He wore a white beard, a white shirt, and a plain white sheet of silk wrapped and tucked around his waist, hanging to his ankles. "Please, ma'am," he whispered, guiding Jessabelle away from the elephant. "Myuri gets cranky when disturbed from her meditation, and nobody likes a cranky elephant."

"Is she really meditating, or just sleeping?" she whispered back.

"I assure you she's meditating. She always does before the noon arati, and since she hasn't yet figured out how to turn herself into Tommy, she does it out here."

When he said the name Tommy, he pointed to a four-foot chimpanzee walking up steps of concrete and stone, toward the double doors of the Free & Blissful Yogi's shrine, a small stone temple. Walking on all fours using his knuckles for support, Tommy moved with a cool civilized air, followed by Johann and Vishva.

"The arati?" Jessabelle asked.

"I assume that's what you're here for."

"Correct," Jessabelle said.

The saronged man escorted her up the stairs, then handed her a laminated card, "Verses from the Bhagavad Gita." He welcomed her inside. She stepped into a large corridor, and before entering the main room, pit-stopped in a small shoe room where she left her black lace-up clompers.

The temple's main room had a long rectangular shape with occupancy of two hundred. Jessabelle strode up the center aisle, past seven rows of chairs in the back, and took her place crosslegged on the floor at the front of the room. Her eyes fell on a life-sized bronze statue of a man she recognized as Lalli's guru. Richly dressed in a silk cape and adorned with jewels, he resided in an alcove, the inner sanctum, seated crosslegged on a stone pedestal. Flowers and oil lamps decorated his platform. A dome-like tower rose over the niche where he was installed.

Humming sounds rippled in her right ear. She swiveled her head. Tommy smiled, instigating her to smile back. He was cute, all right, but with her past burning inside, she couldn't bring herself to show her crooked horse teeth, not the way he displayed his extra-large chimp chompers. Further down the row, Fuzz sat in front of Doc, who sat next to Johann and on the other side of him, Vishva. Vishva glanced at her. Again Jessabelle tried to smile but lacked the spirit for it.

She turned her head left and saw many people with eyes closed. She tried to imitate them, attempting to enter into a relaxed meditative state, but only found herself anxious and staring.

A bell jangled, and everybody stood. A harmonium player up front tapped a few keys, starting up the music. They sang the verses printed on her chanting card. Afterward, everyone dropped onto their knees and bowed before the likeness of the Free & Blissful Yogi.

They again took their seats, crosslegged, and chanting loudly, sang Om Namo Bhagavate Shivanandaya in a call-and-response fashion for about ten minutes. Tommy extended his disproportionately long arms, gesturing like a conductor, producing a range of sound wide as an opera singer's.

Om Namo Bhagavate Shivanandaya cocooned her, bringing peace to her heart, solace to all those burning emotions. When the chant ended, Tommy covered his heart with his hand while the elephant bellowed outside the temple walls and Fuzz lay curled in Doc's lap, snoozing. She loved this congregation so much, she felt like putting a hand over her heart and bellowing. Dare she say she felt right at home here?

Several people formed a line and came before the Free & Blissful Yogi. Some bowed and prayed. Others placed gifts of flowers, fruits, sweets, or money in straw baskets at his feet.

Seeing all those hands opening, Jessabelle smiled inside, thinking about the best job she had in the time after she fled the Cozies—typing a manuscript for Mrs. Acorn, an eighty-three-year-old widow who wanted to leave an autobiographical record of her life for her grandkids. At fifteen dollars an hour, the pay was better than minimum wage. Another thing Jessabelle lied about: "I can type sixty-five words per minute."

When Mrs. Acorn saw Jessabelle searching out and pecking keys with her two index fingers, probably thinking, *Why'd I hire her? I can do better with my arthritic hands*, she didn't even get mad. She let Jessabelle continue working for her because she could see how badly she needed money, but lowered her wage to eight dollars an hour because in her words, "This is going to take a whole lot longer than I thought. I just hope we finish before I die." Jessabelle agreed to the new wage; it was more than fair.

Keystroke by keystroke, she came to love the old lady like a cool salve lavished on fresh burning-hot wounds. When Mrs. Acorn found out Jessabelle hadn't graduated high school, she helped her get her G.E.D. When Jessabelle showed her various pictures of Pops as a Chinese man, an African-American man, a very old Caucasian man, Rabbit Man, Alien, Monster, Zombie, and a Giant Fairy-man with wings (pictures she still had because they weren't worth anything on the open market), Mrs. Acorn helped her bind them into a portfolio, and suggested she use the portfolio to apply to art college.

When Mrs. Acorn found out Jessabelle no longer had a computer, she let her type her application on her computer when she wasn't typing the manuscript.

Why couldn't there be more Mrs. Acorns? If everybody in the world were like Mrs. Acorn, the whole world would be good, not a place where people took advantage of each other.

She'd planned to go back and visit Mrs. Acorn during her first Christmas vacation in art college, but Mrs. Acorn didn't even make it past Thanksgiving. Jessabelle spent part of that Christmas holiday in her room drawing pictures of Mrs. Acorn's hands.

Funny she should find herself thinking about those hands now. Without those hands, she never would have gone to art college.

Witnessing all those people placing gifts in baskets, she wanted to give something too, but had nothing to give. Maybe one day, once she got her hands on that solid gold Shiva, she would have something to give.

Back out on Liberation, Vishva waited with her hands tucked into the jacket pockets of a cream pantsuit, accessorized with a lavender silk camisole, a genuine fine gold necklace and earrings, and gold pumps with a kitten heel. "Everything okay? You seem sad."

"I'm not the least bit sad! Why do you think I'm sad?"

"You look sad."

"I'm happy! Very very happy!" Jessabelle forced a smile and put a skip in her step.

Vishva's expression of concern didn't change. "Sometimes things come up when we go inside."

"Go inside? Inside the temple?"

"No, inside ourselves."

Inside? Is that what Jessabelle was doing? Going inside? With all the bad stuff hidden there, why would she want to do a thing like that? "Not me." She felt her head shaking; from side to side it went. "You must have the wrong girl. I'm not the going-inside type."

"Well, you must have wanted to now," Vishva persisted. "Otherwise you wouldn't have come to Lalliville."

Hah! Is that what Vishva thought? That Jessabelle had come to this place to go inside? *I'll have you know,* Jessabelle thought, *I came here to get rich!*

"If you ever need somebody to talk to, you know where to find me."

Hah! She didn't have a problem, and even if she did, surely it was one way too delinquent to discuss with a woman as high-class as Vishva. How could Jessabelle tell Vishva anything about herself? She nodded to Vishva, managed a "Thank you" before hurrying off.

The saronged man led Myuri along Liberation. She wondered where the elephant lived, at the same time becoming aware of a great sadness inside. How long it had been there, she couldn't say.

She blamed Vishva's ability to detect this sadness on her own capability to make prosthetic appliances strong enough to use several times over, but flexible enough to emote in. Well, human touch appliances were not what she needed right now! What she could really use is a tin suit, a place to cry all day, shielded from everyone else's sight.

Why was she so sad?

Deep inside, she knew. She knew that long ago, she had lost herself. Art college was supposed to take her back. Wally's knife and gun shop was supposed to take her back. Selling brass bars for several thousand dollars a pop was supposed to take her back. But she never found her way back to herself. She was lost with no idea how to get back home, and that made her feel very, very sad.

Chapter 13

With her morning sadness over memories of how the Cozies had starved her assuaged by a lunch of cornbread and beans, Jessabelle plodded to the shed, telling herself everybody in this place had to work, and that included her. Doc did security, Johann finance, Madeline halls, Chet cooking, and Vishva welcoming.

Jessabelle didn't want to labor. She was used to making two to four thousand dollars a day for essentially making faces and lying, not paying $500 a week to live in a place where she was required to work.

Sure, making faces was work, but in that kind of work hours went by like minutes. Scrubbing mold off a floor hardly compared to creating a wart on the side of a prosthetic nose that kind of grossed everybody out because they thought it was real.

She didn't know if she could take one minute of scrubbing and cleaning. Just thinking about it made her wince. But to make a good impression, she had to endure some labor. At some point Pierre would be by to check her progress.

She opened the door to the shed and entered, moved to a box of cleaning supplies, and selected a pair of rubber gloves and a sponge.

Later, after she had spent two hours cleaning a corner of the room, she was on her way to Pierre's office. "Omigosh," she mentally rehearsed. "I just remembered I have a doctor's appointment. Dr. Hardy's supposed to give me an allergy shot. I'm allergic to mold. If I don't go, a serious attack might strike me!" How could Pierre say "no" to that? Once she'd produced her alibi for not being in the shed, she'd find Doc and confirm her discovery about him.

She was remembering the time she first saw Doc, when Doc and his fuzzy companion came up beside her. "I hear you're cleaning the shed," he said.

Doc didn't seem to notice her startlement. She half nodded. "Word travels fast."

"Around here, word moves faster than three gallons of chai." When she stared at him blankly, he explained, "That's fast. All that sugar and caffeine make it a popular beverage."

Doc had never seen her before she came to Lalliville, but oh, how she'd seen him. She wished it had been under different circumstances. Looking at him now, the whole thing almost made her feel guilty.

The beads of Shiva slowly vibrated against his chest to the rhythm of his walking. "That's a unique necklace," she said.

"My mala?" Doc asked.

"What kind of beads are they?"

Doc laughed. "You're here and you don't recognize japa

"I do," she lied, ashamed of her ignorance. "I know what they are. For a second, I just forgot. I also forgot how to spell jop-uh. Could you tell me?"

"J-a-p-a."

"Oh yeah," Jessabelle said and silently repeated the letters j-a-p-a. "Just so I don't forget again..." She took out a small pad she carried in her breast pocket and wrote *japa* on it.

She turned the way Doc's beads went. "Looks like we're going to the same place." Doc held the door to Krishna's Corner open for her.

Dozens of people packed the place. Scattered about the room, they sat clustered around tables in groups, eating sweets off paper plates and drinking milky tea from plastic cups. "Welcome to afternoon tea time, the unofficial part of the daily schedule," Doc said with a smile. "Can I buy you a chai?"

"No thanks," Jessabelle said.

"How about a cup of coffee?"

"Sorry, I don't do caffeine."

"Not a drinker, eh? Me neither. My get-up-and-go comes from morning meditation. Where do you get your energy?"

Morning meditation sounded good, so Jessabelle said that, although she'd never even tried meditating.

"So we're alike," Doc said.

Jessabelle wished it were so, but knew in reality they were nothing alike. Right down to their teeth. His were perfect. Hers were cracked, crooked horse teeth. And those were just her fakies. While her real teeth didn't provide as much to gape at, they were still far from perfect. Four of her incisors twisted as if they danced. That was okay by her; she liked teeth with character.

She cherished the full spectrum of toothlines on planet Earth, in fact, including turning and overlapping ones.

Overbites and underbites sort of fascinated her. She preferred teeth the way nature produced them. It gave them such personality, abundant in eccentricity for her to replicate in her own wearable art.

Doc exhibited naturally straight, white teeth.

He was clean-shaven. His fingernails were trimmed and scrubbed. Neither the black jeans nor the loose-fitting turquoise and purple plaid short-sleeve cotton shirt he wore bore any spots, rips, tears, or holes.

The terrycloth patch she'd cut from a white bath towel (compliments of the Good Night's Sleep chain of motels) and sewn on the elbow of her white shirt was there for geek effect, but also to hide a real hole that came with the shirt when she picked it up at a thrift shop for twenty-five cents.

Of course the shirt was part of a costume, but in costume as in real life, she had no beef with garment flaws. The most comfortable article of clothing she owned was her faded blue jeans, not the ones she wore as part of her blonde-haired country girl disguise but the ones ripped laterally over the knees. Those she liked just fine. She wondered if Doc would ever wear ripped jeans.

She'd bet that he was just as clean on the inside as he was on the outside. She could tell by the open, unaffected way he smiled at her now.

Before she put on her face every morning, she showered and brushed her teeth, but she never felt clean. Her insides were soiled with hundreds of her own lies, a kind of dirty she couldn't get out with a toothbrush or washcloth. If she shoved a scrubbrush down her throat, it would only hurt.

"Can I buy you an Anzac cookie?"

Maybe a cookie was just what she needed to soothe the uneasiness forming in the pit of her stomach. "Sure."

He clasped the knobby handle on top of the glass lid over the plate of Anzacs, tilted it up, and selected two of the baked goods, which he placed on two small paper plates. He glanced at the watch fastened around his wrist. It had a brown leather band, a silver case, a black dial, a date window, and a compass subdial. The watch of an explorer. "I've got about twenty minutes. Do you want to sit together?"

"Sure," she said again. "I'll get us a couple of waters."

He paid the cashier and they took seats across from one another at a table for two. He put a cookie in front of her and one in front of him. She did the same with the glasses of water. He took off his straw hat and set it on the square tabletop, leaving himself with a bad case of hat head.

He gave the fuzz ball at his right foot a puppy treat from his pocket. Then he took a bite of his cookie, and with his mouth closed, chewed in smooth, genteel motions.

The impression of softness he emanated was so strong, it wouldn't have surprised her if he possessed the ability to transform himself into a rose pink cashmere blanket—make that a freshly laundered rose pink cashmere blanket—to keep a girl feeling snuggly and warm on a cold winter night.

Snap out of it! He's not a cashmere blanket. Besides, with temperatures at ninety degrees by eight o'clock in the morning, who needed one of those?

She raised her cookie to her mouth.

"I'd love to hear more about your inventions," he said. "Do you have more than three?"

She wanted to tell him the truth, No, in fact I have no inventions. Instead she muttered, "Umm hmm," from behind the cookie she held before her mouth.

"Sorry?"

Again she wanted to tell the truth, but said, "Yes, I have more than three." She didn't want to lie to him, but there, she'd just done it again.

She'd lied so many times and for so long, she didn't know how to stop.

"I'd love to see your wingsuit," he said.

She searched several possibilities for the correct way to respond, but couldn't find it. She put down her cookie without having taken a bite. She picked up her water glass and held it a moment, and then put it down without taking a sip. She again picked up her cookie and again put it down.

She realized she was being fidgety. From inside, Uncle Trix scolded her. *It's okay to be nervous,* he said. *Just don't look nervous! It's a sure sign you're lying.*

But how? How could she hide her nervousness when she had a man with such a clean and honest face gazing straight into her eyes and saying, "I'd love to see your wingsuit," an invention she had led him to believe she had but didn't?

"Yeah, well, uh…" She had to deflect attention off her and onto him, fast. "Why do they call you Doc?" she asked.

"No big reason," he said in a relaxed manner. "One day Chet called me that, because I'm a doctor, and my last name's Halloway."

There was the confirmation of what she already knew. Doc was the young man in the picture she'd seen in the Halloway living room, a part of the family, probably Mr. Halloway's son. His hair the color of sand with the light of the sun shining on it, his sweet eyes. They'd made an impression on her even then, as they were now.

"The name kind of stuck," he was saying.

"Doc, as in Doc Holiday the outlaw?"

"Well, yes."

"Are you an outlaw?"

"Well, no. I don't believe in outlawry in any form—thievery, lying."

Jessabelle sighed so loudly, she was afraid it sounded as if she'd just uncorked a windstorm. She had to admit, it was weird. He gave her an odd look and the space to explain the sudden gust, which she chose not to do.

"What does Isa mean?" he asked. "Smart? I hear you're a direct descendant of Sir Isaac Newton."

Crap, crap, crap. Why had she told Chet that last night? She had to remember: Around here, word travels faster than three gallons of chai.

Ashamed, she turned her body away from him and crossed her legs. She needed to get the attention off her and steer the conversation toward Shiva. Now that she was sure of his identity, she recognized him as a good person to question about the golden statue. She crossed her arms, trying hard to close down to him, to concentrate on theft. But her heart would not follow her mind's lead. "What kind of doctor are you?"

"An anaplastologist. You know what that is?"

"Yes."

"Really? You'll be the first layperson I've met who does." He paused and smiled. "Do you really know what that is?"

"Yes."

"Tell me then, what is it?"

"Somebody who restores lost or injured parts of the body."

"Wow, you really are smart!"

She loved his voice and not just because he'd said she was smart. It was his tone. He spoke in a way that evoked the soft rustling of trees. Jessabelle felt as if she could listen to that stirring all day. He didn't even have to make sense. He could string together sentences of incomprehensible words; she would still listen.

She could hear Uncle Trix telling her how stupid she was for falling for the closest thing to law enforcement in this town. Besides, he'd just said he didn't like thievery and lying, and that's all she was, a thief and a liar. She didn't stand a chance with him.

She had to get her mind back on business. She resolved

to question him about Shiva. She opened her mouth. Out came, "So what made you want to be an anaplastologist?"

"I want to help kids and animals."

"Animals?" She'd made humans look like animals, and fit humans with prosthetics, but it never occurred to her to place an artificial anything on an animal. "How do you fit an animal with a prosthetic?"

"Same way I fit a human."

"And this is something you've actually done?"

"Sure. Fuzz was the first."

"Fuzz?" She spotted Fuzz in the children's corner, next to a basket of toys, swinging a stuffed giraffe in his mouth.

"His foot got ripped apart by a bear trap."

"A bear trap? How'd he get into one of those?"

"I wish I could get inside his head and know. But I can't. When I found him, he was sick, hollow-eyed, all alone, and close to death. I took him home and nursed him back to health. But without his leg, he slept all day. That artificial leg I gave him changed his life. He can walk again, and now he plays all day. He's growing so fast, soon I'll have to make a new leg for him."

The sweetness of that story clotted her throat. She held back tears, knowing she couldn't cry. With all the specialty makeup she wore, things could get ugly, messy, or both.

She glanced at Doc from the corners of her eyes. He gave a warm smile as if he were enjoying this conversation and felt delighted to tell his story. And who wouldn't be pleased to share the fact they'd saved a dog's life? Gave a puppy back his spirit? Those were things to be proud of.

She wanted to share herself with him, pour her heart out about all the things that really meant something to her. She uncrossed her arms, straightened her legs, and turned to face him. She opened her mouth to tell him about the nine anaplastology conventions she had attended in her pursuit of mastering the art of prosthetics.

A few feet from her right ear, she heard a tiny, low growl.

She started in unison with Doc. They turned their eyes toward the sound.

Fuzz cinched a stuffed bear in his teeth, tossing his head from side-to-side. He pawed the bear's body.

Doc whistled, but Fuzz didn't stop his play. "Better get him before he decapitates the thing," he said. He got up, joggled the bear from Fuzz's mouth, lifted Fuzz in his arms, and holding him against his chest, returned, consulting his watch.

His good-bye was polite. "I'd like to stay and talk, but really must get back to work." He exited, cradling his K-9.

What was that pain pinching Jessabelle's gut? Was it her stomach growling, telling her she needed one more Anzac? Or was that discomfort something else?

She knew in her heart that her uneasiness had nothing to do with food and everything to do with Doc. Romance was not part of the plan, and under the circumstances—could not be.

She didn't like these feelings that confronted her, but they were too strong to push away.

Chapter 14

At the end of her first day in Lalliville, Jessabelle was alone at a table in a corner of the dining hall, scarfing down a dinner of peas and carrots, curried brown rice, and French lentil soup.

Her phone had rung twice that day, and both times it had been Uncle Trix. The first time he called, she'd been standing in the library balancing a book entitled *Yoga Defined* on her open hand, reading the definition of japa. It said, "Japa is the repetition of a mantra. You can say it aloud or to yourself, and you can count your repetitions on a string of beads called a japa mala." The entry included a photo of a japa mala almost identical to Doc's.

Uncle Trix wasn't interested in any of that, only wanted to know if she had any updates. After less than one day, he'd wanted to know if she'd found the statue. Well, no.

He'd just called again, no more than three hours later, wanting to know the same thing. The man had the patience of a drug addict working on a big fix.

With a mouthful of vegetables, she'd told him, "Gimme time." While Lalliville had only nine streets, she still needed at least a few days to get acquainted with the place. The untold truth was she felt no need to rush things; she wanted to take her time charting Lalliville to be sure she didn't miss any part of it.

He argued that there was no time. At forty-five, he was already at his designated retirement age.

"Okay, okay," she finally said. She promised to begin combing the place right after dinner. And when she made that pledge, she meant it. But as soon as she clicked off her phone, Vishva, Johann, Doc, Chet, and Madeline joined her one by one, and she stayed.

Picking up on the discussion from the night before, they hammered her with questions and comments. "Where do the ideas for your inventions come from?" "Were you always smart?" "Your father and mother must be very proud." "What do you think of Amelia Earhardt?"

That lie about the wingsuit felt so old, she wished they'd let it die. She didn't like having to keep it on life support by answering questions about it, hated being forced to concentrate so hard to be sure nothing she said today contradicted anything she had said yesterday.

This kind of accountability was a new experience for her. In the company of any of the people she met on the road, she could make up any crazy story right there on the spot, knowing she would never see the same people again. But this wasn't the road, she had to remind herself. Tonight she was eating dinner with the same people she'd eaten with the night before.

If you want to succeed, you have to remain sharp as a pin. That voice inside her head sounded like Uncle Trix, and she couldn't agree with him more. If she wanted to find the statue and not get caught in the process, she had to take her game to a new level. So she kept smiling, focusing, navigating their line of questioning with the skill of somebody well practiced in the art of deception. "My ideas come from pure inspiration…As a baby, I was already really smart. My parents often joke that I came out of the womb reciting mathematical formulas…My father and mother placed so much faith in me, between the two of them, they worked five jobs to send me to M.I.T. ..Amelia Earhardt, she was great. I really admire her pioneering spirit." If Uncle Trix could only see Jessabelle now, he'd be proud.

When the bell signaling the start of the chant tinkled, everyone got up to leave, and recalling the previous night's chant, Jessabelle followed like a baby bird in search of the open sky.

With the group, Jessabelle chanted Hari Rama Hari Krishna for forty-five minutes in a call-and-response fashion. Exiting the hall, she felt much better than when she'd entered it. Once again the chant had transformed her state, renewing her enthusiasm for finding Shiva. In her brightened mood, she followed the others to Krishna's Corner to further energize herself for the search.

Jessabelle and Vishva settled at a table together, each with a mug of chamomile tea and an Indian coconut cookie. "How was your first day of service?" Vishva asked.

Many adjectives sprang to mind: stressful, turbulent, depressing, disgusting. "Great," Jessabelle finally said, and in a weird way, felt it wasn't too much of a lie. "I talked to Doc." What strange reason prompted her to relate that fact to Vishva?

"He's quite nice. Don't you think?"

Jessabelle nodded. "How come he doesn't come here after the chant?"

"He meditates instead. Do you have a crush on him?"

"No," Jessabelle pronounced, perhaps a little too emphatically. "I definitely do not have a crush on him. Besides, have you seen me lately? I'm hardly romance material." Jessabelle took a huge bite of coconut cookie, and then another, polishing off the sweet. With puffed out cheeks full of coconut cookie, she chewed.

Vishva took a small bite of her cookie and chewed in slow, dainty motions. "I bet you can be quite pretty, if you want to be." Vishva glanced at Jessabelle's body. "You've got a cute figure." Vishva's gaze traveled up, her eyes resting on Jessabelle's wig of kinky red wire. "I can help you do something with your hair, if you want."

Jessabelle swallowed the commingling of sugar, coconut, and flour that was in her mouth. "Can we please change the subject?"

"Sorry Isa." Vishva laid a hand over Jessabelle's. "Didn't mean to offend you."

"You didn't," Jessabelle said over the buzz of conversations going on at other tables. "It's just that there's something beside my hair I want to talk about."

Fingers wrapped around a paper cup, Vishva held her tea, poised for a sip. "Go ahead."

"I don't get meditation."

Vishva sipped her tea, set her cup back on the table. "What don't you get about it?"

"How to do it. You just sit there?"

"Surely you've done it before."

Jessabelle nodded an agreement while gulping chamomile tea.

"What do you usually do?" Vishva asked.

"Usually," Jessabelle lied, "I just sit there, but nothing ever happens."

"You could try a new mantra."

"Which one do you use?"

"Jaya Shiva Om."

"Why do you use Jaya Shiva Om?"

"Because that's the mantra Lalli's guru gave her, and in turn she gives to all of us. It's enlivened by her grace and has the power of stilling the mind."

Approximately thirty minutes later, Jessabelle's mind was anything but still. After tea and cookies she'd wandered down Liberation, looking through windows for the statue, when she saw a sign for a meditation cave and halted.

A cave seemed impossible in this terrain, with its flatlands and zero rock formations. She'd heard about the magnificent underwater caves in Florida. But wouldn't it require an ocean and special scuba equipment to meditate in a cave like that?

If there really was a cave back there, what better place to hide a three-million-dollar statue? But if that were the case, why make a public announcement, complete with a sign pointing the way to it?

She set foot on the dirt trail and started through the woods in the direction of the meditation cave as shown by the arrow. She needed to see this cave, and if she didn't find the statue there, she could at least eliminate the meditation cave from the list of places the statue could possibly be. As she trod along the trees grew thick, shrouding the path, making it hard to see.

She heard a shriek. It echoed in the darkness, turning her body cold. With a racing heart, she whipped her head to the top of the path, where the sound had come from. The grizzled gray coat of something—human, beast, or both!—emerged there. It progressed in her direction, sending her adrenaline soaring even higher.

She stepped to the side of the path, hid in thick brush,

and watched as a gray hog lumbered past.

More squeals spiked the darkness. Afraid to move a muscle, she stayed put and from her observation deck of forest floor, saw two more hogs, one after the other, walking the path.

Hogs. She'd never studied one of them, or even seen one up close. She thought of a man in overalls and workboots she and Uncle Trix had met in Boise, Idaho. That man had told Jessabelle he had lots of hogs on his farm. He said, "I love my hogs. Aren't they friendly?" And she said "Yes," as though she knew all about hogs. She lied and told that man, "I used to play with the hogs on Grampa's farm." He smiled as if he knew exactly what she was talking about. Then she pretended to cry as she said, "I don't know what will happen with all my hog friends now that Grampa's been taken to the hospital."

In reality, the hog was one animal she'd spent no time with or knew anything about. She'd never read about them the way she'd read about other animals.

She could hardly believe three hogs had just trotted past her now. If they hadn't startled her and she'd had her camera, she might have taken a picture and added it to her vista of inspiration, in the event she ever wanted to make a pig face.

She tried to recall the way those hogs looked as her heart rate returned to normal. Short snouts, canine teeth. No, couldn't be. Hogs didn't have canine teeth, did they? She decided if she saw another hog, she'd meet it face to face, maybe even wrestle it in order to see it up close.

At the very moment she made that decision, she heard the snap of brush. As if that crack was a signal that her decision was a good one, she rose up, moved to the center of the path, and stood with feet squarely planted.

She waited for a shriek or a squeal, but nothing came. She thought she saw the slow-moving figure of something, perhaps an ambling rambling hog straggler.

Her heart raced. Fear knotted her gut. What if the hog now coming down the path wasn't inclined to play, only in the mood for dinner? Did hogs ever eat people the way people ate hogs? A few sides of Jessabelle-back-ribs could make for some good eating.

If she wasn't scared out of her mind, she probably would've laughed at the concept of Jessabelle-back-ribs, laughed until she cried. As it was, she wanted to cry out of fear that she was doing a crazy thing, a terribly demented thing in facing a wild animal.

Hogs are friendly, she told herself. That's what the Boise farmer had said just before he purchased a brass bar from her. *Stay calm.*

She heard another crack of brush and took a deep breath as the soft padding of hooves approached. She huffed and charged head up.

She saw a straw hat, sweet eyes beneath it. A japa mala dangled from a man's neck. Doc!

By the time she realized the hog was actually Doc, it was too late. She was already moving forward with full momentum. Just before her body crashed against his, she tried to stop, laying her hands on each side of his waist to keep them both from falling, but to no avail. They tumbled to the earth, she landing on top of him, his straw hat flying off, her glasses falling on the dirt path.

He flipped her on her back, squishing her body beneath his, his japa mala whipping her cheek. She gazed into his discombobulated eyes. He may have been stunned, but her momentary lack of glasses gave her a crystal clear view of him. His handsomeness stunned her!

"Are you nuts?" he asked.

"Sorry," she said. "I thought you were a wild hog."

He shot her a look of disbelief.

"I swear I'm not crazy. I saw three feral pigs and thought

you were another."

"And you decided your best strategy would be to tackle a wild pig? Tell me again you're not crazy." He rolled off Jessabelle and sat up. "If you mistook me for a hog, it's time for me to go on a diet."

"No, you're perfect." Jessabelle scrambled to collect her glasses and get them back on her face. "Really. Maybe I am crazy." Glancing around, she didn't see Fuzz and became terribly worried that a hog had gotten him.

"Where's Fuzz?"

"He got eaten by a wild pig," he said, confirming her fear.

She gasped.

He rose to his feet. "Just kidding." He took a couple of steps, squeaking as he went. "Actually, he's with Chet. Lalli suggested it, so he can learn to be around other people besides me." The bottom half of his left jean leg crumpled. He started limping. The smile rushed off his face.

"Doc, are you all—"

"You hit the lock button," Doc said and collapsed.

Jessabelle moved to his side, where she saw an unattached prosthetic foot hanging out the leg of his jeans. His cheeks reddened.

"Doc," she said. "It's okay."

He sat up, rolled up his jean leg, and began reattaching his foot.

"Do you want help?" she asked.

"Just go away."

"It's okay," Jessabelle said again. "I can help you."

His eyes bulged with anger. "Just go!" The fury in his voice pushed her off.

She staggered along the path toward the meditation cave. Was every person and animal in this town missing a foot? She stopped and bent down to feel her own lower extremities, ensuring she still had two legs and two feet.

In lingering fear of a wild hog attack, she straightened up fast and took stock of her surroundings. Would it really matter if she turned into a gourmet meal for a few hogs? She could think of only one person who would mourn the carnage, and it would be because she messed up his plans for getting his hands on a solid gold statue. Besides, being ripped to shreds by a few hogs couldn't be any worse than Doc getting mad at her, just because she'd seen his prosthetic foot. Another animal she knew little about—guys!

In a clearing she found the meditation cave, its mouth measuring about seven feet tall and two-and-a-half feet wide, the size and shape of a standard door. In fact, its opening was a door leading into a dome-shaped structure.

Jessabelle passed through that portal into a dark vestibule, through a set of double doors, and into another room so dark, she had to stop for fear of colliding with something she couldn't see. While her eyes adjusted to the darkness, nothing stirred except a quiet so profound, it lived like a colony of nocturnal creatures hanging from the ceiling in hibernation, fused by the rhythm of their slow silent breathing.

As if for the first time in her whole life, she heard the respiration of stillness. That made her suck in her breath so fast, her gasp echoed in the cave. *Relax. Just relax,* she told herself. Then she heard her breath come in easily and go out slowly.

She continued breathing, a bubble floating in the life force of silence, and her eyes adjusted further as fingers of soft blue light reached toward her in the darkness, luring her further into the center of the cave.

The blue light illuminated five stone statues of people crosslegged in meditation, positioned in a circle with their backs around a center pole, carved in the shape of a red serpent spiraling all the way up to the center of the dome ceiling.

She circumnavigated the statues, examining them. She saw the figures of Lalli's guru and Shiva, but no Shiva made of solid gold.

Just for fun, Jessabelle decided to become a statue of Jessabelle. She sat crosslegged on a cushion against one of the wide curves along the thick cave wall, closed her eyes, and started silently repeating Jaya Shiva Om.

She had only repeated Jaya Shiva Om three times before her mind wandered to the earlier conversation she'd had with Vishva. What did Vishva mean when she told Isa, "I bet you can be quite pretty, if you want to be"? Did Vishva really think Isa stood any kind of a chance with Doc?

Forget it.

Bringing herself back to the mantra, she again repeated Jaya Shiva Om, until her recollection of the odd meeting she'd just had with Doc took over her mind. The weirdness was all her fault; she felt sorry she had confused him with a wild pig.

Forget it!

Jaya Shiva Om, Jaya Shiva Om, Jaya Shiva Om, she thought over and over in a desperate attempt to refocus on the mantra before she was off considering where she might find Shiva.

In fact, she couldn't think more than three Jaya Shiva Oms before her mind ran off, lugging her with it. She just couldn't seem to concentrate on the mantra, and after a few minutes she stopped trying, because she couldn't see what was so great about stilling the mind in the first place.

She liked to think about things—especially the prospect of being a millionaire. So she sat thinking about the golden Shiva, and plotting where she could find it.

Chapter 15

The morning after Jessabelle mistook Doc for a wild pig, a blunder resulting in a head-on collision with the man, she unlocked the door to the shed. She stepped inside that dark pit of despair. Glancing around, she realized a whole lot of work *was not* getting done here.

Today was the day that was going to change. She had to make some progress so she didn't appear incompetent and get booted out before she got any closer to Shiva.

She lifted a bucket, took it outside, filled it with water, brought it in, and set it on the floor, ready to get down to some serious scrubbing. She thought about Doc, wondered how she could've mistaken him for a hog. She considered apologizing and found herself talking to him. "I am so sorry. Because of my near blindness, hence the reason for these big glasses, I just couldn't see a thing."

No, that made her sound sort of pathetic.

She tried again. "I am so sorry. Really, there is no re-semblance between you and a big pig. None at all! On the contrary, you're as fit and handsome as a movie star."

No, that made it sound like she worshipped him. She didn't want him thinking she had the hots for him or any-thing like that.

Perhaps she should keep it simple, say something like, "Hey, sorry about last night. Hope there's no hard feelings between us."

She wanted him to know the fact of his prosthetic foot didn't bother her. Not one bit. Maybe to some women it would be an issue, but not to her. It certainly didn't detract from his appeal.

It occurred to her she had no idea how to get in touch with him. She didn't know where he lived or his phone num-ber. A residue of mold on the sign next to the phone obscured its lettering, but she was still able to make out Dial 33 for Security Emergency. She couldn't see how her apology con-stituted an emergency.

Her shoulders sagged. *Forget about apologizing.* What did she care if his feelings were hurt? She hadn't come here to make friends. She had applied to this place to get rich. And what did guys like Doc know about crawling through the mud to get rich? They were born with everything—well, ev-erything except maybe a foot. She wondered if he was born without his foot or if he'd lost it in an accident.

Why was she interested? She and Doc shared nothing in common, nothing at all, except a love for fabricating and wearing body parts, and a distaste for caffeine.

Guys like Doc, their parents paid for their college, bought them houses and cars. They could work if they wanted to, but didn't have to. They could have whatever their hearts desired.

She would too, once she found the golden Shiva.

If she ever found the golden Shiva.

She and Uncle Trix had this place all wrong. Before she came, well, she didn't know what she thought really. She had only vague impressions. She had imagined the people here would sit in meditation all day like dopey-eyed zombies.

She had thought she would sit like a dopey-eyed zombie, and search for Shiva when she wasn't doing that. She didn't expect to have to clean a moldy shed.

This place was totally different than what she'd expected. For all she knew, the golden Shiva didn't exist. Wrench was not exactly the brightest tool in the toolbox, a man with poor dental hygiene who called a Caribbean vacation a caribou vacation. Why had Uncle Trix listened so wholeheartedly to him in the first place?

She would call Uncle Trix and tell him she wanted to leave. "There is no three-million-dollar statue here," she'd say. "Let's get back on the road."

Seriously Smart Nerd was starting to feel seriously dumb and old. She really wanted and needed a new face.

On the road she could change faces and costumes with regularity, as frequently as suited her whim. She missed having the opportunity to follow her fancy. She didn't really want to spend another two-and-a-half weeks cleaning this place. The air in this room felt stifling and damp.

She drew her smartphone from her back pocket and stepped outside for better reception and fresh air. She called Uncle Trix. His phone rang at the same time she heard the sound of a motor. She glanced up to see the apple-red Cherokee wheeling across the grass. It stopped right in front of her.

Uncle Trix's signature greeting boomed through the earpiece. "Yeallo." A combination of yeah and hello.

"Sorry Unc," she said. "Got to call you back. Something

came up." She hung up without waiting for his response.

The door to the Cherokee swung open. Fuzz dropped out, romped toward her. Doc followed his canine companion. Plastic spray bottles protruded out the top of a brown cardboard box he carried in both hands against the red and white vertical stripes of his shirt. "I'm really sorry about last night," he said, and set the box on the grass before her.

He's sorry about last night?

"I hope you can forgive me," he said. "I had no right to bark at you the way I did."

"No hard feelings," she said.

"I'm going to drop all shyness about my foot right now, just like this." He snapped his fingers.

"You are?"

"Yes, and you can help."

"I can?"

"Yes. Just watch." He sat down, rolled up the left leg of his blue jeans, detached his prosthetic foot, and tossed it on the grass. "There! There's the bottom of my leg." The body part slumped alone on the grass, dressed in Doc's crew sock and sneaker.

The way he'd just popped off his foot, ankle, and lower calf, and thrown it on the grass, as easily as if he'd just removed his straw hat and cast it aside, she couldn't believe he'd ever had any shyness about it to begin with.

He stripped off a sock and a stiff liner of foam rubber he wore over the bare nub. "Look! It's a stump," he said, pointing. "It doesn't mean anything—nothing at all—except that I have a stump for a leg. There's a foot at the bottom of your left leg. At the end of mine, there's a stump. So what?"

"Yeah," she said, shrugging. "So what."

They both laughed.

His confession seemed very brave if not a little deranged. In his madness he seemed so carefree that it tempted her to doff her teeth, wig, glasses, and prosthetic face (if she could get it off without adhesive remover) and throw them all on the grass. "Look!" she could say, pointing. "There's Isa Newton."

Wouldn't that be an accomplishment? Yeah, one she didn't have the guts to actually perform.

She thought she was supposed to say something. He'd just lain himself wide open before her. She felt she should at least look interested, and in fact, she was. "Can I see that?" she asked, eyeing the foot on the grass.

He passed his foot to her. "When you're wearing it," she said, "I can't tell you are." She undressed the foot, removing the sneaker and sock. She probed it with her fingers. "It's very well made."

"Why thank you. I made it myself."

"The skin covering is so natural-looking." She caressed the foot's surface. "Did you use silicone or foam?"

"Silicone."

"Did you design the socket and suspension system too?"

"Yes." He twisted his face. "You seem to know a lot about prosthetic feet. Did somebody you know wear one?"

"No," she said.

A moment of silence followed. It seemed he was giving her that space to explain how she knew so much about prosthetic feet. She wanted to tell him about the tooth technique she'd invented, one that allowed people to eat in prosthetic teeth, if necessary. A real feat that was. But she remained quiet; the moment passed.

"I should get going," he said. "Can I have my foot back?"

She passed him his foot. He reattached it to the bottom of his leg, beginning with the insertion of his stump into the stiff liner of foam rubber material. He swathed it in a sock, then inserted his stump into his prosthetic leg. He rose up and, balancing on his right foot, stepped into his other foot with a click.

"How did you lose your foot?" she asked.

"Saving my nephew's life," he said, matter-of-factly. "One day, when Aaron was only three, he wandered into the street. Before anybody noticed he was about twenty feet from a speeding SUV. I didn't think. Instead I ran. I dove at him and rolled him out of harm's way. One of the truck's tires smashed my foot, pulverizing it." He gazed straight at Jessabelle. "Everybody knows I don't have a foot but nobody ever saw. Not even Chet, my best friend, or my mother or father. If you hadn't crashed into me the other night, I wouldn't have realized just how much fear I carried about that. So thank you."

"Thank me?"

"I want to be a good role model for Fuzz and others," he said.

"I just hope he's a good role model for you," she said. They both glanced at Fuzz batting blades of grass with his tiny paws.

"He is," Doc said with a smile. "And if I'm ever going to help children and animals with their disabilities, I've got to be over any fear about my own. So thank you again."

She still didn't understand exactly why mistaking him for a wild pig was good. But who was she to argue? If he thought she'd done a good thing, then so be it. She'd scored points with a virtuous man.

She opened her mouth to say "You're welcome," but got distracted by the word "Vinegar" on the side of a one-gallon plastic container in the box Doc had dropped at her feet. She bent and lifted another one-gallon container next to it. "Demold," its label read. "What's all this?" she asked, shifting her gaze to a bottle of tea tree oil.

"All natural, environmentally safe mold cleaners," he said.

"You've got a funny way of thanking a girl."

"Oh no no," he said. "These aren't from me. I just wanted

to get my apology out of the way first."

"If not from you, then where did they come from?"

"Lalli."

"Lalli?"

"Yes."

"But why?"

"To help you."

"What does she care?"

"Well, she cares a great deal. If she gives you a direction, her support is with you all the way."

"What are you talking about? Pierre Dubois told me to clean this shed."

"I'm sure it's because Lalli saw a reason for it."

"If you were me, would you clean this shed?"

"Yes."

"Have you seen how moldy this place is?"

"No. Have you seen what you're cleaning?"

"No."

"I'll bet it's precious."

A thought formed at the edge of Jessabelle's mind, making a mad dash front and center. She felt so stupid for not thinking of it earlier that she could have reached up and whacked her own head. She hadn't really seen the full contents of the shed. Shiva could be sitting right under her nose.

"You're right," she told Doc. "I should get to work." She hoisted the box of environmentally safe cleaning supplies in her arms and rushed inside, yelling over her shoulder. Now she was the one telling him "Thank you."

Inside, she dumped the box beside the cleaning supplies that had come with the shed. She found a mask and rubber gloves, then searched the place from top to bottom, discovering nothing new except more cobwebs.

Disheartenment settled over her like a heavy metal blanket. Once again she'd had the chance to question Doc about the statue and didn't. Letting him off like that was just plain negligence.

Oddly, his presence made her forget all about the statue. Besides, holding his prosthetic foot in her hand while he poured his heart out to her hardly seemed the appropriate time to launch into, "Now about that Shiva statue..."

And then there was that conversation about Lalli. Jessabelle got lost there, trying to figure out what Lalli had to do with her service assignment.

If she was ever going to find Shiva, she needed to get serious about finding Shiva. She made up her mind to stay focused on the statue in the future, even with Doc in the vicinity.

And what about Lalli? Doc's father may have given Lalli the statue, if indeed the statue existed, but it was Lalli's statue now. Certainly she'd be able to provide some clues as to its whereabouts. Hmm, how exactly did one go about tracking down a guru for the purpose of figuring out where that guru kept her three-million-dollar statue?

Chapter 16

Jessabelle had no idea where to find Lalli or how to talk to her about Shiva. Not that it mattered; as in art and everything else, she often had no understanding of what she was doing, but plunged forward and did it anyway, until that magic moment when comprehension descended and she achieved the desired effect. In her experience, any achievement, big or small, was a process of trial and error.

"Operation Obtain Information about the Golden Shiva from Lalli" began after a five-minute lunch of hummus and pita bread, as Jessabelle trotted around town, trying to figure out where Lalli lived. She spotted a large, soft pink house with a wraparound porch, shuttered windows, and a fresh coat of paint. Since it was the largest house in Lalliville, she assumed Lalli must live in it as she passed on by, continuing all the way to the end of Generosity Street.

When she reached the beginning of the meditation gardens, she glanced around. Confident nobody was watching, she U-turned and hoofed it in the opposite direction.

Jessabelle went all the way to the start of Generosity Street, spun on her heels, and headed back in the direction of the meditation gardens with the hope of a "chance meeting" with Lalli. If she ran into her on her way there, she'd pretend she was going to the gardens to meditate. If she bumped into her on her way back up the street, she'd pretend she had just come from sitting in the gardens. Then she would nonchalantly start a conversation.

"Hi, Lalli," she rehearsed. "My name is Isa Newton. You may or may not remember me from our first meeting. I feel I know you from your pictures on the walls. They're nice pictures, by the way, especially the one of you seated on the beach with the rising sun in the background. Anyway, I'm interested in Shiva. Can you tell me anything about him?"

Eventually she got tired of rehearsing and sang Om Namo Bhagavate Shivanandaya until her voice cracked. Then she entertained herself with jokes Uncle Trix had told her that weren't really jokes. "I'm never going to pay taxes and if Uncle Sam comes to lock me up, I'll tell him it costs a lot of money to keep people in jail. Let me keep my money, and I'll let you keep yours."

On and on she strode, until she put about three miles on her black lace-up shoes. She paced the length of that street for one hour and fifteen minutes. The only moving life she encountered was a groundhog and a female deer with her two fawns.

The deer family feasted on the lush green grass in front of the big pink house with wraparound porch. She considered marching right up to the front door and ringing the bell. But who even knew if Lalli lived there?

She thought about actually entering the meditation gardens to sit and meditate, but didn't have much time. Her clonker of a wristwatch read one-thirty; by two she was supposed to be working again.

With all that walking, she'd worked up quite a sweat. It pooled under her arms and soaked her underwear. What she really needed was one of her other two white shirts, a fresh set of underwear, maybe even a shower.

The Cherokee whirred up the street. Doc waved from the driver's seat before he turned into the driveway of the big pink house. Seconds later he stood before her.

"You live here?" she asked.

He nodded.

It figured; he always got the biggest house. "By any chance, do you live with Lalli?"

"No. I live with Chet and…"

His words trailed off and he gawked at her as if he was viewing Glinda the Good Girl turn into a three-hundred pound werewolf in that classic of horror, *Werewolf at Heart*. After all, she'd been standing at the edge of his lawn when he came upon her. He probably thought the Seriously Smart Girl named Isa was pursuing him now.

She was well aware of what a scary prospect that might be, standing there in her white shirt and denim overalls with crisscross suspenders, their bottom hem resting on her knees so the legs of the overalls kissed her knee-high tube socks. Two navy stripes circled their band. Even she had to laugh at the outfit when she'd seen it in the mirror that morning. She was sure the huge sweat stains under the arms of the white shirt added nothing to its elegance.

"I swear, I was just on my way back from the meditation gardens where I…meditated!" she blurted in defense of any stalking charges he might be conjuring against her. "I just happened to see the deer family! That's why I'm standing here…admiring the deer!"

"Oh," he said as if he hadn't noticed the deer before now. "It's okay."

If it was really okay, then why did he have that look on his face? She wanted to question him about where Lalli lived, but didn't like that glare. It made her feel as though she'd already overstayed her welcome. "Okay," she said and took a step back. "I guess I'll see you around."

His eyes stayed on her face. "You have something on your cheek," he said, reaching his open hand toward her face. He wiped her cheek and examined his palm. The sheen of powdery goo spread over it turned his expression quizzical. Before he could say another word, she yelped, "Gotta go," spun on her heels, and dashed all the way back to her house, straight to her private bathroom.

She gazed into the mirror, cursing the Florida heat again and again. It had melted her makeup, and in the liquidizing, tinted it metallic gray.

Arrgh! No wonder Doc had stared at her the way he did. Glinda had turned into the Tin Man.

Acquiring an interview with a guru regarding the existence of a solid gold statue was not the easiest task Jessabelle had ever had. Despite her failed lunchtime mission to engineer a chance encounter with Lalli, her enthusiasm for the project remained high as she hurried down Liberation toward the shed, makeup refreshed, wearing another white shirt beneath her denim overalls with crisscross suspenders. She planned to regroup at the shed and figure out her next move toward interacting with Lalli as she worked.

To assuage her parched throat, she swerved into Krishna's Corner for a to-go drink. A sign posted on the door announced BOAR SIGHTING. Beneath that headline, details cited the time and place that three boars had been spotted on the path to the meditation cave the previous evening, the three boars she had witnessed with her own eyes. The sign included tips regarding what to do in the event of seeing a boar: Remain quiet, avoid quick movements, don't feed or corner the animal. The sign was a duplicate of the one she'd seen on the door to the dining hall when she went for lunch. She later discovered the signs to be the work of Doc, who'd consulted a wildlife expert and posted the fliers in public spaces around Lalliville as a safety measure. "Turns out boars are docile creatures," he'd said, looking straight at her. "A boar won't hurt you unless you do something stupid—like try to capture it."

Once inside Krishna's Corner, she surveyed the rows of canned and bottled beverages on metal shelves behind the glass door of a refrigerator case. Ginger Beer, Root Beer, San Pellegrino water. A glass pitcher filled with a milky-orange substance that reminded Jessabelle of melted Creamsicles. The simple sign squatting in front of it indicated it was Mango Lassi, $1 a cup.

A woman's voice called, "Hello." Jessabelle wheeled toward the sound's origin. Lalli flowed through the door in a simple white cotton sari.

Jessabelle froze. Her eyes darted around the room. Nobody else was present. The on-duty cashier was a slotted wooden box with a sign. "Please pay here," it read. *It must be me she said hello to,* Jessabelle thought. "Hi," she said.

Earlier, Jessabelle had walked for what felt like an eternity hoping to bump into Lalli and didn't see her. Now that she wasn't looking, Lalli just happened to be a mere ten feet away. Was it by chance she had shown up this way?

Lalli moved toward her, quick and supple.

"Let's have something to drink," she said. Like a perfect host, she brought the pitcher of mango lassi out of the refrigerator and poured the refreshment into two small plastic glasses. Lalli started toward the tables, carrying a glass of lassi in each hand. No doubt, she wanted Jessabelle to follow.

Jessabelle took a seat at the table Lalli chose near the window. Lalli's gaze met her own. Jessabelle relieved herself of her eyeglasses under the pretext of polishing them, when it was really to get an unobstructed view of Lalli.

In those moments she wiped her glasses with a paper napkin, Lalli seemed to her the most beautiful woman in the world. With her chiseled features and high cheekbones, she could've been a high-paid model, if she'd chosen to be a model instead of a guru. She was no longer in her twenties, Jessabelle felt sure about that, but how old she was, Jessabelle couldn't decide with any certainty.

Lalli's skin dazzled! In the pictures Jessabelle had seen around Lalliville, Lalli's skin looked healthy and radiant. But Jessabelle was privy to the tricks of corrective make-up artists. She'd seen the professionals convert women with pasty skin or bad cases of acne into potential spokespeople for skin care products.

Wow! Jessabelle thought, sitting across a two-foot span of table from Lalli-in-the-flesh. *Her skin really is lovely.*

Even in the bright sunlight coming through the window, Jessabelle couldn't see one wrinkle on Lalli's face, a face that shone luminous as three suns. So splendid was that glow, Jessabelle had to avert her eyes.

Outside the window a brown squirrel foraged for its food at the base of a large oak. Jessabelle regarded the squirrel a moment before putting her glasses back on, tucking the napkin in her pocket and returning her gaze to Lalli.

When Jessabelle noticed Lalli's skin had lost its special luster, she felt as if her heart had fallen out the front of her chest, dropping on the table beside her cup of lassi. She was tired of having to see through two chunks of distorting glass.

Her artificial lenses may have been transparent; but still, their density dulled her ability to fully see Lalli and the children's artwork displayed on the window behind Lalli's head, pictures of mountains, trees, sun, and flowers.

Lalli swirled the lassi in her cup as if it was wine and she was a connoisseur. She inhaled its aroma, then took a small sip. "Mmm," she declared.

Jessabelle thought Lalli had just demonstrated the way a person was supposed to drink lassi, and wanting to express proper etiquette, she imitated action-for-action. The lassi slid down her throat, sweet and refreshing.

Observing Jessabelle mimic her, Lalli laughed, and politely asked, "Is this your first lassi?"

Jessabelle nodded.

"It's good to try new things," Lalli said matter-of-factly.

The statement was followed by a silence so complete, Jessabelle felt herself disappearing into it. A powerful desire took hold of her, a yearning to speak in a way she hadn't in a long, long time. To speak without motive for riches, without guard standing or defenses up.

She wanted to tell Lalli about herself, her family, her ambition to bring smiles to people's faces through the use of prosthetic makeup. The whole truth and nothing but the truth!

An impression of Uncle Trix's face loomed up in front of her like a hologram beamed from a distant constellation. *Are you crazy?* he was saying. *You want to get thrown in jail?*

Obviously, telling Lalli the whole truth could produce some negative effects. Jessabelle wanted liberty, not imprisonment. Her longing to be free rang inside like a cowbell, clanging so loud it drove her to the subject of Shiva. "Can you tell me about Shiva?" she asked in a casual manner.

"Certainly."

More silence. Lalli sipped her lassi. She seemed so

ordinary, Jessabelle couldn't figure out why anybody would give her a statue worth three million dollars in the first place.

"Well," Jessabelle encouraged, growing impatient. "Would you tell me about Shiva?"

"What do you want to know about Shiva?"

"Anything you can tell me."

"Why do you want to know anything?"

"Curiosity."

"Isn't that what killed the cat?"

"What?"

"A proverb, is it not?"

"Oh yeah. Curiosity killed the cat."

"Did it ever make the cat rich?"

"I don't know. Can we just get back to Shiva?"

"Not until you tell me what you want to know about Shiva and why."

Exactly what she wanted to know about Shiva: Where is his solid gold form? Why she wanted to know: So she could steal it and become rich. Naturally, she couldn't tell Lalli that.

Jessabelle found herself pretending that she and Shiva were best friends in an effort to trick Lalli into talking about him. "In fact," Jessabelle said as part of the ruse, "I know a lot about Shiva. I might even be able to tell you a thing or two about him you don't already know."

"Then speak."

"In order to tell you something you don't already know about Shiva, I've got to know what you do know about Shiva. So you speak first."

Lalli raised an eyebrow. *She knows I'm BSing her*, occurred to Jessabelle. She could see it in the way Lalli narrowed those black onyx eyes at her, her vision penetrating straight through to Jessabelle's heart.

Jessabelle feared Lalli could see she was anything but

good and felt annoyed at herself for trying to pretend she knew more about Shiva than the woman with the eyes of Shiva.

Lalli remained unperturbed. Never had Jessabelle seen anyone so comfortable in her own skin.

Lalli's easeful state gave Jessabelle the courage to make another attempt at gaining information. "I know what I want to know about Shiva."

"What is it?"

"Where is Shiva?" she simply ventured.

"Your question doesn't make sense."

Jessabelle quickly pieced together an argument that the question made perfect sense, but before she got a chance to articulate it, Lalli spoke.

"Would it make sense to you if Shiva asked where Shiva was?"

"What?" Confusion enveloped Jessabelle, and from the midst of it came the odd sensation that she'd messed up, missed her mark. All this talk about Shiva may have been making her real intentions clear to Lalli. "Did you know I'm working on that project in the shed?" Jessabelle asked, changing the subject.

"I'm sure you're doing your very best on it, right?"

"Ah, ah, ah," Jessabelle stammered. She cleared her throat. "I'm working very hard." Jessabelle again cleared her throat and gave Lalli a nervous smile. "It's very dark there and moldy." With the hope of garnering some sympathy, Jessabelle told Lalli a story about a guy who accidentally ingested mold and then died when the mold turned toxic.

Unimpressed, Lalli's face didn't change. She said, "Perhaps you could use the help of someone who isn't afraid of a little mold."

"Yes, I sure could use some help," Jessabelle agreed, "because I'm in that shed all alone. And it's not just a little mold, but a lot."

"I know just the person for you."

Jessabelle perked up. "You do?"

"Bennie."

"Name doesn't ring any bells."

"He's a mighty soul."

"Strong?"

"Very strong."

Jessabelle's spirits soared. She was getting just what she needed, a strong man. Like a warm wind blowing, a hero was coming to save her from the mold.

"He arrived today and is just itching for some work to do."

"Well," Jessabelle said, pushing her chair back from the table and folding her hands on her lap, "I've got plenty of that for him."

"I'll send him to the shed this afternoon."

With that settled, Jessabelle wanted to take another crack at obtaining information about Shiva.

But Lalli was already standing. "Speaking of work, I must get back to mine."

Chapter 17

Jessabelle left the shed door open for the strong man. While she waited for Bennie to arrive, she carried two buckets of water into the shed. This whole episode induced a fit of crazy laughter. Why was she acting like a damsel-in-distress who needed the help of a strong man to combat mold?

Her Lalliville experience possessed a surreal quality. But when she compared it to her real life, she couldn't decide the winner in the peculiarity contest. She laughed harder.

Ever since she'd left her chance meeting with Lalli at the café, everything seemed hilarious to her. On her way back to the shed, she spotted a robin tugging an earthworm out of the ground. "Gor for it!" she told him, raising a hand in tribute to his efforts. From there she sprinted to the moldy pit, laughing all the way.

Jessabelle did not know why, merely sensed the knowledge hidden somewhere in her own body, that it was Lalli she should be paying homage to. Lalli, the woman with the strange effect on her. Lalli, the one who gave off a vibe that made Jessabelle feel so happy, she found joy in a bird fetching a meal.

Jessabelle began to sing in the liquid movements of a bird. "Chippily chip chip chippio, chippily chip chip chippio." The volume of her singing became so loud, she neglected to hear the tap, tap, tap of small feet, although she would've sworn she felt the presence of something, if not another person.

She was turning, reaching for the vinegar, when she beheld, in the dimness of the shed, what appeared to be the scrawny apparition of a boy about three and a half feet tall, wearing a long purple shirt with a four-button placket, bordered with fancy embroidery. Half a foot of white cotton pant stuck out the bottom of the shirt. Faced with the unexpected sight, she screamed.

The apparition shuddered. "If this is the way you welcome people who come to help, you won't get any help."

He speaks.

Astonished, Jessabelle asked, "You're here to help?"

The ghost-child nodded. "Guruji sent me."

Realizing the ghost-child was indeed an actual boy, Jessabelle relaxed. Lalli must really care about her; in addition to Bennie, she had also sent a boy to help. "I was just planning our task," she told him. "We can start once Bennie gets here."

"He's here," the boy said.

"He is?" Jessabelle asked, excitement flooding into her voice. She glanced toward the door. "Where?"

The scrawny boy waved his arms. "Hello, earth to whoever-you-are, I'm Bennie!"

Jessabelle rolled out of her lofty state, crashing fast. She glared at Bennie. She'd expected her hero, the strong man, the one who was going to save her from the mold, to actually look strong. She'd pictured him as one of those types who model flannel shirts in catalogues for the outdoorsman, not this boy with a physique so slight, his long, loose shirt fit him like a dress.

Puny boy in a dress? An odd sense of familiarity settled over her. She moved closer to examine the boy's features. Bright green round eyes. A mass of tousled moussed-up blonde hair that added two, maybe two-and-a-half inches to his height. What he lacked in size, he made up for in hair.

While checking out the thick, luxurious texture of his mane, she recognized him as the Short Kid afflicted by two Troubles who had tried to throw him into a slimy pond in a field behind his school. Her stomach cinched. Anger heated her cheeks. *Yeah right, strong man.* This had to be a joke. Jessabelle bet Lalli was having a good laugh over it right now.

"What's your name?" he asked.

Of course, he didn't recognize her. She was no longer an elephant. "Isa."

"Isa," he said, "if we're ever going to get this place clean, we'd better get to work."

"You really want to help?"

"I wouldn't be here if I didn't."

Small or large, she needed all the help she could get, and he hadn't even squirmed or balked at the smell, the dimness, or the fungi. "Our first step is to clean this room," she said. "Can you handle that?"

"Why couldn't I?" He moved toward the box of cleaning supplies Doc had brought, found a diffuser, poured a few drops of tea tree oil on a cotton pad he placed in it, and plugged the diffuser into the wall. Within seconds the whole room smelled fresher, lighter.

"We're scrubbing the room with vinegar and water,"

Jessabelle said. She offered him a pair of rubber gloves.

"I won't need those," he said. "I'm not scared of a little mold."

She put the rubber gloves on her own hands.

Bennie dumped some vinegar into one of the buckets of water. Then he dropped to his knees, dunked a sponge in the bucket, and started scrubbing, getting into a rhythm that bobbed the curls on his head. Observing him, Jessabelle got the impression that cleaning the shed was an easy task, and with soaring spirits she went for her own sponge.

"How are we supposed to clean this place?"

Jessabelle turned back toward Bennie, who had stopped scrubbing and sat up straight on the back of his heels. He wadded his face. "I can hardly see in here!"

"Complaining already."

"I'm not complaining. It's a fact we need more light. Otherwise, how will we know whether we're doing a good job?"

"Pierre said the lights can't get fixed until they fill the electrical position."

"Until then, let's borrow one."

"Borrow a light? From where?"

Following Bennie's suggestion, they walked to Johann's office. Pointing toward a standing lamp beside his desk, Bennie asked, "Can we borrow that light?"

"And in the meantime," Johann grumbled, "what am I to do? Go blind looking at all these numbers? No, you can't borrow my light. Get your own."

In the kitchen, above the place where Chet was chopping scallions, there were only fluorescent ceiling lamps, nothing Jessabelle and Bennie could carry away with them.

Jessabelle flat out refused to go anywhere near the security office.

En route to the welcome center, the balls of her feet

throbbed with pain. Her black lace-up clompers were beginning to take a toll, especially after all the traipsing around town she'd done earlier that day, attempting to arrange a chance meeting with Lalli. Still, she forged onward.

When Bennie asked Vishva if they could borrow the lamp, hooded by a stained glass covering that rested on the welcome desk, Vishva asked what they needed it for. They explained and she told them, "This little light is not going to do the trick. Check with Hanuman and Bhisma to see if they have what you really need, high-powered lights."

Jessabelle followed Bennie behind the maintenance building, a structure with metal walls and a sloped metal roof, where they found two guys. One of the guys ruffled a side of Bennie's hair, looking down as if he were talking to a squirrel. "Hey, Big Man."

Bennie tilted back his head as if he were looking up at a skyscraper. "Hi, Peewee."

The second guy ruffled the other side of Bennie's hair. "Hello, Sir Grande."

Bennie turned slightly, and adjusted his neck as if now he were watching a plane fly over the skyscraper. "Hi Teeny-weeny."

Judging by the way that plane looked down, thought Jessabelle, Bennie must have appeared to him like a toy automobile.

The skyscraper and plane had just hopped down from each side of a box truck backed against one of two loading-dock bays. Following their exchange of greetings with Bennie, they introduced themselves to Jessabelle.

The skyscraper was Bhisma, a black man with a shaved head who stood at least six-feet-five-inches. He wore gym shoes and gray track pants with white stripes running down the outer seams of the legs. His bright yellow form-fitting T-shirt showcased the well defined muscles of his chest and

shoulders, tapering down to a taut abdomen. Obviously he
lifted weights, and not just a little, but enough to bring impressive girth to his biceps.

At a lofty seven feet high, Hanuman was even taller than
Bhisma, and twice the height of Bennie. Even Jessabelle, a
good two feet taller than Bennie, had to tilt her head back to
see the men's faces. Hanuman had a dark, unpruned shrub-in-
full-bloom on top of his head. He shared Bhisma's naturally
thick-boned, thick-muscled physique, but without the same
muscle definition. Jessabelle guessed Hanuman maintained
his shape somewhere outside a gym, maybe in the woods.
On his massive feet he wore a pair of low shoes designed for
hiking trails. The rest of his trek-wear outfit included khaki-
colored lightweight nylon cargo pants with zip off legs and a
sage green half-zip short-sleeve pullover.

Hanuman was rugged, Bhisma the envy of gym rats.
Hanuman shopped at the camping store, Bhisma the sport-
ing goods store. Or maybe their wives did their shopping for
them. Plain gold wedding bands circled both their left ring
fingers.

"Can we borrow some high-powered lights?" Bennie
asked them.

"Sorry," Bhisma responded, "right now the high-powereds
are all out on loan." He put an arm around Bennie's shoulder
and guided him through a door with a combination lock. "Go
ahead and check the stock room," he said, gesturing in the
direction they should go. "See if there're any other lights you
can use. In the meantime, we got a truck to unload."

Jessabelle was relieved to lower her face. Her neck was
hurting from gazing up at the guys. She massaged the back
of it as she and Bennie wandered into a room full of simple
furniture for bedroom, living room, and office. They followed
a well delineated concrete path cut through the furniture,
weaving through a maze of beds and dressers, metal desks

and office chairs. They didn't see one single light.

"Nice recliner," Jessabelle said. She plunked down in a yellow leather recliner with wooden legs, sank into its padded back. She rolled up the foot stool and propped her feet on top.

Bennie threw his body on the matching sofa, stretching out, resting his head on one of its pillow arms.

Along came Hanuman, hauling a three-cushion cappuccino fabric sofa on his back. With his head lifted, Bennie closely followed Hanuman's movement with his eyes, all the way across the room, until Hanuman slid the couch off his back, and positioned it in a cleared space before them. "He makes carrying a couch on your back look so easy," he mused.

Hanuman left without saying a word, and in came Bhisma with a matching loveseat. After he set it down, he moved over in front of Jessabelle and Bennie. "You didn't find anything?"

"Nothing," Bennie said, "except an unfortunate lack of lights in storage. There's got to be something around here we can use."

Bhisma's face grew pensive. Then he snapped his fingers. "There is one light. It's up in the office. I'll bring it on my next trip." Bhisma left.

Hanuman returned, lugging a dresser on his back. Again, Jessabelle and Bennie spectated in awe until he set it down. He was such a show of raw strength and grace, Jessabelle felt she could sit all day in that recliner and watch Hanuman and Bhisma move furniture into storage.

Bhisma entered again, carrying a three-drawer file cabinet in his arms the way another person might tote a plastic laundry basket loaded with heavy sheets and clothes. He set the file cabinet on the far side of the room with the rest of the office furniture, and then walked over to Jessabelle and Bennie.

Bhisma slipped a silver pen light from his pocket. Holding the power switch with his thumb, he shined the light in Bennie's face. "Might not be high powered, but right now, it's all we got."

"Thanks," Bennie said, springing to his feet. "I guess it's better than nothing." He took the light and clipped it in the side pocket of his long shirt.

"The instructions said it's good for ten thousand hours of use," Bhisma said.

Kill me, Jessabelle thought, *if I'm in the shed with the mold that long.*

"Let me know if you need new batteries," Bhisma offered. "And make sure you return it." He pointed a finger straight at Bennie.

"I will."

The finger moved. Now he pointed to Jessabelle, rising to her feet. "Would you make sure he returns it?"

"Yes, definitely. You don't look like the kind of guy we want to upset." *And neither does he*, Jessabelle thought when she turned and saw the other lean mean lifting machine, Hanuman, winding through furniture stock with an end table poised on his head, held steady by one hand.

On Jessabelle and Bennie's way out, they saw the open back of the box truck still butting the loading bay. Bennie stopped in front of the mass of furniture in the truck bed yet to be unloaded. He zeroed in on a sofa in the mix. "Would you put that on my back? I wanna see if I can carry it."

"No way. I'm not putting a sofa on your back." Jessabelle didn't want to add accidental manslaughter to the list of things she worried about going to jail for.

"C'mon."

"Even if I could get it on your back, you can't carry it."

"C'mon. Let's just try."

"No."

"You're no fun."

"Have you ever carried anything on your back?"

"A backpack."

"There's a big difference between a backpack and a sofa. Why don't you try a few things in between. A kitchen chair, an ottoman. Work your way up to a sofa."

Bennie fell quiet a while. On their way along Peace Street, his face grew long with dejection. "Let's face it," he said, "I'm never gonna be able to carry a sofa on my back."

"Why do you want to, anyhow?"

"Just to feel strong."

"Lalli told me you are strong."

He brightened up. "She did? When?"

Jessabelle related her earlier contact with Lalli, to which Bennie emitted a "Hmm," rich in meaning.

Back in the shed, Jessabelle held the pen light on, positioning it in the air so it shined over the spot Bennie was scrubbing. "Mind if I ask you a question?" she said.

"That was a question," Bennie said and laughed.

"Hah hah. Mind if I ask you another question?"

"That was another question."

"Stop!"

"Okay. What's your question?"

"Would it make sense to you if Shiva asked where Shiva was?"

"No."

"Lalli asked me that."

"Sounds like she gave you a riddle." He smiled. "Time to switch."

Jessabelle traded with him, the light for the sponge.

At six-thirty in the evening, Jessabelle was seated with Madeline, Vishva, Johann, and Doc at a table in the dining hall. The night's conversation centered on the subject of meditation, although Doc stared at Jessabelle and not Johann, the one who was actually speaking about what he called a breakthrough in his meditation.

"I was practicing a dharana," Johann said, "visualizing the Swiss Alps. I breathed in through the third eye, then out through the third eye, repeating 'I'm still as a mountain.' Then everything fell away and I was the mountain, completely still. When I came out of meditation, I was totally awake and alert, not tired at all. It was sheer elation."

"Meditation hasn't been going well for me," Jessabelle said, referring to the one meditation she'd tried in the cave. "Maybe I should try visualizing a mountain."

"I've been doing that a while," Johann said. "It was hard in the beginning. I'd say 'I'm still as a mountain' and nod off. Then I started imagining certain mountains, the Matterhorn, the Swiss Alps. I'd seen them, so I could easily picture them."

Jessabelle considered the mountains she'd seen, and from the corner of her eye, saw Doc with his eyes fastened on her. Why was he observing her so carefully?

"Just out of curiosity," Doc said to Jessabelle, "can you design an ear or a nose?"

Jessabelle took in a sharp breath. Was he on to her disguise? "I might be able to if I tried," she answered evenly.

"Could you also fabricate those body parts and fit them to a human form if you tried?"

"Doc," Vishva said. "She's not a...What do you call yourself?"

"Anaplastologist," Madeline interjected.

"Yeah, Doc," Jessabelle said. "I'm not a doctor."

"She's an inventor!" Chet said.

"That reminds me," said Madeline. "Talent show acts are filling fast. You want me to slot you into one?"

"Talent show?" Jessabelle shook her head. "I don't think so."

"A wingsuit in a talent show with freedom as its theme," Johann said. "It's perfect."

Jessabelle saw another thought forming in Madeline's mind. Before she could get it out on the table, Jessabelle hopped up and announced, "I must get ready for the chant."

"I don't believe it exists," said Madeline.

A collective gasp rose from the mouths of those seated at the table.

"Madeline!" Vishva said like a mother shocked over the rudeness of her child.

Indignation jabbed Jessabelle. "It exists!" The emphaticism in her voice surprised her. She'd lied for so long, she'd forgotten she'd ever been lying to begin with. She reminded herself there was no wingsuit. "It's just that…"

"It's just that what?" Madeline asked.

"The talent show will be held in the multipurpose room, right?"

"Right."

"In order to get off the ground, I need a mountain to jump from."

"How high a mountain?"

"One hundred feet." Jessabelle smiled wide, confident that Madeline couldn't move a mountain into the auditorium.

"I'll change the talent show venue to an outdoor one and ask Bhisma and Hanuman to erect a one-hundred-foot platform!"

"O…kay. Put me down for an act."

"We'll call it Bird Woman," Madeline said.

"Bird Woman," Jessabelle repeated. "Sounds great." Had she really just agreed to demonstrate a wingsuit? Could she design and build one capable of making her airborne before the talent show? Impossible! Panic seized her.

Chapter 18

Now that Jessabelle had boldly agreed to exhibit her non-existent wingsuit at the upcoming talent show, she had no choice but to comb the internet via her smartphone for a nearby store that sold anything that might help her fly. Once she found the Fly Supply, she called Uncle Trix to come get her and take her there. Then she walked down Way of Truth and out onto Route 54.

Alarm racked her when she found Uncle Trix at their meeting spot on the hard shoulder of the road. With his arms crossed over his chest, he leaned against a faded white pickup. A fancy sign on its door read "Dave's Plumbing." Its bed overflowed with toilet seats, faucets, shower heads, pipes, and fittings. The face of a water heater emerged from the flood of plumbing supplies.

"Where's the step van?"

"Back at the motel."

Her eyes fell on the wrench that hung out the front pocket of his dungarees. Until that moment, the only bottoms she'd ever seen him in were on-duty designer slacks or off-duty cotton lounge pants.

"What're you up to?"

"Do I always have to be up to something, little Miss Suspicious?"

"Yes. If you're not, what's with the plumber persona?"

"I'll have you know, I met a woman. Feel like a new man. Got an honest profession now."

"Yeah, right." Uncle Trix and honest profession were like oil and water; they just didn't mix.

"Seriously." He slid a small photo out of the breast pocket of a T-shirt so white and crisp, it appeared fresh out of a Hanes three-pack. It was definitely not a T-shirt that had ever experienced the rigors of a plumber's life.

He held out the picture of his "fiancée."

Jessabelle stared at a pretty brunette with the kind of all-American smile that really showed off her veneers. Probably a generic photo produced in a print shop along with about 99,999 others exactly like it. It could've been something he swiped from inside a plastic picture frame up for sale on a Wally's shelf.

"Her name is Sarah," he said. "Ain't she the loveliest thing you ever saw?"

"Umm hmm." She rounded the truck to get to the passenger side. Climbing up onto the bench seat, she noticed a document resting on the dashboard. She took off her glasses and tucked them in the front pocket of her denim overalls. Then she rolled down the window for air and lifted the document for closer inspection. It said, "Certificate of Achievement, Awarded to Dave Drogan, for the successful completion of

Plumbing Training School." The certificate bore an official seal and the signature of the president of Plumbing Training School.

Cruising along Route 54, she noticed Uncle Trix watching something in the rearview mirror. She thought she could make out a black car in the distance. She was still engaged in figuring out what Uncle Trix was up to when he brought the truck to a stop on the road's hard shoulder. He reached under the dash and opened the hood. Outside, he propped the hood open. Thick black smoke jetted out from it, rising in a steady stream toward the sky. She thought she saw flames!

Jessabelle gasped, jumped out of the truck fast as she could, and dashed up front, her nostrils and lungs burning from the smoke in the air. "What the hell is going on?" She hitched her fingers around Uncle Trix's elbow, trying to evacuate him to where the air was clear.

"Get off me," he shouted over the smoke's hiss. He wrenched his elbow free.

She coughed several times.

A black Continental parked in front of the truck. An old man got out, and with the help of a cane, shuffled slowly toward Uncle Trix. "Looks like car trouble."

"I'll say! And I just spent every last penny on a one-carat diamond for my lady."

Oh no, Jessabelle thought.

"What terrible timing," Uncle Trix continued. "My business runs on these wheels. I'll need to have them towed and repaired. And I just spent my last dime on an engagement ring. Sure is pretty, though."

He dug a black velvet jewelry box from a front pocket of his blue jeans. The box had a gold ribbon tied around it, knotted in a small bow at the top. "I have no choice," he said. The corners of Uncle Trix's mouth turned down. His eyes drooped as he untied the ribbon and opened the box. A large diamond sparkled from inside it. "I'll have to sell it now."

"It must have cost a bundle," Old Man said.

"Only my life's savings, five thousand dollars. Say, you wouldn't want to buy it? So I can get my wheels towed and repaired?"

Old Man snorted. "I don't have five grand on me."

"A fiancée ain't no good if I can't get back home to her. I could get these wheels rolling again for less." Uncle Trix's gaze penetrated Old Man's eyes. "Do you have one thousand dollars?"

Old Man considered it. "My sixtieth wedding anniversary is approaching fast. My wife never had anything that special. Mind if I take a look?"

"Not at all." Uncle Trix handed over the fancy jewelry box. Old Man received it with a shaky hand.

"A wife of sixty years deserves something special," Old Man said, studying the ring.

"You bet she does. You'd be giving her a treasure for a fraction of a treasure's cost."

"Okay." Old Man snapped the box shut. "I'll take it." He slid it in the front pocket of his trousers, its shape bulging slightly beneath their polyester fabric. From his back pocket he slipped out his wallet, opened it, and handed Uncle Trix a pile of $100 bills.

Uncle Trix seemed surprised, but only for a nano-second. Then he started counting the money.

Jessabelle dipped her eyes and hustled back inside the truck. *You shouldn't have called him*, she scolded herself.

She could've stopped Uncle Trix. She'd known he was up to something. She should've just been firm, told him when she got in the truck, "Look Trix, no tricks."

She should've said something to stop Old Man from buying. But, remembering the time she'd tried to prevent Blondo from buying an imitation gold bar, she wasn't even sure she could have. Sometimes, trying to be good only brought more trouble.

She sucked in a slow deep breath to ease her guilt. A whiff of silicone, her mask's material, filled her lungs. At the back of her throat, it tasted slightly rubbery.

The raised hood of the truck obscured her view of Uncle Trix and Old Man, but she didn't have to view the action to know what was going on out there. In her mind's eye, she saw Uncle Trix folding Old Man's money, tucking it into his back pocket, offering a handshake to seal the deal.

She imagined Old Man waving good-bye and starting back to his car.

She heard Uncle Trix's voice. "Hello, ABC Towing? I need your help." No doubt his cell phone was propped to his ear with nobody on the other line.

The roar of the Continental's motor muffled Uncle Trix's voice. Jessabelle heard it head off down the road.

Uncle Trix slammed the truck hood shut. Then he kicked something. It skittered across the shoulder of the road, stopping in the tall edge of grass between the road and treeline. A burned-out smoke ball.

Uncle Trix joined Jessabelle in the truck, whooping and hollering like a man whose team just won, as he situated himself behind the wheel. "That's the first time it's gone that smoothly. The guy just handed over a thousand bucks he had sitting right in his back pocket. That's a Continental driver for you. I didn't even have to give him an appraisal certificate. I love the suckers!"

"That man was like eighty years old. You ought to be ashamed of yourself."

"Actually, I feel rather proud. You know how much I paid for that ring?" He didn't wait for her to guess. "Twenty dollars! That's how much. Wouldn't you say that was a good investment? I got two hundred bucks in the glove compartment that I'll turn into ten thousand by week's end. Go ahead and take a look."

Jessabelle opened the glove compartment, not so much because she wanted to see two hundred dollars, but because Uncle Trix's elbow to her side prompted her to.

Ten black velvet jewelry boxes exactly like the first, ribbon and all, stood crammed inside. She took one of the boxes out, untied the bow, and opened it. A diamond, indistinguishable from the one Old Man had purchased, beamed at her.

"Lucrative side job, don't you think?"

Jessabelle separated the ring from its fancy box. She raised it into the light pouring through the front windshield, twirling it in different directions. Depending on which way she moved it, it appeared blue tinged, milky, faintly yellow, or a little oily. But it never looked colorless.

"You give it a try," Uncle Trix said.

"Nah. I'm not in the mood right now."

"Not in the mood for a thousand dollars? What's the matter with you?"

She remembered how stainless and pure Lalli had appeared to her the day before. She thought about her new friends. She wanted to be like them—trustworthy, somebody to count as a friend.

Uncle Trix handed her a smoke ball and lighter. "Tell the motorist your wealthy fiancé dumped you because his mother doesn't think you're pretty enough for him. You're selling the ring to help me. Call me your father."

"It's okay." She returned the smoke bomb.

"Well, ain't you the uppity one. Hope you haven't forgotten what it's like to work for a living."

"No, I haven't." She slid her glasses from her pocket and wiggled them in Uncle Trix's face. "You try wearing these all of your waking life. See if that doesn't feel like work to you."

"Hey, the glasses weren't my idea."

"But Lalliville was; hence, the reason for the glasses." She tapped the face of her computerized wristwatch. "Can we just get going? I want to get there before the place closes."

Begrudgingly, Uncle Trix got the pickup truck back on the road. As per instructions from her phone's GPS, he drove her to Ferretsville, a town fifty miles north of Lalliville. The man who owned Fly Supply introduced himself as Soaring Sam. His sales uniform consisted of a bright orange jumpsuit, commando boots, and white helmet. He assured Jessabelle that flying was an easy matter. All she had to do was get into the air. He slapped a picture of an airplane on the counter, the single-engine kind with four seats, designed for personal use. "This will do just that for ya."

"What else you got?" she asked.

In a type of descending order, Soaring Sam tried selling her a helicopter, a plane rental, a parachute and helicopter rental combo, and a paraglider with directions to the nearest mountain, all without success. Finally he said, "You could always start on the ground and go up."

"How do I get up?" she asked.

He placed a rocket belt on the counter.

"How much?"

"Two grand."

She glanced at Uncle Trix who shook his head.

"Do you have anything cheaper?"

"The only thing cheaper than that is this," he said, erecting a pile on the counter, comprised of one-inch-diameter steel pipes and three metal drums, two silver, one blue, each a foot high. "It's called Make Your Own. Three hundred dollars. For an extra fifty bucks, I'll throw in the instructions. You can't go wrong here." Soaring Sam scooped the pile in his arms and dropped the tanks and metal piping on the counter. One of the tanks rolled off and hit the ground. Jessabelle covered her head, but nothing happened. "These are non explosive materials."

Jessabelle glanced again at Uncle Trix. His sour expression told her the return trip to Lalliville held a tongue-lashing. It started a second after he climbed in the truck, settling himself behind the wheel. She felt his gaze upon her. With nothing but two feet of vinyl upholstered seat between them, there was no way to avoid what was sure to come. He said, "I think you should spend less time figuring out how to fly and more time looking for the statue."

Her hands were folded over a drawstring bag resting on her lap, the bag stamped with a set of wings, the Fly Supply insignia. It contained the materials and a complete set of plans to make a device to propel her into the air. "I spend all day looking for the statue."

"If you spend all day looking for the statue, and you've been there three days, how come you haven't found it?"

"Because there's also a lot of other stuff I have to do to appear as if I fit in."

"Like what?"

"Breakfast, work, lunch, work, dinner, chant, go for a snack."

"Maybe you could skip all that eating."

"And then what—faint from hunger? I'll have you know it takes a lot of energy to be in that place, especially with all the cleaning I have to do."

"Can you skip work?" he asked.

"Impossible," she said. "Everybody has to work."

"That right there sounds like a scam. What do you mean, everybody has to work?"

"Just what I said. Everybody has to work."

He aimed a disapproving look her way. "But I paid for you to stay there, and you still have to work?"

"It's not my fault. That's how it is. Everybody works."

"Eight hours a day?"

Jessabelle nodded, although she couldn't say it made a lot of sense to her either, considering she saw work as more of a responsibility than a choice a person would freely make. People had jobs so when they were not at their jobs, they could eat at nice restaurants, see movies, take vacations, and in other ways, have fun. Right?

Jobs themselves were not necessarily fun. Her job as a con artist was just a means to buying supplies, so she could have fun creating characters. "It's service to the guru," she said, more to herself than Uncle Trix, in an attempt at understanding.

"Is that how they sold it to you?"

"No, that's what they call it."

"Who?"

"Vishva, Johann, Doc, Madeline, Chet."

Uncle Trix grunted. "Are they sane people?"

An inexplicable calm washed over her, increased by the lull of the moving vehicle. *I'm on my way back to Lalliville.* That thought comforted her.

She wished she was already in Lalliville, and not here, getting grilled by Uncle Trix. If she was there, she'd be coming out of the chant, uplifted in a way she couldn't explain, walking with her new friends to Krishna's Café for snacks. The longing for that obliterated Uncle Trix's voice for a few moments.

He had to repeat his question. "Are they sane people?"

"Huh? What? Who?"

"Vicky, John…Doug…and whoever else you said."

She nodded gravely. "Umm hmm, very sane."

"Wow! I could learn a few things from this guru—like how to get people to pay me to work for me."

It was after dark by the time they made it back onto Route 54. Uncle Trix drove his customary five miles over the speed limit, a pace he considered leisurely, one he believed no cop would ever stop him for. He drove, one hand on the steering wheel, his other draped over the seat back, his eyes passing from her to the road and back again to her.

"What's this guy got that I don't?"

"What guy?"

"The guru."

"Oh, didn't I tell you? It turns out the guru's a she."

"Hmm," he pondered. "Is she married?"

"I don't think so."

Uncle Trix rode up behind a fourteen-foot U-Haul and quickly crossed the yellow dashed line to pass before drifting back into the right lane, without ever placing both hands on the steering wheel or pausing in his line of questioning.

"Does that woman live in a mansion?"

"I don't think so."

"Does she drive a Rolls Royce?"

"I don't think so."

Uncle Trix socked the dashboard in irritation. "I don't think so, I don't think so, I don't think so," he mimicked. "Well, what do you think?"

She shrugged.

Several minutes later Uncle Trix took the steering wheel with both hands and made the left onto Way of Truth. Jessabelle scanned the darkness for any late night strollers, not wanting Doc or Vishva to see her in the plumbing truck with Uncle Trix.

Uncle Trix slowed the pickup to a crawl, trundling onto the dark, grassy shoulder of the road. In the glow of the dashboard lights, his expression turned pensive. "Maybe I can get a date with the guru," he said. "Figure out what she's got that's so special." Before he came around to questioning Jessabelle about his prospects for a date with Lalli, she jumped out of the car, blurted "See you later," and slammed the door, hastening toward Lalliville's front gate.

She heard the rumble of the truck coming up behind her and slowing down. "Jessie, get in the car."

She shook her head.

"I said, get in the car!"

"What for?"

"We're not done talking."

"Yes we are," she said, walking faster. For some strange reason, she even considered running.

"Why you being so stubborn?" Uncle Trix leaned halfway out the window, following her like a mugger. "C'mon. I don't bite."

Her heart pumped wildly.

Uncle Trix slammed the pickup to a stop, jumped out, and ensnared Jessabelle by the arm. He shoved her against the back of the truck, her arm locking around her Fly Supply bag, her ticket to being airborne. He spewed, "I get the impression you like it in Lalliville."

"So what if I do?"

"I'm afraid you're being brainwashed."

Jessabelle grinned. "Of course I'm being brainwashed."

"It's not funny. You might like Lalliville, but Lalliville isn't the real world. The real world is a tough place without cash in your pocket. Now get focused on what you came here for."

He made her promise that she'd make finding the statue a priority and call him as soon as she got any clues. She had to repeat her promise three times, until he believed she meant what she said. Only then did he get in the car, engineer a perfect U-turn, and head back out toward Route 54.

Chapter 19

Jessabelle rested her eyes on the sign beside the front gate of Lalliville. For entrance after 9:00 p.m., it said, call Security. No way was she dialing security. The last thing she needed was to have to explain to anybody why she was returning to Lalliville at ten-thirty p.m. Best to keep that entry out of the log books.

She studied the gate, surmising it was not climbable. If she tried scaling it, she might make it several feet up, but would eventually only slide back down, becoming a smear on the symbol Om, akin to being a dark spot on the sun. In order to get over the gate, she'd need a pole to vault over it, and she didn't happen to have one of those tucked in her pocket.

Where the fence ended, a tall row of bushes started. She walked to the bushes, heaved her Fly Supply bag up over them, and heard it land on the other side, a jangle of grating metal. She tapped the caps of each of her colored pens, ensuring the entire set was fastened to the pocket protector inside the breast pocket of her white shirt.

She clawed the bushes with one hand, lifted the opposite foot, and shoved a toe of her black clomper into the green brambles. She fastened upon the bush with her other hand, climbing higher along the clusters of shaggy branches. She tossed a leg up and then another, crawled across the top of the bushes, and plunged to the grass on the other side, ending flat on her back. She again checked her colored pens just to be sure they had all made it over the bushes with her.

She rolled to her side.

The second she saw the dark feet in flat white-strapped sandals, she knew whose feet they were. Maybe it was the white cotton of the sari billowing above those feet that told her. Or the feet themselves. They expressed perfect anatomical structure, with lots of space between fanned out toes. The arches sloped up to medium height, well supported by the bones and muscles at the heels and balls of the feet. In addition to being structured the way nature had designed feet to be, they were healthy, pretty feet. They were not dry, cracked, or callused, but well hydrated, young-looking feet.

"Out looking for Shiva?"

Jessabelle whipped her glasses out the pocket of her overalls and got them on her face, as if she needed them to see. "Who's that?" She gazed up at Lalli, who offered Jessabelle a hand.

Jessabelle raised an arm and took that hand. Lalli hoisted her to her feet with so much power it surprised Jessabelle. "Actually," Jessabelle said. "I was just out shopping for a few things."

"Where'd you go?"

"Wally's," she lied. "Do you know what that is?"

"Of course. I'm not a prisoner here."

Jessabelle smacked a piece of grass off her elbow. "Then you know it's not the place to find Shiva."

"Absolute Truth exists everywhere."

There she goes talking about Truth again. Jessabelle said Shiva, and Lalli said Truth. Was Lalli trying to keep her in a state of bafflement? *Focus*, Jessabelle told herself. "I mentioned Shiva," she said with all her concentration. "Why do you talk about Truth?"

"Shiva is ultimate Truth."

"What is the *ultimate* Truth?"

"One day you will know."

"How will I know if you don't tell me?"

"Meditate on the Self and ultimate Truth will reveal itself to you."

"Meditate? I can't do that. I tried last night. It's too hard."

"Let me ask you a question or two. The first time you tied your shoes, was it difficult?"

"I don't remember."

"How about the first time you rode a bike?"

Jessabelle tried to recall that event but drew a blank.

"How about the first time…you did anything? Did this thing get easier after about ten times? It's the same with stilling your mind. The more you do it, the more natural it becomes, and the more you will know Truth. Meditation practice makes Truth evident."

"How long do I have to practice before I find ultimate Truth?"

"That depends on you. The Upanishads say, 'If you want Truth as much as a drowning man wants air, you will realize it in a split-second.'"

Before, Lalli had said Jessabelle needed to practice to know ultimate Truth. Now she was saying Jessabelle could find it if only she wanted it urgently enough, as if it were the thing she needed to save her life. Internally, Jessabelle wrestled with the paradox.

"Grace is there," Lalli said as if speaking to her thoughts. "You do have to make the effort to let it in. And of course to know truth of any kind, one has to give up lies."

One has to give up lies.

The thought of giving up lies turned the pit of Jessabelle's stomach to a hard rock of discomfort. That sounded tough. Sure, she wanted a life of integrity, but give up lies? She had to admit that part of her liked lies and the fast cash they brought her way.

She hankered after the things her lies bought, like silicone, cold foam, gelatin, and all the other stuff she used in her art of making and applying prosthetics. Did she really want to sacrifice all that? Where would she be without dental acrylic powder, shim, plaster of paris, slip latex, hair lace, urethane, and oil clay?

She couldn't imagine a life without lies. Would it be boring, or turn her penniless?

Lalli wished Jessabelle a "Good night" before she went on her way.

Jessabelle wandered back to her house, where she found Vishva in the living room, lounging on a recliner with her legs resting on its raised foot stool. A Styrofoam toe spreader, wedged in place, splayed Vishva's toes so her freshly polished red toenails wouldn't get messed up.

Vishva wore a white cotton poplin pajama set, combining a button top with a collar and short sleeves with simple pants. They probably had a drawstring waist. Jessabelle couldn't really tell, the way Visha sat in the recliner reading a book, *Astavakra Samhita*, by the light of a standing lamp.

When she heard Jessabelle come in, Vishva lowered the book. "You're late." A thick paste of moist green clay coated her face. A pink stretchy fabric headband kept her hair back. "Missed you at the chant."

"I was out shopping for a few supplies I need for my wingsuit." On the floor Jessabelle set the fly supply bag, containing all the ingredients she needed to bake a contraption that would propel her into the air. One of the steel pipes unexpectedly poked its head out the bag's drawstring opening. Vishva leaned forward for a peek.

More than the fact Lalli and Vishva were both Indian and possessed slender-without-being-willowy-or-frail body types, Vishva hinted at Lalli. It was something in her constitution, a dignified presence. Vishva struck Jessabelle as being statelier in her pajamas, with her face buried in clay and Styrofoam stuffed between her toes, than the average Wally's shopper, dressed to go out of the house. All Vishva said about the bag with the steel pipe sticking out its top was, "Hmm, interesting."

Jessabelle plunked down on the couch, similar to the one Bennie had stretched out on in the warehouse earlier that day. Completing the furniture setup were the recliner where Vishva was parked and a loveseat. There was no TV in the room.

"Are you by any chance related to Lalli?" Jessabelle inquired.

"She's my second mother."

Jessabelle had two mothers. Why couldn't Vishva? Of course, neither of Jessabelle's mothers was like Lalli. "Who is Lalli?" Jessabelle asked.

"A true guru. She is Shiva."

"Shiva?"

"Yes. Her mind and body have become pure consciousness. Living in a thought-free state, she is one with the Truth. She makes others lovers of the Truth."

"How does she do that?"

"By giving the experience of the Truth."

"I don't understand. Can't I experience the Truth just by telling the truth?"

Vishva waved an ethereal hand. "I'm talking about absolute Truth, oneness with pure consciousness."

Absolute Truth? Pure consciousness? These expressions went right over Jessabelle's head. In an attempt to bring the conversation to a level she could understand, she asked, "Did Lalli ever steal anybody's money?"

Vishva looked appalled. "No! The only things she's ever taken from anyone are their ignorance, sins, and impurities."

"Did she ever take anybody's house or car?"

"Stick around and you won't ask me these questions. You will understand how great she is." Vishva's mask of green clay had begun drying, solidifying like plaster. "Lalli will bestow her grace upon you, take away your sadness, and turn you into a new person. Because that's what she does. She transforms a person's ordinary life with their family into a sacred existence."

Jessabelle suppressed a laugh. Obviously, Vishva did not know who she was talking to. Turning Jessabelle's life with Uncle Trix into a sacred existence seemed as impossible as turning a beast into Prince Charming, something that only happened in fairy tales. "Not me," she said, swinging her head from side to side.

"Yes you."

Jessabelle's head came to a stop. "I have another question for you, and I'm just speaking hypothetically here, okay? Can you remember I'm just speaking hypothetically?"

"Hypothetical. Got it. What's your question?"

"Okay, let's suppose I'm a really bad person who has never done one single thing to deserve anybody's grace. How could Lalli bestow her grace upon me?"

"Lalli's not just anybody, and I'm not talking about

ordinary favor." Vishva's mask was hard now. She spoke, hardly moving her lips. "Whether you think you deserve it or not, in her boundless compassion, Lalli will bestow her grace upon you. In fact, she probably already has, but for whatever reason, you're not aware of it."

Jessabelle wondered what Uncle Trix would say here. No doubt he'd be making fun. *What are you trying to sell me?* she heard him say. Part of her wondered if indeed Vishva was trying to sell her something and why.

Another part of her desperately wanted to understand, as if indeed her very life depended on this understanding. Jessabelle said, "Lalli asked me, 'Would it make sense to you if Shiva asked where Shiva was?' What do you think that means?"

"I would have to know the context before commenting."

"I can give it to you." Jessabelle became quiet, realizing she couldn't really give Vishva the full context: She'd been questioning Lalli about Shiva with the hope of stealing a golden Shiva from her.

"No," Vishva said, her mask cracking around her lips, "on second thought, I've said enough for one night." She rolled the recliner's foot rest down and got to her feet. The Styrofoam toe spreaders forced her to keep her weight on her heels. "I've got a face to rinse." Before she waddled off, walking on her heels with her toes in the air, she said, "Lalli's words are subtle and profound. You have to listen in a subtle and profound way to understand them. They are not just facts to store in your brain, but words capable of transforming your whole state of being. I suggest you contemplate what she said and tell me what you think they mean."

Jessabelle had no time for contemplation, not when the pressure was on to design a wingsuit, one that actually flew. She carried her supplies off to her bedroom and locked the door. She spent over an hour getting ready for bed, stripping

layer by layer, beginning with her clothes, and then removing
her wig, fake teeth, and face, ending with her bald cap. Finally,
in her Creativo T-shirt and underwear, she sat crosslegged on
her bed and spread open a sketchbook she had packed in her
suitcase to a clean new page.

She drew her face with a plumped-up, puffed-out deep
orange breast and belly, and black head and back, ending in
dark tailfeathers that extended out from her body. She gave
herself brown legs and feet, white eye rings with intense
glossy black eyes, and a thin yellow bill for a nose.

She had chosen a robin, a small bird just like the one
she'd seen earlier that day, reasoning the lighter she could
make herself, the better her chances of actually flying.

And who was to say she couldn't make a RobinSuit fly?
If only she could figure out how, it could happen. Who was
to say it wouldn't have already happened if she'd chosen a
profession more focused on mathematics and physics instead
of anatomy, physiology, and art?

Terror gripped her as she recalled stories she'd heard of
birdmen throughout history who had died falling from tall
buildings, bridges, or jumping out of small planes, flapping
their wings to keep them in the air, all the way to their fatal
crash to the ground.

For the first time it occurred to her: *I could die trying to
protect the lie.* Oddly, it almost didn't matter. She'd rather die
than admit to her new friends that she was not who she said
she was.

The problem in creating a wingsuit wasn't with her. It was
in the fact there was too much going on here. It left no time
for designing a wingsuit. She spent an hour each evening removing, cleaning, and picking glue off her mask, and another
hour the next morning reaffixing it, ensuring it was on just
right.

Originally she'd toyed with the idea of creating several

individual pieces—forehead, nose, upper lip, lower lip, cheeks, and chin—to be glued overlapping each other for a complete face. In the end, instead of a face divided into multiple parts, she'd settled on one large piece, basically a mask, in the interest of saving time. And her mask fulfilled that purpose.

However, the time she saved in the daily application and removal of her face was getting eaten every other way. Cleaning a shed, attending the evening chants, meditating, trying to figure out who Lalli was. It was all starting to wear her out, making her feel crazy and disoriented. How was she supposed to focus on a task as monumental as creating a wingsuit with all these other things commanding her attention? Uncle Trix was right. She'd lost her focus.

She inwardly swore to stay centered on her reason for being here, the golden Shiva. She hoped she'd find it before July 21, the date of the talent show, just a month away. Then the robin's ability to fly would be a moot point, because Isa Newton would be long gone, never to be seen or heard from again.

And if she couldn't find the golden Shiva by then?

Tomorrow she would tell Madeline she'd changed her mind. Instead of jumping off a platform to get her wings started, she'd begin on the ground and go up.

From a bird's point of view, it seemed safer to be stuck on the ground than to drop from a platform in the sky, headlong to the earth.

Chapter 20

With the morning sun on her face, Jessabelle sat with her rear on the grass and back against the side wall of the shed. She was wondering what Lalli had meant the night before, after Jessabelle had dropped at her feet: "Shiva is ultimate Truth."

The sound of laughter broke into her reverie. She glanced up to see Lalli approaching, walking hand-in-hand with Bennie. Vishva was with them too. They all looked pretty, including Bennie, who sported a long teal cotton shirt with fancy gold embroidery around the collar, sleeves, and hem. Vishva and Lalli wore long shirts, Lalli's white cotton over an ankle length straight white skirt, and Vishva's purple cotton with striped pants bearing all the colors of the rainbow.

The trio stopped in front of Jessabelle. Lalli asked, "Is this what you call working hard?"

Jessabelle knitted her eyebrows in bewilderment.

Lalli explained, "Yesterday, you told me you're working hard in the shed."

"Oh, that small remark," Jessabelle said. "Generally speaking, I am working hard in the shed. Right at this particular moment, I'm getting ready to work hard in the shed."

"Did you see Shiva?" Lalli's face contained an inkling of a smirk.

How many times was Lalli going to ask Jessabelle that same question? "No," Jessabelle snapped. "Did you?"

"Of course, I see him every day." Lalli's inkling of a smirk became a full-fledged smile. She turned toward Vishva and told her, "Isa." She flashed a glance at Jessabelle. "That's your name, right?"

Jessabelle nodded. Had Lalli really forgotten her name? Or was there something more behind her question? *What is really going on here?*

"Isa is looking for Shiva," Lalli told Vishva. "Have you seen Shiva?"

Jessabelle wanted to shout, "Enough about Shiva already!" but stayed cool. *Is Lalli playing a game with me?*

"Yesterday I saw Shiva in the bookstore," Vishva said, "and then the temple. And today I saw him in the park, when I meditated under the big oak tree. He shimmered in the morning light."

"Maybe we'll see him in the auditorium," Lalli said. "That's where we're headed. Vishva is going to give me her advice about starting a theater."

"A theater?" Jessabelle asked. "What for?"

"To act out spiritual stories," Vishva said, "and put on plays about the lives of saints."

Indignancy bit Jessabelle. That was the kind of service assignment she should have gotten. "What do you know about starting a theater?" she asked Vishva.

"Virtually nothing," Vishva said. "But Lalli asked for my advice. I'm always happy to give her whatever I've got."

Maybe I can give advice about starting a theater, Jessabelle thought, *and you, Vishva, can stay here and clean.* Jessabelle never got a chance to pose the suggestion before Lalli and Vishva moved on, leaving Bennie with her.

"They didn't ask us if we wanted to come give our advice about starting a theater," Jessabelle grumbled.

"Our job is here," Bennie said.

"Thanks for reminding me."

"Today we're going to Johann to get a requisition to buy some high-powered lights from Wally's."

Bennie explained how he'd told Lalli he and Isa had been taking turns holding the penlight for the other while he or she cleaned. Surpise, surprise. Lalli deemed it an inefficient system and helped him come up with another, more practical solution to their lack-of-lights problem.

Bennie began describing why their system was inefficient. Jessabelle told him to save his breath, as she full-well knew. The only reason she hadn't said anything when they'd been working using their method was because she didn't care whether this place ever got cleaned. It didn't matter whether they used a toothbrush to scrub the floor, a handkerchief woven of fine thread to wipe the walls, or a penlight to see by. The only thing that mattered was that it looked as if she was cleaning so she could remain in this place long enough to get rich.

"So you're on board with my idea?" he asked.

She nodded her agreement.

On their way to Johann's office, she got to work on her real goal. "You heard Lalli say I'm looking for Shiva," she said. "Have you seen any Shiva statues around here?"

"Umm hmm."

"Where?"

"Guruji's."

"You've been in Lalli's place?"

"How could I not have been in Lalli's place when I'm staying on her couch?"

"What does Lalli's Shiva look like?"

"Shining."

"Like gold?"

"Her Shiva is gold. And big."

"Big too?"

"At least sometimes he looks big, and sometimes small."

"How big and how small?"

"Sometimes he looks this big." Bennie held his thumb and forefinger close together. "And sometimes he looks this big." He spread his arms as wide as he possibly could, trying to spread them even wider. "I can't even stretch my arms as wide as Shiva, or as high. His head reaches the sky."

Jessabelle blew out a frustrated breath. "Can you just give me the actual height and width of Lalli's Shiva?"

"I don't know. He's a thing, but he's not just a thing. What's the actual height and width of Consciousness?"

Clearly, Jessabelle needed to see Lalli's Shiva herself. "Where does Lalli live?"

"I can't tell you that. What if you're a guru stalker?"

"A what?"

"Somebody who follows Lalli around, just because she wants something."

"I don't want anything from her!"

"Then why do you want to know where she lives?"

"I'm just curious."

He cocked his head and studied her with his bright green round eyes. She returned his gaze. His lips weren't moving. "Tell me about her habits," she coaxed.

"Don't you know anything about her?" asked Bennie.

He sounded suspicious. She wondered if he really was. "I know she likes mango lassi," she said, trying to sound innocuous, "and wears white. I just don't know about her habits."

"I'm not sure she has habits." He sniffed. "Nobody knows what she'll do or won't do. She walks, but always at a different time of day. She can sit in meditation all morning or all evening. She eats some days, and some days she fasts. Other days, I've seen her eat only three grains of rice and a plum. Oh, I know a habit she has."

"What?"

"She works many hours every day."

"When and where?"

"Always different times and places."

Jessabelle skipped lunch and went searching instead, desiring to feast her eyes on the golden Shiva. "Yesterday I saw Shiva in the bookstore," Vishva had said, "and then the temple. And today I saw him in the park when I meditated under the big oak tree."

In the bookstore, Jessabelle passed shelves of yoga books, snacks and food, toiletries, and homeopathic remedies for common ailments like cold and flu. The only kind of Shiva she found was on a shelf filled with one-inch statues of various Hindu deities, carved from limestone, not the kind of Shiva that would make her rich.

She didn't search the temple. She'd seen the small porcelain Shiva statue that sat on a pedestal cut into one of its side walls.

Jessabelle couldn't imagine why anyone would place a three-million-dollar statue in a park, but Vishva had said she'd seen Shiva in the park, when she sat under the big oak tree.

From the edge of the park, Jessabelle saw many oaks, but

not a single Shiva statue. Jessabelle chose one of many majestic oaks in the park, sat crosslegged in its shade, and gazed in every direction. No Shiva. She changed position, shifting her weight from one rear cheekbone to the other, and gazed around again. No Shiva. She stood up and circled the tree halfway. On its other side, she again took a seat and searched all directions. Again, nothing.

She lay face down on the ground, raised her head, turned it to the right and then the left to see what she could see, but all she could see were a few picnic tables, grass, trees, and a lake shimmering with sunlight.

She rolled a couple of yards across the grass, came to rest on her back, interlaced her fingers behind her head, and gazed along the treetops. She definitely did not see a gold statue hidden up there.

Ridiculous searching for Shiva this way! She sprang to her feet.

But just to be sure there was no Shiva statue whatsoever in this park, she strode its perimeter, looking this way and that. For the last time, she came up with nothing. Vishva seeing Shiva in the park had to be a joke.

Jessabelle bet the statue was in Lalli's house.

Lalli didn't live in the largest house on Devotion Street. Jessabelle had finally gotten that much out of Bennie. From the corner of Devotion, the pastel houses on the street looked equal in size, except for one all the way on the end, the smallest of all. Jessabelle decided to walk to it.

Apparently the residents of this town liked decorations and were slow on sidewalk repair. Strings of rich green, orange, yellow, red, pink, and blue lights decorated three of the houses she passed. Jessabelle turned her head to admire some blinking white lights on a pine and nearly tripped over a crack in the sidewalk.

"Whoa," came a voice from overhead, and Jessabelle

raised her face to see Hanuman high up on a ladder, winding a metallic garland around the pole of a street lamp. "Are you okay?"

"Oh yeah," Jessabelle said. "A little trip—no big deal, unless you're talking about an LSD trip. That could be a big deal."

Hanuman glanced at Bhisma, who stood at the foot of the ladder holding the garland's spool. "We wouldn't know anything about that," he said rather seriously.

"Actually, I don't either. One time my uncle tried to talk me into trying some. He thought I'd like to see things. But to tell the truth, I've got enough pictures inside to last a lifetime." She was babbling, all the while surveying the house on the end. About forty feet wide, some would think it a perfect vacation cottage, others a sweet starter house. It had a stone walkway and five steps leading up to a front porch.

She wasn't so sure the house belonged to Lalli. She wished she'd pressed Bennie further for a more specific description of the house in which he was currently a guest.

"We'd love to stay and chat," Bhisma said, "but we're on a tight schedule. We've got to get these decorations up by the end of today."

Jessabelle nodded, briefly wondering what they were decorating for, and proceeded toward the house on the corner. She didn't know exactly why, call it a hunch. To her eyes, that house, the color of blue sea, shone brightly. Something told her the source of this town's life dwelled in that house.

She sneaked around the house, and standing in the backyard, peeked through the kitchen window, over a stainless steel sink that stood between an old-fashioned stove and a dishwasher. On the other side of the room, Bennie sat with Lalli at a small wooden table. At the same time it pleased her to know her hunch was correct, she felt disappointed that Lalli didn't live in a mansion, drive a Rolls Royce, and mercilessly order people around. It would be so much easier to steal a three-million-dollar statue from a woman like that than the person Jessabelle saw now, the woman eating cheese quesadillas with Bennie.

Around here, people called her a great being and treated her as such. How could a great being live in such a simple house on a plain street in an average small town with ordinary people and eat cheese quesadillas for lunch?

Why didn't Lalli live in a mansion? If indeed people gave her gifts like three-million-dollar statues, she certainly could and should. Shouldn't she?

"You already told me this story," Lalli was saying.

"I know," Bennie said. "I just wish you could've been there." Something had magnetized his attention, and from the level of excitement that played on his face, he might have been staring at a shooting star or some other natural phenomenon. "I prayed to Shiva and Ganesh appeared right then and there to rid me of my Troubles."

Jessabelle followed Bennie's gaze to his point of interest, a small gold-plated figurine of an elephant-faced god. It stood on the shelf next to a figure of Lord Shiva in the same size and style.

"And you say Ganesh had a female voice?"

"Yeah."

"And a pair of white tennis shoes with purple smiley faces?"

"I know," Bennie said. "It surprised me too. But you taught me to be open in thinking about the deities." He shrugged as if to utter, What more can I say? Then he actually said, "Those mantras of yours are power-packed."

"Thanks. I didn't invent them. Bhaktas have recited them for thousands of years. Through war and peace, sickness and health, the mantras kept those Bhaktas connected to their own true source of strength. Sounds like the mantras are yours now too."

"Can you teach me how to fight like Ganesh? Huh? Can you?"

Lalli gave Bennie a level stare.

"What? You don't believe in fighting?"

"What do you believe?"

"That sometimes you have to put your foot down. Otherwise two boys twice your size will just kick you around until you're dead."

"It's true. Sometimes you have to defend yourself. There's no other way."

"But how? Look at me! I'm small and weak.'

Lalli laughed and said, "You have a small weakness. It's that you *believe* you're small and weak."

"But I am! Against two boys twice my size, I am weak!"

"Don't believe everything you see. They may look bigger, but that doesn't mean they are."

"What do you mean?"

"They are no bigger or smaller than you."

"But they are bigger!"

"Only in physical form." Lalli clasped Bennie's hand and held it. "A great pool of strength resides in you. Once that strength flows out into your limbs, you will know how strong you are."

"So, does this mean you'll teach me to fend off my attackers?"

"I'm not a street fighter."

"But my mom said you do everything."

"No one person can do *everything*. If Ganesh defended you, why don't you ask Ganesh to teach you to defend yourself?"

Lalli turned toward the window. Jessabelle sucked in her breath, pivoting away from the screen and plastering the back of her body against the wooden siding of the house. Her heart beat wildly with the fear that Lalli had seen her.

She considered running and hiding behind a nearby bush. Hearing the conversation continue, she relaxed. Her eyes rested on a small pond. Several white lotus flowers as big as soccer balls floated on its surface.

"My mom's not even sure who I saw was really Ganesh. She said Ganesh was probably just an actor who had the role of an elephant in a play. But there aren't any theaters near us."

"What do you believe?"

"That I saw Ganesh."

"Well then, ask Ganesh to teach you how to fight like Ganesh."

"I'm not sure how to get hold of Ganesh."

"Obviously Shiva does. Pray to Shiva and he'll tell Ganesh."

"Okay." There was a shuffling inside the kitchen. Jessabelle pictured Bennie moving to stand before Lalli's Shiva. He started reciting mantras.

Nonsense! How can a pipsqueak become strong by praying to Shiva? Shiva was no bigger than her palm. She should leave Lalliville at once! Pursue real business, the kind that would make her enough money to be free and never again have to be or do anything she didn't want to be or do. She slid down the wall of the house, easing into a seated position. She deeply breathed the aroma of the lotuses.

Something in her frowned over the thought of leaving. Even now, with all these doubts swirling inside, she would've sworn the walls of this house vibrated with peace. Very real peace, not something she imagined, but a force that made her feel calm and sleepy.

She closed her eyes and listened to Bennie. "Please Shiva, in the face of my Troubles, make all my bodies strong as bulls." She may have even fallen asleep. It was hard to tell. All she knew was that when she again opened her eyes, Lalli pillared over her.

Jessabelle jumped, hitting the back of her head on a wood shingle. She managed to get to her feet. It didn't seem possible. A second ago, Lalli was inside. Now she stood right before her with an annoyed expression. "Creeping around this house like a thief!"

"I wasn't…creeping around your house…like a thief."

"Then what are you doing?"

"I came to get my co-worker," she lied. "You know, we're going to Wally's to get some lights."

"Were you planning to hoist him over the sink and out the window?"

"Yes," Jessabelle said, thinking fast. "He is small, after all. I thought I'd give him a piggyback ride. Loading him on my back will be a lot easier if he comes out a window." To prove she wasn't lying, she stuck her nose against the screen and called Bennie.

Bennie ran to the window. He squinted at Jessabelle as if she were an alien who had just landed in Lalli's backyard. "What're you doing here?"

"It's okay," Lalli told Bennie. "She wants to give you a piggyback ride. Meet her out front; that's where you'll board your vehicle." So much for telling Bennie to crawl over the kitchen sink and out the window to get onto her back.

Jessabelle followed Lalli toward the front of the house. "You could make Bennie's prayer your own," Lalli said.

"Huh?"

"We all need to be strong. The spiritual path is not for weaklings."

"Spiritual path? I'm not on a spiritual path."

"You could have fooled me."

One thought tumbled into the next, disarranging the contents of Jessabelle's head, tossing it all into disorder.

"If you don't want to continue," Lalli said, "then don't. I'm not insulted if you don't. You're welcome to walk whatever path you like. By your own experience, you will know your true path when you find it."

All Jessabelle thought to say is, "Just so you know, I'm very strong." She bent her arm at the elbow, flexing her bicep. It bulged like a juicy, but slightly squished grapefruit.

"Impressive." Lalli laughed and then said, "Physical is not the only kind of strength there is. Turn your vision within. There you'll find unwavering strength."

At the front of the house, Lalli helped Bennie hop up on Jessabelle's back. "See you later," she told him. Jessabelle carried Bennie off as he blew Lalli a kiss. Lalli returned the gesture, puffing out a kiss of her own, carried through the air.

Bennie started out weighing about eighty-three pounds, but with each step he grew heavier, until it felt as if he weighed eighty-three hundred pounds. Hauling the cargo promoted a sweat.

She saw bracketed pole banners on the streetlights now, the work of Hanuman and Bhisma, no doubt. "I love Day of Practice decorations!" Bennie yelled. In his joy, he threw his hands in the air, becoming a no-hands piggyback rider. His weight pitched backward.

Afraid of losing him to the pavement, Jessabelle shrieked and bent her chest forward, too busy trying to keep him from falling to ask what the heck a Day of Practice was. His chest thudded against her back. He regained his hold, tightening his grip on her neck.

"I just love decorations!" She'd heard him the first time. That voice of his came in loud and clear since it hung right next to her ear. "Wait until you see the balloons," he went on. "That's my favorite part of a Day of Practice. The kundalini balloons! Spiraling like snakes! This is the only place you'll ever see balloons like that! The party lady makes them special, just for us!"

Never had she seen a boy get so excited over decorations.

Up ahead, Doc set a yellow caution sign in front of the sidewalk crack Jessabelle had tripped over earlier. Bennie extended an arm and wagged his hand side-to-side in greeting.

Doc's face contorted. He gave Jessabelle his "I'm viewing Glinda the Good Girl turn into a 300-Pound Werewolf" look.

"What's the matter?" Jessabelle asked.

"Nothing," Doc said.

Jessabelle and Bennie continued up the street. "You like Doc!" Bennie exclaimed.

"I do not!"

"I can tell, because your face got all weird after we saw him."

She had the sinking feeling something was wrong with her face. "You mind stopping by my place? I need to freshen my makeup."

"You wear makeup?"

"Just a little."

Chapter 21

In Jessabelle's private bathroom, she cupped both hands together, forming a bowl, a handmade bowl one could say. She held her bowl under the spigot. When it pooled with water, she raised it to her lips and guzzled.

Piggybacking Bennie to her house at high speed and in high heat, she had worked up such a thirst, she would've gotten down on all fours and drunk from a plastic dish like a dog, if that's what it took to wet her throat.

After chugging three "bowlfuls" of water, she shook out her hands and dried them on a towel. Then she turned off the water and glanced in the mirror, not pleased by what she saw: A face the color of a silver dollar, except for the far sides of each cheek, which were slightly pink. The skin oozed down in a scaly look. Overall, it wasn't a pretty picture.

Curse this Florida heat! It was making her sweat; perspi-

ration was known to weaken spirit gum, what was happening 11
here. Tiny pockets were forming where the glue had dissolved. Her face had slid about an eighth of an inch, causing
it to be slightly misfitting.

his was where good planning came into play, showing a
professional couldn't be too prepared. Quicker than refitting
this face was getting another. She selected one of two more
masks, replicas of the first that rested on two additional cold
foam copies of her face, zipped in airtight plastic and stored
in her trunk.

She conducted the adhesive-removing process of freeing herself from the first mask. She considered treating her
face with Sweat Halt before placing the second mask on her
face, but nixed the perspiration inhibitor in favor of adding
tiny vent-holes in the replacement mask, ones that wouldn't
be noticed when the makeup was final, and using Bond-It, a
stronger glue, reputedly unaffected by heat. Flowing naturally
from this change would be the need to later switch her brand
of adhesive remover to Bond-Be-Gone.

She reached into her tackle box for her eight-ounce bottle of Bond-It, when a knock at the door made her jump.

"Isa!" Bennie shouted, "Hurry up!"

He was supposed to be waiting patiently in the living room, not in her bedroom, rushing her. "Get out of my
room."

"Hurry up and I will."

In response to his pounding two more times at one-
minute intervals, she said, "If you bang on that door one more
time, I'm never coming out."

According to legend as related by Mom, when Jessabelle
was five, she'd called the hospital. "Can you send us a little
boy?" she'd asked the person who picked up the phone. She
couldn't remember doing this, but knew it was true, because
she had always wanted a little brother, and even after she

learned babies didn't exactly come from the hospital, she held tightly to her desire.

Currently, Bennie was doing the type of thing she'd imagined a little brother would do by beating on the bathroom door. But instead of being cute and lovable, as it always had in her fantasies, it annoyed her. He finally must have decided to put his waiting time to good use, because shortly afterward, she heard him chanting. When she finally emerged from the bathroom, Bennie sat crosslegged on her bed with his hands joined palm to palm, praying.

He opened his eyes, glanced at her, and reared back like a startled pony. At first she thought it was because he was so into his prayer, he hadn't heard her come into the room and was surprised to see her. That thought got blasted to pieces when he said, "Whoa. You're like a whole new you." And she realized his start was caused by something he saw in her.

Jessabelle moved toward the door. Bennie followed. His line of vision lasered the side of her head. "You went into the bathroom with a disease that made you look like a fish and came out completely cured. What did you do in there?"

"Be careful!" she yelled. He whipped his head around, but too late. His foot caught on a leg of the bed. He fell to the floor, his face landing at the foot of her closet door, resting ajar. Through its opening, Jessabelle could see her broken-in white leather tennis shoes with the purple smiley faces painted on their sides.

Bennie gazed at them for a long time, and then back to Jessabelle's face. His expression turned quizzical. He looked at her sneaks again, and then back to Jessabelle as if his head were a tennis ball moving back and forth across a net. He pointed to her sneaks. "Those are yours, aren't they?"

"No," Jessabelle said. She charged out her bedroom door. "C'mon. We've got to go."

Bennie scrambled up and trailed her to the front of the

house, then out onto the walkway. From behind her, she heard him say, "Ganesh, it's you." He ran to her side. "It's you! It's you! You're Ganesh!" He hooked his arm in Jessabelle's and tried to twirl her around.

She didn't budge. "I don't know what you're talking about," she said.

"You do! Admit it! You're Ganesh!"

"I am not!"

"Why won't you just admit you are?"

Jessabelle turned onto the sidewalk.

"Ganesh! Ganesh!" he called after her. "Most girls have boring makeup, but yours is cool. That's how you made yourself look like Ganesh, and a geek. Right?"

A gray-bearded man passed on the sidewalk, glancing in their direction.

Jessabelle brought a finger to her lips. "Shhh!"

"Ganesh! Ganesh! You must teach me to defend myself."

"I said *shhh*," Jessabelle grouched.

He jumped in front of her. She stopped.

He plopped down on his knees and clasped his hands to his chest. "Please, please, pretty please. I'm begging you. Have mercy on this poor little weakling."

Jessabelle laughed.

Bennie continued his petition. "Before school starts again, I've got to know how to fight. If I say don't touch me, they don't listen. I've got to make them listen. They've got to know I'm serious. If I could fight like you, they'd know I'm serious! Please. I'm a quick learner."

Jessabelle took Bennie by the elbow and pulled him up. "I don't know what you're talking about."

They went to the transportation department to pick up the key earmarked for their use in buying lights from Wally's, a task deemed official Lalliville business. On the way to the van, Bennie led Jessabelle on a shortcut, across three streets and through six yards. "Please," he said along the way. "Teach me to fight like you."

"I'll think about it."

"How long will it take you to think about it?"

"I don't know. I'll think about that too."

They stopped on the lawn between two houses, one teal, the other marigold, so Bennie could determine if they were headed in the right direction. He wouldn't know for sure until they came out onto the next street. They kept moving until Bennie said, "Oh, there he is," referring to a four-armed man, dancing in the midst of a flame. "Dancing Shiva."

This new rendering of Shiva, a bronze sculpture about four feet high and three feet wide, stood on the lawn of a small peach house, one Bennie informed her belonged to Hanuman. Jessabelle mulled over the irony of such a large man residing in such a small house.

"Why is Shiva standing on a baby?" Jessabelle asked.

"That's not a baby!" Bennie crowed. He explained that it was the dwarf demon Apasmara trampled afoot, Shiva's victory over ignorance. "Just say yes," he said, suddenly jolting them back to the subject of her teaching him self-defense.

"Maybe later," she said, stalling.

"Later? Like after they've killed me."

"Don't be so dramatic. It can't be that bad."

"It is."

They started moving again. A warm breeze brushed past her, nipping her rubbery cheeks. A black hawk perched in a tall pine. They watched it until it flew off. Then Bennie stamped his foot. "If you don't teach me to fight, I'll tell everybody you're a fake."

"I am not a fake."

"Are too. You wear all this stuff on your face, and you don't even know who Apasmara is."

"This is my first time here. Of course I don't know every little detail of the place."

"You don't know anything. What do you really look like, anyhow?"

She ran her fingers along the sides of her face and upper body. "This."

"Do not, and I'll tell everybody, unless you teach me to fight."

"Blackmail won't get you anywhere with me. I said I'll think about it. Until then, keep your mouth shut." She placed her hands on his shoulders and turned his body to face hers. "Can you do that?"

He nodded.

They arrived at the van. She climbed in, fitted the key in the ignition, and cranked it. She fidgeted with the knobs until she figured out how to turn on the a/c. The initial blast of it was so steamy, she thought it would melt her onto the bucket seat she sat on. In her peripheral vision, she watched him take his seat, becoming quiet and still.

Rumbling out the front gate, he inhaled a deep breath and began chanting mantras. She wondered why she didn't just tell him yes. He was a good kid. He was also a nice kid. She really didn't want him getting beaten up. Maybe it was just the seeming impossibility of the task that made her refrain from agreeing. Bennie was awfully small compared to just one of his Troubles, and there were two of them.

She doubted he'd ever have what he wanted: to be intimidating to Trouble and Trouble. Is it even possible to train a mouse to scare two pythons? That sounded like a real responsibility and a challenge. Bennie could get chewed to pieces in the process. Why had they chosen Bennie as the target for their savagery, anyway? What did he ever do to deserve their brutishness?

She ventured a little humor. "Why do they pick on you?

Why don't you tell them to go pick on somebody more their speed, like a ten-foot bear?"

Bennie glanced over at her and smiled, but said nothing. He kept humming. She guessed he was too preoccupied concocting a way to get her to say yes to actually speak.

Jessabelle said, "In this case, talking to the principal might not be such a bad idea."

Bennie shook his head emphatically and stopped humming. "The principal can't be with me twenty-four hours a day, seven days a week."

"Maybe he can talk to them, get them to stop."

"Yeah. Right. If the principal talks to them, it will only fuel their misery, misery they'll take out on me."

"Fighting them could make them go from just annoying to angry or even violent. Sometimes the best defense is doing what you can to avoid fighting someone who annoys you."

"Sometimes there's no choice. You find yourself boxed in a corner. It's either do or die."

It seemed he really wanted her to teach him to fight. Did she even know how to fight? Three years as Uncle Trix's partner certainly had familiarized her with manners of defense. Body block, shin kick, throat jab. The punch to the solar plexus. How would she impart that knowledge to Bennie?

They arrived at Wally's; she parked and turned off the van.

"If you teach me self-defense," he said, "I'll tell you a secret about Doc."

"Why would I want to know a secret about Doc?"

"Because you have a crush on him."

"I do not!"

"You do too! It's obvious from eight miles in every direction."

"I don't know what you're talking about."

"Then you wouldn't be interested in my secret."

"What is it?"

"My lips are sealed until the deal is sealed." Bennie pantomimed zippering his lips.

Her curiosity stood piqued. "What caliber of secret are we talking about?"

"Caliber?"

"Like is it a big secret or a little one?"

"What's a big secret and what's a little one?"

"A big secret is like Doc's an undercover cop. A little one, he's afraid of mice. What've you got? A big or little one?"

"Hmm," Bennie twisted his face as he thought about it. "A medium-sized one."

Jessabelle considered the possibilities.

"Wait right there," Bennie said. He hopped out of the van, ran around, and opened the door on Jessabelle's side for her.

There were coin-operated video games in the retail entrance of every Wally's, and according to Bennie, Trouble and Trouble were known to hang around at this one for hours, playing Street Fighter or Frogger. He moaned over how their regular presence near the video games prevented him from taking his own chances with the claw. If Trouble and Trouble were there now, he wanted to avoid them. So Jessabelle granted Bennie's request to enter Wally's through the grocery entrance of the store.

Once inside, he invited her to pick out some candy he'd buy her with his own money. Moved by his generosity, she wondered if he'd still open car doors and offer gifts of candy after he got what he wanted.

She declined his proposal of candy and stopped a mocha-skinned woman with kind brown eyes, clad in a Wally's uniform. "Can you tell us where we can find lights?"

"Ice," the woman repeated in an accent that drew out the I.

"Lights." Jessabelle said the word slowly, enunciating loud and clear.

The woman pointed to a freezer up front loaded with bags of ice. "I-ss there."

Jessabelle figured she and Bennie could roam the store and find the lights faster than it would take her to explain to this speaker of English-as-a-second-language what she and Bennie were after. She smiled at the woman and said "Thank you." Then to Bennie, "C'mon. We'll find them on our own."

She led Bennie toward the not-food portion of the store. They traveled along a row of makeup displays. "How about a lipsmacker?" Bennie asked, whisking a tube of strawberry-flavored lipgloss from a shelf. "To make your lips soft. You want that?"

"No," she said without stopping.

"If you don't want strawberry, you can have vanilla, bubble gum, banana, or watermelon," he called after her.

With a movement of her head, she nudged him onward. He tossed the strawberry lipgloss back on the shelf and ran to catch up with her.

They rounded the corner of the aisle and came face to face with a display picturing a little girl in a green aqua bathing suit walking along a strip of white sand at the edge of a blue ocean. Bennie lifted a spray bottle from a shelf of the display. "How about some perfume so you can smell pretty?"

"That's suntan lotion!"

"Oh." He looked at the price on the bottle. "Do you want it?"

"No!"

They traipsed all over the store looking for lights to the tune of Bennie's offers and her declines. "How about an ex-foliating glove?" "I know, I know" he said, pointing. "I don't know why I didn't think of it before…a makeup bag."

"I've already got enough makeup bags, and if you get me

that Tinkerbell makeup bag, I will get so mad, I will never teach you to fight. In fact, I may even beat you up myself."

"Geez. You don't have to get snippy." He may have looked hurt, but only one beat of silence passed before his song started playing again. "How about Sponge Bob party plates?" "Six Loopy straws?" "A lint brush?" "Tie dye tank top?" "A pair of flip-flops?" "Charm bracelet?" "Picture frame?" "Foam football?" "Hula hoop?" "One of the movies in this bin over here?"

"No, no, no, no…"

"There must be something in this store you want! Something under five dollars."

"To tell the truth, there's nothing in this store, even over five dollars, that I want. Now c'mon," she said, heading into the hardware department. "Let's get the lights and get out of here. And no, I don't want a box of nuts or bolts or anything else in this department."

Bennie became quiet and fidgety. Out the corners of her vision, she could see his eyes dart this way and that.

She found some portable clamp lights. Their box said they had enough amperage to light up a whole backyard for a barbecue—surely strong enough to illumine the shed.

At the cash register, Jessabelle and Bennie got on line behind a man who looked pregnant. Under his left arm he clutched a stack of frozen dinners with several packets of beef jerky balanced on top. With two fingers on his right hand, he hooked the paper handle on a twelve pack of Budweiser.

While Jessabelle and Bennie settled into waiting, Jessabelle searched the covers of tabloids for reports of aliens landing. She couldn't find one, but did see that a famous star had turned into one. There on the cover, lined up side by side, were before and after photos. Jessabelle examined the "after" picture, deciding in what ways she would have made the alien look different if she'd designed it.

"It's a really hot day," Bennie said.

"So what's new?"

"New could be a key lime ice."

"A what?"

"A key lime ice. You ever tasted one?"

"If I did, I don't remember."

"The Pizza Palaces in Florida are different than any of the others in America. Wanna know why?"

"Why?"

"They serve key lime ices. A key lime ice could be very refreshing on a day like this."

"Are you offering to buy me one?"

Bennie nodded.

It seemed the only way to get him to stop asking her if he could buy her something was to let him buy her something. So she said, "Okay. Hook me up."

In a flash of excitement, he went off speedily, deviating around the pregnant man, hanging a quick left when he came out the other end of the checkout, like a missile with a few kinks in its trajectory. "Pucker up! Here it comes!" he called back over his shoulder, dashing toward the Pizza Palace.

The cashier rang up the pregnant man's groceries and sent him on his way with his beer and two gray plastic bags full of frozen dinners and beef jerky.

When Jessabelle's turn came, the cashier said "Hello," reaching out to pull the first floodlight toward the scanner. Through the din of noise, Jessabelle heard a menacing voice.

"Look who it is."

"What's that you got in your hand, shortie?"

"Mmm, lime, my favorite kind of ice."

It clicked at the same time the price of one floodlight appeared on the cash register display. A lime ice carried by a short person. She reeled to the right. Sure enough, Bennie stood before his Troubles, gripping a funnel-shaped paper cup domed with a rounded mound of shaved ice.

Bennie held the ice aloft the way the Statue of Liberty bears her torch. That brought it just above eye level for his Troubles. Trouble #1 tried to swipe it. Bennie brought it down, swinging it behind his back. Trouble #2 plunged for the ice. Bennie twirled, swung his arm out to the side, and held it as far away from his Troubles as his hand would reach.

Every way Bennie moved, one Trouble or the other tried grabbing the ice, but missed. It transformed him into a frenzied dancing form of the robed Miss Liberty. "I just paid for this!" he shouted. "If you want a key lime ice, get your own!"

"Do you have a Wally's rewards card?" the cashier asked Jessabelle.

Jessabelle shook her head.

"It's free."

"I don't care!"

Trouble #2 clenched Bennie's upper body with his arms, locking Bennie's arms against the sides of his torso. Bennie caned his wrist, struggling to hold the ice upright. He kicked at his Troubles.

"You get one bonus point for every dollar spent at Wally's."

"Just ring me up! Hurry!"

"You get one hundred points for every store visit, special member only discounts and…Where'd that frizzy-haired woman go?"

Trouble #2 lifted Bennie up and hurled him to the polished concrete floor.

Jessabelle pushed her way between two onlookers gathered at the scene, a gray-haired woman resting on a cart full of cat food and a young girl with oily blonde hair and pimples, eating a peanut butter cup. Jessabelle sprang between Bennie and his two Troubles and splayed her hands against each of their chests, terminating their advance.

"Eww!" said Trouble #2.

"You know the ugliest girls," Trouble #1 said to the collapsed Bennie.

"That's right," Jessabelle said. "I'm ugly, and if you don't leave now, I will hold you both down and kiss each of you on the lips."

"Eww!" Trouble #2 scrunched up his face. "That's so gross it'll kill me."

"Let's get out of here," said Trouble #1. "She's so ugly, if I just look at her another second, I'll die."

Trouble and Trouble sidled along.

Jessabelle spun toward Bennie, bent on one knee beside him. He lay flat on his back with his neck and head bent up against the coinstar machine. Two legs and his left arm sprawled across the floor. His right arm remained taut, bent at the elbow with his hand anchored in the middle of his belly. In that hand, he held the ice. Untouched by Bennie's Troubles, its dome faced straight up to the ceiling, smooth and unperturbed.

"Are you still alive?" Jessabelle asked.

"Yes," he croaked out, and extended the ice toward her. "Here."

She wanted to tell him he didn't have to protect the ice the way he had. If it had been her, she would've thrown it at them, used whatever she had in either of her hands to stun them. But she knew this was no time for a lecture. She took the ice from his hand and held it against his forehead to soothe any pain he might be feeling there. "I'll teach you to fight," she said.

The corners of his lips curled up in a small smile.

"But don't get your hopes too high. I'm not a miracle worker."

"Don't you know? Around Lalli, miracles happen all the time."

Chapter 22

Three hours after Jessabelle agreed to teach Bennie to fight, she was eating dinner with Vishva, Johann, Chet, and Doc. Vishva, Johann, and Doc were talking about something, although it was a bit hard to tell what. Jessabelle was preoccupied designing a plan of action for teaching Bennie to fight, and grappling with the corresponding doubts about whether it would work.

"Jessabelle," Vishva said, ushering her into the conversation, "I think you're ready for Samudbodhana."

"What's that?" Jessabelle asked blankly. She rested her eyes on Chet, quietly gobbling down a plate of two black bean burritos, Mexican rice, and salad.

"The great Awakening, a spiritual initiation Lalli gives." Vishva lifted a biodegradable brown paper napkin from her lap as if it were made of fine linen, part of a place setting at the wedding of an aristocrat, and dabbed at a spot of sour cream on the corner of her mouth.

Jessabelle picked at her own food, suddenly more interested in understanding what Vishva was talking about than eating. "How do I get this great Awakening?"

"Different ways," Vishva said. "You could get it if you sign up for a Day of Practice."

"A Day of Practice?"

"It's a day-long program in which you chant and meditate all day with Lalli. They only happen about once every six months."

Jessabelle felt a flood of excitement. "How do I sign up?"

"Come to the Welcome Center," Vishva said. "You'll need to bring a check or credit card. The cost for a Day of Practice is three hundred dollars."

Ah ha. So this is where they get you! Uncle Trix was right!

Jessabelle forgot all about the calming energy she perceived at the chant every night as she inwardly exclaimed, *Lalliville is nothing but big business! This great Awakening is— just has to be—a con.*

Jessabelle's voice went flat again. "I may have to pass."

"A Day of Practice is too great to pass on," Doc said. He held Fuzz on his lap, palming a tiny mound of puppy kibble Fuzz eagerly demolished.

"Truly," Johann said, "a Day of Practice is transformative." He scooped up some of the black bean, onion, bell pepper, and garlic mixture on his plate that had dropped out of his burrito and brought it to his mouth.

They seemed like sensible people. That didn't mean a Day of Practice couldn't be part of some moneymaking scheme.

"What does Lalli use the money for?"

"It's not her who makes the money," Vishva explained, cutting a piece of her salad. "The money goes into the association to help keep Lalliville running, so that more people who want Awakening can receive it." Vishva brought a freshly trimmed bite of salad to her mouth.

Even worse than Awakening being a con, what if it was legitimate, and Jessabelle signed up for a Day of Practice, but nothing happened to her? "How does Lalli give this great Awakening?"

Vishva swallowed her bite of salad. "Different ways. These days, she does it through her sankalpa."

Jessabelle blinked. "Her sanwhat?"

"Her sankalpa," Vishva repeated. "That's her intention or will."

"She thinks I and a lot of other people are going to receive this great Awakening, and we do?"

"Basically." Vishva sipped water from a plastic cup.

"But how does that happen?"

"I don't know how it works. I guess it's one of life's great mysteries."

Ugh! One of life's great mysteries was not concrete enough. Jessabelle wanted this thing spelled out for her.

"Awakening is great," Doc repeated.

"Truly," Johann said. "Awakening is transformative."

Frustration clamped Jessabelle's head like a vise. What she wanted was something like, "Animatronics is the technology used to animate creatures built by hand. The creatures can be programmed or remotely controlled." What she got was, "Animatronics is cool."

If they'd said, "Animatronics is great" or "Animatronics is transformative," it would've been okay, because she knew about Animatronics. The word "Animatronics" made her think of Gremlins, E.T., and other characters from old-time movies, produced before computer-generated effects took over.

"Awakening" conjured no images for her, and that started

to make her feel a little crazy. "But *what* is Awakening?" Jessabelle persisted. "Can't you just say what it is?"

"Come and see for yourself," Doc said.

"Yes, Isa," Johann said, "make it your own personal experience."

A hundred doubts closed in on her. They all said the same thing: Awakening is a con. At the same time, a longing began deep within her chest and enveloped her whole body. In this feeling, Jessabelle wanted to experience a Day of Practice for herself.

This longing grew and grew until it was a lot bigger than any of her doubts about Awakening being part of some moneymaking scheme. "Okay," Jessabelle said. "I'll do it."

Doc, Johann, and Vishva clapped. It struck Jessabelle as rather odd, them cheering her on to something, and her not understanding what they were rallying her toward. But genuine excitement beamed on their faces. It made Awakening even more tantalizing. Now she just needed $300.

Before the sun rose, Jessabelle passed the Dave's Plumbing truck, loaded with all its parts, parked at the Good Night's Sleep motel.

She didn't want Uncle Trix coming to her, riding in his new pickup, talking her into selling fake diamonds. So she was on her way to him, having thumbed it down Route 54. Finding a ride at five in the morning wasn't easy. A newspaper delivery person had stopped for her, and before Jessabelle finally made it to the Good Night's Sleep, her driver had pit-stopped at about two dozen mailboxes in line with her duty.

Jessabelle whizzed up to Uncle Trix's motel room door and started banging. Uncle Trix opened the door. "What's up?" he asked.

She squinted in the terrible glow of his hair, a helmet of

hair, with a color so pure, it looked as if it had been spray-painted blond. "What happened to your hair?"

"I was sick of wearing all that stuff on my head just to appear young again." A towel circled his waist, tied at the hip. A smear of red lipstick tarnished his cheek.

She ignored the obvious question, eager to get on with her petition. "I need three hundred dollars."

"What for?"

"A Day of Practice."

"What are you gonna practice?"

"Chanting, meditating."

"All day?"

Jessabelle nodded.

"Three hundred dollars to chant and meditate all day?"

Jessabelle bounced her head excitedly.

A scowl broke his face. "I'm afraid I can't give you the money."

"Why?"

"Because I don't know what I'm giving it to you for. To chant and meditate all day? Sounds like a waste. Get the statue and you'll have plenty of dough to blow on whatever you want."

His towel moved an inch, threatening a fall, but not before his hands darted to his waist. He retightened the knot. With one hand he held the knot secure, preventing the towel from crashing down around his thin ankles.

"Darling," came a woman's voice from inside the room. She appeared in the doorway in a short kimono-style robe patterned with blooms of roses, tied with a sash. Toenails pedicured French-style with a cream base and white square-shaped tips sloped into heeled gold slipper sandals on her feet, each with a pompom of metallic fluff. "Please come back to bed."

The woman caressed Uncle Trix's chest. Turquoise-colored imitation jewels embedded into a design of pink and orange acrylic coated her artificial fingernails, giving the impression that an abstract painting of a Florida sunset hung on the tip of each of her fingers.

The pedicure, manicure, and robe could not obscure the woman's own industrial-strength blonde hair or her desperate eyes. Add to that the transverse frontal lines (wrinkles) across her forehead maturing into grooves, the lateral orbital lines (crow's feet) around her eyes, the slackening of her jawline, and there was no mistaking her for anyone else but Blondo, the crazy lady she and Uncle Trix had conned once upon a time.

The fair-headed couple stood in front of their room at the Good Night's Sleep, he stubborn in his refusal to cough up any money, money Jessabelle knew he had, she softly strumming his chest with her fingernails, her lips at his ear, whispering as if he was the only person or thing in the whole wide world, the weathered walls of the motel appearing sad in the early morning light. The overall scene suggested a bad movie about a blonde-haired hooker, the grumpy pimp she loved, and his disturbed niece. If only Jessabelle was at the cinema!

In this film that was Jessabelle's real life, Uncle Trix shooed Blondo away, saying, "Go back to bed. I'll be there in a minute."

"I'm counting." With a lick of her lips, Blondo disappeared into the darkness of the room.

Uncle Trix stepped outside and shut the door.

"What is she doing here?" Jessabelle asked.

"Let's just say I ran into her, and she recognized me. I had to do some major damage control, if you catch my drift. A manicure, pedicure, new haircut and color, and the upgrade to her bathrobe and slippers just weren't enough. I had to give her something else."

Jessabelle rolled her eyes. "Well, aren't you generous." What did he see in that silk-robed hyena? Why would he allow himself to get close to her, so close, he actually— The thought of the two of them wrapped in each other's arms made Jessabelle convulse.

Blondo threw open the door and called, "Time's up."

"Give me another sixty seconds," he said, pushing her back inside.

"Find that statue, Jessie. If you can't, I've got somebody interested in your job."

"Oh please," Jessabelle said. "Your hyena can have it."

"Yeah, and what are you gonna do? Become a dental assistant?"

He didn't wait for an answer before heading back into his motel room, his hand clamped on the tuck of his towel. Following the slam of the door, Blondo's voice emerged. "Come here, darling. Let's see if I can loosen your grip on that towel, get Trix Junior to come out again and play."

Uncle Trix had never lain a finger on Jessabelle. So why did she feel she'd been beaten up, kicked out, and thrown down? Seized by disheartenment, she turned to leave.

A manicure, pedicure, new haircut and color, and an upgrade to her bathrobe and slippers, Jessabelle tallied. How much did all that cost? It had to be $300 or more, depending on where Uncle Trix took Blondo to get all that. Blondo's fingernails were handpainted. Chic nail art done by a professional. That right there cost a pretty penny.

And that robe. It was made of the finest soft silk. Definitely not cheap either. He'd probably blown at least $500 on that woman. Why couldn't he just give Jessabelle $300?

She fell into the deep dark chasm she was walking between two worlds. From this fissure, her life with Uncle Trix seemed strange. Lalli's world seemed more normal, but beyond her grasp and comprehension. With each step she sank further into depression.

It was the hope of $300 that drove her to hitchhike here. With that expectation snuffed out, she was damned if she was hitchhiking back.

The step van slumped all alone in the corner of the parking lot. She stroked its side with her hand just before she kissed it. "Great to see you again." She noticed birdshit on its front silver fender. "You got shit on too." She retrieved a napkin from a garbage can with an ashtray on top out front of the main lobby, then used it to wipe off the birdshit. "Don't worry," she said. "You won't be shit on again."

Jessabelle drove the step van out Route 54 toward Lalliville. She attempted a rendition of Jaya Shiva Om to a melody she made up on the spot. The chant ran strong for several stanzas, until anxiety leaked in, dampening her spirits. Before long, Jaya Shiva Om dripped out in a labored whisper.

She had to admit, it had rattled her, seeing Uncle Trix with Blondo. The realization that something had changed when she wasn't looking rocked uneasily in her gut. These new developments meant only one thing—Trouble for Jessabelle.

Jessabelle considered what she was doing, moving the step van from the Good Night's Sleep to Lalliville, as if transporting a friend to safety. Who knew what kind of danger she and it were averting? If Blondo found her way into the step van, if she hadn't already, one thing would turn up missing and then another. Mrs. Cozie all over again!

The door between the cab and cargo area glided open. Wrench appeared like an oozing sore with crimped hair and groggy eyes. Her rendition of Jaya Shiva Om died with a shriek.

By the unfazed manner he plunked down in the other bucket seat, yawned, and stretched his arms overhead, it seemed he was accustomed to women screaming when they saw him.

Camouflage covered him from his neck down to his ankles. The man would probably attend his mother's funeral in a camouflage suit and tie.

She braked the van to a stop on the shoulder of the road.

Wrench examined her a good long moment and said, "Hey, sugar. Where we going?"

"*We're* not going anywhere. Get out!" She shooed him out the door on his side.

He fastened his large fingers around her wrist. "You get out!"

With his hard grip on her wrist, she recalled their fight in the Halloway home. He was a strong one. Uncle Trix was not in sight this time around, nor did she have a handy bag of brass blocks. "Truce," she called.

"Does that mean we're friends?"

"Yes, friends," she said, biding some time, holding this cease-fire until she figured out how to shake him off without getting killed. "Did you spend the night back there?"

"It's quieter than my mom's."

"Don't you have a home of your own?"

"I did, but the Halloways came back."

She neglected to point out that the Halloway home had never actually been his home, so high was Jessabelle's fear that he'd made himself at home in her space. Pictures of Wrench having sex with a friend or sister of Blondo crawled inside her head like maggots. She shivered. "Is anybody else back there?"

"No. We're the only ones home." His eyebrows twitched in attempted seduction. "Wanna climb in back and get kinky with the body parts?"

She refused to let his perverse expression shake her.

"Okay," she said in an agreeable tone.

"All right!" He slapped his thigh, lurched out of his seat, and gripped her forearm, coercing her with brute muscle toward the back of the step van. "Before we start, I want you to change back into the blonde-haired cutie you were the day we met."

"Okay." Jessabelle squeezed her buttocks and tightened her abdomen, remaining firm in her seat. "But before I do that, let's eat breakfast." From behind the step van's soft wheel, she pointed through the front windshield to a red plastic-sided Burger Barn hunched by the side of the road, neighbor to a Dippin' Donuts.

Wrench snarled, "Breakfast comes after."

"With me, it must come first. Otherwise, I can't get in the mood. How about buying me breakfast special number one?"

"I don't have any money. You got some I can borrow?"

"Sure. Breakfast is on me."

"I don't need sausage and eggs to have sex."

"Well, I do. So why don't I buy me breakfast. You can get something if you want. If not, you can watch me eat."

Before he had a chance to think about it, she started up the van and gunned it to the Burger Barn. An oil-stained parking space bordered by a row of landscape bushes waited there for her. She backed into it carefully so as not to hit either of the SUVs on its haunches.

"Can't we do the drivethrough?"

"I want this to be a real date, the kind where we sit at a table together and talk."

"Aw, geez. Next you'll want a white tablecloth and one of them smelly romance candles."

Jessabelle opened her door.

"Wait a minute," Wrench said, pointing to the key in the ignition. "Gimme that."

"I can't. It's stuck in the engine."

Wrench reached over and jiggled the key, but he could not dislodge it. "If I had known that, I would've gone for a ride."

Good thing you didn't, she thought, seething.

Inside the grimly lit Burger Barn, Jessabelle ordered breakfast special number one (french toast with home fries) and the tallest orange juice available on the wooden menu nailed on the wall behind the front counter. When she got her food, Wrench decided it looked good after all. The glutton demanded a double order of the same thing. Maintaining her pretense of agreeability, she said nothing, only smiled, as she uprooted two tens from their nesting place in the breast pocket of her white shirt and paid the cashier.

Then they headed for the seating area, where Jessabelle led Wrench to a two-top close to the ladies room. On opposite sides of its marbled Formica tabletop, they ate their food. Jessabelle humored him when he shared his ultimate dream of getting stuck in an elevator with a Victoria's Secret model. "If that doesn't work out for you," she told him, "maybe you can become pen pals with one."

She refrained from smacking him across the face when he expressed his disgruntlement over how flat-chested his last girlfriend was, something he felt he could confide in Jessabelle now that they were friends.

She'd hoped to finish her breakfast before making her escape. But after only one piece of French toast, with two more still left on her plate, her stomach churned; his company poisoned her food. If she sat any longer or ate any more, she'd decline into instantaneous illness.

She rose from her seat of woven metal. With hopes of climbing out the bathroom window, she announced she had to go to the toilet. She set off for the ladies room. He tried to follow, saying he wanted to keep an eye on her. She told him, "You're not allowed in the ladies room. Besides, what'll I do there? Climb out a window?" Begrudgingly, he turned around.

It proved a fruitless ruse as she found not one single window carved in the white tile walls of the block of a Burger Barn women's restroom, possessed of a single toilet and sink.

She returned to the table she shared with Wrench. Sinking down in her seat, she felt two inches shorter than when she left. He asked her what her ultimate dream was.

"Not sure I have an ultimate dream," she said. "Right now I'd settle for finishing school."

"School," he spat. "A lot of good that'll do you, getting your head crammed full of useless information. Why not let me teach you a few useful things, like bad girl sex tricks."

She stared at him, maintaining an expression barren of any interest.

"In another subject area, I can teach you how to use a B-B rifle. Helps get rid of them birds, the birds outside the window, the ones that just won't shut up, even when I'm sleeping."

"And killing birds is something you do regularly?"

"Yeah. Taught my little brother the trade too. Just yesterday he killed two robins. Threw them in the gutter. Those two won't be waking me up tomorrow." Wrench laughed uproariously, giving her an unobstructed view of the mashed particles of French toast and home fries lodged in the crevices between his plague-ridden teeth.

The hair on the back of her neck bristled. She felt as if she'd been pelleted in the head. Wrench had shot a creature just for singing, what the creature does. He annihilated exactly what she was plotting to become. He dispensed cruelty toward the birds in his neighborhood, senselessly destroying this other life form. All of it made her blood burn.

Unable to hide her true feelings for Wrench any longer,

she snatched her cup off the table and heaved thirty-two ounces of orange juice at his face. She dropped the cup. It hit the table with a pop. Wrench's hands went to his eyes.

She bolted, slammed her hands against the glass pane of the front door, and out she flew. She made a mad dash for the step van. Her escape route led across a stone walkway, past a playplace. Halfway across a lawn, a steel hand wrapped her ankle, sending her toppling forward. Her face fell on a bed of Astroturf. She glanced back over her shoulder to see the orange-juice-specked top of Wrench's hair, buzzed in a crew cut.

She wiggled free, losing a heavy black shoe as his hand slid over her heel. She flipped onto her back, hooked the shoe with her toes, and flung it into his face. He flinched, covering his eyes.

She lost no time getting to her feet.

He rose with her.

She ripped off her other shoe and pitched it, his head as the plate. He caught it and threw it right back. She ducked, but not fast enough. The shoe skipped off her head, then landed somewhere behind her.

She darted toward a two-tiered outdoor play area with brightly colored tubes, towers, and tall cages for kids to scurry through and climb. She ran straight for the Burger Barn mascot, guardian of the playplace, a plastic man in a tuxedo and top hat with a cheeseburger on a bun for a head. A bulbous tomato was his nose, pickle slices his eyes.

Just before she reached him, she dropped into a ball, curling her arms tightly around her knees. Wrench's heavy body crushed her back as he tripped over her, and in that grinding, she rose up, threshing her arms wide, catapulting him into the manburger.

While he crumpled at the feet of the manburger, she tore off in the direction of the van. In her Neptune-blue plaid skirt, white shirt buttoned all the way to the top, vest, and bowtie made from the same material as the skirt, she was sure she appeared as an overgrown and slightly deviant prep school girl running in white knee socks and no shoes. She kept going until she got to the van, the bottoms of her feet firing with pain from small rocks she'd stepped on while running across the parking lot. She felt one tear right through her sock, cutting a hole in her flesh. With no time to check it, she tumbled into the van.

Speeding out of the Burger Barn parking lot, the last thing she saw was Wrench, who'd made it to the edge of the blacktop. He cupped his hands around his mouth and shouted, "I'll get even with you."

Her breathing and heartrate didn't return to normal until she'd driven all the way back to Lalliville, having to speed to make it in time for her early morning appointment. She left the step van in the parking lot. A quick inventory of the contents told her everything was still there. Later she'd return to wash the sheets on her air mattress and sanitize the air mattress itself. Maybe even burn some incense. Did Lalli do exorcisms? she wondered.

Chapter 23

"No offense to your training," Bennie told Jessabelle, "but if I'm going to succeed, I need to be more threatening than this." They both struck the tree pose on side-by-side yoga mats at Pierre's early morning yoga class.

Bennie stood on one foot, his other leg bent up so the sole of that foot rested on the inside of his standing leg. He'd gotten into the posture, she had to applaud him for that, but his back and leg wobbled, so unstable he appeared more like a fragile weed tossed about at the mercy of a demented windstorm than an elm, maple, or birch rooted deep in the earth.

"Focus on something in front of you," Pierre told Bennie. "It will help maintain your balance."

"I'm trying!" he yelled as he collapsed to the floor.

"Of course, falling over can be half the fun!" Pierre said,

extending a hand to help Bennie back to his feet.

"Now we're going to move into sitting postures," Pierre told the class.

Bennie frowned. "I just got off the floor!" he exclaimed to no one in particular.

Originally, yoga poses hadn't even been part of the Teach Bennie to Fight plan. Then Pierre had told Jessabelle that yoga was the only physical activity he ever did, and while he was well over forty, his body remained firm. The way Jessabelle figured it, yoga couldn't hurt.

Jessabelle copied Pierre move for move as he demonstrated a seated twist to the right.

Bennie's voice filled her right ear. "Just so you know, in this position I'm a sitting duck." Balled up in the twist, he proved to be more flexible than strong.

"Just so you know," she said, "I'm not telling you to sit and twist in front of your Troubles. This is all just part of your fitness training."

Pierre's eyes hit her like darts. "Isa, you'd get more out of this class if you tuned into your breathing instead of chattering with your co-worker."

Chattering? That's what birds did. This was strategizing. Or at the very least, discussing. She wanted to tell Pierre that, and the fact that the chattering, if that's what he wanted to call it, was actually Bennie's fault. But she didn't want to go on talking in class when he had just reprimanded her for talking in class.

"Now let's twist to the other side," Pierre said. Bennie twisted in reverse, curling tightly to his left. He rolled off one of his cheekbones, tipped, and plunked to the ground, maintaining the twist. She'd never seen anybody fall from a seated position.

Pierre announced, "It's time for shavasana, final relaxation." He dimmed the lights.

Jessabelle and Bennie followed the rest of the class as they lay flat on their backs, arms and legs apart. The sole of Jessabelle's right foot throbbed where a rock had broken her skin while running in the Burger Barn parking lot earlier.

"Just so you know," she heard Bennie whisper, "if they catch me like this, I'm dead meat."

Jessabelle smiled, but said nothing. She had her own Troubles to think about, like how to get $300. She considered breaking into Uncle Trix's motel room and stealing the money.

"Focus on your breath," Pierre said in a tranquil voice. "Feel it moving in through your nose and out through your mouth." He paused for a few seconds. "Listen to your breath."

Jessabelle closed her eyes. Per Pierre's instructions, she concentrated on her own breath, relaxing deeply into it.

On Jessabelle and Bennie's walk along Liberation toward the dining hall for breakfast, Jessabelle considered other ways of gaining the money she needed for a Day of Practice. In a flood of new ideas, a solution floated, so simple she didn't know why she hadn't thought of it before. Was she stupid or something? No. Uncle Trix just hadn't sufficiently pissed her off before now.

She already had all the prosthetic materials she needed to become Samuel Sheldon, one of Uncle Trix's aliases. She also knew the name of Samuel Sheldon's bank, a bank with branches all across the U.S. She and Uncle Trix had stopped there at least once a week over the past three years. She knew the account number. She had seen it once and memorized it. On the pad of her phone, it spelled bonanza.

The bank statements were delivered to a post office box in Wichita, Kansas, the last place Uncle Trix actually had a residence. It could be several months before he again picked up his mail and figured out she'd absconded with half their money. She began roughly calculating how much money was in Samuel Sheldon's bank account.

"You think I'll ever really get rid of my Troubles?" Bennie asked, interrupting her thoughts.

"If you really want to get rid of your Troubles, how about changing your clothes?"

Bennie stopped. He looked down at his red and green kurta embellished with beads and embroidery. One size too big, it hung to his right side, leaving the shoulder seam about two inches below his shoulder line. "What's wrong with my clothes? This is my loose-fitting kurta, for yoga class."

She wasn't sure what he meant, since all his combinations of long shirt and matching bottoms appeared baggy. This one must be his extra-loose-fitting kurta. "It conveys peace-loving Christmas ornament, not pit-bull."

Bennie frowned. "I told you before, they'll always find a way to pick on me. It doesn't matter what I wear."

"Still, I think it would help if you dressed the part of a strongman."

"I don't want to dress the part. I want to be the part." He drooped his head, staring at the ground. "You don't think I'll ever really defeat my Troubles, do you?"

Some teacher she was, depressing her student like this. Who was she to balk at anybody else's clothes, anyway, when she was standing in a one-piece footed yellow cotton pajama jumper with deep kangaroo pockets, minus the slippered feet? She'd cut them off and hemmed the legs after she'd decided to wear the jumper to yoga class.

She'd brought the jumper to Lalliville for sleeping, but never wore it for that, or for walking around the house she shared with Vishva. It was too hot. But it seemed the perfect outfit for yoga, kind of like a loose-fitting one piece bodysuit, a nerd's version of a yuppie-yogi's unitard.

Together, she and Bennie made quite a pair, he in his

opulent ethnic clothing, she in a pair of pajamas. Now that she'd lost her black lace-up clompers to the Burger Barn parking lot, she wore the pajamas with her tennis shoes. She'd made the purple smiley faces on the outside edge of each disappear, covering over them in white paint.

Bennie needed building, not tearing down. She could see that. "I guarantee, someday you will kick their butts." She tried to sound as if she believed in him. She hoped she was convincing.

His head came up. "Really?"

"Really." She didn't have the heart to tell him the truth, that his Trouble-conquering abilities were shaky. But who knew? Maybe one day he would, in fact, kick their butts. Lalli had said Bennie was very strong. With Lalli's penetrating gaze, maybe she saw something Jessabelle couldn't.

"I'll wear a muscle shirt and powerlifting pants like Bhisma," he said, confidence returning to his voice, "if you think it will help."

She centered his kurta, laid both her hands flat on his shoulders, and smoothed its silken fabric. "On second thought, you're dressed perfectly."

She took hold of his hand, which fit in hers like a plum ripened in a sun-filled window, soft and warm. She led him by the hand, along Liberation and over to the dining hall for her second breakfast of the morning. It was bound to be better than her first breakfast with Wrench at Burger Barn.

Later, in the field beside the shed, Jessabelle faced Bennie and said, "I'm coming to throw you in a slimy pond." She'd wrapped heavy layers of foam padding around her torso, arms, and legs, and secured them with electrical tape. She also wore a thick helmet of the stuff. The foam padding and tape obscured the outfit comprised of Neptune-blue plaid skirt, white shirt buttoned all the way to the top, vest, and bowtie Jessabelle wore beneath it.

When Bennie saw her, he started laughing, and laughed so hard he fell on the ground laughing. He could barely get out the words, "You look funny."

"Do you want to succeed or not?"

"I want to succeed."

"Then you'd better take this seriously!"

"Okay," he said, and put on a serious face. "I'll try again."

She stood in front of him a second time and said, "I'm coming to hang you on a lamppost by your underwear. Try to get around me. If I touch or grab you, strike me."

His expression became pained. "But I don't want to hit you."

"It's the only way you're going to learn," she said. "I'm protected. I won't get hurt!"

"Okay. If you insist." He cocked his fist and threw it. His knuckles grazed her stomach. It was supposed to be a punch, she knew that, but it was a punch with less power and coordination than one thrown by the feeble granny Jessabelle once impersonated.

She clutched her stomach, imparting the impression the punch had some effect.

He rushed forward and attempted to kick her shin, at least she thought that's what he was aiming at. It was hard to tell. He missed her whole body by a foot.

"Be fast!" Jessabelle snagged his leg while it was still in the air. "If you're not quick enough, I'm going to catch your leg, disturb your balance, and flip you to the ground."

"First I have to kick you, and now I have to do it fast."

"Yes. Let's try that kick again. But first, put on your most menacing face, something to psych out your opponent."

He puffed his nostrils, grunted like a horned bull, and stormed.

He heaved his foot back, then thrust it forward, landing it square on her shin bone.

"Not bad." Jessabelle smiled her approval. "Your fist and feet should be your last resort. Use the other tools you have at your disposal first."

He tipped his head to one side. "Like what other tools?"

"Your speed, for one."

"My speed?"

"I saw you run for the key lime ice at Wally's. You may not be as big as a plane, but you sure can fly like one."

"And I wasn't even going my fastest."

"Let me see your fastest. Do a perimeter of the field."

Bennie sped off, dashing around the edges of the field while Jessabelle observed. When he returned, he bent, resting his hands on his knees and breathing hard. Jessabelle propped a hand on his bony shoulder. "I see definite potential there."

On their way to lunch, Jessabelle told Bennie, "I just want to point out that your fitness training has begun and you haven't told me the secret."

The way he stopped, squinted his eyes, and shifted his gaze off into the air over her shoulder, he seemed puzzled by the statement.

"About Doc. Remember?" She tried to sound casual. In reality, the suspense of it had held her since Bennie had promised to tell her the secret if she taught him self-defense. She'd just been waiting for the right moment to ask.

"Oh, oh yeah. That secret." Excitement funneled into his voice, as if he'd just been appointed the prestigious role of slumber party storyteller. She felt ten years old again as he cleared his throat and began.

"One night I heard Doc and Chet talking about you. Chet said, 'Doc, I notice you been staring at Isa.'"

Jessabelle went down on one knee, coming eye to eye with Bennie. "I'll say he does. Makes me feel like an amoeba squished into a plastic slide."

Bennie giggled. "Chet asked Doc, 'Is your interest in her

merely scientific, you know, because she invents things?'"

She leaned in toward Bennie. "What did Doc say?"

"Doc said, 'My interest in her was merely scientific, and then it turned to...' 'Love?' Chet asked. They both laughed, and Doc said, 'Oh no, not love...let's just call it general interest. I think there's more to Isa than meets the eye, and I'm trying to figure out what that is.'"

Bennie paused.

"Is that the end of the story?"

Bennie nodded. "Maybe he likes you, but doesn't want to admit it."

Could a handsome guy like Doc possibly have a crush on Isa Newton? The thought of it sent a streak of red-hot laughter bolting through her lips. "A guy would have to be crazy to like a girl like me," she said through her hilarity.

"Remember?" He winked. "You're not who you are."

Her blood went from humorous hot to fear-filled frigid. "You didn't tell anybody about me, did you?"

"No."

When Jessabelle and Bennie rounded the corner onto Liberation, she saw something out of her peripheral vision— a bush waving at her. These things happened in Lalliville. For split seconds in time, she thought she saw clouds smile at her or would've sworn she felt a bright blue sky fall around her shoulders like a soft cape.

Mother Nature was particularly friendly in Lalliville, so when Jessabelle saw the bush waving at her, it didn't surprise her. But as she drew nearer to it, the waving became more vigorous and she experienced the odd sensation the bush was trying to get her attention. "If you want him to like you," Bennie said, "you'd better wave back."

Huh? Jessabelle turned her head, actually looking at the bush, and realized it was Doc waving at her. He stood next to the bush, wearing a green shirt and tan jeans, a combination that blended perfectly with the bush.

"Speak of the celestial being," Bennie said, "and the celestial being will appear."

Jessabelle waved to the one Bennie referred to as a celestial being, the nicest smile plastered on her face, all the while fearing that Doc knew more about her than he'd disclosed. After all, they shared the same artistic craft, working it toward different goals, he in the name of helping animals and children, she for fun and profit. Of all the people here, he'd certainly be the one most capable of discerning her use of prosthetics. If he had, that would explain why he dissected her face with his eyes, as she and Bennie passed on by, the same thing he did every time their paths crossed.

Chapter 24

At Krishna's Corner for afternoon snacks, Bennie stayed inside with Vishva and Johann while Jessabelle sat at a table outside, pen in hand, sketching a picture of Uncle Trix on a napkin.

She glanced up to recall the exact shape of Uncle Trix's nose and caught sight of Doc walking toward her. One of his hands was open. In his palm sat two cookies coated in powdered white sugar. "One is for you," he said. She selected one.

He took a seat opposite her, munching his cookie. "What are you doing?"

"Sketching a picture." She turned the napkin so he could see the drawing on it.

"Somebody you know?"

"My uncle the saint," she said, not hiding her sarcasm.
"He won't give me the money for a Day of Practice."

"I will."

"What? Why?"

"Because I have at least six hundred dollars, and I believe there's no point in having a dime if you can't give a nickel away. But don't let that statement fool you. I'm thinking of the money as a conditional gift."

"What are the conditions?"

"I give you the money if you show yourself to me."

She uttered a cry of shock, dropping her pen and moving her fingers to her distressed lips. "This isn't a strip club! I'm not getting naked for you. No sir, no way."

He laughed. "I don't want to see you buck naked. Your face will do."

"Have you gone crazy? What're you talking about?"

"You know exactly what I'm talking about. To prove it, I'm going to tell you a little story."

"I wait on the edge of my seat."

"One day," he said, "a girl named Isa Newton attacked me, because she thought I was a wild pig. My foot fell off. It embarrassed me. But the more I examined Isa Newton, the more I noticed she wore prosthetics too, maybe even a wig."

Indeed, she wore a mask, covered in makeup, matching the color of her skin. She wore clothes on her body, and a red wig on her head. Yet she felt as though she was standing in that dream where she suddenly discovered she was naked. Her heart pounded in her chest. She forced a laugh, eked out words. "Now that's a story," cough, cough, "if I've ever heard one."

He ignored the comment. "I'm dying to see what you really look like."

"Well, you're looking at…what I really look like."

"I know you wear prosthetics. I just can't figure out why.

STEALING SHIVA

Is it to hide a deformity? If so, I'm wondering what's so bad that this face and that wig make it better."

"I don't know what you're talking about."

"You do too." He darted a hand across the table and tugged a chunk of her kinky red tresses.

"Oww!" she caterwauled like a wounded cat. She smacked his hand away.

"What do you mean, 'Oww'? All I did was tweak your wig."

"It's not a wig," she insisted, clenching her crooked and cracked horse teeth.

He attached his hand to another chunk of her hair and pulled. Thanks to the lessons of one of her teachers who specialized in wigs, nicknamed Mr. Hair, her artificial hair budged only slightly. "Oww!" she yelled again, louder than before. The cry of a wounded cat had become the roar of a distressed tiger.

Doc reeled from the sound of her howl.

She brought her hand to her head, grimacing in pain. Holding that hand flat open, she moved her wig a pinch forward, realigning it.

"Wait a minute. Did you just straighten your hair?"

"No," she said, massaging her head. "I'm rubbing my head…to ease the pain…of you pulling my hair," she blubbered out in great heaving sobs, her fear adding a necessary element of authenticity to her performance.

"You're really crying." Suddenly, Doc looked horror-sticken. Guilt spread over his face. "I'm sorry," he said. "I don't know what came over me. I've never done anything like that. I was sure…I thought…" As if the violence of trying to rip out a woman's hair was more than he could bear, he stood up and slowly backed away. "I should go now."

*   *   *

The day after Doc accused Jessabelle of wearing prosthetics, going so far as attempting to snatch her wig off to prove it, Jessabelle hid behind a tree. Armored in her finest array of foam padding, blanketed over a white shirt and denim overalls with crisscross suspenders, she waited.

Along came Bennie.

She jumped out in front of him. "You little worm," she shouted. "I'm going to throw you in the mud where you belong."

Fear knocked him into a stupor, freezing him hard as an ice statue of himself.

She rushed to him and stood over him wiggling her arms. "This is an attack!"

When he heard her voice, the ice melted a bit. "Oh." A smile cracked his face. "It's you." He sighed in relief and put a hand over his heart. "You scared me."

"That's the point! I was trying to scare you, and you got scared, but didn't do anything! Just froze!"

Bennie hung his head.

"If you really want to fight, you have to act even when you're scared." Jessabelle backed up a few paces. "Let's try again. Remember, your fist and feet should be your last resort. Use the other tools at your disposal first."

"Running?"

"Right. And your voice. Let's say you're at Wally's and you see your Troubles coming toward you. If there are people around, yell for help. Let's practice that."

She closed in on him for the pretend attack. He opened his mouth, and a cry for "Help!" emerged from that childlike triangle with all the force of rolling thunder. This time Jessabelle froze, stunned. A moment later Doc whirled onto the scene. Along with him came a small crowd of people, charging across the grass like the cavalry.

Doc hopped out of the security vehicle. "What's

"It's okay," Bennie told the crowd. "We were just practicing."

"Practicing for what?" somebody asked.

Bennie explained about his Troubles, that Jessabelle was helping him resolve them.

"This is work time," somebody else said. "You should be working, not playing."

This might look like play to others, but standing in the middle of a field, covered in foam and tape, with about forty pairs of eyes pressed upon her did not feel like fun to Jessabelle.

Lalli emerged from the back of the crowd. Everybody parted for her. "Show us how you're practicing."

Way to put Jessabelle on the spot. How did she get to this spot, anyway? Fighting was not even an area of her expertise. Sure, she knew a few things. That didn't classify her as a professional fighter. Now Lalli wanted her to give a demonstration in front of all these people of how she was teaching Bennie to defend himself. Absurd! She should be out earning money to return to Creativo, not standing here doing whatever it was she was doing.

Jessabelle glanced at Lalli and her insides melted. How could she refuse the woman with the black onyx eyes of Shiva?

Jessabelle paced back five steps from Bennie and said to the crowd, "I'm one of his Troubles closing in on him. He'll try to get around me. If I tag him, he can strike."

Bennie crouched like a tiger eager for combat, something Jessabelle had never seen before. They discovered his strength: Getting loud! And an audience seemed to fuel his enthusiasm for a fight.

"Your mother is a rat!" Jessabelle approached Bennie. "I'm going to throw you down the sewer where you'll feel

The crowd cheered. "Go, Bennie!"

Bennie went right. She blocked.

He spun on his heels and went left. She tagged his arm. Bennie tried to kick, tried to hit. He swung his foot and punched air. Not the least bit embarrassed, he kept going. Finally, Jessabelle moved toward his fist, letting him punch her.

Lalli said, "Stop!"

Bennie and Jessabelle obeyed.

The crowd became quiet.

"I'm not sure you're headed in the right direction," Lalli told Jessabelle.

Jessabelle wanted to say, *For God's sake, I'm a special effects artist, not a self-defense expert.* But something in Lalli's expression, so firm and strong, made Jessabelle stay quiet.

Lalli addressed the crowd. "Does anybody have a message for Bennie, something to help him overcome his Troubles?"

Vishva raised her hand. Lalli called on her to speak. "Instead of fighting," Vishva said, "why not use common sense? If your Troubles are in a certain place at a certain time, you be in a different place at that time. Like if they're entering school through the front, you enter through the back."

Madeline was the next to speak. "Program the number of the police into your cell phone. If your Troubles harass you, call the police."

For Jessabelle, a girl who had spent her life avoiding the law, she'd never even have thought to program the number of the police into her phone, but she had to admit it wasn't a bad idea for a boy with no fear of the law.

"I think you should keep coming to yoga class," Pierre told Bennie. "It will help you develop a posture of self-confidence. Right now your back is curled like the stem of a dead flower."

"But—" Bennie began in protest.

"Right now," Lalli said, "you're not defending yourself. You're listening."

Bennie closed his mouth.

"When I was a little girl," a woman in the crowd began. A whole minute later, her message sounded more like an autobiography than a message.

"This isn't story hour," Lalli told the woman. "Make your point."

The woman shrugged. "I don't know what that is."

Doc raised his hand. "You could try de-escalation to prevent things from getting so bad that somebody gets hurt."

Bennie's face knotted in confusion. Lalli asked him, "Do you understand what Doc means?"

"Not a clue," Bennie said.

Jessabelle understood de-escalation. What she didn't comprehend was how trying to rip a woman's hair off her head classified as that.

Lalli told Doc, "Show him what you mean."

"Sure," Doc said. He moved to where Jessabelle stood. "Excuse me."

She stepped aside.

"Now," Doc said to Bennie, "pretend I'm one of your Troubles. Whatever I say, just agree with me." Doc raised his hands over his head, assuming a towering, menacing demeanor. He ran toward Bennie shouting, "Your mother is a rat."

"But that's not true," Bennie said.

Doc stopped before Bennie. "I know that, and you know that, but it doesn't matter. You don't have to believe it. You're just using words to get out of a dangerous situation."

"Oh," Bennie said. "Okay. You're right. Come to think of it, my mother is a rat. She's got sharp teeth, like this," he said, baring his canines, "and hands like this." He curled his fingers, clawlike.

"Now," Doc said, "I'm standing here stumped because you just agreed with me. Redirect my focus."

"What?" Bennie asked.

To show Bennie what Doc meant, Jessabelle moved behind Bennie, and squatted so the top of her head was even with the top of his. In her best Bennie voice, she said, "Look over there! What a beautiful bird!" She raised one of Bennie's arms, pointed his index finger off in the distance.

The crowd erupted with laughter.

Doc turned his head and gazed in the direction Jessabelle was pointing Bennie's finger.

"Now run," Jessabelle whispered in Bennie's ear.

Bennie took off running. The crowd cheered. "Go, Bennie!" Pumped on excitement, Bennie started on a perimeter of the field.

As per Lalli's request, Doc asked everybody to return to work. The crowd dispersed along with Lalli.

That left Jessabelle and Doc standing all alone. Anxiety tightened her gut. What would he do now? Tear off her mask, destroying it and leaving her face with bloodied patches where the adhesive tore off her skin? She shivered. "If you're still here when Bennie comes back," Jessabelle said, "tell him I'm in the shed." She turned to go where she felt safe, anyplace Doc was not.

"Wait a minute." Doc reached into his back pocket and came up with some cash he turned over to her. "After what I did," he said, "I feel I owe this to you."

Guilt stabbed her when she glanced down at three one-hundred-dollar bills in her hand. "It's okay," she said and tried returning the money.

"No really," he said. "Keep it." He smiled. "I won't bother you anymore."

"You really haven't bothered me," she said. By the way he

stared at the grass in front of his feet, she could tell he felt bad about what happened. She should be the one feeling bad, and she did. She'd led him to believe he was wrong when that wasn't the case. "You were right," she admitted. "I wear prosthetics." It came pouring out before she had any time to think about it. "You really want to see what I look like without them?"

"Yes."

"Okay," she said, dropping her voice, "but I warn you. You might not like what you see."

"I'll take my chances."

She folded her arms, holding her elbows. "How will we do this?"

"Just do it—throw off the mask."

"Some of the things I'm wearing are not things I can drop like a raincoat. There's a process involved. You of all people should know."

"Can you meet me at the lake after the chant, at say eight forty-five?"

She nodded her agreement without looking at Doc. Instead she kept her gaze on Bennie returning from his perimeter.

"Come without prosthetics," Doc said in a low voice.

Chapter 25

Jessabelle tightened the white wool blanket that wrapped her head, neck, and shoulders. The way it covered her whole face except the eyes made it necessary to kink her neck forward in an L shape to see her way out to the lake where she had agreed to meet Doc. Holding her head down gave her a view of her geek outfit of white shirt, denim overalls with crisscross suspenders, and knee-high tube socks.

Along Strength Street, across Liberation, over toward the park she walked, wearing no mask, no cracked horse teeth, no wig. She had nothing on her head except the blanket she'd found neatly folded on the end of her bed the day she arrived and had never used until now. She stopped, lifted her head, and held the blanket steady as she glanced around. Where were those wild boars when she needed them? If she could get eaten by one in the next three minutes, she wouldn't have to go through with this meeting.

Who was she trying to kid? She knew in her heart she wanted Doc to see who she really was. Embracing this opportunity for a genuine connection, she again began moving her feet.

She spied Doc seated beside the lake with his back against a tree, one leg extended and the other bent up toward a clear starry sky. When she came close, he hoisted himself up. Ironically, he wore an orange and blue striped Henley along with a pair of easy-fitting blue jeans, an outfit similar to the one rolled up and stuffed in a side pouch of her suitcase, a pair of easy-fitting blue jeans and short-sleeved crew neck orange and blue striped T.

It was the kind of thing she wore when she wasn't working. The clothes had been reserved for the time she'd be leaving Lalliville, when she was done with this job. She'd considered wearing them for this occasion, but dropping her geeky clothes and prosthetics all at the same time seemed too dangerous. She now felt especially glad she hadn't worn them. It meant she didn't have to worry about Doc thinking she was trying to play "twins" with him.

With Fuzz nowhere in sight, she asked, "Where's the boy?"

Doc mumbled something about Fuzz staying with Lalli and Bennie before saying, "I thought you were coming without your disguise."

"I'm not in disguise."

"Then why do you look like an Arabian ghost?"

"The blanket was just until I got here."

He raised his hand and held the edge of the blanket. "May I?"

She nodded.

"I'll take that as a yes," he said. "All I saw was a bobbing blanket."

He walked a slow circle around Jessabelle, unwinding the blanket as he went. He lifted it off her neck, and then her mouth and cheeks. The blanket rose higher and higher, until her whole head breathed in the starlight. "Wow!" he said, waving a hand from her head to her toes. "Who would've thought Isa Newton actually looks the way you do?" After a pause, he asked, "Is there a Mr. Newton?"

"You met him."

"I did?"

"Umm hmm. The day he dropped me off."

"That's your uncle. But do you have a husband?"

"No."

"How about a boyfriend?"

"No," she said, hoping the reason he was asking was because he had a romantic interest in her. The possibility of Jessabelle and Doc as a couple enlivened her. At the same time, she was acutely aware she couldn't hide the things she'd done forever. Any relationship they started would come to an abrupt halt once he discovered her true identity.

She felt exposed, longed to run home and lock herself alone in her room where she felt safe. She reached for the blanket he clutched in his hand.

He swung it behind his back. "Let's sit a few moments." He shook out the blanket. "I want to get to know you." The blanket came to rest on the grass, opening like a welcoming yet risky invitation.

She wavered between her desire to get closer to him and her need to protect the lie. She wanted him as a friend, maybe even more. At the same time, doubts about whether she could ever have him as a friend nagged at her. How could they be friends when he was he and she was she?

She'd let the desire for money control her life. She saw that she'd done so at the cost of the kind of life she really wanted. It was a trap, and she wanted out. "It'd take more than a few minutes to tell you about me," she said, taking a seat.

"Maybe you can start with the thing I'm most curious about. Why did you come here in disguise?"

There it was: the question, the most obvious question, the one she'd ask if she were in his shoes.

How was she going to explain this one? She'd tried to prepare earlier, but lacked the inspiration to come up with a great answer. She'd also considered telling him the whole truth. *Just start talking*, she told herself now. *See what comes.* "Just for fun and practice," she ended up saying, in a rather lame tone, not brave enough to tell the truth but too tired of lying to do it with enthusiasm.

Quickly, without even looking at the sky, Jessabelle said, "Aren't the stars just beautiful?" She followed the line of his gaze as it drifted up toward the night sky, continuing with, "It's spectacular the way they light up the clear sky and that row of trees."

Doc brought his attention back to Jessabelle. A moment of silence passed between them, accentuating the song of the cicadas to such a degree, the insects seemed as loud as a rock band. "Practice?" Doc asked. "What are you talking about?"

Having failed in her "look at the sky" diversionary tactic, she quickly adopted a new approach to getting past the "why the disguise" question. "I work in show business."

"As in movies?"

"Yes, movies."

"Which ones have you worked on?"

"None you've heard of, I'm sure."

A slight smile danced on his lips. "Try me."

"My Sister the Demon." Being honest seemed like the simplest thing in the world. So why couldn't she just be honest? she wondered at the same time her lips moved, formulating a lie. "The Nine Faces of Sasimoto Toyota Hungaya. That was a Japanese production."

"You were correct, never heard of them. Isa Newton, that is your real name, right?"

"Of course," she said. "I had to present two photo IDs to get into this place."

"Part of the application process. It ensures the applicant is who they say they are. But I'm a little confused. Did you major in physics or art?"

"I majored in physics with a minor in art, but decided I liked the art part of my degree so much better than the physics part."

He nodded.

Wow. He believed it all, and that made her feel worse than if he hadn't believed one word of it. She wished he'd said, "You're lying. I know all about you. I'm going to call the cops, send you straight to jail."

She deserved punishment, not the warmth and friendliness of that smile of his. What exactly was he smiling at, anyhow? Could he see something in her that she couldn't see in herself, something that would actually make somebody smile, and not just any toad but a very handsome man capable of creating his own artificial foot?

"Where were you born?" he asked.

You don't have to relate the circumstances of your birth. You don't have to tell him your mother was shackled when she gave birth to you. You just need to say where. "Wyoming."

"Tell me something about your family."

What was there to say about them that wouldn't make him run away? Did he really want to hear that her mother died in prison? And that her adoptive parents went to prison? And that her uncle was a con man who talked her into becoming a con woman? Probably not. "Not much to say about my family. They're really boring people."

"C'mon. There must be something you can tell me about them."

"Well, if you really must know, my parents made a fortune selling art. Then they became philanthropists."

"Really?"

"Really. They donated large sums to community institutions, things like schools and art centers. They even bankrolled the construction of the Wyoming Science Center."

"Really?" he said again.

And "Really," she said again. "We were honorary visitors at the science center on opening day. We had so much fun seeing the life-sized animated models of Triceratops and T-Rex, although they scared my brother who was still just a baby. So we went to the cafeteria for cheesemelts and milkshakes.

"In the evening when we got home, after my mom and little brother went to bed, I sat in my living room with Pops, eating popcorn and watching creature features."

Suddenly the ruse dropped, and she found herself pouring her heart out in a real way, telling him about how Mom and Pops supported her in developing her skill in the art of special makeup effects.

Oh, what a tangled web she weaved. Doc knew what she really looked like, but didn't really know why she dressed as Isa. Bennie knew she wasn't Isa, but had no idea who she really was, had never seen what she really looked like. Everybody else assumed she was just Isa, or at least that's what she assumed everybody else believed.

Keeping a record of all the variations of herself was getting tough. It felt like trying to keep track of the color nuances of a cloud. The lines between each were so fuzzy, it was easy to miss where one shade ended and the other began.

She was sick of remembering all the fluctuations of herself, and the appropriate places to bring them out. The person she was with Doc. The one she was with Bennie. The one she was with Vishva, Chet, Johann, and Madeline.

She wanted the luxury of being the same person with everyone, of existing inside her own skin with the same ease and stability Lalli exhibited wherever Jessabelle saw her.

Doc looked at her, his expression so open and trusting.

She wanted to be trustworthy. "Doc," she said. "There's something I want to tell you—the truth."

"The truth," he said, "that you're a crazy Martian from outer space? I already knew that."

"I mean the real truth. It just might shock you."

"What's that?"

"I was adopted," she began. "I never had a relationship with my biological mom." She toiled onward, telling him the story of her life. How her adoptive parents got thrown in jail, how she got thrown to the Cozies, how she ran away, went to Creativo, left Creativo, became a con woman.

When she got to the end of her story, Doc said, "That's a good one." Then he laughed like a clown in a funhouse, proof that she and Doc could never be a couple. Their backgrounds were so different, he thought hers was a joke.

She wanted to tell him she was serious.

The sound of men and women's laughter shuffled into Jessabelle's ears. Her heart hopped in her chest like a skittish Mexican jumping bean. "Doc," she said. "Promise you won't tell a soul about me."

He gave her a collaborative wink as if to say, "We're in this together now."

A sigh of relief emanated from her. Her heart paused from its leaping.

"I signed up to be Juggling Baba at the talent show. I can do his features, his skin, but not his hair," Doc said. "I'm not a wigmaster. Maybe you can help."

"Yeah, sure." Jessabelle shoved Doc off the blanket. She

wrapped her head with it. They both got to their feet.

"Hey, Doc," Jessabelle heard someone say.

Someone else said, "It's such a clear night. We came out to see the stars." The voice had a punchiness she recognized as Chet's.

"Isa," a voice asked, "Is that you?"

She looked to her right, but all she could see were tufts of wool blanket. "Yes."

"Are you catching a cold?" The voice was proper, unmistakably Vishva's.

Jessabelle turned her whole body to face Vishva. "How could I? It's like eighty degrees outside."

"That doesn't mean you can't catch a cold. And if you're not, why do you have that blanket on your head?"

"Actually," Jessabelle groaned, changing her tune, "a cold might be why I feel so horrible." She hacked and coughed like an actor in a B-movie. "My throat feels scratchy. The chills increase by the minute. I thought the blanket might help."

"If that's the case," Vishva said, "you should be in bed. C'mon." Vishva took Jessabelle by the elbow. "Let's get you home."

Vishva led Jessabelle across the grass toward Liberation. "But," Jessabelle protested, "you didn't get a chance to do much stargazing."

"It's okay," Vishva said. "Right now your well-being is more important."

Jessabelle stopped, feeling bad that she'd just been led off without saying good-bye to Doc. She bent slightly. "Okay, just give me a minute to catch my breath." She inhaled deeply, exhaled slowly. She straightened up, turning back. Johann and Chet stood near the lake, heads tilted back, viewing the stars. Doc moved along Liberation, away from Jessabelle. Maybe he was heading home.

It occurred to Jessabelle, as she watched Doc recede into

darkness, her mother may have been sad, really sad, the day
Jessabelle was born.

Jessabelle had been told her mother was two months
pregnant when sentenced to nine years in prison. At first her
mother wasn't sure whether she'd be able to keep her baby.
Then the prison board made its decision. She'd have to relin-
quish the baby.

Her mother had life growing inside her at the same time
she knew she'd have to give that life up. Was it any wonder
she cared not whether it was a girl or boy? After Jessabelle
was born, her mother had been given twenty-four hours with
her baby. The guard called her cold-hearted for not wanting
to even lift the baby in her arms and cuddle her.

Jessabelle suddenly gleaned the most obvious thing: Her
mother wasn't cold-hearted. She'd already been grieving her
loss, a life she lacked rights to.

Jessabelle grieved too, seeing Doc disappear in the darkness. He was part of a life she could not claim as her own. She
hated the fact that he'd laughed at her, that she'd made him
swear he wouldn't tell anybody she was playing a character.
She wanted to yell to Doc, "I'm not cold-hearted! I told you
the truth. And you laughed!" But he was already gone.

"Why does somebody get nine years in prison just for
wanting money, anyway?" Jessabelle's thoughts raged so loud,
she realized she'd just verbalized one.

"I don't know," Vishva said. "Who are you talking
about?"

Her mother! That's who! Suddenly, anger toward Vishva
arose. For her perfect accent, perfect clothes. Perfect grades,
no doubt. Perfect in every way. And kind on top of all that
perfection!

Jessabelle felt angry toward her for showing up with Chet
and Johann when she had. Vishva's sudden appearance had
forced Jessabelle to throw the blanket on, shielding herself all

over again. If Vishva hadn't entered the picture when she did, Jessabelle's need to conceal herself would not have arisen!

Jessabelle had enjoyed not being covered, relished the moonlight on her cheeks and the breeze in her hair. She wished Vishva would just leave her alone.

Jessabelle wanted to run away from this place, forget she had ever seen or even heard of it. Everything was getting complicated. She felt edgy and uncomfortable. But pretending to be calm, she managed to say, "I'm speaking in general."

"I don't really know. Did the person merely desire money, or did she try to take something that wasn't hers?"

"I don't know." She heard the ire rising in her voice. "Maybe she was just trying to feel good! To be happy!" Instead of saying it, she yelled it out, protecting somebody she never even knew.

Vishva laid a hand on Jessabelle's shoulder. "Are you okay?"

"Yes, I'm okay," she shouted in a way that made it clear she wasn't. She brushed off Vishva's hand.

They crossed under a streetlight and Vishva gasped. "Your eyes. I don't think I've ever seen them sparkle so. How can you see without your glasses?"

"They're called contact lenses."

Vishva raised a hand to the blanket. "Can I see the rest of your face a moment?"

"No!" Jessabelle snapped.

"Okay." Vishva returned her hand to her side. After a moment of silence, she said, "Maybe it's best if we remain quiet." And so they did, all the way back to their house.

Jessabelle went to her room, shut the door, and unwrapped the blanket. She balled it up, tossed it in a corner. She heard a knock. She rewrapped the blanket and opened the door a crack.

Vishva stood in the hallway, holding in one hand a box of

tissue with a bottle of cough medicine balanced on top, and in the other a steaming tea. "Feel good," she said and handed the items to Jessabelle.

"Thanks." Jessabelle took the items one at a time, setting them on the dresser along with the three one-hundred-dollar bills from Doc, a flattened paper cone left over from the key lime ice Bennie had purchased for her, and a biodegradable napkin with the words Vishva had printed on it in green pen, Om Namo Bhagavate Shivanandaya. The generosity in that small pile of gifts surged up so strongly it nearly choked her. She wanted to tell Vishva "Thank you," but with all that emotion clotting her throat, she simply nodded, mouthing the words, and quietly closed the door.

Chapter 26

The afternoon after Jessabelle met Doc at the lake, she and Bennie finished cleaning the outside room of the shed so well, it was fit for a princess to sit on and eat a lunch of delicate foods. They seated themselves on the floor, cross-legged, not to eat, because they wouldn't chance messing up the floor, but to decide how to proceed with cleaning the pictures stored in the interior room.

Jessabelle scratched her head, and then her mask. Back in wig and prosthetics, it seemed everything itched. That included the long sleeve white cotton shirt and red plaid skirt with suspenders she wore. She suggested she and Bennie set up a folding table outdoors and clean the pictures one by one in the sun.

"That's a good idea," Bennie said, "since next to Lalli,

there's no light brighter than the sun. We need a good strong light to be sure we get the pictures really clean."

They went to the maintenance building to get a folding table from Hanuman and Bhisma, one that could be easily collapsed and brought inside at the end of each day. On the way there, they further planned to store the pictures in the clean room for the time being. When they finished cleaning all the pictures, they'd then clean the interior room, before moving the pictures back into it.

They found Hanuman and Bhisma in their office, and after explaining what they wanted, Hanuman disappeared into the storage area while Jessabelle and Bennie waited.

Hanuman returned a few moments later with a rectangular folding table. Despite that its speckled gray plastic top stretched about five feet long and three feet wide, he swung it in his hand as if it was a home and garden magazine he was bringing to his kitchen table to read in leisure while he drank his coffee on a Sunday morning. Hanuman set the table down in front of them.

Jessabelle lifted it slightly by its metal frame, testing its weight, about half Bennie's body weight.

"Shall we deliver it for you?" Hanuman asked.

"No," Bennie said. "We've got this one." He eagerly took the front, Jessabelle the back. Together they carried it out the back door of the maintenance building.

They were carrying the table along Peace when the apple-red Cherokee stopped on the road beside them. From the driver's seat, Doc called through the window. "Isa, may I have a word with you?"

Jessabelle motioned to Bennie. They set the table on the grass. Over at the security vehicle, Doc said, "There's something I want to ask you." Fuzz looked at her from the passenger seat as if he too had a question for her. Meanwhile, the person who'd announced he had a question for her anxiously scratched the back of his neck, just above the collar of the lived-in loganberry and white two-pocket plaid short-sleeved shirt he wore with black jeans and his red sneakers with green stripes. Nervousness was not something she'd seen in Doc, and she worried that he'd done some research and discovered her true identity, was getting ready to accuse her of something.

I swear, she was thinking, *it's not how it seems,* when his question came out: "Do you want to meditate with me this evening?"

"Oh," she said, exhaling the breath she held. "You want to meditate with me?"

She guessed this was how the men in this town asked women on first dates. They didn't ask, "Do you want to go to the movies?" or "Do you want to go to the local watering hole for a Budweiser?" Instead they asked, "Do you want to meditate with me?" It made sense, considering there were no bars or movie theaters in Lalliville. Among the town's finer establishments were a chanting hall, a meditation cave, and an Indian temple. That left chanting, meditating, and praising God as date activities.

She accepted Doc's invitation.

On the lawn beside the shed, Bennie and Jessabelle set up the folding table. Wearing rubber gloves, Jessabelle carried the first picture to it, setting its three-by-three-foot frame flat on top. She squirted the glass with a mixture of vinegar and water, then began wiping it clean while Bennie stood by.

First she saw beautiful brown eyes. She continued wiping, revealing the whole picture of the Free & Blissful Yogi seated on a sheepskin. Demonstrating flexible hip joints, he sat crosslegged with one heel against his lower belly and the bottoms of both feet perpendicular to the ceiling. He wore a loincloth and a sweet blissful smile. Gray streaked his curly dark hair. A red spot the size of a fingertip dotted the space

When she met his gaze, a vibration of joy moved through her, a joy she would have sworn emanated from the picture as it traveled up her arm and through her chest, exploding into the rest of her body.

"Pictures of saints convey their states," Bennie said.

"No kidding?" She laughed, giddy over the concept of a living picture, capable of breathing bliss.

At eight-thirty in the evening, Jessabelle stood at the entrance of the path leading to the meditation cave, where she and Doc had agreed to meet. She wore full prosthetics, along with her short sleeve white cotton shirt with suspenders and red plaid skirt. She'd considered meeting Doc without disguise, but quickly vetoed the idea in favor of playing it safe. The whole revealing-herself-thing the night before had put her on edge, producing a discomfort she wasn't keen on experiencing again so soon.

When Doc came, she gave him a once-over and blinked her eyes, just to be sure she wasn't seeing things. When she opened her eyes, he appeared just as he had before she closed them—as if he was physically morphing into someone else.

He wore a colorful long shirt, designed with longitudinal turquoise, purple, and orange wide stripes over black jeans. The shirt was tied at the waist with a turquoise sash. Its hem fell to his knees. Doc's skin was darker, his nose a different shape.

"It's like you're halfway to another man."

"Halfway to a saint," he said with a laugh. He brought an old four-by-four-inch black-and-white photo from a side pocket on his shirt, holding it so Jessabelle could see. "This is who I'm shooting for."

In the picture, a fit and slender Indian man from a

different era stood barefoot on a dirt road, his shirt a black and white version of the one Doc had on. The man wore his shirt over pants that fit tightly around his calves. Thick wavy whirly hair streamed in all directions from his scalp. He was juggling knives, clasping two by their handles with his eyes on a third in the air.

The name "Juggling Baba" came into her mind. Then she remembered that on the prior evening, down by the lake, she'd told Doc she'd help him become Juggling Baba for the talent show. "Juggling Baba."

Doc nodded.

"Who exactly is Juggling Baba?"

"A saint with juggling skills. He took samadhi in 1961."

It was clear by the way Doc used the word samadhi, it meant that in 1961, Juggling Baba had died.

They started toward the meditation cave while Doc explained that as a young man, Prahlad Jishnani made his living as a street performer, a trade he learned from his father and grandfather. He traveled all over the central states of India on foot, sleeping in a tent at night.

Doc's story about Juggling Baba was interrupted by four people sitting on lawn chairs, two each on opposite sides of the meditation path, drinking sparkling spring water. One of them, a man, came to attention, sitting upright in his chair, as Jessabelle and Doc approached. "You ain't no boars. Ever since you put up those signs, Doc, we've been out waiting for boars. That's five nights, and we haven't seen no boars."

"Hang in there," Jessabelle encouraged. "You'll see them."

At the cave, Jessabelle and Doc were greeted by a sign on the door: Closed for Repairs. "I know another spot," Doc said, leading her toward the forest.

Making their way through the forest, Doc continued on about Juggling Baba. At first Prahlad performed street acts traditional in India, juggling brass bells and knives, skills passed through the generations of his family. An Englishman taught him pantomime, magic tricks, and tightrope walking, numbers he added to his street acts.

One day Prahlad fell off a rope stretched over a Bombay street, but instead of dying, he opened his eyes and, for the first time, saw his guru. He ended up in the ashram of his guru. Eventually he became a saint in his own right and juggled every day as a meditation. People started calling him Juggling Baba. They came from all over to watch him juggle. Sometimes he gave teachings as he juggled. Other times he juggled in silence.

So engrossed in the story of the performing saint, Jessabelle lost track of where they were going, although she knew they were nearing a river. She could hear the sound of moving water growing louder.

"People used to leave money that Juggling Baba distributed to the poor," Doc said.

"A powerful performance he must—" She stopped in mid-sentence when she felt the shadows of the giants. Her mouth dropped as her eyes caught sight of a huge tree trunk. It must have had a diameter of twenty feet. She followed its line up, up, and up about 125 feet in the air.

With her neck craned to its maximum, she saw the dark green overlapping branches that formed its tree canopy. The branches weren't even flinching under the weight of hundreds of pounds of Spanish moss that hung from them.

"Holy cow! Look at that!" She shifted her gaze to a neighboring tree even bigger than the first.

Through laughter, she heard Doc say, "It's a tree, not a cow." Then he briefly explained, "These are seven- and eight-hundred-year-old cypress."

She no longer heard the sound of the wind in the trees. Instead she heard the trees singing scales of Om, but not with her ears. This singing was something she felt with her whole body as a kind of primordial vibration. These trees were the big ones, the old ones, the ones who'd thrived through hundreds of years of heat and storms, and in their presence, she was drawn deep inside.

It occurred to her: These cypress trees didn't have to put on a nice skirt or fancy tie to impress anybody. They simply inspired by the very thing they were—grand old cypress trees. They didn't have to shout to get her to be quiet. They roused her silence with their very presence. Their world existed beyond sight and sound.

Doc motioned for her to have a seat.

She gazed at the ground. A group of ants hovered in frozen motion near where he wanted to sit.

"Look!" Doc said. "The ants are meditating."

"Are they really meditating?"

"Sure," he said. "At this very moment those ants are probably receiving telepathic transmissions from their queen."

"Transmissions about what?"

"'Come back to the nest', 'the little ants need food,' and stuff like that."

"You're kidding."

"I'm serious," he said. "Ants are very evolved beings. They don't have ears but they find their way around, search for food, and take good care of each other."

"Hmmm."

"They can lift things weighing fifty times more than their own bodies," he said, and described a time when he'd seen five ants carrying half a piece of toast across a counter. "That kind of strength doesn't come from the barbells in their nests. It's got to come from somewhere inside of them, maybe from their commitment to the colony. After all, half a slice of toast is a lot more than five ants can eat."

She took a seat a few feet from the ants, crosslegged at

the base of the cypress tree, back-to-back with Doc, who sat in her same position facing the opposite direction. They chanted Jaya Shiva Om for a minute, then closed their eyes for meditation. She quietly repeated Jaya Shiva Om until a bright light illumined the inside of her head. She slowly opened her eyes, staring at the moon.

Meditating with Doc became part of her daily routine. She began each morning when she awoke at five-thirty. Once inside her mask, horse teeth, wig, and one-piece footed yellow cotton jumper with deep kangaroo pockets, the one fashioned for sleeping, she met Bennie at Pierre's early morning yoga class.

Breakfast followed yoga class, and after breakfast she zipped home to change into one of the three geek outfits she wore in rotation. Then it was off to work, which began at nine.

Day by day, she and Bennie cleaned one picture after another, each an image of a saint. The Free & Blissful Yogi, sitting in his courtyard, walking along a beach at sunset, standing before the gates of his ashram. Sometimes Bennie referred to him as Svairin ca Krtapunya Yogin.

Bennie told her the names of other saints they uncovered. Anandamayi Ma, Hari Giri Baba, Sai Baba, Jnaneshwar, Peace Permeated Saint. The last two were ink on paper renderings of the saints, as they had lived in a time before photography. Jessabelle cleaned pictures of Juggling Baba too. Soon the pictures they had cleaned stacked up to over a hundred. This collection told her the saints of India were a motley-looking crew, male and female, old and young, ranging from homeless and ragged to well-groomed and gorgeous, with everything in between. Theirs was a look vast as the leaves of the forest.

At noon each day Jessabelle trained Bennie. Their usual

practice consisted of low kicks to the abdomen, groin, and knee, along with ways to throw a punch. These sessions always ended when Bennie said, "I'm pooped. Time for a recharge." At that point he ran off to have lunch at home with Lalli, or in the dining hall if they were serving his favorite vegetables. As a boy particularly fond of all plants in the cabbage family, he was the only warrior she'd ever known who fortified himself on Brussels sprouts.

By two p.m. she was usually back in the shed with Bennie, cleaning pictures, and in the evenings, following dinner, she attended the kirtan before going to the river with Doc, to the land of the giants, each night sitting beneath a different one to meditate.

To get there, they always walked the path to the meditation cave and then out into the woods and down to the river. And each night, on the path, they passed the same four people, waiting for a boar sighting. The man's moan went from, "We've been out here five nights and haven't seen no boars" to "We've been out here eleven nights and haven't seen no boars." Finally, it happened that the four were no longer there, having entirely given up on seeing pigs.

At dinner one evening, after Jessabelle had signed up for a Day of Practice, Chet suddenly piped up. "A Day of Practice means a special meal," he said, "and a special meal means dessert. I'm thinking about carrot halwa. Do any of you have other ideas?"

Carrot halwa sounded as Indian as a burfi. Jessabelle wasn't sure if the carrot halwa was a random possibility Chet had come up with, or if in Indian tradition carrot halwa was always served on a Day of Practice, as in America a turkey was always served on Thanksgiving. "Do you have to make carrot halwa? Is that some kind of a rule?" she asked.

"It doesn't have to be carrot halwa," Chet said.

"How about a sheet cake decorated with a picture of

Lalli?" Jessabelle suggested.

Vishva gasped.

Shocked by the depth of despair expressed in the utter-ance, Jessabelle asked, "What?"

"That's a terrible idea," Vishva said.

"But people love Lalli," Jessabelle said.

"I love her too," said Vishva, "but a cake is not just for looking at. Eventually people will want to eat it, and then... and then somebody will have to cut into it!" A violent shud-der rattled her body. "I couldn't bear to see Lalli's image cut up that way."

"I'm sorry," Jessabelle said and placed a hand on Vishva's shoulder. "Didn't mean to be as insensitive as an ax murderer."

Chapter 27

"We are gathered here for a Day of Practice, to awaken to our highest self." Madeline spoke from behind the podium, dressed in a patchwork sari, composed of pieces of silk cloth sewn together, each with a different design. In one square an elephant ate grass; daffodils bloomed in the next; cardinals perched in another; plaid and paisley patterns followed. Madeline also wore cosmetic makeup, including blue eye shadow, blush, and lipstick.

On Madeline's right, Lalli sat crosslegged in her chair, so still and stable, Jessabelle doubted a bulldozer could budge her if she didn't want to be moved. Lalli seemed rooted right through her chair and down into the earth. She listened to Madeline, her face in a state of natural repose, her eyes focused on the space before her.

"Through Lalli's sankalpa," Madeline said, "or intention, everyone in this room will receive her grace. Not one of us will leave as quite the same person we were when we entered. Personally, I love Days of Practice, because of how peaceful and content they make me feel."

Peace and contentment seemed as far from Jessabelle as India from America. Irritation was much closer to home. In her crooked horse teeth, hook nose, thick glasses, and coiled red hair, she was sure she had never looked so ugly. Underscoring this feeling of ugliness was the contrast she felt with Vishva, who sat beside her in a sari of turquoise and purple silk with rhinestones running along its bottom and top edges. She wore bangles, a necklace, and long earrings; with her hair rolled up and held in place by a jeweled tiara, she exuded majesty.

Why am I here? Jessabelle asked herself again and again, and couldn't come up with an answer. Whatever happened to her search for Shiva? She felt she should be out looking for the golden god, not sitting here in her white shirt buttoned all the way to the top, Neptune-blue plaid skirt, matching vest, bowtie, and white knee socks, gazing at a bunch of people in celebration clothing. She saw dresses and suits, slacks and ties. Doc wore a silk suit for the occasion. Bennie dressed pretty much how he always dressed, in a rust-colored silk kurta. He'd tied a three-foot spiral-shaped balloon to his finger, something all people aged eight to twelve received at the door. (The minimum age requirement to sign up for a Day of Practice was eight.)

"During this particular Day of Practice," Madeline said, "we will chant and meditate. It is through the age old mantra Jaya Shiva Om that the power of the guru's grace flows. When we sing this sacred verse with all our hearts, the power of consciousness fills us and expands outward into our everyday experiences.

"It's almost time to get started but before we do, I have a few reminders. First, there will be plenty of breaks during today's program in which you are invited to enjoy a variety of dishes made with so much love and devotion, they are going to make your stomach sing its own praises." The part of Jessabelle she sat on rejoiced to hear there'd be plenty of breaks.

"Don't compare your experiences with others or have expectations about what should happen during this Day of Practice."

Jessabelle silently screamed, *I don't have any expectations! I know nothing is going to happen!* Wait a minute. Was knowing nothing will happen an expectation?

She considered this while Madeline concluded her second reminder: "Way of Truth is a very personal path. Everyone's experiences are unique. Yours will be exactly what you need at this point in time."

Arriving at her final reminder, Madeline said: "The program is going to begin shortly so please turn off all your watch alarms, pagers, and cell phones." Jessabelle clicked off her smartphone, wishing that with a simple twist of her ear, she could click off her own penchant for deception.

At the conclusion of the reminders, Madeline said, "Through chanting, music, and meditation, we will now awaken the eternal light." And with those words, the chanting and meditation began.

Jessabelle chanted Jaya Shiva Om with the group in call-and-response fashion, meditated afterward, chanted Jaya Shiva Om again, meditated afterward, and then chanted Jaya Shiva Om some more. By noon she had racked up the repetition, both silently and aloud, of over three hundred Jaya Shiva Oms.

When lunchtime came, despite the crooked horse teeth, hooked nose, thick glasses, and coiled red hair, she felt more beautiful than ever. She also felt as if she'd grown about three feet throughout the morning. Literally, it seemed as if the room had gotten smaller while she got BIGGER.

For lunch, she sat at a picnic table in the park with Vishva and others to eat eggplant parmigiana, marinated green beans, and salad. Chet's dessert, berry trifle, stood tall on her tray. She admired the lovely colors in the clear plastic, stemmed glass loaded with layers of cubed angel food cake, strawberries, blueberries, raspberries, and vanilla pudding, topped with whipped cream. It was almost too pretty to eat.

Everybody observed the spiritual practice of silence, which meant no talking.

She felt that energy, the same energy released each evening from the kirtan, only it seemed much thicker, far more concentrated. This energy made a nearby gardenia tree smell like a whole gardenia forest. It made the eggplant parmigiana, green beans, and salad on her plate tastier than a five-star meal.

With her senses heightened this way, Jessabelle beheld a leaf falling from the branch of a large tree. It drifted past her and landed on the grass behind her and Vishva. Jessabelle noticed a brightness to its color she had never discerned in any "green thing," and it touched her in a way no leaf ever had.

Jessabelle elbowed Vishva in a good-natured way, saying, "You dropped a piece of your lettuce." She pointed to the leaf. "You'd better pick it up."

Vishva studied the "green thing" for a moment. Once she realized it was a leaf and not a piece of lettuce, she beamed Jessabelle a playful look that Jessabelle read as "Stop being so silly! Can't you see I'm trying to be silent here?"

Jessabelle started to laugh. She laughed harder and harder until she was laughing harder than she could remember ever laughing in her whole life. Mirth shook her body; her ribs trembled.

A mass of what felt like warm white light exploded below her belly button, and she started to cry as hard as she'd laughed the moment before.

She glanced through her tears at the others at the picnic table. Oddly, they didn't seem fazed by her behavior. Still, she couldn't help but worry they'd soon find it crazy. She didn't want to end up as anybody's recommendation for a psych ward, so she set her plate aside, stood up, and wandered off to find a place she could be alone in her madness.

She ended up sitting on the pavement, her back against an outside wall of the dining hall, where she…

Cried and cried and cried and cried and cried and…

Cried. This crying wasn't sad, not at all like the crying she'd done when Mom and Pops had gone to jail or the Cozies liquidated her makeup supplies.

As she cried, it seemed she cried not just through her eyes but in ten thousand different places all over her body. With all these tears oozing from her, Mr. and Mrs. Cozie came to mind, and for the first time ever, Jessabelle thought about them with love and gratitude instead of anger.

As she cried, she felt lucky to have had Mom and Pops in her life, even if their time together had been nipped short. As she cried, resentment over their being taken away from her at an early age disappeared, along with the chronic disgust she'd held for Mr. and Mrs. Cozie.

For forty-five minutes, tears poured out of her as fast as they rained from the sky on a stormy day. When the torrent ended, a great calm pervaded her and her whole perspective had changed. The personal grievances she'd accumulated over a lifetime were gone, and she was left with nothing but a clear and profound feeling of love. She felt this intensified love for the trees, the grass, the sky, the clouds, and every other thing she saw, including the Dumpster behind the dining hall.

This love wasn't the personal attachment she had to Mom

and Pops. It wasn't the desire she had to roll in the grass with Doc. Nor was it her passion for special makeup effects. Affection, amour, and passion were drops of saltwater; this love bubbling from her was the great wide ocean from which they sprang. With its magnificent waves, the ocean was as vast and deep as this love.

From this love's point of view, money seemed like nothing. She saw paying $300 for this feeling of love to be like standing on the beach on a really hot day and casting a penny Doc gave her into the ocean in exchange for an opportunity to swim in its cool blue waters.

Inside this love in which she swam, she experienced deep currents of gratitude for everything that existed in her whole life, including the bad. She inwardly thanked the Cozies for starving her in a locked basement. Their cruelty had prompted her to run away and go to Creativo, which led to dropping out of Creativo, working the knife and gun counter at Wally's, hooking up with Uncle Trix, meeting Wrench. If it weren't for all of that, she wouldn't have ended up here, where she found this love, perfect in and of itself.

Vishva approached, her sari sweeping across the pavement. "I found you," she said. "Are you okay?"

Jessabelle nodded.

"Do you want some company or would you rather be alone?"

"Your company would be nice," Jessabelle said.

Vishva sat down on the pavement beside her. "What is going on with you?"

"I feel so much love and gratitude," Jessabelle whispered.

The two sat in silence for several minutes, and then Vishva told Jessabelle, "I first met Lalli when I was sixteen."

"Was that yesterday?"

Vishva smiled. "It was nine years ago, outside of Mumbai. Lalli has an ashram there, and I went one night with my mother to see her. The hall was dark. There were all these smells of incense and we sat on the floor. There was chanting, and Lalli gave a talk.

"I didn't understand a lot of what was going on, but Lalli was such a dynamic figure that I ended up returning to that place a couple of weeks later for a Day of Practice.

"I stayed in her ashram on Saturday night, and the following day there were a couple hundred people in the hall, and I remember at one point Lalli was walking around the room Awakening people by touch.

"We were supposed to have our eyes closed, but I was kind of peeking so I could see her. Just before she came to me I shut my eyes. She pushed them, and it felt like they went into the back of my head.

"Then she pressed on the space between my eyebrows and touched the top of my head, and I just started to cry. I wasn't bawling or anything, but I had tears rolling down my face. I didn't cry back then. I didn't cry much at all. At least, nobody ever saw me cry. And I didn't know what I was crying for. There was no content to it so I knew something had happened. After that I felt so much joy and love."

When Jessabelle heard the word "love" she again started crying because of all the love she felt in that moment. As she cried she thought about all the time and energy Vishva and the others donated to make Lalliville a viable place.

Jessabelle had never really understood the work they did that they called service—until that moment. Suddenly she recognized that it was the many hours of service performed by a variety of people like them that kept this town going. Through their service, she received an experience of true love. With watery eyes, Jessabelle told Vishva, "Thank-you."

Vishva laughed and asked, "For what?"

"For all this love I feel."

"You're welcome. You can also thank Lalli."

"But she's not even here."

"By the looks of Isa Newton, I'm sure she is." After a few moments, Vishva got to her feet. "When you're ready for it, your dessert awaits you." Vishva handed Jessabelle a tissue before she walked off. "Here," she said, "Looks like your makeup got messed up." Oddly, the comment didn't even make Jessabelle paranoid.

After she refreshed her makeup and ate her dessert, she returned to the hall, occupying a seat beside Vishva. The entire F.B.I. could have been in Vishva's spot, their captain holding a warrant for Jessabelle's arrest, and somehow Jessabelle wouldn't have cared. So solid was her internal happiness, nothing could shake her. Her usual concerns didn't exist as more than shaded spots on the surface of a deep body of warm, liquid, moving energy that she could only describe as love, or gratitude. The two seemed interchangeable; she couldn't experience one without the other being present.

Waves of love and gratitude, gratitude and love, love and gratitude continued to wash over her. They were there when she listened to the musicians chant OM on different scales. She slipped beneath these waves during the time she again chanted Jaya Shiva Om with everybody else and meditated afterward.

During the last segment of the program, she chanted Jaya Shiva Om with the group, to a melody she'd never before heard. As always, it began slowly. Her serenade of Jaya Shiva Om increased in speed and intensity alongside the progressing chant. Soon it was moving so fast, she didn't know Jaya Shiva Om could glide so quickly.

People clapped to the beat or slapped their hands against their thighs, adding to the rhythm. Jesabelle's body swayed, and with each swinging movement, she had the sense of becoming bigger and bigger.

Suddenly Chet leapt out of his seat and began dancing in

a lively style to match the high energy of the chant. Shaking and shimmying with head and hip rolls thrown in, he inspired others to dance, until half the people in the room were on their feet dancing freestyle.

Johann pranced catlike over the carpet, throwing his head from side to side in sharp movements. Madeline rotated in slow sensuous circles with open arms as if she were dancing to a tender love ballad and not an energetic chant, while Bennie did a happy dance. The way he simultaneously hopped up and down, blinked his eyes, and opened and closed his fists made him look like a party light twinkling at high speed.

If she hadn't known Doc had a prosthetic foot, she would not know now, by how he moved his feet one-two-three, one-two-three. Spinning and twirling in perfect time to the music, he came across as a man whose background check would turn up ballroom dance lessons.

Lalli and Vishva also danced, side-by-side, an exotic dance they knew by heart. With stylized hand and foot gestures, they scintillated like dancing fire.

Jessabelle rose to her feet, and with no clear plan, began moving to the rhythm, improvising, chanting. She felt the chant inside her, as if that was where it had always been. Only now she heard it, expressing it with her whole body. It poured out her limbs.

She caught Doc watching her from across the room. She smiled as if to say, "Not bad for a nerd, huh?" Then she let go, allowing herself to be swept up by the energy of the kirtan, and danced until she forgot everything.

The music slowed, and one by one the dancers took their seats wherever they stopped dancing. Jessabelle found her seat on the floor, once again remembering she had a body.

Lalli began a talk, her voice moving like a soft tide. "The Free & Blissful Yogi was not much of a dancer," she said with a laugh, "but he loved dancing. He loved to see people dance, freely expressing the energy of their hearts." Her eyes sparkled and shined, recollecting her own guru.

That led into, "My guru saw everyone as no different from himself." Lalli glowed with the energy of love. In that light, Jessabelle felt luminosity and heat.

"The Free & Blissful Yogi was God incarnate. He was love, and love was him. He could not be confined; his love was unlimited. One with the universal energy, he belonged to the whole of humankind, existing in a state beyond sect, place, or country, free from barriers of caste, creed, race, and color."

Lalli continued speaking about her guru, saying things like, "He lived in bliss." "All virtues resided in him." "In his boundless mercy, he bestowed his compassion on all."

Lalli's voice held Jessabelle spellbound, as Lalli began speaking about Shiva. In her enchantment, Jessabelle found Lalli's words to be as slippery as wet fish. She caught them as they jumped out of the sea and held them for a moment with perfect understanding. Then they escaped her grasp and disappeared into the love that was all around her while she unsuccessfully tried to remember what Lalli had just said. She couldn't hold a stash of Lalli's words, just a minnow and a big fish.

The minnow was: "Have the understanding, I am Shiva, and everything else is Shiva. It is the true awareness of equality. Experience Shiva everywhere and in everything: the plants and trees, gods and people, animals and creepers. See the one in the all."

The big fish was: "Shiva is the Self, that immaterial consciousness beyond space and time. It is not born and does not die. It is bliss, freedom, and contentment. And it exists within you. Stop looking for something that you are."

*   *   *

On the night of Jessabelle's Day of Practice, she lay in bed with eyes so heavy, she could barely hold them open. At the same time she couldn't sleep, with the words "Stop looking for something that you are" rolling back and forth inside.

Was it really true that Shiva—the supreme Truth—was inside her? If so, where was it? Squeezed between her liver and kidneys?

Shiva is that immaterial consciousness beyond space and time, Lalli had said. Shiva is bliss, freedom, and contentment, Lalli had said.

On that day Lalli had not said that Shiva is vast and endless love, but from Jessabelle's own experience, she knew it to be true. As another wave of that oceanic love washed over her, she felt totally energized.

Somewhere in the course of her Day of Practice, she'd experienced love as expansive as the wide and deep blue sea. It sounded so simple and yet it felt completely profound.

Like a precious eagle swooping out of the sky and landing in her hands, the experience seemed to come out of nowhere. It had showed up in her life like a surprise gift of gold, delivered to her doorstep on an ordinary day.

With great gratitude for this bounty she had received, she started to cry all over again. Lalli's figure appeared in her mind's eye. Jessabelle spoke to it. "I don't even know who you are but thank you."

As another wave of love rushed through her, she repeated the words "Thank you." In the past, "Thank you" was a throwaway line, an automatic response to receiving a birthday present, drummed into her head by Mom and Pops.

Now, she couldn't imagine receiving a greater gift than this love. She had never felt the words "Thank you" more deeply. It was with a profound sense of gratitude that naturally inspired reverence and respect, not only for Lalli but also for the love itself, that she thanked Lalli.

When the tears subsided, she realized that this love was the only thing she had ever really wanted. It was never three million dollars she was searching for but this love, which was absolutely magical. She wasn't kidding when she cried out, "I wouldn't trade the way I feel now for a hundred million dollars."

Chapter 28

At breakfast on the morning following her Day of Practice, Jessabelle sat with Vishva, Madeline, Johann, and Pierre. She wore her full costume of white cotton shirt with suspenders and red plaid skirt, wig, mask, glasses, and horse teeth.

Pierre talked about something Lalli had said at the Day of Practice. "There is no permanent happiness in anything outside the Self." Jessabelle hadn't remembered Lalli saying this until Pierre brought it up.

"When I got married," Pierre said, "I lived in a state of bliss. I couldn't wait to get home every night to see my wife." He laughed. "That definitely did not last." Apparently, he was divorced now.

"It's like when I buy clothes," Madeline chimed in. "I

get a new skirt, one I really like, and a rush of elation goes through me. After a time, if I don't get food on it, it wears out, and my joy in it goes."

"It's true," Johann said. "It's like that with everything. As a kid, I loved *goetter speise* until the day I ate so much of it, I threw up. To this day, I can't even look at the stuff."

Jessabelle listened to them speak, her feeling of love for them intensifying, growing so big she feared her body might crack like an egg. She managed to hold back the tears. Her chest ached.

Experiencing such a strong love for these people, she recognized that when it came to other people, she was usually so intent and focused on making herself seem equal if not better that she often neglected to really see them.

She could see Vishva, Madeline, Johann, and Pierre now. All competitiveness was gone. She wasn't comparing herself to them. In this moment of connectedness she was inherently as good as them. This wasn't something she thought about or tried to convince herself of by telling herself, I am as good as them, I am as good as them, I swear I am as good as them. The feeling of equality was simply there, just as the sun was there.

"How about you, Isa?" Vishva asked. "What do you think?" All faces spun in Jessabelle's direction.

Tears burst from Jessabelle's eyes. In the midst of all these tears, she broke out in laughter over the fact that she was doing it again, crying in front of everybody.

"What is happening to you?" Pierre asked.

"That's a good question," Jessabelle sobbed. She knew absolutely, unequivocally, and without a shadow of a doubt that something profound was happening to her, and that it was connected to her Day of Practice and all these tears she was shedding. But she couldn't say exactly what was happening to her.

She could see she'd been flashing in and out of two different states. The first was the newfound state in which she experienced a sense of gratitude for everything in her life. Having touched this state, she realized she had what could be called a "usual state," which seemed to be gratitude's opposite. In her usual state, she wanted something; a three-million-dollar statue, for instance.

The times she'd cried since her Day of Practice, the tears had transported her from her "usual state" of wanting to the state abounding with gratitude.

All her life she had feared tears because she associated them with grief, sorrow, and pain. Now she saw her tears as mysterious little friends that washed away the grief, sorrow, and pain of a lifetime and made her new again. They showed her love, and when she left the place of love to go back to her "usual state" for too long, the tears came and gently returned her to love. This love was much bigger than her; it made her feel like a particle of salt floating in the sea.

"I feel like I've been taken hostage by a force of love the size of King Kong," she blubbered. "It's at least a hundred and fifty times my size. I'm just sitting in its palm with no choice but to go where it carries me."

"That's Awakening," Vishva said.

"When I received Awakening," Madeline said, "I cried for at least thirty minutes. It was the most cleansing, relieving experience I ever had.

"When the tears subsided, I felt as if I'd been carrying a thousand-pound pack on my back throughout my whole life that was gone. I was emotionally uplifted and felt so light, it was like my body didn't have any weight on it at all.

"Shortly after that my perception totally changed. I suddenly became aware that what I consider 'I' was not my body at all. It's like being in a house and looking out the window. The house isn't you, and you know it, and that's your experience—that you're not the house.

"But I had lived my whole life thinking I was the person I see in the mirror. Awakening made me realize I merely inhabit this body in order to function in the physical world, in this life—just the way we inhabit a house."

"At the time of my Awakening," Pierre said, "I did a spontaneous yoga posture. I stretched into a backbend from a seated position with my forehead touching the sacral part of my lower back.

"I was in this position for what felt like an eternity, but it must have only been twenty minutes. In that time, I experienced this wonderful rush of love throughout my whole body and I felt completely connected to the universe.

"Then a fear arose that I was going to be paralyzed in that position forever, and as soon as I felt that fear, I came out of the position." He laughed and added, "I could never do that posture now. I couldn't even do it back then in a regular state."

It was probably a good thing Jessabelle hadn't heard these experiences before she took a Day of Practice. If people had spoken to her then about imaginary thousand-pound packs falling off their backs and spontaneous impossible yoga postures, the stories would not have seemed real. But in this context, she didn't doubt the truth of any of them, given her own experience during her Day of Practice. And when she listened to other people's experiences, she relived her own. There was something in them that felt so familiar. She could relate to Madeline's lightness of body, and the rush of love that went through Pierre.

Jessabelle reflected on Lalli. Doing spontaneous backbends, being out of body. Jessabelle didn't know anybody who produced these effects on others; undoubtedly, there was something special about Lalli.

"Sometimes in the right lighting," Johann said, "I can see

a subtle glow or a ring of light emanating from a person. It gives me clues about what that person is like.

"I wanted to see Lalli's aura, and during my first Day of Practice, I looked at her as she sat at the front of the room talking. I thought it would be a perfect time for me to see her aura.

"So I gazed at her, not really focusing on her but looking behind her. I did this for about a minute, but didn't see anything. I thought it was really unusual that I couldn't see *anything*.

"The same instant I had that thought, I watched the whole room fill up with light. This light was sort of like a fog that hung over all the people. It was really bright around Lalli.

"I kept closing my eyes and opening them again to see if it was going to stay or go away, and it just kept staying. Then I became immersed in this light of her aura, and I had the feeling that everyone in the room was engulfed in her energy. I became that energy, and when I did, my mind seemed like a pea over in a corner."

Yes, Lalli was definitely unique. And so was Johann. What an unusual thing—a number cruncher who read auras.

Jessabelle's wonder about Lalli grew while considering the things she'd just heard. If there was a scale ranging from one to ten for measuring the intensity of the wonders in her life, Lalli was on her way to busting the scale.

On this scale, a one was something like: "Why is white sugar more expensive than brown? Don't they take something out of brown sugar to make white?" A one was the kind of day-to-day thing that aroused her curiosity for a moment or two.

A five involved various archaeological sites like Chaco Canyon or the Great Pyramids of Egypt. These things were intriguing enough to spark her speculation about the grand

and ancient cultures of which they were a part.

Lalli, on the other hand, aroused the kind of speculation Jessabelle felt when she gazed up in the sky on a clear night to see thousands of stars blazing with light and considered the origins of the solar system. Every time she thought about Lalli, it felt as if a giant crack had opened beneath her feet and she'd fallen into something as deep and primal as the mystery of life itself.

A new day had dawned, and with this rising, Jessabelle's enthusiasm was high as the sun. Following breakfast with her new friends, she strode along Liberation, no longer as just a woman with feet moving in alternating motions, arms swinging at her sides. Instead she coasted on a boat, sailing across the great wide ocean of love.

She started chanting Jaya Shiva Om. Repeating the mantra, she felt like crying, but didn't want to. All her crying was beginning to make her feel wrung out. *You'd better not cry*, she ordered herself. She choked back tears. At the same time, she felt utterly compelled to continue chanting Jaya Shiva Om.

A prickling sensation ran up her spine. Within seconds of it, tears spouted from her eyes, clouding their surface. She felt the tears striate her cheeks with warm rolling lines before they fell from her body, melting in the waters of divine love extending from all sides of her body, as far as her eyes could see. When salt merged with salt, she felt nothing but love, inside and out.

Feeling the full magnitude of this love, she felt good thoroughly, deeply, and completely, from the top of her head to the tips of her toes. She no longer wanted a cut of three million dollars, if to get it she had to steal from Lalli. Dared she say, her heart belonged to Lalliville.

She wanted to live in Lalliville and get to know Lalli the

way Vishva, Bennie, and the others did. She wanted to be like the others. Maybe if she stayed here long enough, she'd turn like them. Maybe without even knowing it, she'd already been reformed. After all, she hadn't stolen anything in four weeks, and didn't miss it.

Indeed, she was beginning to feel like one of them, devoted, virtuous, and hard-working. Hah! A woman like her could hardly be called virtuous. But hard-working? That she could almost believe by the considerable progress she and Bennie had made in the shed.

She proceeded in the direction of the shed, eager to finish what they had started. Her body felt so light and fresh, she started jogging. She hung a right after the dining hall and motored along making vrooming sounds, holding her arms out from her sides, as if she were an airplane.

The sight of him sank her boat and crashed her plane, made her suddenly feel dead. She cursed, squeezed her eyes shut, and when she opened them again, the last person on earth she wanted to see was still there.

She slowed and came face-to-face with Uncle Trix, his painted blond hair in sharp contrast to the third-of-an-inch of speckled-gray, dark roots that blossomed from his scalp since she had last seen him, a man in serious need of a touch-up. In his white T-shirt and dungarees accented with a wrench, he was all dressed up, ostensibly speaking, to go off and fix somebody's toilet, a plumber with designer footwear, Italian shoes he'd pilfered from a men's store, a proud accomplishment he refused to relegate to his closet at the Good Night's Sleep.

"I brought you a present," he said.

"If it's three hundred dollars, it's too—"

"It's not money."

"What then?"

He fell silent, studying the mat of red wire that passed for her hair. "Did you get a new wig?"

"No."

He examined the white cotton shirt with suspenders and red plaid skirt she wore. "Did you get a new costume?"

"No."

"Something is different about you. What is it?" After piercing Jessabelle's extra thick glasses with his own steady gaze, he stamped his foot and snapped his fingers. "I know what it is." He raised an eyebrow. "You're in love, aren't you?"

Her hair, makeup, and clothes were the same as the day he'd dropped her off. She wondered what he saw in her that made him think she was in love.

Laughter tickled her, spurting from her, when she realized the love she felt inside was so strong, he had perceived it through layers of disguise. She decided to play along, at the same time distracting him from the statue, the step van, or whatever else he had come to harass her about. "Yeah," she boasted. "I'm in love."

"Who's the lucky guy?"

Jessabelle paused for a very long moment. She didn't know how to answer that question. It wasn't *a* guy, but the "Indian guru," Vishva, Johann, Chet, Bennie, and Doc. How was she supposed to explain this to Uncle Trix?

You wouldn't give me $300, but I got it anyway. I went to a Day of Practice. Now I'm swimming in an ocean of love and gratitude so deep it makes me cry and fills me with love for everybody and everything.

Uncle Trix was too degenerate to accept that. In fact, if Jessabelle wasn't experiencing it herself and somebody told her that, she'd probably be too depraved not to laugh out loud.

"C'mon," Uncle Trix urged. "Tell me. Who's the lucky guy?"

Jessabelle paused for another very long moment. She

wanted to share her Day of Practice with Uncle Trix. In fact, she wanted to tell the whole world about it. While her experience may sound a bit strange or unbelievable, she felt as if there was nothing more natural than to experience love and gratitude as deeply as she had. At the same time, the experience was so valuable to her she felt she needed to protect it, just as somebody might guard an expensive jewel. She didn't know if she could trust Uncle Trix.

"Maybe, just maybe," she finally said, "I'll tell you about it sometime."

Like a man bit by a scorpion while simultaneously polishing off a bottle of whiskey, Uncle Trix flew into sudden rage. "Damnit!"

She took a step backward. "What's wrong?"

"Don't play dumb with me, Jessie. You know this is not the time to be falling in love. I found an antiquities dealer with links to the Russian Mafia. The guy will pay cash for the statue. You just need to find it."

"What's so great about finding the statue, anyway?"

"What's so great about finding three million dollars? Only an idiot would ask a question like that!"

Uncle Trix's exclamation made her feel like she was five years old again and had just met Uncle Trix for the first time.

He'd stayed the night at Mr. and Mrs. Macadoo's, and before he left the following morning, the four of them shared a breakfast of blueberry pancakes. When they finished, after a short conference with his watch, Uncle Trix rose from the table. Jessabelle heard a coinslide as all his spare change rolled to the bottom of his pocket. He picked up his coffee cup and plate, carried them to the sink, and smiled at Mrs. Macadoo. "Thanks for the finest grub I've eaten in months."

He returned to the table carrying the chink, chink, chinkling of the change in his pocket. Mr. Macadoo got to his feet and held out a hand. They shook.

After they separated, Uncle Trix placed an arm on Jessabelle's shoulder.

"I hear you have a piggy bank," he said.

Jessabelle bobbed her head.

"Before I go, I want to give you something you can feed Mr. Piggy for breakfast." He scooped a handful of coins from his pocket and selected a nickel, dime, and quarter that he set on the table before Jessabelle. "Choose the one you want."

Jessabelle quickly surveyed her choices. She understood that twenty-five was a higher number than ten or five, but she picked up the dime. "I'll take this one."

"Why?" Uncle Trix asked.

"Because it's so shiny and small, it's the prettiest of all."

"But the quarter is worth more."

"I know, Uncle Trix, but Mr. Piggy isn't that hungry. He doesn't want something big, just something that makes his stomach feel pretty and good."

"That is the stupidest thing I ever heard. You can buy more candy with a quarter than a dime."

"So? Too much candy puts holes in your teeth and brain."

Mr. Macadoo laughed and said, "Can't argue with that logic." He lovingly rubbed the back of Jessabelle's hair.

"I could," Uncle Trix said, "if I had the time. If I didn't have to get on the road, I'd stay and educate this stupid kid you're raising."

"She can already identify one hundred and twenty-five parts of the body and knows two hundred animals by name," Mrs. Macadoo said. "If you ask me, that's smart."

"Whoopee! It doesn't matter if she can name one thousand animals if she doesn't know two thousand and five hundred dollars is better than one thousand dollars."

Jessabelle blinked, staring off into the clusters of bushes

along the front gate of Lalliville. She realized Uncle Trix had just said something she didn't hear.

"Look at me when I'm talking to you." The sharp prongs of his thumb and fingers clamped onto the sides of her jaw, and Uncle Trix twisted her head. She had no choice but to face him. "What's so great about finding three million dollars?" he repeated as if she hadn't heard him the first time. "What kind of an idiot are you?"

She wanted to tell Uncle Trix she wasn't an idiot. She just wasn't that hungry. What difference did three million dollars make to a person with one hundred million in the bank? That's how rich she felt. But he was gripping her jaw so tightly, it made moving her mouth difficult.

"Answer," he insisted.

"Please," she managed. "Please let go."

The tips of his digits slackened; he dropped his hand, but not his ire. "You want to go back to working at Wally's?"

She massaged her jaw. "No."

"Well, that's what you'll be doing if you don't find the statue."

She burst out crying, not because of what he'd said, but because she had never realized how deeply sad she was. She was also crying because she had never realized just how much love it was possible for her to feel.

"Yeah, go ahead and cry, because that's what you'll be doing if you got to go back to Wally's."

In the face of his insults, she felt nothing but gratitude toward Uncle Trix. "Thanks for everything, Uncle Trix."

"What the hell is wrong with you?"

She shook her head. "Nothing."

"I can handle that you borrowed the step van without telling me. What I can't handle is you messing up our chance at three million dollars."

The dam broke. She couldn't hold it anymore. She told

Uncle Trix about her Day of Practice and all the experiences
of love she'd had since.

After, he said, "Love, love, love. You keep talking about
love, but what is so great about love?"

"I'm not talking about love as we're used to thinking
about love," she sobbed. "The love I'm talking about gives me
profound gratitude for everything, including you."

"If I didn't know you," Uncle Trix said, "I'd swear you
were on drugs."

She wanted to tell Uncle Trix how this newfound love
made her feel clean and unfettered, like a newborn or a person without a past. But she couldn't because all the tears
prevented her from putting more words together. Finally, she
managed, "It's the love that's got me crying."

"You may be in love now, but this isn't the real world. In
the real world, you can't live on love alone!"

Insecurity knifed her from every direction. Maybe Uncle
Trix was right. She might be full now, but she was scheduled
to leave this place in a month. If she didn't leave with the
statue, she wouldn't have the money to return to Creativo.
Without that, her choices looked grim. The reality of working
at Wally's the rest of her life closed in on her.

He dredged up a handgun from somewhere down the
side of his pants and slapped it in her palm. "Here's your present, something actually useful."

She glanced at the high-caliber weapon with the sleek
handle, and all at once, her good feeling turned to fear. "I
don't want it." She attempted to stuff the gun back in his
hand.

She heard a voice from behind. "Isa."

The handgun fell to the ground. Expecting it to fire upon
impact, she covered her head, but the gun didn't go off. Uncle
Trix snatched it up and shoved it back down the side of his
dungarees, its place of concealment.

Bennie bounced up, smiling and happy. Panic spread through her. If Uncle Trix found out Bennie was special to her in any way, he might use it against her. She needed to protect Bennie. "You slimy toad," she yelled at him. "If you don't get lost, I'm going to throw you into a green pit where you belong."

Bennie smiled, drew his foot back, and kicked her shin so hard it hurt.

"Oww!" She took hold of the injured body part.

Seeing her in real pain, Bennie shrank back in horror. "This is practice, isn't it? That's why you were yelling at me, right?"

"No! This is for real! Get out of here!"

Stunned, Bennie said, "But we're friends." Bennie glanced up at Uncle Trix. "Are you a friend of hers too?"

"I'm her best friend," Uncle Trix said.

"My name's Bennie. What's yours?"

Uncle Trix extended a hand to shake Bennie's. Bennie raised an arm, but before their two hands touched, Jessabelle pushed him. "No joke! Get out of here!"

"Okay already." Bennie moved off in a huff.

"Friend, huh?" asked Uncle Trix

"He's no friend. Can't you see the way I treated him?"

"You can't kid a kidder." He patted the place over the handgun. "If you won't use it, maybe I will." He leveled his gaze at her. "Find the statue, or you just might find your friend with a bullet hole in his head." He laughed. "And if that doesn't inspire you to get moving, maybe we'll kidnap this Lalli person and torture her until she tells us where it is."

Chapter 29

Jessabelle parted ways with Uncle Trix, his threat to shoot Bennie or kidnap Lalli floating over her like a flesh-eating creature tied to her finger by a string. When she reached the shed, Bennie was sliding the folding table on its side, inch by inch, out onto the grass.

"If you ever again see that man in the dungarees and white T-shirt," Jessabelle told him, "run the other way."

"Why?"

"He secretes an odorless body odor. It's highly toxic. If you breathe it, you will die." Jessabelle pushed the back of the folding table, speeding its movement across the grass.

"But you stood right next to him and you didn't die."

"I'm immune to his poison."

They laid the table face down on the grass. Bennie opened

the legs on one side of the table, clicking them into place, while she did the same on the other side. "I'm not afraid of that man," he said.

"You should be."

"You're the one who scares me. You're acting really weird."

"I just want you to be safe." She turned the table right side up, setting it on its legs.

Bennie pressed his hands on the table, testing its stability. "Oh, now you want me to be safe. Earlier, you wanted me to go away. Make up your mind. Do you want me to go away? Or do you want me to be safe?"

"I want you to be safe."

He rolled his eyes and then went off toward the shed. A moment later he returned, his arms spread to each side of a picture frame. He set it on the table and began cleaning, clearing a circle in a coating of filth over its glass. Through that opening shone the Free & Blissful Yogi's face. When Jessabelle met his gaze, it was as if his two eyes became streams of light confluencing into a sacred river that surged into her heart and flowed through her, carrying her in a definite course, returning her to love.

While she did not deserve this love, there it was, inside, its rippling current urging her onward, encouraging her to be strong.

She didn't realize she was crying again until Bennie stopped what he was doing and asked, "Hey, you okay?"

Jessabelle nodded.

"Then why are you crying? You mad 'cause I kicked you?"

"No. I'm happy you kicked me. It hurt."

"You're happy it hurt?"

"It means you're progressing." All the time they'd spent training seemed to be paying off. A street fighter recharging on Brussels sprouts had seemed odd at first, but she could no longer argue with his formula for success. "Defending against someone with a gun, it's time to put all niceties aside."

"A gun? Who said anything about a gun? My Troubles don't carry guns."

"You never know when you might meet some who do."

At their training session that day, she taught him advanced fight moves, including the headbutt to the face. She also showed him how to knock someone out by going for pain sensitive-spots, like the liver, kidneys, shin bone, and testicles, and striking these spots repeatedly. She instructed him on how to hit the chin, temples, top of the head, and not let up, all the while wondering, *Will we make it through alive?*

Fifty yards from the shed, Bennie's body slumped inert, splayed face-down on the grass. He'd been trying to run when Uncle Trix fired the lethal shot, riveting the back of his head. Now his head weighed upon the earth, blasted open like a cantaloupe smashed by a crowbar, exhibiting a bloody mess. The cavity where his brain used to be gaped at Jessabelle.

Jessabelle rolled Bennie in her arms, lifted, and carried him. Blood soaked her white shirt, gushed onto her red plaid skirt, dripped onto her white tennis shoes. "It's all my fault," she wailed.

Her eyes flew open; she almost screamed.

The bark of the cypress tree was grinding through her white shirt, into her back. She adjusted her position, moving closer to Doc. Eyes closed, breathing steadily, he was lost in meditation.

She'd hoped meditation might help alleviate the horrible visions she'd been having of a dead Bennie. But no matter where she went, there they were: figments of Bennie gunned down.

Helplessly, she stared at Doc, just as he opened his eyes. He returned her gaze. "What's up?"

A commotion roared inside. All she had to do was tell him her real name and why she'd come here, tell him who and what he must be aware of. Maybe he could call for reinforcements, get the police or some other law enforcement agency to help him protect Lalliville from danger.

But she just couldn't bring herself to tell him. If she did, all that love, the good feeling she'd amassed, this new life she hoped for—she could kiss it all goodbye.

Was any of it really hers to begin with? There was no such thing as a life of truth founded on deception. She might as well just dump it down the drain now and accept feeling bad about herself for the rest of her life. There was nothing wrong with being messed up. Crap! Ninety-nine percent of the people she met out there in the world were, if not fully, then at least slightly deranged.

She could live with being a societal outcast; she'd already been one for some time. What she couldn't live with was Bennie getting hurt on account of something she didn't do. All she needed to do to keep him out of harm's way was figure out the location of the golden Shiva and inform Uncle Trix about it.

She didn't want to locate the statue for Uncle Trix so he could steal it.

But it's for the best, she told herself. She had to do it to keep Bennie and Lalli from getting hurt.

This man seated before her now—he was Doc Halloway. Surely he knew something about the statue. *No more pussy-footing around*, she told herself. She planned to just say, I hear your father once gave Lalli a statue. From there, depending on his response, she'd escort him through a line of probing questions until she got what she wanted, a solid lead on the golden Shiva.

But she couldn't bring herself to do it. She couldn't use Doc to reach her own goal. He'd been nothing but a gentleman to her, except for that one digression when he'd tried to rip her wig off. That hardly compared to traveling around ripping off people's wallets and trust. If tearing a woman's wig from her head was Jessabelle's only sin, she wouldn't be in her current jam.

"Are you okay?" he asked.

"Yes." The word came out as weak as a single drop of beige paint mixed in a gallon of water.

He placed his hand over hers. "Are you sure?"

"I'm worried about Bennie."

"Why?"

Because she had to give a reason, Jessabelle muttered something about being afraid his Troubles might get him.

"You're worried about his Troubles getting him here? That doesn't make any sense."

Jessabelle got to her feet and announced she was going off to find Bennie. "I need to see he's okay. It's the only way I'll stop worrying." Doc rose too, volunteering to come with her on the basis that he knew where they could find Bennie. He took her hand and tugged her along with him.

About twenty minutes later, Jessabelle stood beside Doc as he rapped on Lalli's door. Lalli and Bennie appeared behind the screen, fit and healthy as ever, him in a bright silk kurta, her in a white cotton sari. Doc explained they'd come to make sure Bennie was okay.

"Maybe I can sleep here," Jessabelle offered Lalli, "on your floor, to protect you and Bennie."

Lalli put a hand on Bennie's shoulder, gazing down at him for clues about Jessabelle's concern. He shrugged. "I told you she's been acting weird."

After a moment of unresolved confusion about why Jessabelle felt the need to pose as a guard dog, Bennie changed the subject by hopping up and down, begging Lalli, "Can Doc and Isa play charades with us? Huh? Can they?"

Lalli declined Jessabelle's offer to sleep on her floor, but she invited Jessabelle and Doc to join her and Bennie for the game. Jessabelle wasn't sure if the invitation to charades was a concession for not being able to sleep on Lalli's floor; nonetheless, she was more than willing to accept what she could get.

Doc and Jessabelle left their shoes at the door, then followed Lalli and Bennie into the living room while Bennie explained the rules of the game. With no words, only gestures, they were to act out Way of Truth teachings. Sounds were allowed.

Lalli's living room contained simple furnishings—a couch and a loveseat, upholstered in fabric patterned with vines of pink roses. A framed portrait of the Free & Blissful Yogi, etched in glass, lit from behind, graced one wall. Beneath it, a long shelf ran the length of the wall. It held a stereo with a turntable, AM/FM radio, and CD player, flanked by speakers. At the far end, next to the speaker on the left, was "Merging," Vaughn Fabrizzi's twelve-inch-high statue of a mermaid. Scales flecked her skin. She had long hair, a woman's breasts, and the tail of whale. Seated on a short stretch of beach, with her head turned over her shoulder, she gazed off into the distance (presumably out to sea), her face filled with yearning.

Jessabelle had heard that Fabrizzi, the famous marine life artist, lived somewhere in Florida. In mediums of painting, sculpture, and photography, he captured the majesty of dolphins and gray whales. "Merging" was the only mythological figure he'd ever sculpted. As one of a kind with no reproductions, it was worth a small fortune, somewhere in the neighborhood of half a million dollars. Before now she'd seen it only in pictures, as an art student.

In art college, the mermaid hadn't caught her interest the

same way it did in this new context of Lalli's living room.
Gazing at the mermaid from the place on the loveseat Lalli
offered her, Jessabelle felt a kinship with the figure, and not
just because of the day the heat had scorched her makeup,
making her face appear rough and scaled. Taking in the figure, possessing the upper body of a woman and lower body of
a fish, Jessabelle felt like a woman divided, trapped on Uncle
Trix's beach while hungering to exist in an environment of
deep love—her true home.

What was "Merging" doing in Lalli's living room? She
wanted to ask, but the question seemed too abrupt.

Doc and Bennie moved Lalli's light mahogany coffee
table into a corner of the room. It was an artistic table, rectangular in shape with a hand-carved rendering of a banyan
tree on its inch-thick top. The table's displacement freed a
bushy area rug, a perfect stage for their game of charades.

Bennie took his place front and center of that stage. He
held up six fingers.

"Six words," Lalli said.

Bennie again held up six fingers.

"Sixth word."

Bennie tugged his earlobe.

"Sounds like."

Bennie squatted, wrapping his hands tightly around his
knees. Maintaining that position, he did three front sommer-
saults. Then he rolled once to his right and five times to his
left. His curled form spun on a diagonal, and then out on a
straight line.

Lalli, Jessabelle, and Doc guessed "gymnast" "turning"
and "rolling" as Bennie tumbled around Lalli's floor. With
each hypothesis, Bennie only stopped long enough to close
his eyes and shake his head emphatically.

He looked so serious, Jessabelle had to suppress a laugh,
the first one that had arisen since Uncle Trix had threatened

to shoot the boy if she didn't find the golden Shiva.

Lalli and Doc threw up a few more conjectures about Bennie's sixth word, but missed. Lalli finally hit it with "ball." When she did, Bennie's arms and legs flew open. He sat up, and with a satisfied smile, gave a frenzied nod.

The laughter Jessabelle had restrained earlier erupted. She just couldn't help herself; it felt so good to see Bennie alive and well.

Bennie jumped to his feet. Chopping the top of his arm, he indicated that while the sixth word rhymed with ball, it began with an A.

"All."

Another frantic nod. Bennie held up one finger.

"First word."

He cupped a hand over his eyes, gazing out from under that hand as if he was noticing something.

"Look," Lalli guessed.

Bennie waved his hands in circles toward his body as if to say, You're close. Keep your guesses coming along those same lines.

"See," Lalli said.

"See the One in the All," Doc guessed.

"Yes!"

Doc and Bennie switched places. Bennie took his seat on the loveseat while Doc assumed his place on the carpet.

Through gesture, Doc communicated that he was beginning with the third word of a five-word teaching. Then he stood erect with his hands raised straight overhead, palms together. He rumbled and shook. Explosive sounds streamed from his mouth.

After much guessing on the part of the other three players, it came out that Doc was a huge rocketship lifting off the ground, taking flight into outer space. Space. That was the word he was shooting for. Live in Space, Not Time. Word by word, syllable by syllable, that was the teaching he expressed.

Since Lalli had guessed it, her turn came next. For the first word of a seven-word teaching, Lalli sat crosslegged on the floor, arranging her sari so it covered her legs. She placed both hands on her thighs, holding thumb and forefingers together. She closed her eyes. Her breath came in and went out slowly. Jaya Shiva Om whistled on it, musically, like the sound of a flute lilting on a breeze.

Jessabelle, Doc, and Bennie quietened, listening. Jessabelle relaxed; her eyelids became heavy with pins and needles. She fought to keep them open as Doc and Bennie closed their eyes, falling into meditation. Doc's head drooped.

After a few moments Lalli unfolded her legs, got to her feet. She moved to the edge of the room, picked up a small brass mallet, and clocked a small gong. With its sound vibrations reverberating through the room, Doc's head suddenly popped up, his eyes alert. "Meditation Brings You into Alignment with Universal Consciousness," he blurted.

"You're correct," Lalli told him.

Doc forfeited pantomiming another teaching, insisting Jessabelle go instead of him, since she hadn't yet taken a turn.

Jessabelle stood front and center carpet, arms at her sides, gazing at the ceiling. Her mind whirred past all the teachings she'd heard since arriving in Lalliville: *Don't Believe Everything You Think. Make the Present Moment Your Friend. You Create Your Own Reality.* So many to choose from. Finally she decided on Dance Your Spirit High. It was from a small book Lalli had written, *Practical Spirituality.* Jessabelle had found it one afternoon among the books in Krishna's Corner.

Jessabelle held up four fingers.

"Four words," Bennie said.

She held up one finger.

"First word."

Jessabelle thrust up her arms, holding them parallel to the ground. She moved, evoking the illusion of a wave traveling from her right fingers through her wrist, elbow, shoulder, and chest, cockling all the way to the tip of her left fingers. Further movement on Jessabelle's part had the wave rolling in reverse, receding all the way back to where it started. Jessabelle undulated, creating a rippling motion through her body, from the top of her head out her right toes, and back again. The wave swept up and down her body and from side to side.

"Liquid," Doc guessed.

Jessabelle shook her head.

"Wave," said Bennie.

Jessabelle gave him the signal that he was on the right track.

"Ocean?"

Jessabelle shook her head, realizing with her chosen hip hop dance moves, she was leading them astray. The residual sound of Jaya Shiva Om playing in her head became a fast and furious tempo, fueling her animation. Before she knew it, she was doing a coarse imitation of the break dancers she'd seen on the streets of some of the big cities she'd visited. She glided back and forth on Lalli's floor. She jumped to the left, and jumped to the right. She kicked her feet, one and then the other. She drove her left arm high into the air, chucked her right arm out low. Her fingers smacked "Merging." The mermaid rocked unsteadily. Jessabelle's heart thudded over the lady's potential crash. With both hands, Jessabelle held the feminine form at the navel until she came to a stop.

"I'm sorry," she told Lalli, patting her heart in an attempt at easing her own internal distress. "Got a little carried away there. Didn't mean to hit 'Merging.'"

"Ooh," Lalli said, "you know the name of the sculpture."

"I know something of sculpture." Seizing this opportunity to find out where the statue came from, Jessabelle asked, "Was it a gift?"

Lalli nodded. "As with everything else I have received in my life."

"Your house isn't even locked. Aren't you afraid somebody will take it?"

Lalli gave a small shake of her head. "If somebody takes it, then I guess it's not mine anymore."

Jessabelle moved out of the wings and back onstage, to the center of the area rug, wondering whether she should dance again or move on to enacting her chosen teaching with other physical clues.

"You must know about a lot more than just sculpture if you've made a birdsuit fly." Everything was going well again. Why had Lalli had to remind her of the birdsuit?

"You know about that?"

"I'm informed about the people and happenings in this town. So tell me, Isa Newton, what do you know about sculpture?"

"I'm a sculptor of sorts," Jessabelle told Lalli. "I draw people and make models of what I draw." She decided to leave out the part about how she fits prosthetic appliances to the models.

"I want to show you something that as a sculptress, I'm sure you'll find inspiring." Lalli told Jessabelle to meet her on the corner of Strength and Liberation the next day, when the sun reached its highest point in the sky. Then Lalli would take her to this thing of interest.

"Hey," Bennie pleaded, "can we get back to the game? Dance, right? The word just hit me."

Chapter 30

Jessabelle couldn't wait to see what Lalli's surprise was. Lalli hadn't called it a surprise, but this thing Lalli thought Jessabelle would find "inspiring" bore all the mystery and excitement of one.

In the absence of a sundial, Jessabelle checked in on the sun all morning, waiting for the time it ascended to the highest peak of its daily trip across the sky. Then she zipped over to the corner of Strength and Liberation, where she found Lalli waiting. It was the exact moment of noon.

In the clear dome of sky overhead, the sun burned like fire and shone like gold. Sweat stuck to the front and back of Jessabelle's white shirt, making her feel sticky. "It's hot out here," she said, stating the obvious. She could hear that voice sounded anxious.

"Maybe you should try fewer layers," Lalli suggested with a sly smile.

Jessabelle glanced down at her clothes. Along with her white shirt buttoned all the way to the top, she wore her Neptune-blue plaid skirt, vest, and bowtie, the same boring outfit she'd donned at least ten times in the past month. If she took that off, she'd be left walking through Lalliville in nothing but white knee socks with white cotton bra and underwear. She wasn't sure that was the kind of de-layering Lalli had in mind.

Lalli rested her eyes on Jessabelle's face, then rolled them up to her wig. *Oh, all that*, Jessabelle thought, and experienced one of those moments when she felt sure she couldn't confess anything to Lalli she didn't already know.

"Don't get me wrong," Jessabelle said with a nervous half-smile, "I really love it here." As Lalli led Jessabelle along Strength, Jessabelle listed everything she loved about the place: the brilliant red-orange sunsets, the pigs, the kind people. "Oh, and the trees," Jessabelle said. "I just love that grove where the cypress reign."

Lalli listened. With her long white shirt undotted by sweat, she seemed untouched by the heat, a moving statue of herself placed here from who knew where, incapable of being effected by the extremes of this world.

They walked all the way to the end of Devotion before Lalli stopped in front of one of the houses, a single-story house, soft red.

"You want to show me a house?" Jessabelle asked.

"Not just any house, but the House of the Deities." Lalli unlocked and opened the door. An alarm beeped. Lalli punched the code to silence it.

Jessabelle followed Lalli as the guru wound through rooms, introducing her to the deities they passed along the way. There was Hanuman, with the face of a monkey and a well-built human body strong as a gorilla's. Cast in bronze, his stance was courageous, exuding physical strength, intelligence. He clasped a club with a long shaft funneling up into a large head. With this weapon in hand, the monkey-like humanoid seemed the perfect hero, capable of delivering powerful blows.

Jessabelle's phone rang. She took it out of her breast pocket just in time to see the name Uncle Trix flash across the top of the screen. She powered off the phone and shoved it back in her pocket, out of sight.

"This is Lakshmi, goddess of wealth, love, and beauty."

Jessabelle faced a painted plaster statue of a fair-skinned lady with four arms, standing on a lotus, wearing a soft pink sari. Another lovely lady stood by her side. Clothed in a white sari, seated on a white lotus, she played a stringed instrument with a long neck and a gourdlike chamber, an unusual violin. "Who's this?"

"Saraswati, the goddess of speech and learning, who plays her veena for God."

Lalli guided Jessabelle into the main room. "I'm sure you know Shiva."

Jessabelle gaped at Shiva with his glowing eyes. His long locks of hair, streaked with light and drawn up at the sides, spiraled into a bun that sat on the crown of his lustrous head. Precious rings hung from his ears. A bright serpent adorned his neck and two more his biceps. He wore three exquisite malas around his neck. Two were molded as part of the statue; the third was loose, a gleaming replica of the others.

He sat crosslegged, in meditation, holding up his left hand, palm toward her, with the thumb and index finger joined in a circle. His right forearm rested in the U-shaped crook of his carved stick, a small resplendent mala dangling from between his thumb and ring finger.

Jessabelle was hardly able to believe her eyes as she gazed

upon the golden Shiva, appearing bright but not shiny, radiant but not glittery, just like genuine gold.

When her tongue again began working, she turned toward Lalli, trying to sound cool. "He must do a lot of japa if he needs a stick to hold up his arm."

"His danda stick keeps him comfortable through hours of japa meditation."

Turning toward Shiva once again, Jessabelle's cool melted. "Wow!" She caressed Shiva's abdomen, running her fingers over his surface, soft like gold. She walked around the statue, searching for any discoloration that might reveal any other metal beneath the gold. She found none. Coming out on his other side, she'd concluded he was the real deal, not the kind of fool's gold she and Uncle Trix peddled in front of Wally's.

In this knowing, Jessabelle felt Lalli's gaze upon her.

Fear bolted through Jessabelle, jolting her with the belief that Lalli saw everything about her. Lalli knew she'd come to this town for the golden Shiva.

I just wanted the money to go back to college! Jessabelle nearly blurted. She didn't want to buy a mansion, yacht, or fancy island vacation. She was not a lavish person. Couldn't Lalli see she didn't want or need a lot of things? Just room + board, tuition, supplies.

Her propensity for lying was not even hers. It was more like a family tradition she'd gotten sucked into. But no. Family tradition was cake on your birthday, or a visit to Grandma every summer. Her problem was more like a malady, a genetic disease she'd inherited at birth, something she didn't want but was forced to live with. Some people got blonde hair or blue eyes from their parents. She'd acquired an inclination toward dishonesty from hers.

Thievery never even felt like it belonged to her. But was it just a pipe dream to think she could ever live a life of truth? Was there any point in striving for moral health? Or was it only a matter of time before she was completely eaten by her disease, going the way of the rest of her family and ending up in prison?

Maybe she was and always would be nothing but a thief and a liar. Maybe that's why she'd known so many thieves and liars in her life. Why, she was thinking right at that moment that she needed to return Uncle Trix's call at her earliest possible convenience.

"Shiva was a gift," Lalli said, "from one devoted to the Truth, Jordan Halloway. Do you know him?"

"No." Jessabelle's voice cracked.

"His generosity knows no limits," Lalli said. "He often pays for special food served here in the dining hall.

"Of course he can afford to be generous. He has lots of money."

"I thought you didn't know him."

Jessabelle paced the circumference of the Shiva statue, restlessly. "I never met him." She scratched her side, wild as a dog with fleas. "I've only heard about him, from Doc."

"Doc told you his father has lots of money?"

As someone who had spent three years conning people, why wasn't Jessabelle better at it? Because Lalli was not the average Wally's shopper, capable of being conned, and Jessabelle knew that. Lalli had power, real power. Jessabelle felt it now as a vibration of love that flowed toward her, chipping away at her facade.

The confusion over who she was that started the day Jessabelle arrived in Lalliville escalated with each step around the Shiva statue.

Lalli invited Jessabelle to have a seat beside her and relax a moment. Jessabelle accepted. But as soon as her butt hit the ground, she started twiddling her thumbs.

Lalli took Jessabelle's hand. "Generosity doesn't come from a big bank account but an open heart." Jessabelle felt herself relaxing as Lalli continued. "I heard that Jordon once paid off fifty dollars on a struggling father's layaway gifts for his son. He was twenty at the time, he himself a struggling young art dealer whose daily wage was about fifty dollars." Lalli's gaze penetrated Jessabelle. "Jordon is not afraid to give. With one hand he receives; with the other, he gives. Giving is an attitude that opens the heart. In an open heart, abundance flows both ways."

Jessabelle mulled that over, trying to understand. "I know a man who has lots but won't give anybody fifty dollars, unless he gets something in return."

"Who is this man?"

"An enemy."

Lalli leaned toward Jessabelle. She dropped her voice, becoming intimate and personal. "Then why not make him your friend? We fight our enemies and keep on fighting them. Our vices never leave. Make friends with them and the fighting ceases."

Jessabelle didn't understand why anybody should make friends with their vices, or a guy like Uncle Trix.

"Could you explain what you mean?"

"Vices have power. If you resist them, they will persist. Make friends with them and you take away their power. Hatred can take the form of anything, but not if you make peace with everything. There is only one in all."

Make peace with everything? Jessabelle wasn't sure Lalli really understood her unique situation. In an attempt to explain it to some extent, she said, "That man I mentioned, he has this niece, Jessabelle. Jessabelle travels around with her uncle. One time in Alaska, it was so cold, Jessabelle's breath puffed out as fluffy white as clouds in the sky and her snot froze before it dripped out her nose. Her uncle had two scarves around his neck; Jessabelle had none. She asked if she could borrow one of his. He said no. 'Please,' she said, 'I'm really cold.' Still he said no." Jessabelle paused. "What do you think about that?"

"What do you think about it?"

"I think Jessabelle's uncle is greedy."

"Does Jessabelle still travel with him?"

"Sort of."

"Why does Jessabelle stay with him?"

"I guess she thinks someday their relationship will pay off in a big way."

"That makes Jessabelle sound greedy."

"Jessabelle has nothing. How can you give if you don't have anything to give?"

"Everybody's got something to give."

Jessabelle tried to remember a time she had given someone something. Between the period when she was about six and ten years old, Mom's refrigerator was covered with pictures of monsters and animals Jessabelle drew for her. After that, monster and animal masks graced the walls. She liked giving them to Mom, but who but a mom liked receiving something like that?

"You give your time to clean the shed," Lalli said, "and help Bennie rid himself of his Troubles."

It was true, although she wasn't cleaning right now, and she hadn't exactly transformed Bennie into a bulldog. Not yet, anyway.

"Jessabelle doesn't want to be greedy," Jessabelle said. "She wants to be a devotee, learn to be more like Jordon Halloway."

"How do you know what she wants?"

"I'm a close friend of hers."

Silence followed. Jessabelle thought Lalli might tell her to invite her friend to come to this town. Then Jessabelle could tell Uncle Trix about the statue, thereby saving Bennie and Lalli. And once that was done, she could leave today as

Isa and return another day as Jessabelle. Lalli's invitation was not forthcoming.

"Do you think Jessabelle can be a devotee like other people here are devotees?"

"If she wants. Of course, she would have to apply like everybody else. At any rate, I don't care whether she becomes a devotee. I don't need devotees for the sake of having more devotees."

"She would not be a usual devotee. That's for sure."

"There are no usual devotees. Whoever you are, you can realize Truth from wherever you are, in whatever you are doing."

Truth. Hearing the word from Lalli's lips almost brought tears to Jessabelle's eyes. Truth. She felt so near to it. "I want Truth."

"It's easy to say 'I want Truth,' but quite another thing to realize it. But it can be done. Has been done. The goal of creation is to realize the Truth. It's the purpose of human life. Many people pursue only worldly things. They're born and live their whole lives without getting one step closer to the Truth. You cannot find Truth in books. You must experience it."

Jessabelle was so content listening to Lalli, she felt she could sit right where she was, just as she was, all day into forever, listening to Lalli.

"Tell me more about Truth."

"Truth is indescribable, yet as humans, we speak about it. Why don't you tell me about Truth?"

"I don't know anything about Truth."

"Don't pretend to be ignorant of Truth."

But I am ignorant of Truth.

Lalli gestured toward Shiva. "Reciting his mantra is a vehicle that will carry you to the Truth."

Lalli became silent, and in this silence, she began

repeating the mantra aloud, Jaya Shiva Om, turning her japa bracelet. After a moment she stopped, and handed Jessabelle her beads. She instructed her to hold the japa beads over the ring finger of her right hand, just like Shiva was. Starting at the odd hanging bead that Lalli called the "guru" bead, she was to move the beads one-by-one with her thumb, repeating Jaya Shiva Om at each bead. Lalli told her to go around the mala until she reached the guru bead again, and then turn and go back round again, never crossing over the guru bead.

Jessabelle passed the beads through her fingers the way Lalli prescribed. As if the beads were infused with Lalli's energy, they drew her inside. Lalli repeated the mantra. Jessabelle joined her, sinking deeper into meditation with each turn of the mala.

The golden Shiva appeared in Jessabelle's mind's eye, seated in a house, much like the one she was in now. Saints Jessabelle recognized from their pictures in the shed were there too, alive and doing japa. Lalli walked toward her. She said, "You can have what you want." She motioned, inviting her toward the Shiva statue.

Jessabelle took a step toward him, and his golden beads started to move. He came to life, a golden person seated on radiant earth, repeating the mantra. He beckoned her closer.

Another step toward him, and he opened his eyes—black onyx set in gold. She stood before him staring. Mesmerized by his beauty, she couldn't take her eyes off him.

The symphony of Jaya Shiva Oms vibrated throughout her body.

Shiva stood up, moved toward her, spread his arms wide, and wrapped her in them. And she felt them encircling the length of her whole body. Their two bodies dissolved, becoming one, and in the fusing, they both became clear, glimmering, glowing light. She knew it was the light of the one in the all, of conciousness, of Truth. It was in her and she was in it.

Like the soft melody of a song interjecting itself into a dream, Lalli's voice came from far off, Jaya Shiva Om, guiding her back to the House of the Deities.

A moment after Jessabelle opened her eyes, Lalli stood up. Sadness hooked Jessabelle, for she knew her time in this house had come to an end. She returned Lalli's mala.

On their way out, Lalli reset the alarm and locked the door.

Back on the sidewalk, Jessabelle wanted to follow Lalli wherever she went, all the way to the end of the earth if that's where she was going. But Lalli said, "You can go now." It was an even statement void of any emotion, a simple instruction.

Jessabelle didn't want to say goodbye, but knew the choice wasn't hers. She glanced at her high-tech watch, realizing it was already getting close to two o'clock. Two hours had passed since she'd met Lalli. She shook her head in disbelief. It seemed no more than one. She'd missed lunch, but didn't care; her stomach wasn't even growling. Absorbed into Lalli's aura, she was swept into a world that no longer felt like Earth, a dazzling place where hunger and time didn't exist.

"Before we part ways I want to tell you something. It's a message for your friend Jessabelle."

"A message? For Jessabelle?"

"Do you want to hear it?"

Jessabelle nodded.

"What's the use of dwelling on your life with your uncle? Of feeling sorry for yourself?" Lalli's expression was serious. "Of saying 'I am weak in the face of my bad habits?' Of believing you've been treated unjustly? If you want to get from here to there, the bridge must be crossed, and for that to happen, you must take responsibility for yourself. Nobody else can do it for you. I can initiate you, tell you how to meditate, give you dharanas, techniques. But I can't cross the bridge for you. You must make the effort." Sparks of light flew from

Lalli's eyes.

Jessabelle was sure Lalli had just chewed her out, and yet she perceived love in Lalli's words. The corners of Jessabelle's eyes stung. Warm tears rolled down her cheeks. Never had she cried before Awakening, and now there seemed no end to it. "Thank you. I'll tell her, and maybe I'll be able to do it without crying."

"Let the tears roll if they must. They're purifying tears. They come from love. A day may pass, a month, or a year, but love never passes. It's always there. You may cry for a long time, even forever."

Leaving Lalli felt like stepping out of eternity. Moving along Liberation after her talk with Lalli, back into the realm of clocks and work, Lalli's words flitted around Jessabelle's skull, tumbling through her brain in no particular order. "If you want to get from here to there, the bridge must be crossed." "Giving is an attitude that opens the heart." "Hatred can take the form of anything, but not if you make peace with everything." "There is only one in all."

Remembering the way Lalli had looked at her, Jessabelle felt beautiful. It didn't matter that she wore a red wig, mask, crooked horse teeth, big chunky glasses, and dressed like a nerd in a white cotton shirt with suspenders and red plaid skirt. She could be wearing a dress made of black rubber tire treads, accessorized with a hubcap on her head and diesel oil for perfume. Still she'd feel beautiful.

She saw this beauty up in the sky, and in the buildings she passed on Liberation, the gym, the education building, Krishna's Corner, and the Welcome Center.

She saw it in the whole spectrum of this town's shapes. With that array of forms spreading across her inner space, reflecting their loveliness, her sense of beauty opened wide as the sky.

She used to think of beauty as something that could only

be perceived with the eyes. It was either something small and ineffective or something powerful in a way that was not to be trusted.

In many of the movies she'd seen, the beautiful women either ended up as the victim of something, or their beauty disguised the fact that they were manipulative bitches, sociopathic killers, or grotesque aliens from other planets.

The beauty she felt now was not small, trifling, or dangerous. On the contrary, it was power. The power she felt in the world's forms seemed inherent in their very shapes, sizes, and colors, an ever-present beauty residing in everything.

In the face of this beauty, appearances seemed small and unimportant. She'd spent her life designing appearances, as if outward impressions were the most important thing in the world. As if that was all she was, this or that person, this animal or that bug.

On this street called Liberation, she felt like something much bigger than any single form or shape, as if she'd expanded into the shapeless presence behind every one of the world's figures.

It was as if she was the formless, carrying a picture in her pocket. The person in that picture was Jessabelle Knox. In Jessabelle Knox's pocket was a photo of Isa Newton. She was the creator behind the creator, Truth, the Life of the World. In perceiving the essence of all material things, she'd merged with the one in all. In this merging, she understood that just as she'd assumed many shapes, Shiva in his abstract form of pure consciousness animated all the forms of this entire world. Shiva was the most skilled special makeup effects artist of all! She laughed out loud.

Suddenly a fear hit Jessabelle, shattering the beauty of her landscape like a mudball slung at the Mona Lisa, a mudball that stuck, its mucky grime obliterating the Mona Lisa's nose and casting her other features into darkness. Having been in

Lalli's company, Jessabelle was on Liberation, experiencing the bliss of the great Self while Bennie could be off in some corner of Lalliville, dead. She was supposed to be protecting him, not out looking at the world a whole new way.

Swept up in the fear all over again, she started to run. With all these beautiful experiences she was having, she couldn't figure out the reason for the fear. It was a wasp buzzing among fluttering butterflies. While it didn't seem as though it belonged among the experiences, Uncle Trix roamed on the loose, which meant Bennie was in danger.

Back at the shed, she was relieved to find Bennie in his usual sassy mood, hauling out the folding table. "It took you long enough to get here," he said when he saw her. "We've still got plenty of pictures to clean."

Chapter 31

Jessabelle and Doc walked from their meditation in the
Cypress Grove, through the woods to the step van, stopping along the way to surveil the elephant. In a clearing
behind a house the color of green leaves, Myuri stood on
strong, straight legs, her trunk dipped into a wooden trough.
She sucked water into her trunk, then curled the appendage
and squirted the water into her mouth.

Beside her was a circus tent, a giant wheel of a thing with
triangular stripes of rhubarb and peach radiating out from its
axis, a blue flag on its top. An opening at the side of the canvas formed a doorway, over which a marquee read "Myuri's
Place."

Doc told Jessabelle that Myuri made a pilgrimage to
Lalliville every summer; Vishva had arranged this year's food
and accommodations for her.

"That's what you call a guest with special needs," Jessabelle said.

Doc laughed.

A squeaking drew her attention to Fuzz, running around in circles. The sound was coming from his mechanical paw. Earlier that day, at breaktime, Doc had explained that Fuzz had trouble running and needed a new leg. Doc had made the new leg and put it on him, a flexible silicone paw with matching fur, but it creaked. Jessabelle had invited Doc to her workshop on wheels, offering to take him there so he could modify Fuzz's leg with her Allen wrench.

When they arrived at the step van that evening, Jessabelle unlocked the back door and rolled it open. Smells of rubber, foam, and clay wafted out, tickling her nose like good friends. She hopped up and clicked on the light.

Doc followed her inside. "This is really yours?" he asked.

She nodded.

He took in the tiny sink, small oven, and idle space heater in the corner. "Do you live here?"

"Sometimes."

"You're just full of surprises," he said. He glanced at a small drafting table with plans on top. His eyes roved to her wheeled plastic three-door file cabinet, piled on top with professional sculpting tools mixed with a Popsicle stick and a few others, makeshift or handmade. "You actually know how to use all these tools?"

"Umm hmm."

"Where's the Allen wrench?"

She opened the top file cabinet drawer, extricated the wrench from her silver pliers and her pink-handled four-in-one screwdriver, and tossed it to him.

He snatched it midair, and as he did, he caught sight of her vista of inspiration. "Whoa!" He studied the images of different kinds of people and animals, with close-ups of eyes, ears, noses, and other human and animal features. "Where did you get them?"

"Some I snipped from magazines. Most I took myself. Whenever I see an interesting face or body, I march right up to the person, if it's a person, and ask, 'Mind if I take your picture?' With an elephant, you've gotta ask a different way."

"Nobody's ever trampled you?"

"No. Most creatures are glad to have their photo taken, happy somebody has noticed them and wishes to snap their picture. Don't you think people want to be seen?"

"Definitely, but only for their good qualities, not their bad."

His eyes dropped to an assemblage of dark material, wings, and metal tanks on a corner tabletop. "Your birdsuit!"

She scurried to clear the mass.

"Wait!" he said as she spread a plain white bedsheet over the RobinSuit. "I want to see it."

"You can't. Right now it's a robin without its appendages. Not a pretty sight. I had to disconnect the wings to do a flight test."

"I can't wait to see it fly. I still can't believe you've made a birdsuit fly."

She could just tell him, "I haven't. I said I had a birdsuit that could fly just to make myself sound smart and good, but I don't. And right now I'm just winging it, trying to figure out how to make it fly so you won't know I lied, so I won't look bad in your eyes." But if she did, all that good opinion he had of her would be out the window and gone with the next wind. And she'd rather die than lose his good opinion of her. *I have to make the birdsuit fly.*

Fuzz yipped. She wished she knew dog language, in case he had just passed along a tip on how to make this thing work, something he'd picked up from a couple of birds in the neighborhood.

Changing the subject, she indicated a sand-colored wig propped upon a wooden head. "Let's discuss your hair."

"That's my hair?"

Three nights ago she'd measured his head for the wig, cut some flesh-colored nylon lace to fit, and shaped the lace over the wooden head. Her drawer where she kept packets of European, Asian, Angora, goat, and synthetic hair that she ordered from the hair emporium was running low. The closest thing she had to Juggling Baba's hair was fifteen-inch synthetic light blond, so she used it. With a knotting hook she had filled the lace, five synthetic sand-colored hairs at a time, weaving the long blond hair as if she were upholstering a carpet. She'd worked two hours a night, three nights in a row to get it the way Doc saw it on the wooden head.

After pinning up the front of his real hair and slapping a wig cap over his head, she placed the wig on him. The hair fell halfway down his back.

"What do you think?"

"It fits nicely."

"Of course, I still need to cut and style it. Get that whirly wavy thing going. Oh, and the hair color. Tomorrow I'll go to Wally's and get some dye. Next best thing to ordering mahogany-colored hair, rush, and paying for overnight delivery. Soon you'll have Juggling Baba's head of hair."

Doc whipped a ten-dollar bill out of his pocket. "For the hair dye," he said, attempting a hand-off.

"It's okay," she waved, "the product is on me."

"Okay," he said, putting the money away, replacing it with the car key he dangled before her. "Then the gas is on me."

"I don't even know what car is yours."

"Bennie knows Lona."

"Lona?"

"That's my other girlfriend. Take Bennie with you, and he'll show you where she is."

She tucked the keys in her pocket.

"Do you have a name for your truck?"

Jessabelle nodded, made up "Steppy" there on the spot. From there, they moved onto Fuzz's leg.

She covered the table with a clean towel for added comfort, disentangled Fuzz from Doc's arms, and laid him on the table. "I'll hold him while you tweak his leg." Fuzz squirmed. Obviously he didn't like being held on the table. Jessabelle lifted the little guy off it and cradled that large ball of Fuzz called Fuzz in her arms, stroking the top of his head with her index and middle fingers. He calmed.

Doc gave Fuzz's mechanical leg a few turns of the wrench. Then he took Fuzz, hopped out the back of the step van, and transported the puppy to a grassy field on one side of the asphalt. Fuzz ran a few feet, then fell on his side with a whimper.

"Ouch," Jessabelle said for Fuzz.

"It's the lock," Doc said. "Now it's too loose."

Jessabelle went with Doc to Fuzz's side and lifted Fuzz in her arms while Doc tightened the lock.

She set Fuzz back on the grass. He ran a few steps, making snapping sounds as he went.

"There's that sound again," Doc said. "If it doesn't drive him crazy, it'll drive me crazy when he's running around in the middle of the night."

Jessabelle chased Fuzz, scooped him in her arms, and held him. With one more turn of the wrench, Doc made another adjustment.

When she set him on the grass this time, he bounded off with a spring in his gait. No screaking sounds could be heard, only the rustling of wind through the trees beyond the grass.

Doc smiled. Fuzz ran a happy circle and started on another.

"I want you to meet my parents. I was thinking maybe we

could have dinner together. Have a barbecue in the courtyard. Maybe I can even talk my brother into coming with his wife and little boy." The more Doc talked, the more his excitement over the idea grew.

Panic pinched Jessabelle from all directions as she pictured herself seated in the courtyard with Doc's family. She'd already seen their lovely house, and the faces of the people in the family photo looked genuinely kind. She had a biological mother who had died in prison, a missing set of adoptive parents who spent time in jail, and an uncle who was a thief. Most days she was nothing but a thief herself. Under these conditions, how could she talk to them?

They'd do that thing well-bred people did: polite conversation. But they could talk about the weather for only so long before they'd want to know about Jessabelle. Where she went to school, what her parents did for a living, how it was that she came to Lalliville.

If she answered any one of their questions truthfully, they'd gasp and give each other looks they thought she couldn't see, and those looks would say, This girl is all wrong for our Doc. Later, when they were alone, one would tell the other, "I just don't know what Doc sees in that girl."

Could she blame them for their response? "Auntie Isa met Uncle Doc when she went to Lalliville to steal the golden Shiva from our beloved Lalleshwari. The golden Shiva we gave Lalleshwari!" It wasn't a story they'd be proud to tell their grandchildren.

"Well," Doc said. "What do you say?"

"I can't."

"Why not?"

"I've got to finish cleaning the shed."

"That's not something you do every hour of every day, is it?"

"No, but—"

"Well, think about it."

Jessabelle pictured how Mr. and Mrs. Halloway would be dressed. If the elegance of their living room was any indication, it would be well. She compared it to what she had on at that moment, her Neptune-blue plaid skirt, vest, bowtie, and sneakers with painted-over smiley faces.

The headlights of a station wagon coming into the parking lot sent Doc off to locate Fuzz. "Don't want any accidents," he said, shooting off to collect the frolicking pup.

On his way back to Jessabelle, she asked, "What does a girl wear to meet your parents?"

"Oh, I don't know. How about a bear suit? Do you have something like that in your effects?"

"Yes."

"You do?"

"Yes. But would you really want me to wear it to meet your parents?"

"Why not? They're open-minded people. They'll like your creative side."

She smiled at Doc. No one had ever told her she had a creative side—at least not since Mom and Pops. She never thought of her passion for special makeup effects as being anything except survival, something she needed as much as air and water. Take it away and she might as well be dead. Doc's statement that she had a creative side made her feel special in some way, more important. It made it sound like she wasn't all wrong after all. She was just creative.

The next morning, that's what she told herself: *I'm just creative.*

The declaration occurred at about six a.m. She'd arrived at the field beside the shed, encased in her RobinSuit, which came all the way up around her neck. She'd constructed it from Kevlar, a highly durable, lightweight fabric, creating webbed surfaces between her legs and the spaces between her sides and the tips of the wings outstretched. The RobinSuit's only rigid part was the carbon fiber tubing she'd sewn at the front of each wing.

She'd painted the RobinSuit brown with deep orange over the breast and belly, an area she plumped up and puffed out with additional Kevlar. She'd coated the suit all over with feathers the same colors, finishing it with long dark tailfeathers that extended out from the back of the suit.

She positioned herself at the top of an incline, her wingtips resting on the ground, gazing with longing at the sky. She wore the three tanks she'd purchased from the Fly Supply in long pockets on her back. The center tank was filled with pressurized nitrogen, the two on each side hydrogen peroxide.

She pushed the launch button underneath her right wing, activating a process whereby the nitrogen, working through tubing connecting the tanks, converted the hydrogen peroxide into high-pressure steam that shot downward through steel pipes, their nozzles four rocket-shaped metal pieces strapped around her waist, aimed away from her body. Steam poured out of those rockets. Heat emanating from its flow pulsated against her legs, outside their Kevlar covering.

That jolt of propulsion, lasting thirty seconds, launched her twenty-five yards up into the air, half the distance she'd designed her rockets to take her. The sound of the fizzled-out rockets acting as her cue, she stretched her arms wide and spread her legs, straightening her limbs and opening the RobinSuit, fully utilizing its twenty-foot wingspan.

The RobinSuit functioning as an airfoil, she felt herself aloft, coasting into the wind. In those glorious moments, she'd done it! She was flying!

Not being up so high, she descended fast. Not sure how to come down gracefully, she landed hard.

Then *bang! Clang!* Oh, that hurt. That crack could've been

her skull, or at least her front horse tooth getting chipped, if 333
it wasn't already chipped.

That's when she convinced herself she wasn't all wrong
after all. *I'm just creative.*

With Bennie's help, Jessabelle found Lona in the corner
of the parking lot, slumped under a shady oak tree: a 1970
Chevy Chevelle covered in rust, its paint badly faded.

While Lona wasn't much to look at, she ran on brand
new tires, strong as the wind. On the way out Route 54 to
Wally's, sitting in freshly reupholstered bucket seats, Bennie
told her an old dying neighbor of Doc's had given Doc the
Chevy. When he first got her, her tires were flat, her insides
icky.

Doc had polished her interior right down to the silver
ashtray, and what he couldn't make shine, he replaced, and
that included the sun visors. He gave her a brand new steering system and four new tires. He was now working up to a
new coat of blue paint, maybe even some thick white racing
stripes.

Despite Lona's current appearance, she was a welcome
relief to the sleek black late-model SUV speedily passing on
the left, strutting its four-wheel drive and flashing its boxy
tail. She liked Lona's candorous "I am what I am" feel.

Just before the black SUV disappeared around a bend,
Jessabelle spoke to it. "You are just a machine, but our Lona
has character. While you run yourself into the ground, our
Lona is in the process of becoming." Together, she and Bennie
laughed.

Considering the surgeries and cosmetic procedures Doc
performed and was performing to bring Lona back to full life,
Jessabelle decided he was the artistic one. She felt moved that
he trusted her with his work in progress as she and Bennie

arrived at their destination. If Uncle Trix was here now, he'd probably scold her for getting out of such an obvious head turner in the middle of Wally's parking lot.

Bennie started toward the store's retail entrance, where Trouble and Trouble were known to hang around playing Street Fighter and Frogger.

"Don't you want to go in the grocery entrance?" she asked

"The time has come—to face my Troubles," he said, continuing on his course. "If they're there, they're there."

On the threshold of the retail entrance's sliding glass doors, Jessabelle and Bennie looked right and left, but Bennie's Troubles were nowhere near any of the coin-operated video games. They passed a pinball machine and a claw crane arcade game, full of a bright and eclectic array of stuffed plushies: red unicorns, pink flamingos, orange caterpillars, yellow sunflowers, green aliens, and blue UFOs. "Maybe on the way out, I'll play this game." Bennie tapped his index finger on the glass, pointing to a purple rabbit, the only one in the heap. "I always wanted that."

Jessabelle and Bennie went into the store and quickly located the hair dye. While they stood in the checkout line, Bennie announced he was going off to play the claw. "Pick me up on your way out," he instructed.

By the time Jessabelle had paid for the hair dye and headed out, Bennie's two Troubles were in his face. She froze.

"We learned a new word," Trouble #2 said.

"What's that?" Bennie asked, releasing the breath he'd been holding. "Jerk?"

"Hah, hah," Trouble #1 said. "The word we learned is pygmy. You know what it means?"

Bennie nodded.

"An umimportant short person," Trouble #2 offered.

"There's no such thing as an unimportant person," Bennie

boldly stated.

"Yes there is," Trouble #1 said. "He's called a pygmy. You're a pygmy in a dress."

"Go ahead, insult me," Bennie said. "But insulting the pygmies, that's just mean."

"Yeah," Trouble #2 said. "What're you going to do about it?"

"Invoke grace." Bennie began chanting mantras.

Trouble #1 slammed him against the glass front of the claw game and held his neck tight. Fear surged into Bennie's eyes. Beside him, a stuffed brown bear stared out from beady-black stud-eyes. A three-pronged metal grabber dangled behind his head. The mirror at the back of the claw reflected Bennie's scalp butted against the glass, hair squished flat.

He kept chanting. Jessabelle stepped forward to protect him.

Bennie squeezed his eyes shut, his mantras becoming stronger, more forceful. Resolve mounted on his face. He fisted his hands.

Jessabelle stopped.

All at once, Bennie opened his eyes and swung his right fist. The punch brushed Trouble #1's chin.

"Ha! Is that all you got?" Trouble #1 gloated. "A mouse can do better than that."

Bennie squeaked like a mouse, just before his left fist hit Trouble #1 in the throat. *Nice job,* Jessabelle thought.

"Akk!" Trouble #1's hand fell from Bennie's neck. Bennie shoved him away.

Trouble #1 doubled over with both hands on his neck, panting for air.

Trouble #1's shock gave Bennie the space to escape, but he didn't run. Instead he straightened up. Bolstered, he stared right into Trouble #2's cold eyes.

"You little...pyyg-my." Trouble #2 drew out the word

pygmy. He closed in on Bennie.

Bennie moved into him, directing his foot to Trouble #2's gut. It was a high kick for him, one that made him look more like a swift ballerina than a fighter, but it had its effect. Trouble #2 folded forward, the wind knocked out of him.

Bennie closed the distance between him and Trouble #2. He clobbered him on the back of the head with both elbows.

"Ugh!" Trouble #2 grunted like a caveman.

Trouble #2 tried to straighten. His head waggled from side to side.

Bennie pushed him. He collapsed on the rubberized rug beside Hoop Dreams, the basketball game.

Bennie stood over Trouble #2. "You had enough?"

Trouble #2 nodded.

Trouble #1 moved forward.

"You wanna be next?" Bennie asked him.

Trouble #1 backed off, shaking his head.

"Now if you'll excuse me, I got a game to play." Bennie swaggered toward the claw. Jessabelle joined him. He slipped a dollar in the machine, grasped the joystick.

Trouble and Trouble slinked off. "You think he's on steroids?" one Trouble asked the other on their way out the door.

"Maybe," the other Trouble said. "How else can you explain it?"

When the sound of their voices faded to nothing, Jessabelle patted Bennie's back. "You weren't kidding when you said the time had come to face your Troubles."

The crane skimmed over the head of the rabbit and returned to its position, empty.

"Sorry," Jessabelle offered.

Bennie shrugged. "You win some, you lose some. It's being able to play the game that counts. Dropping the fear of playing, it's like being liberated."

Chapter 32

The same day Bennie defeated his own Troubles in the video arcade at Wally's, he took on Jessabelle's. It happened at about noon. Jessabelle and Bennie were on their way to lunch, having an innocuous conversation that started when Bennie told Jessabelle, "You should change your name from Isa to Issie, with an i.e. on the end."

"Why?"

"My name ends in i.e."

"So? Does that mean mine has to too?"

"Yes, because if both our names end in i.e, we can be the two ies." He pronounced "ies" like the word ease. "You've heard of the Three Musketeers. Now there's the two ies," he said, wrapping an arm around Jessabelle's waist. "I.e. stands for intelligent earthling."

"I'm in." Jessabelle draped an arm over Bennie's shoulder. "Who doesn't want to be an intelligent earthling? Maybe we could get somebody else to join, and be the three ies."

"We could get lots of people to join! Vishv*ie*, Johann*ie*, Chet*ie*. Lall*ie*. Hmm, Lall*ie*, Guruj*ie*. No fun. They sound no different than Lalli or Guruji. I guess she's already an intelligent earthling. She doesn't have to join the club."

They had started up Liberation when Jessabelle heard a haggling voice. "Where is it?"

Jessabelle and Bennie snapped to attention. Further along Liberation, Wrench was shoving Lalli. "Tell us where it is!" he demanded.

"In your hearts," she said.

"Stop playing games."

"You heard the man," Blondo said. "Tell us where Shiva is or we'll kill you." She stood with one hip jutting, waving a finger at Lalli, its tip decorated with orange, red, purple, and green dripped on a background of opaque blue polish that reminded Jessabelle of a stained glass window. For such an ugly woman, Blondo had the nicest fingernails. Was she going to use them to kill Lalli?

Wrench tightened his grip on Lalli's wrist.

"Guruji could die!" Fear rattled Bennie. His eyes darted about, frenzied and wild. "Nobody else is here! We must act!" In a flash, he bolted off.

"Wait!" Jessabelle followed. "You'll get hurt."

Running along the street, Bennie tripped over a branch. Twisting, the side of his body landed on a rock. He screeched as if he'd been stabbed. Then he rose up, and without a glance back, kept going, running until he arrived on the scene.

"Leave her alone!" Bennie jumped on the back of Wrench's knees. Wrench's knees buckled and he fell forward.

Bennie rolled from Wrench's side and sprang to his feet. He got between Lalli and the thugs, and spread his arms wide. "Don't worry. I'll protect you," he told Lalli over his shoulder.

Wrench got to his feet.

Bennie got loud. He danced from one foot to the other, growled, and barked. He yelled, "Help!" He growled and barked some more and again yelled, "Help!"

The idiosyncratic display of movement and sound shocked Blondo and Wrench. They appeared to have both been blasted in the head, one right after another, with tasers from the same stun gun.

Then they regained their senses, and as if they were seeing Bennie for the first time, they started to laugh.

"Laugh all you want." Bennie kept dancing from one foot to another. "I feel it only fair to warn you I'm not an easy target."

"We'll see about that." Wrench stepped toward Bennie.

Bennie splayed both hands against Wrench's guts. For a moment they were at a standstill, Wrench pushing forward and Bennie holding him back. When Bennie just couldn't hold him any longer, he kicked Wrench in the knee.

"Oww!" Wrench doubled over.

The gardeners came from the east.

Blondo and Wrench took off, outrunning one of the gardeners, who chased them out through the front gate.

The gardeners surrounded Bennie and Lalli. One of them said, "We heard Bennie shouting for help."

"We came as fast as we could," another said.

Jessabelle stood in the crowd, flooded with paranoia that Lalli would think she had told these people about the statue.

Bennie stood in the center of the circle trembling. He opened his mouth to say something, but couldn't get a word out.

Lalli wrapped Bennie in her arms and hugged him. Slowly, Bennie stopped shaking and grew calm. By that time

Doc was moving onto the scene. Others followed.

"With great strength," Lalli told the crowd, holding Bennie's hand, "Bennie rescued me. If he hadn't shown up, who knows what those people would have done to me. It could have been the end of this form called Lalli." She pinched her own arm.

"He saved you for real?" somebody asked.

"For real," Lalli said. She lifted Bennie's hand like a champion wrestler who had just won a prize fight. "He's my hero."

Everybody clapped. Jessabelle added her own hands to the patter of applause, although she hardly felt elated. True, it was amazing that Bennie just singlehandedly fought off Wrench and Blondo. She never even had to get involved. But what if he hadn't succeeded? And he and Lalli got seriously hurt?

Uncle Trix must have told Blondo about the statue. Jessabelle bet he had sent Blondo and Wrench here.

"Wow!" Bennie exclaimed, smiling from ear to ear. "I really am strong."

"C'mon," Doc told Bennie and Lalli. "I'm taking both of you to the first-aid station so the nurse can examine you."

"But I don't need a nurse," Bennie protested.

One look from Lalli told him they should go anyway.

"Okay," he told her.

As Doc escorted the two to his vehicle, Jessabelle heard Lalli tell Bennie, "I want to properly thank you. On Monday, we'll have a special lunch in your honor."

"Will you be there?" Bennie asked.

"Of course," Lalli said.

"Well, I'm sorry. I don't think I can make it." After a brief moment, he giggled. "Just kidding. Would a mere peasant boy decline an invitation for lunch with the queen? No. I'd be crazy not to be there!" Bennie turned and waved to Jessabelle.

"See you later, meditator."

Smiling, Jesabelle waved, all the while thinking, *Shit!* The scoundrels hadn't hurt anybody this time, but the next time they showed up could spell disaster. It could mean the disappearance—even death—of Lalli or Bennie, especially if Uncle Trix was getting impatient.

Blondo and Wrench's appearance in Lalliville killed Jessabelle's appetite for lunch. Instead of eating, she wandered, pondering what to do.

She meandered through the meditation gardens. For the better part of an hour, she followed one of its paths past many trees, walking by an occasional statue on a pedestal with rings of green grass around it. She passed Ganesh and Lakshmi and came upon Shiva. She stepped all the way to the opposite edge of the path to take in the full statue. Chips of paint fell from Shiva's fingers, giving him a bit of a weathered look.

A gust of wind blew so hot and humid, it felt as if she and he stood in the stream of a giant blow dryer. Somebody tapped her shoulder. With heart beating wildly she spun around, only to see a yellow and orange flower atop a really long and slender stem.

She was relieved to see that "the person" was not Wrench or Blondo but a swaying flower. The wind stopped blowing, and as her heartrate returned to normal, she noticed the field to which this flower belonged.

The field contained thousands of flowers of various shapes, sizes, and colors. Some were small and plain, others big, bright, and showy. Some were long and elegant, others short and stocky.

Following an internal inclination, she sat on the grass at the edge of the field and closed her eyes to meditate and calm her mind.

The tapping returned to her shoulder. She opened her eyes and turned to see what kind of flower wanted her attention now. Uncle Trix stood in her sights like a dark weed that sprung up from a nefarious place.

"You have no right to be here," she told him.

"Good afternoon to you too."

She got to her feet, meeting him eye to eye. "Why did you bring Wrench and your Hyena here?"

"You haven't been much help in the statue-hunting department. I asked them to join our team."

"It's not our team. I quit, okay?"

Uncle Trix gazed into her face for a long moment. "You found it, Jessie, didn't you?"

"Found what?"

"The statue."

"No." Jessabelle gave him a halting shake of her head. "I don't know what you're talking about."

"Tell me, Jessie. Where is it?"

"I want to do the right thing."

"Telling me what you know about the statue is the right thing."

Was that true? Maybe she was being stupid by not telling. With her cut of three million dollars, she could finish art college and wouldn't even have to work the gun counter at Wally's while she did. That thought put a smile on her face. Why not tell him?

As if Uncle Trix could read that smile, he said, "Go ahead, tell me."

All she needed to do was disclose the statue's whereabouts. Then he could steal it while she went somewhere far, far away and waited for him to deliver her money. Then it would be Uncle Trix who stole the statue, not her.

Passing along a piece of information was not a crime. Like giving people directions to the library or grocery store, she'd simply give Uncle Trix directions to the statue. And it would just so happen, not long after, a lot of money would land in her lap.

And on the day she encountered that stroke of great good fortune, she would become a philanthropist by giving a large chunk of money to charity, especially one that benefited foster kids. She could hear the hero music play.

Why not? Giving somebody directions to a statue hidden in one of the houses in Lalliville wouldn't hurt anybody or anything. The people in this town had everything they needed. She wouldn't be taking food out of their mouths or causing harm to their physical bodies just by indicating the location of a certain gold item.

But if she told him, she'd never be able to come back here, to this place, the source of power. She would cut herself off from Lalli, Doc, Bennie, and her other new friends—all for only a part of three million dollars. That thought swept through her like a great black flood, obliterating every happy thought in its path, turning her inside world to darkness.

Jessabelle looked at the ground and then her watch. It was nearing two p.m. Bennie would be heading out to the shed soon, and she wanted to be there when he arrived. "I've got to go to work," she told Uncle Trix.

"What kind of work? Slave labor? I guess you want to do that forever."

"You need to leave! To take your thieves and get out!"

"Not without the statue."

"I told you, it's not here."

"My guess is that it is here and you know exactly where."

"F you." She clenched her fists. Indignation jabbed her, driving deep into her chest. She lunged with both arms, reaching for his neck.

He ducked and punched her square in the gut. All the air left her body. She gasped for more. Uncle Trix punched her again, and she fell. "I can't believe you tried to choke me," he said. "I thought we were partners."

Uncle Trix placed his right foot on Jessabelle's neck and pressed his foot down slow and hard. Then he eased up the pressure and asked, "Where is it?"

"It's not here."

He pressed his foot down again. She lay there with her head on a bed of flowers, hardly able to breathe, belly throbbing. What would happen if Uncle Trix forced her to tell him? Tortured her until she did? And he stole the statue from Lalli? She couldn't let that happen.

If she was going to be loyal to somebody, it would be Lalli. Lalli had shown her Truth. Right now, Uncle Trix seemed like nothing more than a two-bit thief, someone who'd strangle his own flesh and blood for money.

She wished things were different. But they weren't. His foot was snug against her neck. The pressure of it made her eyes grow big. First they felt the size of golf balls, then baseballs, and then…if he didn't kill her first, she was sure her eyes were going to pop right out of her skull. No SPX here. A woman was about to die from asphyxiation. Soon her skin would be blue and her eyeballs would be rolling along the path.

The pain was almost more than she could bear. Almost. Her tolerance for pain was higher than Uncle Trix realized, because she had never admitted to him that at the hands of the Cozies she hadn't given into starvation until after she considered eating mold off their basement wall.

She decided that no matter how much pressure Uncle Trix exerted, she'd stick to her story. She wasn't going to tell him where the golden Shiva was. Lalli had shown Jessabelle the statue, letting her in on a secret. Jessabelle didn't want to blow all that trust by talking, even if it was under conditions of extreme duress. She wanted to be a loyal friend, someone who could be trusted with valuable knowledge.

The problem was she couldn't get the fact she'd seen the golden Shiva in the House of the Deities out of her head. Under extreme torture conditions, she could fall into an unconscious stupor and babble unaware. Jessabelle had to convince herself Shiva was somewhere else. Shiva is in your heart, Lalli had said. Mustering all her concentration, Jessabelle pictured him there. She muttered, "Shiva is in my heart."

Uncle Trix raised his foot, releasing the pressure on her neck, and a breath of air rushed into her lungs.

"What did you say?"

"Shiva is in my heart."

He pressed his foot down hard, but she didn't care. She didn't want him and the other two thieves scavenging around this place. She would rather hurt than betray Lalli's trust. To help her stay strong, she kept whispering, "Shiva is in my heart," until her tongue turned to melted butter and everything else fuzzy white light.

She heard men shouting and what sounded like a toy train with a squeaky engine. She wanted to cover her ears but couldn't move her arms. She wished it would go away, but it would not. Anger coursed through her veins. Stop! she wanted to yell, but couldn't get her tongue working.

She dropped further. Shiva appeared in her mind's eye; for a moment she saw him, seated in his soft red house, doing japa, singing Jaya Shiva Om as his beads rolled through his fingers. After that darkness enveloped her.

She didn't know how long she was out, but when she opened her eyes, Bhisma knelt beside her.

"You okay?" he asked. She squinted against the bright blue sky backdropping Bhisma's face.

"Yes," she said, wheezing for breath. Her neck beat with pain. She instinctively covered it with her hand to soothe it.

"Where's that man?"

"The one who tried to kill you?" Hanuman asked.

"Yes, him."

"We chased him off."

She heaved herself to a seated position.

"Whoa, easy girl." Bhisma extended a hand to support her back.

Her gaze dropped onto the face of Sarasvati, a goddess she recognized from her visit to the House of the Deities. Sarasvati stood on the gray carpeted deck of a hand truck with a black rubber bumper.

"What's she doing here?"

"She came to give Shiva a rest. As you can see, he needs some rejuvenation." Hanuman clutched the aluminum handle of the hand truck. Rubber wheels turned beneath the goddess as he steered her in Shiva's direction.

Hanuman lifted the goddess from the platform of the hand truck, setting her on the grass at Shiva's side. Then he lifted Shiva onto the hand truck.

Cell phone in hand, Bhisma began dialing, first tapping the number nine. "You can't dial nine-one-one." Jessabelle poked a red "call end" bar on the bottom of his phone's screen.

"You need an ambulance," Bhisma said.

"No," she said. "No ambulance."

Hanuman parked Sarasvati where Shiva had stood and took out his phone. "We should call the police."

"No. No police."

"Somebody just tried to murder you. Call it old fashioned, but that's not right. We need the police."

"Polease. I mean please, I can't talk to the police right now." She hoisted herself to standing. "Maybe after I lie down for a bit. I'm going home. Thanks, guys, for saving me." She took two steps. Her head felt light. The whole spectrum of purple, blue, yellow, white, green, orange, and red of the flowers whirred, making her feel like she might throw up a rainbow. She swooned.

Bhisma rushed to her side. With a firm grip on her upper arm and a tight hand around her waist, he held her up. "You're not going anywhere without us."

Hanuman abandoned the hand truck, telling Shiva, "Come back for you as soon as I can." He took Jessabelle's other arm. They escorted her back along the path.

They were halfway along Devotion toward Liberation when she heard a siren grinding through the air. From her own guesstimations, that siren was headed for Lalliville!

She whipped her face toward Bhisma. "I told you I don't want an ambulance."

"I didn't call one."

She stopped cold, not knowing whether to continue or find a place to hide. She spun on Hanuman. "I told you I don't want the police."

"I didn't call them."

If neither Bhisma nor Hanuman called an ambulance or the police, then what was that sound?

On Liberation, a small crowd encircled a person or thing. "What's going on?" she asked someone when the three got to the back of the crowd.

"I don't know," the person said. "Something with Bennie." The hair on her arms bristled.

She heard the unmistakable voice of Bennie. "Why'd you call an ambulance? I don't need an ambulance," he was saying as the ambulance careened onto Liberation and braked near the crowd.

Jessabelle pushed through the crowd, making her way to the front. "Bennie?" Her eyes widened when she saw him. He had a cut on his cheek. Blood oozed down the side of his face. "What happened?"

Bennie gazed at Jessabelle with an expression of utter bewilderment. A terrible fear captured her.

Lalli held him by the elbow and spoke to him in a sweet direct way. "Bennie. You're bleeding. You need to go to the hospital."

"Bleeding?" he asked with blood dripping off his chin.

Two paramedics came forward.

"I'm okay," Bennie said. "I don't need an ambulance. I've got…" He gazed at Lalli as if he didn't recognize her. He tried to say her name, but never got past a long "LLL" sound. "I've got," he said, and shifted his vision to Doc. "DDD."

Bennie reached up to touch his head. "That tank, it hit me out of nowhere," he said, woozy as a drunken soldier. Bennie swayed. His knees buckled.

Doc held Bennie underneath the boy's armpits, preventing him from falling. Johann stepped out of the crowd. He and Doc helped the EMT lay Bennie on a gurney and load him in the ambulance.

"Doc," Lalli said, "go with Bennie," and Doc climbed in behind him.

The EMT shut the doors, and turning, one of them caught sight of Jessabelle. "There's room inside for one more."

"Medical attention is not what I need right now."

"Sure? Your neck looks like chopped beef."

"Thanks for the poetry, but it's a little over the top. This was just a little accident."

"Accident?" Bhisma said. "Somebody tried to murder her."

"Murder?" Lalli commanded, "Someone call the police."

Hanuman was already dialing.

"Hurry up and go," Jessabelle told the EMT. "Take care of Bennie."

While Hanuman talked to the police, Jessabelle asked Chet, "What happened here?"

Chet told her: "Those two Bennie saved Lalli from—they came back. The guy was trying to drag Lalli into their truck, with Bennie fighting him. The blonde gunned the motor and whacked Bennie." Chet held up a brand new toilet seat. "This fell out of the truck she was driving."

"Was it a plumbing truck?"

"Yes," he said, somber as a man at his best friend's funeral.

Jessabelle groaned, fighting a wave of nausea. Bennie's accident was all her fault for exposing him to bad influences by befriending him. She blamed herself. She blamed Wrench, Blondo, and Uncle Trix. The nausea was supplanted by rising fury. "I'm going to kill whoever did this to Bennie."

"No," said Bhisma. "You're going home to lie down until the police get here."

Chapter 33

In her room, Jessabelle sat up in bed, leaning against a backrest built from her own foam pillow plus two more of fluffy down Vishva had found and propped behind her, so she could drink her tea. The tea, of the herbal variety, what Vishva called "Calming Chamomile," came in a pot on a plastic tray with cream, sugar, and lunch, consisting of a bowl of black-eyed pea soup, a scoop of rice, and a small salad crested with carrot slivers.

From her last consultation with the mirror, Jessabelle knew she looked beaten up. A bruise marred her neck, a blood-red bruise, colored by vessels bleeding internally, shaped like the bottom of a size eight-and-a-half man's Italian designer shoe.

But just because Jessabelle saw an Italian designer shoe in

the ugly mass on her neck didn't mean anyone else would recognize the damages to be the work, specifically, of an Italian
designer shoe. Looking at the injury seemed as subjective as
looking at a cesspool; people saw different things in a cesspool, depending on their perspective.

Bhisma had called Jessabelle's injury "that mess on your
neck" when he'd brought her the icepack. "Here," he'd said,
"hold this on that mess on your neck, keep it from getting any
bigger." She'd put the ice on her neck, swollen into slight dis-
figurement, and held it there; it soothed the burning that felt
as though someone had circled her neck with a blow-torch.

Vishva referred simply to Jessabelle's injury as "the
wound." She'd brought her lunch, set it on her lap so delicate-
ly. "Food and tea to make the wound feel better." Jessabelle
had loaded the tea with so much cream and sugar, she was
sure it cancelled out any health benefits the herbs possessed.

While Jessabelle doubted anyone else could see the outline of an Italian designer shoe in her injury, she knew it was
there, could even define where the edges of its heel and sole
had abraded her skin. The excoriation had probably occurred
after Hanuman and Bhisma appeared on the scene, and in a
sudden movement toward fleeing, Uncle Trix scraped his foot
across her neck. It disquieted her to think she'd worked all
this time only to be branded by Uncle Trix's shoe.

Jessabelle sipped the tea. It hurt to swallow.

Bhisma sat in a chair beside her bed, entertaining her
with a story about how he found Lalliville. He was at the
gym, bench pressing 250 pounds, while his friend, on the biceps curl, told him he'd visited this place, asked him if he
wanted to go with him the next time Lalliville held a chant
open to visitors. He did; they chanted Samba Sadashiva; the
rest was history.

She felt like a bad princess, with everybody doting on her,
and her own actions the reason she needed to be doted on to

begin with.

She wanted to call Vishva back into the room, gather her together with Bhisma, and say, "Hey, guys, this isn't exactly how it looks," and then explain the whole damn story.

But she just couldn't, couldn't tell anybody anything when everyone was being so kind. The truth would sever her from all her new friendships and her love affair with Lalliville, from this feeling of cocooned safety she had with Bhisma by her bed and Vishva hovering nearby like a concerned mother.

"If you can bench press two hundred and fifty pounds," she told Bhisma, "you're strong. Go protect Lalli with that strength. Don't worry about me anymore."

"Hanuman is bodyguarding Lalli, so she's got all the protection she needs." Bhisma told her he might be capable of bench pressing 250 pounds, but Hanuman could lift a car off the ground. He was the only person Bhisma knew stronger than himself.

A knocking sound induced them both to swing their eyes toward the door, filled by a man so fair, he looked like the bright white bedsheets surrounding her. "Isa Newton?" he asked.

"Yes," she said.

Before he flashed his badge at her, she knew he was a cop. She could tell by the conspicuous way he dressed: in a gray suit, the kind that meant serious business, with a pressed white shirt and tie. If a Day of Practice were being held today, he'd probably blend with other guys dressed in suits, but today there were no special events scheduled in Lalliville, so he stuck out.

"Your roommate told me where to find you," the detective said, moving into the room. Despite the fact that the dapper detective's jacket was a bit loose, it didn't hide the contours of his shoulder sling, no doubt holstering his gun. He wore a cell phone and radio clipped to the sides of a thick black belt.

One cuff in a pair of handcuffs was inserted inside the waist-band of his pants; the other dangled outside. Whether this ostentacious positioning was to keep the metal from falling into his underwear or for purposes of intimidation, she wasn't sure.

His presence produced some added anxiety, but it was a steady, composed type of uneasiness. She was confident that the sight of her would promote her role as a victim, someone who had nothing to do with the actual crime itself.

The man introduced himself as Detective Douglas from the county sheriff's office. "I'd like to ask you a few questions." He moved a chair from the desk to her bedside and took a seat.

"Sure," she rasped out. She set her cup of tea on her lap tray, then set the tray on her bedside table while mentally turning her heart to stone. Facing him again, she looked him straight in the eyes. "I'll tell you whatever you want to know." She brought her hand to her throat, drawing his attention to her neck trauma, adding to her own credibility by spot-lighting her bodily damages. "But I must warn you, it's been a rough day." She paused for a breath. "I'm exhausted." She took off her glasses and rested them on her lap, giving him a better view of the ruddy half-moons sagging beneath her eyes.

He gave her a sympathetic look, not quite genuine, pos-sibly something learned in detective school. He said nothing, but dug a small leatherbound notepad and a fine pen with a stylish gold clip from an inside pocket of his suit jacket, and scribbled something. "I understand somebody tried to kill you in the meditation gardens." With his pen poised above the pad, he was ready to write more.

"That's what Hanuman and Bhisma said." She nudged her head toward Bhisma, seeing if she could divert the detec-tive's line of questioning in his direction.

The detective flipped back a few pages in his notebook and read what was written there. Melding both index and middle fingers into one pointer, he poked the air in Bhisma's direction. "Bhisma Norris?"

Bhisma nodded. "That's me, sir."

"I'll need to ask you some questions next."

The detective trained his attention back on Jessabelle. "Tell me what happened out there."

Clumps of disheveled hair, befitting someone recently attacked, shadowed her eyes. "To tell the truth, I don't remember much. It was all so shocking, the whole thing is kind of a blur."

"Tell me what you do remember."

She recited the statement she'd been practicing in her head, in slow halting style and a hoarse voice, explaining how earlier that afternoon, she'd been sitting before the Shiva statue in the meditation gardens to meditate when she felt a tapping on her shoulder. At first she thought it was a flower blowing in the breeze. But when she opened her eyes to see what kind of flower it was, there was a man. "He crept up out of nowhere. I guess that's when Hanuman and Bhisma showed up."

The detective again wrote in his pad. A nervous tremor rumbled through her stomach. She was purposely vague, not giving him anything specific or pindownable, anything he could link back to her. So what the heck was he noting?

"I don't remember anything," she said, "except for this vision I had of Shiva after the man beat me unconscious." She began telling the detective about how Shiva had materialized before her, singing.

He listened politely until she took her second breath. Eager to get back to his own business, he cut in with, "Now, about the man who accosted you—"

"Okay, but Shiva's not just a statue." She wished everybody would just drop all this attempted murder stuff and talk about Shiva.

He jotted another note in his book. "I wonder why he picked your shoulder to tap." He patted his pen on his pad. "Any theories?"

"Maybe he just wanted to mess with somebody, and I was easy to mess with, because nobody else was around at the time."

"Did you ever see the man before?"

"No."

He pointed at her neck with his two-fingered pointer. "He choked you?"

"That's what Hanuman and Bhisma said." She sighed heavily.

"I wonder why he did that."

"There're a lot of crazy people in the world."

"Yes, but still there's got to be a reason he targeted you, of all the—" He glanced in his notebook again. "—two hundred and nine residents in Lalliville."

"Just in the right place at the wrong time, I guess." She dropped further into her stack of soft pillows, making herself look very tired.

Obtuse, the detective plodded on in a frustratingly neutral way. "Describe how the man looked."

"I can't remem—" She pretended losing her voice.

He handed her a piece of paper. "Write down what his voice sounded like."

She wrote, "I'm sorry. I can't. It's all a blur." She returned the sheet of paper to him. Lying to a detective was so much easier than lying to anyone else; it almost felt like fun.

They continued conversing, him verbalizing his questions, her writing her answers on paper. "Did he ask you for anything?"

"I don't have anything to steal."

"Did he ask you for sex?"

"I definitely don't remember anything like that."

"Did he have a gun?"

Jessabelle considered that. She knew Uncle Trix had a gun, but she hadn't seen it on him that day.

"Yes?" the detective pressed. "What is it?"

"It's my hand," she wrote with a stiff palm and fingers. She massaged her hand a moment, then added to her note, "It's cramping."

Finally he told her she could take a deep breath and relax. Satisfied that she'd done a good job at being vague, she took that much-deserved deep breath.

He turned his attention to Bhisma, asking him what happened out there in the meditation gardens.

Jessabelle let her arms go slack, her head fall to one side. She pretended to drift off into sleep, fading Isa Newton into the background while Bhisma gave a fleshed out, detailed account of the matter. Through a millimeter-sized slit she held in her right eye, she saw the detective furiously scribbling away while Bhisma talked.

Thirty questions to her with none to minimal results; one question to Bhisma and he was producing the whole story, delivered in the same helpful tone as when she and Bennie visited the domain of Bhisma and Hanuman for their light and table loans. Bhisma called Uncle Trix "the perpetrator," described his blond hair as "a real shocker," and told the detective exactly what he wore: "a white T-shirt, working man denim, sissy shoes. Definitely not working man shoes. He carried a wrench in the front pocket of his pants. I remember the wrench; I kept my eye on it, so he couldn't club me with it."

The detective closed his notebook and tucked it back in his pocket, along with his fine pen. "Let's stay in touch," he said to Bhisma. "I'll check back with you in a few days, see if there's anything you might have left out."

Anything he left out? It was like telling Tolstoy, "I'll check back with you in a few days, see if there's anything you might have left out of *War and Peace*."

The detective handed Bhisma a business card and left another on Jessabelle's bedside table.

"Do you have any idea who they are?" Bhisma asked the detective. Jessabelle was wondering the same thing, but couldn't ask while supposedly sleeping.

"No," the detective said. "Maybe by day's end, I'll have some leads. I'm off to question Lalleshwari Ujala and Hanuman Maier."

She heard the detective leave, followed by Bhisma. Vishva came into the room and left a note on the bedside table.

Fear jabbed Jessabelle. With the detective poking around, it was only a matter of time before he linked her with Uncle Trix, Blondo, and Wrench. After that, something unpleasant was bound to strike. There may be only hours left before the whole ruse collapsed. With the feeling she had to do something, not just lie there, she catapulted herself back up to a seated position.

A wave of nausea made her sway. She breathed in deeply, regaining her balance. She read the note. "Call if you need anything." She cleared her throat several times, considering herself lucky. Choking by an Italian designer shoe hadn't turned her into a pretty sight, but things could've been so much worse. Her voice wasn't really as bad as she'd made it sound. Her vision and hearing were okay too. Best of all, she suffered no brain injury from lack of oxygen. That meant she still knew how to convert herself into the Uncle Trix look-alike she'd already planned.

*   *   *

A version of Uncle Trix three inches shorter than the original Uncle Trix entered Bank USA. Jessabelle had dialed customer service at this branch forty-eight hours earlier, after studying Samuel Sheldon's online bank records. In her best male voice, she'd told a woman identifying herself as Ms. Smith that she was Samuel Sheldon and that she'd come at this time today to withdraw $103,099.35 cash from his account. "Can you please have the money ready?"

"Carrying that much cash can be risky," Ms. Smith said. "Will you accept a cashier's check instead?"

"No. I want the money in one hundred dollar bills, the ninety-nine dollars and thirty-five cents however you want to give it to me."

Jessabelle heard a long sigh, followed by, "Okay."

Now Jessabelle walked to a table near the window, and with only a mild shake in her hand, filled out the withdrawal form, signed it Samuel Sheldon, and brought it to the clerk.

The clerk came out from behind the counter. "Right this way." She escorted Jessabelle to an office where a woman sat at a desk, sipping coffee and chatting with a gray-suited man on the other side of the desk. Jessabelle froze. "Ms. Smith," the clerk said. "Here is Mr. Sheldon." The clerk handed Ms. Smith the withdrawal form before withdrawing herself from the office.

"Please have a seat," Ms. Smith said. Jessabelle obeyed, reluctantly filling the empty chair beside the man in the gray suit. "This is Detective Douglas."

"Detective Douglas?" Jessabelle's voice went up a couple of notes, a danger for a woman pretending to be a man.

"I asked him to meet us here," Ms. Smith said.

Focusing, Jessabelle said, "It's not illegal to withdraw cash, is it?"

The detective smiled. "Not yet, anyhow." The smile faded as he closed the door. What choice did Jessabelle have but to sit there? She had to remain cool and compliant. Running or resisting would only raise a red flag.

"Can I see some ID?" Detective Douglas asked.

Jessabelle produced one of Uncle Trix's fake licenses and handed it to him. "Hmm," he said examining it, comparing her likeness to the one in the picture. He returned it to her.

"Who was the first president of the United States?"

"George Washington."

"Who is the current president of the United States?"

"What do the presidents have to do with anything?"

"Just checking to see if you're of sound mind."

"Oh," she said as if somehow this strange interrogation made sense.

"Why are you withdrawing so much cash?"

"That's none of your business. I'm free to do what I want with my money."

"This is not an attempt to control how you spend your money," Ms. Smith interjected. "We're trying to protect you."

"From what?"

"Around here," she said, "a $103,099.35 cash withdrawal is unusual."

Jessabelle remained silent.

"It's exactly half your entire savings."

"That's right. Exactly half."

"Is anybody forcing you to withdraw the money?"

"No. I'm acting of my own free will."

Detective Douglas took over again. "Have you heard about bank examiner and pigeon schemes?"

"Yes, as a matter of fact, I have."

"These kinds of things do happen right here in our little town. The other day, Old Man Greely gave some con artist one thousand dollars for a fake diamond."

"I'm sorry to hear that."

"My point is that sometimes even smart people get played. You seem like a nice person. We don't want you exploited."

Jessabelle convinced them nobody was trying to take advantage of her. Ms. Smith left to get the money. Detective Douglas gave her a piece of advice: "Don't trust anybody because he or she is friendly. Swindlers are always friendly. If they weren't, they couldn't steal your money."

"Thanks for the warning," she said in an amicable way. "I've always been impressed by the customer service at this bank. Here Ms. Smith went out of her way to ensure I'm not being taken."

Ms. Smith returned at the tail end of the comment and set the money on the desk, alongside a form printed in black and white. "Before you can take the money," Ms. Smith said, "you must sign that."

Jessabelle eyed the money. Twenty packets, each containing fifty $100 bills, sixty $50 bills, ninety-nine dollars, and thirty-five cents in change.

She read the form, basically a waiver saying the bank was not liable if something happened to the money. Jessabelle scribbled Samuel Sheldon on the signature line, shuffled the money into her GoGreen bag, and stood.

"Don't you want to count it?" Ms. Green asked.

"I already did," Jessabelle said.

Back in the van, she found her way out to the main road. A kaleidoscope of pictures shifted inside. In one pattern of shapes and colors, she saw herself driving, just driving, a hundred miles in any one direction. Once she reached that hundred-mile point, she'd park in the first campground she came upon. She'd call Uncle Trix and tell him there was no statue in Lalliville. That since she could no longer count on him for a job, she had taken her share of the money from his bank account. Surely he'd come to her, bringing his cronies. With his attention drawn to recovering his money, they'd abandon Lalliville.

Other bits of the changing kaleidoscope reflected darkness, obscuring the sight of Bennie. She couldn't just run, not yet. First, she needed to know Bennie was okay. With no idea where the nearest hospital was, she felt lost. Up ahead, a gas station loomed. She'd stop for directions, and to change back to Isa Newton.

Chapter 34

Jessabelle as Isa Newton walked through the doors of the emergency room, wishing she'd gone back to Lalli's house to get some of Bennie's things in case he had to stay in the hospital. What was his stuff, anyhow? Kurtas? It seemed like an odd thing to bring a boy who was in the hospital. Still, this particular boy might find a kurta or two comforting.

Or a treat from the café. He ate a chocolate chip cookie every time they went there and may have liked one now. Or a recording of Brahmin priests reciting Ganesh mantras. Could she have found something like that in the bookstore? Or…something. It felt weird that she didn't have anything to give him, anything to leave him with the last time she ever saw him.

She looked for Bennie among the faces in the waiting

room. Not finding him, she proceeded to the desk. "Can I help you?" the nurse asked.

"I'm here to see Bennie. Bennie…" She realized she didn't even know his last name, and whether his first was in fact Bennie, or if Bennie was a nickname. He might actually be Benjamin or Benedict. She smiled, considering the possibility of Bennie as a Bentley.

"Why did the man come here?"

"He's not a man. He's like eight years old. He came in an ambulance with a cut on his cheek."

"If he's the one I think you're talking about, he's already been admitted to the children's ward."

Jessabelle turned to exit the emergency room, coming face to face with a young family. The man held a girl. Her skin was gray, and her lips and fingernails of the hand draped over her father's neck were blue. Her breath rasped as it came in and went out.

"She fainted right in the middle of kickball with her cousins," the woman said at the desk. "She woke up and now she's complaining her chest hurts."

At the front desk to the children's ward, Jessabelle explained all over again she wanted to see Bennie.

"Hmm, Bennie," the on-duty nurse said. "The boy with the concussion?"

Judging by the way he was acting the last time she'd seen him, a concussion made sense. Jessabelle nodded.

"Well okay. But I've got to warn you, he's not doing too good. Visiting hours are almost over and somebody else is already in the room with him."

"I'll only stay a few moments."

The nurse led her down a hall past other rooms. Jessabelle heard the unmistakable sound of Bennie singing his mantras. She couldn't figure out what the nurse had been trying to tell her; Bennie sounded better than ever.

The nurse stopped in front of the last door on the left. "Here we are." Jessabelle peered into the room.

Bennie sat crosslegged on the floor with his white hospital sheet draped over his head, flowing down around his body. Stitches zigzagged his cheek, and his mouth was wide open, foreign words pouring from it.

Doc glanced up from his seat beside Bennie's empty bed.

"Your neck looks terrible. Why not get it examined while you're here?"

"I'm not here for this." She swept her fingertips over the bruise on her neck. "I'm here for Bennie. How is he?"

"His memory is gone. He's acting a little crazy."

"That's no different than usual."

Bennie stopped singing and stared at her. Then he threw off his white sheet and sprang to his feet. "Welcome," he said, "to my cave." He embraced her, his ID bracelet rippling on his arm. "Please have a seat." He indicated his cast-off sheet, lying crumpled on the floor.

"He thinks he's Jai Ram, a yogi living in a Himalayan cave."

"Please, Jai Ram," the nurse said. "Stay in bed until the doctor tells you it's okay to get up."

Bafflement knotted Bennie's face as he pointed to Doc. "He just said he's a doctor!"

"I am," Doc said. "But I'm not *your* doctor. Just do what the nurse tells you."

Doc arose and playfully carried Bennie back to bed and set him on it. The nurse brought the sheet over and covered him with it, bringing it up around his chest and tucking him in. "I've got to get back up front," she said, and then to Doc, "You'll make sure he stays in bed?"

Doc nodded, and the nurse left. Doc turned to Jessabelle. "Say something to help him remember who he is."

Standing beside Bennie's bed, leaning in toward him, speaking softly, Jessabelle related how they had worked together. She talked about Bennie's Troubles, and how he'd overcome them. How he'd gotten so strong, it took a truck loaded with sinks, toilet seats, and other plumbing supplies to finally take him down. He gave her a blank stare until he fell asleep.

"Time to wrap up your visit," the nurse said from the doorway. "Visiting hours end in five minutes." She disappeared again.

Only the sound of Bennie's breathing filled the room. The idea of leaving him all alone made her nervous. Jessabelle nibbled on a fingernail. The gesture struck her as odd, considering she never bit her fingernails. "What if they give him the wrong medication? Like morphine instead of aspirin, and he dies?"

"That won't happen."

"How do you know it won't?"

"Because he's not taking any medication."

"Maybe he should be. Otherwise, he'll get crazier and crazier until he dies."

"What? That's crazy."

"What if they mistake him for some other boy who's in for a liver transplant, and give Bennie a liverectomy before they realize they got the wrong kid?"

"Well, then they can just put his liver back in," he said with a smile.

Doc was being so reasonable. Instead of soothing, as she was sure he intended, it irritated her. He was thinking like an upstanding citizen, as if nothing bad could happen. "This isn't a joke," she told him.

"Look! They won't accidentally cut out Bennie's liver, because of this chart right here." He lifted Bennie's chart from a hook at the end of his bed and waved it in the air. "Before the doctors take him to the operating room, they will examine this chart and see he's not here for a liver transplant."

"Let me see that thing."

She perused the chart. "I don't care what this says! It could happen! And don't you think it would hurt to have your liver ripped out and sewn back in place? I don't want him to suffer!"

He moved closer and placed his hand on her back. "I know you're worried about him. I am too. But this is a good hospital. Nothing bad will happen to him here. Besides, pain and suffering don't really exist."

"Where did that come from?" she shouted. "Tell me pain and suffering don't exist after I rip your liver out!" She moved to attack him.

He caught her arms. "Why're you mad at me?"

"You're too good!"

"I don't want to fight."

Chet appeared over Doc's shoulder. "I hate to break up a good time, but Lalli sent me to get you, Doc. I didn't even know you were here, Isa. If you need a ride back, you can come with us."

"I don't need a ride, but you can take Goody-two-shoes."

Doc left with Chet, and Jessabelle took a seat by Bennie's bedside.

"Miss, it's time to go," the nurse said from the doorway.

Jessabelle patted Bennie's hand resting on the bed, then lifted it and kissed his palm. She tiptoed out of the room. In the hall the nurse whispered, "He needs his rest."

On her way back to the step van, Jessabelle crossed in front of the entrance to the emergency room, where she again saw the young family. The girl in her father's arms didn't seem any better than before, and in the dusky light, Jessabelle couldn't tell whether she was sleeping or dead. The woman let loose an angry rant. "Where are we going to get $89,648 for a surgery like that, and $2,200 for every day over ten she has to stay in the hospital? It's crazy. I thought hospitals were supposed to take care of people, not send them away because they don't have insurance."

Jessabelle heard herself relating the story she had told so often over all those years on the road with Uncle Trix. "It's Grampa," the story went. "They rushed him to the hospital. He needs an operation, but the hospital won't operate until they have their money."

If it wasn't Grampa who needed an operation, it was a sister, or a fictitious daughter. Heck, she'd once pretended to be this woman standing before her now. That wasn't Jessabelle's kid in that man's arms, but in a sense it was.

"What are you looking at?" the man asked.

Jessabelle realized she'd stopped and was eavesdropping on their crisis in plain view. "Sorry," she said. "I didn't mean to stare. I couldn't help but overhear your predicament. I'm sorry for it."

"Can you believe it?" the woman asked. "Our little girl needs surgery to repair her heart valves, but she can't have it because we have no insurance. They want $89,648 to do the surgery. Up front! Can you believe they want it all up front? Do we look like Prince William and Kate?"

"No."

"Where are we going to get that kind of money? We couldn't even afford eight hundred dollars a month for insurance after he lost his job! And now they want $89,000!"

"There must be something you can do."

"Besides rob a bank?"

"Yes, besides that."

"They said we could try the public hospital in Jacksonville. Jacksonville! By the time we get there, our little girl could be…I can't even say it!"

"I have an idea for you," Jessabelle said.

"What is it?"

"Hold a fundraiser. Invite all your friends. Collect donations for your girl's medical expenses."

"Our friends aren't millionaires."

"Invite people you don't even know. Somebody will come up with the money."

"You think so?"

"I know so. I believe that in their hearts, people are generous. In fact, I'm feeling generous now. I'd like to be your first donor. Wait right here. I'll run back to my van and return with a little something for you."

Jessabelle rushed to the step van and retrieved the GoGreen bag stuffed with cash that she had crammed inside the glove compartment. She brought it back to the family waiting on the pavement. The woman had stopped crying. When Jessabelle held out the bag of money, she took it.

"It's heavy," she said and peered inside. Her eyes grew big. "It looks like a lot more than just a little."

"It's $103,099.35. The money for the operation plus extra in case your daughter needs to stay for longer than ten days in the hospital."

"Why are you giving us all this money?"

"Because I'm rich."

The woman started to cry again. "I don't even know who you are, but thank you."

"I hope your daughter gets a lot better," Jessabelle said.

Out in the step van, she started the motor and let it idle while she stared out the window. Was she crazy giving away $103,099 like that? Absolutely. No doubt, especially since she didn't have another $103,099, only ten bucks left over from the money she arrived in Lalliville with. Oddly, she wasn't all that worried.

Ever since receiving the twenty packets of $100 bills,

sixty $50 bills, ninety-nine dollars, and thirty-five cents, she couldn't really embrace it, actually found it hard to believe that three years of work had only added up to a few metal pieces and about five inches in paper rectangles bearing the faces of dead men. The money numbed her.

For sure, it didn't feel as if it belonged to her. It was money collected under false pretenses for someone who needed an operation. Well, that person had manifested right before her very eyes, riding in her father's arms. It was that little girl's money now. Jessabelle hoped it would give her new life.

It didn't matter that Jessabelle had virtually nothing. If she never made it back to art college, it was okay. If she had to work the knife and gun counter at Wally's just to be an honest woman, it was okay. Whatever happened, it was all okay. Isn't that what Truth was trying to tell her by bringing her face-to-face with those people?

With nowhere else to go, Jessabelle returned to Lalliville for an awful night in which she lay awake, worried about Bennie.

She shut off her alarm long before it went off and waited, staring at the ceiling. At five-thirty she plodded into the bathroom for her ninety-minute makeup/costuming job, the stages of which would transform her from Jessabelle Knox to Isa Newton.

Half an hour later she slammed shut the toilet lid in frustration for having misglued her face, the first time in Lalliville. She unglued it and started all over again. When Jessabelle finally trudged into the living room as Isa Newton, Vishva was there, singing scales, warming up her voice. She stopped when she saw Jessabelle. "I'm sorry. Did I wake you?"

"Impossible to wake somebody who's not asleep."

Vishva smiled. "Are you nervous about the show?"

"Show?" Jessabelle had forgotten all about that. "We can't have a show without Bennie."

"We can't cancel it just because he's in the hospital, not with all the people coming."

An Indian woman, about fifty, wearing a light peach cotton sari with a block print and gold trim, entered from the kitchen with a cup of tea. "This is my mother," Vishva said.

"Mrs. Rajakapanna, did you come all the way from India to watch Vishva sing?" Jessabelle asked.

"Yes," Mrs. Rajakapanna proudly stated, "I wouldn't miss her for the world," and then added, "or the girl who flies."

"This is her!" Vishva exclaimed.

"Ahh. So you're the genius."

"Umm," Jessabelle hemmed and "uh," Jessabelle hawed. "I can't do the show today."

Mrs. Rajakappana gasped and covered her mouth with her hand, an expression that seemed more shocked than news of Jessabelle's act cancellation warranted.

"I need to go to the hospital to be with Bennie," Jessabelle said.

"I know the two of you have become good friends," said Vishva.

Jessabelle nodded in agreement.

"And you care about him."

Jessabelle continued nodding.

"But I don't think it's necessary for you to go to the hospital."

Jessabelle stopped nodding. "But he's all alone there."

"I heard Lalli sent the nurse to sit by his bedside."

"Still, in all good conscience, I can't fly around while Bennie lies in the hospital. I must go back." As she stood up and exited, a disappointed sigh emanated from Mrs. Rajakappana.

Jessabelle marched out to Liberation and headed toward

the parking lot. Along the way, she came upon Lalli, Doc, and a small group of people, under the guardianship of Hanuman, following with wary eyes at a distance of about thirty feet.

From the picture in Doc's living room, she recognized the group as Doc's family. Dressed in a conservative manner, for comfort as well as style, they appeared like an advertisement for an upscale family headed out for a summer day's picnic. Doc's Mom, in a long yellow sundress, a fine knit shrug, and straw fedora, toted a picnic basket. His father wore a light pair of khaki linen pants paired with a black T-shirt, his brother olive chinos and matching short-sleeved shirt. Both men wore loafers and cool black-framed sunglasses, his dad's with square lenses, his brother's wraparound style.

Aaron, the nephew Doc had sacrificed his foot for—there he strolled, holding his mom's hand, clasping a stuffed bird toy, a falcon, in the hand that wasn't occupied by his mom's. He was several years older now than in the picture on the wall of the Halloway living room. Judging by the size of his mom's belly, the boy was due to have a little brother or sister within two months' time. Along with a colorful and blousy maternity top, she wore a wide-brimmed straw hat, capris, and cream flats.

Jessabelle tried to slip past the group without being noticed, muttering to herself, "Not now, not now."

But Doc spotted her. He called her name. "Mom, Dad, this is the girl I told you about," he was saying as she joined the group. After introductions, he told Jessabelle, "They can't wait to see your birdsuit."

"I can't fly today," she said.

"But you must! Everybody wants to see Bird Woman!"

"Bennie is in the hospital! Doesn't anybody care about that?"

"We all care," Lalli said. "But now is not the time for you to go to Bennie. You've agreed to participate in the show.

Now is the time to honor your agreement."

"But I said I'd be in the show before Bennie landed in the hospital."

"His parents will be with him soon."

"What about until they get there?"

"The nurse is with him now. She will stay until they get there."

"The nurse? Why not me?"

"As Doc said, everybody wants to see Bird Woman." Lalli smiled. "Bennie is okay and will be okay. It's time for you to suit up for the show." Her tone left no room for argument.

Jessabelle's heart sank. Why hadn't she fled when she'd had the chance? "Okay," she told Lalli.

Further along Liberation, she passed Johann and Chet, Johann in office attire, carrying a briefcase under his arm, Chet in jeans with a long copper shirt over them. In Chet's hand was a white table linen.

Angrily she called to them, "Where are your parents?"

They stopped and turned. "Huh?" Chet asked.

"Mami and Papi are probably sitting down for weiss wurst und sauerkraut," Johann said. "It's dinnertime in Germany. Why do you want to know?"

"Everybody else's parents are here. I just thought yours ought to be too."

"Whose parents are here?"

"Forget it," she said, dismissing the whole conversation with a wave of her hand.

She sulked onward. If she'd known she could invite someone, maybe she would have. But who would she invite? The one who planted his foot on her neck, choking her in the meditation gardens? Shiva save her and everybody else if he showed up here today.

Once again she thought about running, just getting on the road and driving. Where would she go now that she only had ten dollars? Wherever she ran out of gas.

Wherever loomed as a scary prospect, but at least she'd be off on her own, away from this terrible threat of—of what? Exposure.

She thought about Lalli's words. "Now is the time to honor your agreement." Now was not the time to run. Now was the time to face the music, dance to the song she had written. And when it came right down to it, she didn't want to run. She wanted to make things right. But how would being a bird falling from the sky accomplish that?

Chapter 35

Through the eyes of a robin, Jessabelle surveyed the crowd gathered for the talent show. Her jaw was tight, her breathing erratic, her arms spasming from holding her wings outstretched for too long. Not that heavy but too big to fold neatly at her sides, she'd suspended her wings in the air, floating them over to the talent show venue to avoid scraping them on the ground. Since they made sitting impossible, she stood at the back of the crowd, feeling like a scientific experiment gone awry—a robin injected with growth hormone until its augmentation reached a size a hundred times greater than the average robin. She allowed the tips of her wings to touch the ground, providing the slightest relief of her burden.

Jessabelle wore a thin yellow bill of a prosthetic nose adhered over her own, blended with the rest of her robin face, painted brown. White bars streaked her neck, etched in the same paint as the snowy rings circling her eyes, intense glossy black eyes. A wig of slick brown feathers capped her head.

A ringletted young girl spotted her. With a squawk, she ran to a woman who sat on the bottom bench of aluminum bleachers, rolled out especially for the occasion. "Mommy!" The young girl dove into her mother's lap. "Save me from the monster!" The girl dared a peek from behind her mommy fortress.

Jessabelle smiled, a gesture to show the young girl that behind the dark face resided something friendly, even human. Someone incapable of harming her.

The little girl shrieked and started to cry, blubbering on about scary teeth that would bite. Jessabelle felt sorry her mouthful of black teeth didn't project amicability.

The little girl's mother patted her daughter's back. "It's okay, it's okay," she repeated. The girl's calm not forthcoming, her mother tried reason. "Remember last Halloween, when you dressed up as Princess Mirabai? In the same way, she's dressed as a bird. It's not real. It's just a costume."

Just a costume? Costuming was Jessabelle's life.

The sky shone clear as opaque blue crystal illumined by sunlight. It held not a single cloud while the temperature hovered around a warm and breezy eighty degrees. It was an ideal day, perfect for an outdoor talent show.

Doc was onstage, a grassy rectangle delineated by white field chalk, the kind used to mark out the playing area on football and soccer fields. Dressed in the likeness of Juggling Baba, he wore a long silk shirt, adorned with colorful panels, over pants that fit tightly around his calves. The thick wavy whirly hair she'd made for him poured off his head.

Doc clumsily juggled three water balloons, pink, orange, and blue. "Right now, I'm a person who, ignorant of the self, has become thoughts." He let one water balloon fall, and then the second and third. Bursting, their liquid innards oozed out in puddles on the grass. Doc scrutinized the rubber shreds of the exploded water balloons scattered around his feet. His eyes widened and he cupped a hand over his mouth in mock surprise. "Mercy me, I can't figure out why my life is such a mess."

Doc lifted three new water balloons from a card table before him, holding one of the bright aqueous bubbles in his right hand, and two in his left. "A person who knows the self stays centered in the self." He tossed a water balloon in the air, and getting into a rhythm, he continuously threw water balloons from one hand to another in a smooth loop. "To others it appears as if I am juggling. But to me, I'm just watching my thoughts glide by, acting in the moment."

He laid the water balloons on the card table. In their place, he picked up three flashlights and proceeded to juggle them, effortlessly. "In this way, I can juggle many different things."

He let a flashlight drop and used the inside of the sneaker over his prosthetic foot to bump it back in the juggle. He introduced a rock into the juggle, a small rock with a flat surface; tiny embedded crystals sparkled in the sun as the rock went from one of Doc's hands to the other, and up and around in an arc. Doc lifted two more rocks, one pink-hued and jagged-edged, engrained with pebbles; the other a large, smooth, shiny, igneous type of black rock like those formed by volcanic eruptions. Simultaneously he set the flashlights on the table, until he was juggling three uneven-sized rocks.

Next Doc returned one of the rocks to the table, and while juggling two rocks in one hand, grabbed an apple with the other. He made a snack of it. "It may appear as if I know some tricks," he said between bites. "But really, I'm just watching, free from the hold of my thoughts."

The crowd went wild, cheering and hollering. They loved

Doc. And what was not to love about this guy capable of eating an apple while juggling? He had given her money to do a Day of Practice. He'd returned a 1970 Chevy Chevelle from the dead, saved a puppy's life, given that puppy back his spirit. Recollecting it all, her heart expanded, wide-open as the sky above.

At the same time, she was painfully aware of Doc's family, seated on a blanket near the front of the crowd. Doc's brother whistled; his wife clapped; Aaron sat beside his mom. Behind them, Doc's mother lounged in a low foldout chair, her legs crossed at the ankles. Fuzz was nestled in the folds of her sundress while Aaron had his arms wrapped around the gray and white body of his own cute cuddly thing, his plush falcon. He'd positioned the falcon's head forward, so the bird could see the show she guessed.

Doc left the stage, striding to the back of the crowd. He whispered excitedly in her ear, "Your turn is coming." Because he couldn't stand close without standing in front of or behind her, he assumed his place out next to the tip of her left wing.

She felt the impulse to join her hands palm to palm and recite a silent prayer to Shiva. Since under the circumstances her palms couldn't meet, the prayer would have to do. *Please, Shiva, give me the strength to be free.*

Onstage the host introduced the next act, Vishva. He called her, "Our own celestial singer who brings us the music of the spheres, here today to sing a song she wrote in Sanskrit."

A hush fell over the crowd as Vishva sashayed to the microphone in a full-length Indian dress, red orange with a polka dot border, sequined and beaded, fitted through the chest and torso, flaring full at the hips. Her hair shone like glossy black satin. A necklace and earrings of crystals and beads completed her fancy image.

Vishva launched into her song, repeating a phrase of it

often, "Tatra mama moksah."

Vishva sang so beautifully, Jessabelle could have listened to her sing all day and into the night. She would have been completely swept into its beauty were it not for the terrible state she was in, terrified of being revealed for the fraud she was, but longing to reveal herself; not wanting her turn to come, but unable to run away.

Vishva read the translation of the song. "My body is the holiest of all temples, the place where the almighty has made its home. My faith and devotion in Lalleshwari are my rice and vegetables. Like a rolling river, contemplation and meditation carry me inward. There lies my freedom, there lies my freedom, there lies my freedom."

Applause rumbled up. Mrs. Rajakapanna gave her daughter a standing ovation, cheering, clapping with her hands high. Vishva curtsied. A smile festooned her face.

The forest beyond the field, usually soothing, worried Jessabelle with all the opportunities it afforded for thieves to hide. She searched it for a pattern change, any area where the natural color of foliage fluctuated to human-fabricated green and brown. Dread of uncovering a crew-cutted person dressed in camouflage somewhere out there caught her with each scan of her probing eyes.

Her fear of seeing Wrench unmanifested, Jessabelle breathed in relief, only to nearly jump out of her skin a second later, when as she turned her head, a streak of blonde hair fluttered into her sight. She involuntarily croaked her terror before she realized the wearer of the bleached blonde hair was not Blondo or Uncle Trix, but a teenage girl seating herself with the other teenagers on the bleachers.

"What's wrong?" Doc asked. Luckily, due to the mighty applause directed toward Vishva, Doc was the singular hearer of her falsely rendered auditory distress signal.

"Sorry, it was just a fly. It landed on me. I couldn't smack it off. It's gone now."

"You should've eaten it. After all, you're a robin."

She summoned laughter; not even a smile came forth.

Sweat collected in damp spots under the arms of Jessabelle's RobinSuit as Chet and Johann took the stage for a skit the announcer called an enactment of a story Johann's mother had told him. Chet still had on his jeans and long copper shirt, only now instead of carrying the table linen, he wore it wound round his head like a turban, pinned in the front with an OM symbol brooch. He positioned a lawn chair stage right and settled into it, resting his arm on one of its plastic arms. In his hand he held a two-tone rubber ball, the size of a baseball, a pink and purple carnival prize.

Johann wore a short-sleeved shirt with light blue stripes and a red plaid tie, and navy slacks with a hint of red socks peeping out from under their legs. On his feet were cherry red shoes with tapered toes; between his elbow and ribs, he squeezed a matching briefcase. Standing center stage, Johann gave an introduction to his and Chet's skit, one that turned out to be almost as long as the skit itself. "Once, before the Free & Blissful Yogi took Samadhi, my mother stayed in his ashram in India. She told me about a teaching she got during that time. This skit stars Chet as the Free & Blissful Yogi, and me, as my mother."

With those words, Johann set his briefcase on the grass and kneeled before it. He clicked it open, and huddling over it with his back to the audience, adjusted his appearance. When he again faced the audience, a string mophead rested on the crown of his head, its heavy cotton strands flapping around his face like the hair of a rag doll. A small round sun hat capped the mophead, covering the place the mophead could be attached to a handle, were it currently in use cleaning floors and not as a makeshift wig. Lipstick the color of red wine stained Johann's lips, spilling over his lipline.

Perhaps it was a good thing his mom was in Germany eating weiss wurst und sauerkraut, and not here absorbing her son's parody of her, Jessabelle thought. Sucked into the wave of laughter billowing through the crowd, she couldn't help but chuckle over how ridiculous Johann looked; a small respite from the turmoil raging inside.

Mother-of-Johann approached Chet in his chair and went down on one knee. "Oh Free & Blissful Yogi," he entreated, "you who became one with Truth, and in that becoming, freed yourself, I have come for your help. Please free me of my anger. It has me in its clutches!" He fisted and shook his hands; he ground his teeth and tensed his face.

"I'll help you as soon as this ball lets go of me."

"But the ball is not gripping you," Johann fumed, his whole body trembling. "You are gripping it."

"Your predicament is the same. You are gripping your anger. It is not gripping you. You've got the power." Chet relaxed his hand. The ball fell from his fingers, bounced on the grass a couple of times, and rolled a few feet in a pink and purple swirl.

Johann watched the ball's movement until it came to a stop. "Now I see," he said. Then he loosened his body and relaxed his features, letting go of his anger and coming to rest in a state of peace.

The crowd applauded again, shouting and yelling their encouragement.

The story threw Jessabelle into momentary contemplation. Dishonesty wasn't holding a gun to her head, making her do things she didn't want to do. The power was hers. She really could live her life in tune with integrity. All she needed to do was let go of dishonesty.

"Last, but certainly not least," the announcer said, "we have Isa Newton who will show us how a human can fly free as a bird."

Cheers. Whistles. Teenagers chanted: "Fly, robin, fly, up up to the sky." They stomped their feet, clanging the bleachers.

It's my turn. Jessabelle raised her bird head and tucked in her bird chin to get up her courage. Streaming all her focus into getting onstage, she lifted her wings and stepped forward.

A woman shrieked.

Jessabelle turned her head toward the sound. Madeline's silver clipboard slumped at the talent show planner's feet. Apparently Jessabelle had smacked her with the tip of her wing. The evidence was present: The wing currently dug into Madeline's bicep. "Sorry," Jessabelle said.

She paused to figure out how she could get to the front without knocking somebody or something over. Hanuman and Bhisma came to her rescue, getting on each side of her. They lifted her by her waist and carried her forward to the tune of more cheering. They set her down on the grassy stage.

"Isa Newton is a graduate of M.I.T.," the announcer was saying.

She remembered the last time she had stood on this field in her RobinSuit, when she'd come here for practice—how the rockets had propelled her into the air and she'd stretched her arms and legs, straightening her limbs, transforming her handmade RobinSuit into the airfoil on which she flew. The whole design may not have been perfect, but it had worked. She'd flown! With that thought, something in her rallied. She curled a hand and placed a thumb on the rocket activation button. *Go ahead and push the button,* she told herself. *It will work for at least a moment.* After her inevitable quick descent, she'd make up an excuse, say it had always worked better than that. She needed to tweak it, make it operate the way it usually did. Lying to people who gave her the benefit of the doubt was easy.

Jessabelle saw Doc in his Juggling Baba attire, his eyes hot with expectation. She gazed at Lalli, seated crosslegged in her special chair, off on the side of the stage. All dressed in white, Lalli appeared like something from another world, a bronze angel who drifted to earth on invisible wings, specifically to take her place in Jessabelle's life. Jessabelle had never realized just how beautiful Lalli was.

Jessabelle heard words from inside. "It's your choice." She couldn't tell whose voice it was; it sounded like Shiva, herself, and Lalli, all at once.

It came to Jessabelle: If she didn't tell the truth here today, she might as well let Uncle Trix shoot her now, because if she continued living a life of lies, she was already dead. Standing on the hill with her arms at her sides, wingtips resting on the ground, she could see how she'd evolved into a liar. What began as a single act of dishonesty became her way of life. Years with Uncle Trix had made hiding her identity second nature, cemented her lying habit.

Uncle Trix wasn't here now. Lalli was.

Through Lalli, Jessabelle had received Awakening. With it, a new energy had been unleashed in her, and with this unbinding, she felt her central nature come alive.

The time had come to stand in her own internal power. To embody Shiva, the innermost part of her whole being, that part of her completely separate from happiness and pain, wealth and poverty. To uphold all she had received in this place, protecting the life that had grown inside her like the rising sun.

Like a great ball of fire rolling through black teeth, she yelled, "I'm not who I've purported to be." Her heart beat so loud, she was sure the people in the back row could hear it. Her pulse raced.

Confusion spread through the crowd like a wild blaze.

People turned their heads toward one another, furrowing their brows and pursing their lips.

"I'm not a physicist," Jessabelle continued, "and my name is not Isa Newton. It's Jessabelle Knox. I'm a special makeup effects artist." With a sudden inclination to tell a bit of her life story, she continued. "My mother got sent to prison for armed robbery. She was let out for one day when a guard drove her in a van owned by the state of Wisconsin to the hospital so she could give birth to me." A pang of regret for starting this story struck Jessabelle. She glanced at Lalli, hoping she'd cut her off the way she had when others had started what sounded like an autobiography. Well? she asked with a small movement of her bird head, aren't you going to say something?

But Lalli didn't, and the crowd's foggy expressions forced her to go on. "I used to visit my mother, although I don't remember much about it. She died when I was three. The people who adopted me were kind people and good parents, but they went to jail too, for attempted robbery of a sneaker store. I myself am a thief. I came here to steal a solid gold statue that I heard Mr. Halloway gave Lalli."

The Halloway family gasped, and Jessabelle's voice trailed off as she caught sight of Doc at the back of the crowd, turning to leave. By the disappointment in his eyes and the downturned shape of his mouth, she knew it wasn't a security issue calling him off. What she'd said was the thing driving him away. She opened her mouth to call his name and plead with him not to go. Tell him she'd changed, was different now than when they first met. It would never happen again. It could never happen again, because of how she felt about Lalli, him, everything and everybody in this place.

The spectators scrutinized her, their faces serious and perturbed, but she didn't care. It wasn't her goal to upset people, but in this madness that upset them, she felt free. If none of these people ever wanted to talk to her again, she couldn't help that. All she could do is speak her truth.

She closed her mouth, breathing in deeply through her nose, steadying her resolve. She opened her mouth and spoke to Lalli and the crowd, saying all the things she would have told Doc, followed by, "I'm sorry. I hope you can forgive me." After pausing for several seconds to catch her breath, she ended with, "I don't need these wings to fly. Awakening has shown me what it's like to fly. I don't have to invent a flying machine. The ancient sages of India have already invented several. They're called chanting, meditation, Awakening. In them, I have discovered absolute Truth, and now that I have gotten a taste of it, all I want is to go deeper and deeper into that state, to become established in it." Everything became very still inside, as if something in her had died.

"We'll see," Lalli said. "Many people have high visions and then fall right back into their old habits. It takes strength to live in Truth." Lalli asked everyone to offer Jessabelle messages on how she could establish herself in Truth.

"Make a vow to do it and stick to your vow," somebody said.

"Make a plan of how you will stick to the vow," said someone else, "and carry out the plan."

Johann suggested, "Keep something in your pocket that reminds you of your vow. When dishonesty tempts you, take a good long look at that thing."

"Practice the mantra and meditation until bad habits are forgotten, your system is clean, and all that exists is Truth."

"Ask for forgiveness," called a woman.

Jessabelle thought she already had.

"Not of us," the woman added, "but of yourself."

When no one had any more suggestions, Lalli spoke. "It seems you think Truth is far away, a place you have to get to. Remember, it is not something that has to be attained. Be still and know you are it. It is you. To merge and become one with Truth, all you have to do is be the Self." Lalli smiled. "Spiritual disciplines are not for attaining Truth because Truth is already attained. Spiritual practices exist to purify the mind. When the mind is pure, we experience Truth within ourselves. Freedom is your natural state. Be strong, and your stamina will allow it to be."

Hearing Lalli say those words, Jessabelle experienced an endless longing to live in Truth, a longing so deep it hurt. From out of this longing, her own voice came.

"I promise I will make the effort to be the Self."

Lalli unexpectedly shifted her gaze from Jessabelle to Aaron, who sat motionless, clutching his falcon and staring at Jessabelle with wide-eyed fascination. Lalli called his name, breaking the "Spell of the Giant Robin" that he was under. He revolved his head toward her.

"Did you come here to see a big bird fly?" she asked.

Aaron nodded.

"I see you even brought your own bird out for the occasion."

Aaron's nodding grew more vigorous, now accompanied by a smile so broad Jessabelle could see the space where one of his front bottom teeth was missing.

"What's your bird's name?" Lalli asked the boy.

"Bob."

"What does your bird do?"

"Sleeps in my bed. Eats Cheerios. Talks." Aaron squeezed the falcon's chest and it produced a series of piercing shrill calls, so authentic they could have been recorded in nature. The ringletted young girl squeaked and chirped, communicating with Bob in bird language. Aaron squeezed his toy again, sending more birdsong into the air. Keeping up the conversation, the girl squawked and squealed, chattering like a bird. She and Aaron shared a giggle so refreshing in its purity that it compelled the whole crowd to snicker.

Having engaged the audience, Aaron was on a roll. "He kisses Mommy," he said next. He tapped the falcon's curved bill against his mom's cheek.

"Ohhhhh," the crowd cooed at the sweetness of the demonstration.

"He flies all over the place."

"Show us how," Lalli said.

"Okay."

Fearlessly, as if noone was watching, Aaron hopped to his feet and held the body of the falcon up. Weaving swiftly through the places where people were seated on the lawn, he gleefully bobbed the bird up and down, creating an illusion that the falcon was flapping its wings. Aaron came back to his place and bended the bird into a curtsy to the tune of exuberant clapping and cheering.

Having been upstaged by a stuffed bird toy and his surefooted human friend, Jessabelle was sidestepping with raised wings toward the chalk boundary that marked the stage, attempting to slink off, when Aaron resumed his seat.

"Now let's see what this bird can do," Lalli said. Lalli swiveled in Jessabelle's direction, tossing the crowd's attention from Aaron and his cute little buddy back to Jessabelle.

With all those eyes burrowing into her bird body, Jessabelle stopped in her bird tracks.

"Are you just a pretty bird or do you fly too?" Lalli asked.

"I think I might sort of be able to fly."

"I'd hate for you to be all dressed up with noplace to go. Show us what you got."

"Bob and Aaron are a tough act to follow, but I'll give it my all."

Lalli gave a pleased smile as if that was exactly the thing she wanted to hear.

Jessabelle lowered her wings, resting their tips on the

ground. She pushed the rocket activation button under her right wing. The pressurized nitrogen she wore on her back transmuted the hydrogen peroxide into steam that gushed out the four rocket-shaped metal pieces strapped around her waist. The vapor billowed in such thick white clouds at her base that she felt more like a space shuttle lifting off than a robin hopping into flight.

Moving away from Earth, she rose higher and higher until each blade of grass became indistinguishable from the next and the bleachers appeared as if they were floating like a boat on a green sea, its on-deck passengers taking in some unusual aerial creature with expressions of fear and delight, delight over seeing something new, fear of not knowing if the thing was dangerous.

The rockets sputtered their last breath of steam. A warm breeze ruffled the feathers of her RobinSuit. She stretched her arms wide and spread her legs, embarking on her voyage through a warm sky. For a moment she was flying.

Then the breeze stopped.

She descended, drifting with outstretched wings toward the roof of the shed. She steered the RobinSuit, leaning her weight toward her desired point of touchdown in the middle of the roof, an applaudable stunt she hoped. But the wind started up again, blowing her off course.

Her painted claws glided past the roof while the tip of her right wing smacked it, tossing her as if she were a flexible Popsicle stick, colored brown and deep-orange, flipped the long way. She landed on her back, one wing down and the other one up.

Pulling her wings forward, she strained into a seated position. Using the rigid carbon fiber tubing at the front of one of her wings for support, she got one foot underneath her and from there managed standing.

"I never said I was a perfect bird."

* * *

It took Jessabelle twenty minutes to get from the talent show venue to the bottom of Liberation, walking at a slow pace, dragging her wings.

She saw Doc at the gas pump in front of the grocery store, still in his talent show costume. Her body tensed. She knew if she didn't at least try to make amends, she'd curse herself forever.

He glanced at her as she drew up beside the red-apple Cherokee. She returned his gaze, staring into the eyes of the man she felt was her soulmate. He rolled up the sleeves of the long, colorfully paneled silk shirt, then lifted the gas nozzle off the pump, selected unleaded, and started pumping.

She cleared her throat. "I'm so sorry. Please don't hate me."

"How can I not?"

"I tried to tell you that night at the lake, but you laughed. You should've listened!"

"So now it's my fault? I had no idea you were serious. I thought it was a joke. You should've told me you were serious."

"What can I say? I lost my guts."

"A demon has no guts," Doc spewed.

Out on the street, the ringletted young girl followed a group of people making their way back into town after the talent show. The girl bounced the pink and purple rubber ball Chet and Johann had used in their skit, perhaps a gift from one of the guys, or something the little girl had loaned them. The ball hit a rock and flew off in a trajectory. The girl chased it while her mother glanced around for cars.

"Are you calling me a demon?"

"You are a demon!"

"That's really mature coming from you, Mr. High and

Mighty!"

"Better than being a demon!"

The little girl stood frozen, ball in hand, her eyes pasted on Jessabelle and Doc, eyes stretched wide, as if they were made of soft rubber. That's when Jessabelle realized she and Doc were yelling. The little girl's mother took her daughter by the hand, guiding her off. "It's not polite to stare."

Jessabelle lowered her voice. "I knew this would happen if I told you the truth," she hissed. "I just knew it!"

"This is not the place to talk."

"Where is?"

"Nowhere! I can't talk to you!"

"Please talk to me, even if it's to tell me how much you hate me. Can we go to the park?"

"I'll meet you there in five minutes."

"Can't we just go together?"

"No!" He slammed the nozzle back on the pumpstand, got in the Cherokee, and left.

Walking to the park, Jessabelle worried he was playing a trick. She feared once she got to the park, he wouldn't be there. She imagined the humiliation she'd feel. Desire to turn away, to not go, to trick him before he tricked her, gripped her hard.

Lying is not Doc's way, she told herself. She just had to trust that he would not kick her when she was already down, no matter how pissed off he was.

When she arrived at the park, she indeed found him there, seated at a picnic table, in the likeness of Juggling Baba. She unsuccessfully attempted maneuvering into a seated position across from him, one that would accommodate the carbon fiber tubing she'd sewn at the front of each wing of her RobinSuit. She stood instead, a feathered creature, brown with a deep orange breast and belly, wings resting on the grass.

Impervious to her awkwardness, his eyes were so icy they were like an express train to the North Pole.

"I'm sorry," she said in an attempt to break through the ice and cold. "Can you forgive me?"

"I can forgive that you came here dressed as another person." The ice melting, his eyes began spitting fire. "I can even forgive that you used a fake name to deceive everybody, including me. But I can't get over the fact it was all for the purpose of stealing something from Lalli. That's just evil."

Beneath the area of her RobinSuit plumped up and puffed out with additional Kevlar, her chest tightened and her stomach sank. Her throat felt so dry she thought it might crack. He made her sound so bad, as if she'd committed some terrible crime, when actually she'd only imagined committing the crime.

"I don't understand," he continued. "I just don't. Why didn't you just tell me you're a thief?"

"Uh, duh. Let me count the reasons. For one, you said you didn't believe in thievery."

"When did I say that?"

"The first time we went to the café together. You were… are…so virtuous. So what was I supposed to do? Paint the words 'Isa Newton is a Thief' on your front door in red letters?"

"You could have. At least I would have known up front who I was dealing with."

"And then what? You would've run me out of this town without so much as a second glance."

"You can't tell me what I would've done." A warm breeze swirled the thick wavy whirly hairs of the wig she'd made for him, tossing a few pieces of it into his eyes. He stabbed his fingers into the runaway strands, chucked them off his face. "You made up lies out of thin air. Why did you lie about your family? You told me this whole story about your family. You made it up. I don't understand why."

"I just wanted my family to sound more like yours—a family who keeps a Mercedes in the garage, goes on Caribbean yacht vacations, and gives their kids ballroom dance lessons."

Surely she'd just purchased a one-way ticket out of his life, and there was no returning it now. Even through the multiple pieces of the Indian man mask he'd made for himself, she saw puzzlement in his expression.

"How do you know I took ballroom dance lessons?" he asked.

"It's obvious from the way you dance. I'll bet you won a couple of competitions too."

"Three, which I could never do now because of my foot."

"Of course you could," she said. "You dance like a professional." She wasn't just flattering him to regain his favor; she meant what she'd said.

"Thanks, but that doesn't explain how you know my family owns a Mercedes, or goes on Caribbean yacht vacations."

"I was in your house before I came here." She was digging a hole deeper and deeper. The more she spoke, the deeper it got. But what else could she do? She'd vowed to live in truth no more than thirty minutes ago.

"Before you came here," he persisted, "I didn't even know you. What were you doing in my house?"

She drew a deep breath, then launched into the whole story.

"Omigod," he said when she got to the end. "This keeps getting worse. What else did you lie about?"

"Nothing."

"You expect me to believe that?"

"Yes."

"Do you really do prosthetics?"

"Of course. How could I lie about that? Just look at my face." She squawked like a bird.

"Why'd you make up the thing about the pigs?"

"I saw some pigs," she insisted, in the indignant tone of one falsely accused. Habit prodded her toward sinking her hands on her hips for added effect, but her arms, hooked up at the moment, only strained against her wings.

"If that's true, how come you're the only one who's ever seen them?"

"I swear there are pigs around here. If you don't believe me, you can"—she sighed—"I don't know what you can do."

"You said you weren't married. Is that true?"

"Of course. Why would I make that up?"

"I have no idea. I just think a woman capable of dreaming up a plot to steal a statue from a saint is capable of saying anything. For all I know, you have five kids in a trailer in Tenessee."

"Five kids! I'm only twenty-three!"

"You could've started early."

"Geez, Doc! I didn't come here to find a boyfriend. I came here to steal a statue."

He flinched, as if someone had swatted him with a newspaper. "Thanks for the clarification."

She felt they'd gotten off the subject. "I don't even consider myself a thief," she said, trying to bring their discussion back on course. "I just wanted money to finish art college."

"There're other ways to get to art college."

"Maybe for you, but not for me."

"Scholarships, Pell grants—"

"I tried it all."

"And your parents couldn't help you?"

He just didn't get it, or wasn't really listening. At any rate, her words weren't registering. "Which parent? The father I never met? The mother who died in prison? The adoptive parents who got sent to prison for robbing a sneaker store? The foster parents I ran away from? Which parents did you expect to help me?"

"Is this for real? Or are you making it up to gain my sympathy?"

She could just scream. She'd blown it so badly, he'd never believe another word she uttered. "Yeah." She rolled her eyes and tossed her head back in surrender. "I made it up."

"Look! I just don't know what to believe. If all that's true, how come you never told me?"

Couldn't he figure it out without her having to explain? He felt perfect to her, the one she wanted to be with. Couldn't he see she just wanted a chance with him? "I thought if you knew all that, you wouldn't think I was good enough for you."

"Do you think I'm so superficial I'd make a decision about you based on what your six parents did?"

"I only lied about my family because I liked you," she said. "And I thought you wouldn't like me if you knew the truth."

"So, what is the truth?"

"I told you—and everybody!—the truth."

"That was really the truth?"

She nodded.

"So that's the truth. I just can't believe it." His eyes softened, sparking a touch of the old Doc. He looked down at his hands.

She wished things were normal again. Well, not exactly normal with all the lying and deception, but back to all that was good about the way things were. Encouraging a return to these former times, she asked, "Do you want to meditate with me tonight?"

"Under the circumstances, I'm not sure I want to hang out with you anymore." A long silence followed. He stripped off his wig. "You can have this back." He tossed the wig on the picnic table. And with that, he jumped to his feet.

She couldn't help but think she was losing him, had in fact already lost him. "I don't know what else to say. I was a thief. But I'm not anymore. And you may not believe in thievery, but I believe in second chances. I deserve a second chance, Doc. Can you find it in your heart to give me one?"

"I need some time to think about it." Disappointment and pain written on his face, off he went, without looking back.

Chapter 36

Jessabelle Knox sat as Jessabelle Knox on a molded plastic chair at Krishna's Corner, elbows on table, chin propped in her palms, trying not to think about how much she missed Doc, Bennie, and everybody and everything, really.

A committee had been formed to decide whether her time at Lalliville should be terminated based on whether she posed a threat to the harmony of the environment. Until the committee made its decision, she wasn't allowed to go to chants, the meditation cave, or the shed to work. She could eat, that was it. This arrangement would have pleased her at one time, but right at the moment, it felt like pure torture.

She wanted to go to chants, the meditation cave. She wanted to finish what she and Bennie had started in the shed. Removing layers of grime from images of awakened ones had become an illuminating practice, an experience Jessabelle had come to crave as she wondered what wondrous being or penetrating gaze she might unveil as she cleaned each picture. She wanted to continue engaging in this discipline until there were no more pictures left to clean, and feared that in the end, she wouldn't be able to.

She'd been forced out of every place she'd ever lived. She hadn't even been allowed in her mother's home (prison). Then she was ousted from her home when Mom and Pops went to jail. She got thrown to the Cozies, a family she never would've chosen if she'd had any choice in the matter. When she finally escaped and made it to Creativo, she'd been ejected from there because she couldn't pay her bill. Always the outsider, she'd get booted out of here too, because that was her life—getting kicked out.

That didn't mean she wanted to go back to scamming. No. She'd made her vow, in front of everyone, and whatever happened, she'd honor that vow. She was done with scamming forever, that she knew.

If she had to leave, she would leave, and in her exile, park the step van near a beach, sell oysters for a living. It might not make her rich, but it was an honest profession. When she wasn't selling oysters, she'd honor her vow of becoming one with Truth by chanting and meditating. Maybe she'd even start doing japa.

Who was she trying to kid? She had to admit she'd rather be here than off on her own selling oysters.

Why couldn't she wash the desire for all this out of her system? Like taking a sip of herbal tea, and there, it's gone. To see if it might work, she lifted her mug of tension tamer tea and swigged. She swallowed and then said "Abracadabra" as the liquid rolled down her throat. She closed her eyes, imagined it dissolving in her stomach, and waited to see if it had the magic to make her forget her experiences in Lalliville.

Images of Doc and Bennie danced to the sweet sounds of Jaya Shiva Om. Soon they were doing the fox trot with memories of Lalli seated in her chair at a Day of Practice. Her heart pounded for all of that.

Her life would be so much easier if the pictures didn't make her heart beat so. If she didn't care about any of the people she befriended, or practices she had discovered here, she could rejoin Uncle Trix, content to be a crook and a vagabond headed for Creativo. But she knew she could no longer be content with that, not even for a second. After all she'd experienced in this place, how could she ever again be happy with that? Being here had enriched her life in ways she'd never expected.

Everything will be okay, she told herself. She could still chant, meditate, and practice yoga on her own. But she knew it wouldn't be the same without her new friends. What if she was forced to leave and never saw any of them again?

Arrghh. Her jaw tightened. Her chin sank further into her palms. She glanced at the coconut cookies she had bought but lacked the spirit to eat. They stared back like two bright eyes into a melancholic night that could not embrace them.

She tried to cheer herself by dreaming up her next creation. How about an alligator? She tried conjuring designs, but lacking any real enthusiasm for it in that moment, gave up after only a few seconds.

She tried not to think of how much fun it was meditating with Doc, adjusting Fuzz's prosthetic leg, working with Bennie. Everything had plunged from pretty good to really bad. Now she was suspended; Doc was ignoring her; and Bennie was in the hospital.

In some ways Bennie was such a kid, thrilled by balloons and piggyback rides. In other ways he was more mature than many adults. Who would ever have guessed he'd defeat two people twice his size to protect Lalli?

He seemed to belong here, loved and accepted by everyone. She wanted that. "You'll never have it," she mumbled. "Not after this debacle." She considered packing her bags right now and leaving, saving anybody the hassle of having to kick her out. She'd go to the hospital, say goodbye to Bennie, and then drive to her new destination of oysters.

She heard the sound of the door open and then voices. "Mind if we join you?" Vishva, Johann, and Chet stood beside the table.

Jessabelle perked up. "No."

Johann and Chet plunked down in chairs they brought from other tables while Vishva took her place across the way. "We didn't recognize you without all that stuff on your face," Johann said.

Vishva nodded. "If it weren't for the sneakers, we wouldn't have known."

Johann leaned in toward Jessabelle's face, examining her nose at close range. He reached up and squeezed it.

"Please," she said, recoiling. "Don't touch my nose." She smacked his hand away.

"Just checking to see if it's real."

Chet asked, "Cookies that bad?"

"It's not the cookies," Jessabelle said. "I lost my appetite."

"I haven't lost mine." He reached out and placed a hand on the edge of the plate. "You mind?"

"No. Help yourself."

As he towed the small white paper plate over to his side of the table, Johann said, "For next year's talent show, Chet and I want to take our costumes to new heights."

"That won't be hard," Jessabelle said, recalling their headdresses at this year's talent show, Johann's mop head and Chet's turbanized table linen. She'd never met Johann's mother, but she was fairly certain his mother didn't look like a chic man with a mop on his head. She'd also seen pictures of the Free & Blissful Yogi wearing turbans—rich, colorful silk turbans. None of them were tablecloths.

"So you'll help us?" Johann asked.

"After this trip," Jessabelle said, "I'm not sure I'll be allowed back for another."

"You'll be back."

"Aren't you guys mad at me?"

"For what? Dressing as a nerd to steal a statue from Lalli? That kind of thing happens around here all the time."

"Then why did the committee suspend me?"

"Somebody's got to deal with the insanity."

"Easy for you to joke about it now," Vishva said.

"Who's joking?" Johann asked. "Don't you remember the old man who snuck into the orchard in the middle of the night with a ladder and bucket and picked all the papayas from the papaya tree?"

"He didn't leave a single one!" Chet said.

"Really?" Jessabelle asked. "How did they catch him?"

"Doc caught him when he came back to strip the mango tree," Johann explained.

"But nobody ever exactly became friends with him," Vishva said. "He wasn't like Isa, I mean Jessabelle. He didn't live here."

"Did he go to jail?" asked Jessabelle.

"No," answered Chet. "Lalli was kind to that old man. He told her, 'Nature's bounty belongs to everyone.' She told him, 'That's true, but there's no such thing as a free harvest. And since nature's bounty belongs to everyone, it's meant to be shared.'"

"In the end," Johann said, "she let the old guy come here and work with the gardeners. He learned to cultivate his own fruit trees and shares their bounty with his neighbors."

Chet swallowed the last bite of Jessabelle's cookies and

dusted his hand on his blue and white checked pant leg. "I gotta get back to it," he said, and stood up. Johann left with him.

Vishva leveled her gaze at Jessabelle. "You've got guts, I'll give you that. Coming here under the guise of someone else. I could never do a thing like that, not in a million years."

"No. I'm just a fool. A total and utter fool."

"Let it be a lesson for us all."

Jessabelle considered what kind of lesson this could be for Vishva.

"Now that we know you weren't yourself, it's obvious you weren't yourself. But it was obvious even back then. We just weren't looking. Lalli urges us to have common sense in our spiritual quest."

As always, Jessabelle felt Vishva's love.

"That was quite a vow you made during the talent show," Vishva said.

"I've learned that my satisfaction lies within."

"I thought it was a good idea to have something to remind you of your vow. Did you find something?"

Vishva's integrity reminded her of her vow, but Jessabelle couldn't very well tuck that into her back pocket. "Not yet."

"How about a piece of scripture?"

"I was thinking more along the lines of a mala. In situations that tempt me to be dishonest, I can remember Shiva, and that satisfaction lies within."

"A mala. That's a good idea. I've never seen you wear one. Do you even own one?"

"No, but that's a situation easy to mend. I'll just steal one."

Vishva gasped.

"Just kidding!" Jessabelle held up her hands. "I no longer have the desire to steal anything."

"Good!"

Doc came through the door. Without turning her head, she could tell it was him by the sound of his sneakers on the linoleum floor tiles at the café's entrance.

STEALING SHIVA

"There's Doc," Vishva said, waving to him.

Jessabelle refused to turn toward him.

"Aren't you going to wave?" Vishva asked.

"No."

"I thought something was happening between you two."

Jessabelle winced. From the corner of her eye, she glimpsed Doc purchasing a brownie he carried away with him, leaving without so much as a nod over his shoulder.

"He's mad, isn't he?" said Vishva.

"Really mad."

"I hope he gets over it. He could use a woman who doesn't mind a few body parts lying around the house. A…what is he again?"

"Anaplastologist."

"An anaplastologist and a makeup effects artist. Seems like a match made in Heaven."

Say what you like, Jessabelle thought, *it's just not meant to be.*

Jessabelle was confident in her ability to survive without Doc. Heck, she hadn't even known him two months ago, and before that she lived just fine (if driving from one Wally's to another in search of a sale could be called living). Now if she could just stop thinking about him, she'd be all right.

"How's Bennie?" she asked.

"The same," Vishva told her. "But his parents are here now, and everyone is hopeful."

"Vishva, thank you for everything," Jessabelle said. "You're a really good person. I hope life brings you only the best things."

"This sounds like a goodbye. Are you going somewhere?"

"I'm leaving, so the committee doesn't have to throw me

out."

"You can't leave yet. Lalli wants to see you."

Jessabelle's stomach tightened. Anxiety, sharp as a thousand pins, pushed through her. "Does she want to yell at me?"

Vishva shrugged. "She didn't tell me why she wants to see you. Just told me to give you the message to come to her house after the moon rises."

Jessabelle sought details on the reason for the odd meeting time. Vishva had none to offer, only said, "Lalli is one with the universal energy. Sometimes her requests are practical. Other times mystical. You'll never know why she asked you to do something until you do it, and even then you may never know. But rest assured, her requests are always intended to bring one or more of her devotees closer to the Truth."

Seven forty-five p.m. found Jessabelle standing on the lawn of her house, head tilted back, gazing up into the sky. She was a sentinel on the lookout for moonrise, with irises and retinas unclouded by the tint of any foreign object, such as colored contacts or thick glasses.

A soft haze of light bathed her. Those first rays of moonlight ignited the effulgence within. Jessabelle followed the moon with her gaze. Angling up into the sky, it went from red to orange and then yellow.

In all her roles, that was one thing she'd never been: the moon. Tonight it was a perfect and full circle. Seeing it as never before, she stood mesmerized by that luminous being. In its light, she found herself trying to envision the first person who appeared on Earth five million years ago.

Then she was flooded with impressions of the thousands of civilizations that had risen and fallen since. In that great wide movement, she saw Egyptian pyramids, the Chinese alphabet, the ancient isles of Greece and the Roman Empire, followed by the Vikings, the Aztecs, and the Incas.

When this panoply of history passed, human life struck her as something vast and truly awe-inspiring.

She thought about the billions of people who existed in the past, the billions of people who now lived on Earth, and the billions more who belonged to the future. Then a question arose from someplace very deep: Was there one person on Earth or one person who ever existed on Earth who never saw the moon? And was there one to come who'd never in their life look into the sky, just as she did on that night, to see the moon?

In that moment she felt the moon as some deep and primitive force that had existed since time immemorial. In the quietness of its waxing and waning cycles, it had seen the birth and growth of human civilization and it would see it through to its final outcome.

From its vantage point in the sky, it held the secrets of yesterday, today, and tomorrow, and she felt connected, in that moment, to the entire breadth, the beauty, and the awe of humankind through this moon upon which she gazed.

Jessabelle's eyes roved the surface of the celestial body, studying its features, wondering what it was like to live so high. In the peaceful eyes, tranquil cheeks, and serene smile of its face, Jessabelle recognized Lalli.

Lalli. It was time to go see Lalli.

When Jessabelle reached the bottom of the walkway leading to Lalli's house, her heart skipped a beat. She stopped and sucked in her breath.

There she was, seated on her front step, illumined by the light of the moon.

Lalli.

Lalli with the silken hair and exotic eyes that made Jessabelle feel as if she was on vacation in the tropics. Lalli with lips so full, that uttered words that lived inside Jessabelle's heart like a prayer. Lalli who sat so still, Jessabelle felt her peace as a palpable force that washed up on her like ocean waves rippling to her feet while she stood in the sand.

Motioning with her hand, Lalli beckoned Jessabelle to wade into the water. Jessabelle came forward, took a seat beside Lalli on the steps. Engulfed in Lalli's aura, she felt herself calming and heard herself confessing.

Jessabelle told Lalli how she had traveled around with Uncle Trix, conning people into buying five-dollar brass bars for $2,000 or however much they could get a pop. How they'd met Blondo and Wrench. She talked about how Uncle Trix had come up with the idea to steal the statue. How it was her job to go undercover, find the golden Shiva, and inform him where it was.

Lalli listened without smiling, crying, nodding, or saying "Oh Dear!" While her face bore no judgments, her features remained soft.

Lalli's plain unadulterated expression freed Jessabelle from fear of rejection, gave her hope for redemption. "I've learned my lesson," Jessabelle said.

"What lesson is that?" asked Lalli.

"Deceit is no good. From here on out, I wear no more costumes."

Lalli arched an eyebrow.

"What?"

"Promise you won't neuter your artistic skills. Indeed, it is desirable to pare away our veils to reach the true Self, but being a liar and a fraud is one of your best qualities."

Wide-eyed, Jessabelle drew back. "It is?"

Lalli nodded. "You have come to develop compassion for all creatures through your ability to become them—a realization of the unity of all creation."

Jessabelle considered the statement. Creating and becoming other people, animals, fruits, and bugs was indeed her favorite part of herself. "But look at what trouble my skills have caused. How about those two people who tried to kidnap you? The one who ran over Bennie? And then there's my uncle, the one who tried to choke me, because I wouldn't tell him where the statue was."

"None of those things happened because you were dressed as a nerd."

Pensively, Jessabelle asked, "Well then, why did they happen?"

"They were just obstacles. Like anywhere else, you'll find them on the spiritual path. They must be overcome."

"But some of them happened to you and Bennie."

"My devotees'Troubles become my troubles. It comes with guru territory. I always thrive, and the day I don't, Jaya Shiva Om. Bennie will survive, and will be—already is—stronger for it. I also want you to prosper from your stay in Lalliville." Lalli gazed over her right shoulder, off into the darkness for a moment, then back at Jessabelle. "Maybe it's time you told your uncle where the statue is. When is the latest you can call him?"

"In regard to the golden Shiva, any time."

"Good. I want you to call your uncle and tell him, 'This is your opportunity. We'll be moving the statue tomorrow.'"

"You really want me to do that?"

"Yes. It's all part of my plan."

Lalli revealed her strategy for banishing Uncle Trix, Blondo, and Wrench from Jessabelle's life and the lives of all other Lalliville residents. She let Jessabelle modify it a bit by throwing in a few ideas of her own.

Once they had designed the plan, Jessabelle phoned Uncle Trix, ensuring his participation in it. While transporting the statue in a Lalliville box truck, she told him, Jessabelle would talk Lalli into stopping at twelve-thirty for lunch at

Burger Barn. Jessabelle would secretly leave the keys in the truck while they proceeded inside.

Lalli would probably order Leguminous Legend, because it was the only vegetarian thing on the menu. Jessabelle would probably order the same thing, because she liked being a vegetarian. She'd also feel rude munching two all-beef patties while Lalli ate a mix of kidney beans, tomatoes, and cheese on a bed of iceberg lettuce. Once they got their food, Jessabelle would lead Lalli to a table far away from any windows, so Lalli wouldn't be able to see the parking lot. Jessabelle would be sure they remained there until one-thirty. That would give him an hour to come by and steal the statue.

When she finished explaining it all, she said, "Oh, and Uncle Trix, no guns. Promise?"

"Sure," he said. "I promise."

Chapter 37

In carrying out Lalli's plan, Jessabelle and Lalli traveled along Route 54 in a Lalliville box truck, headed toward Burger Barn. It was twelve-fifteen in the afternoon.

With a full awareness of the spaciousness that existed in the box truck's tall, wide cab, Jessabelle smiled a little smile as she sat high on the bench seat, upholstered in worn and torn black leather. She wore a pair of easy-fitting blue jeans and her orange and blue striped T, the clothes that had been rolled up and stuffed in a side pouch of her suitcase. No prosthetic pieces were glued on her face, a face free from all traces of makeup, cosmetic or stage. She took in the magnificent view of fields and trees from behind the wheel while she and Lalli sang Jaya Shiva Om in a two-person call and response. It seemed the perfect moment. With the breeze through the open window blowing her real hair, brushing her real cheeks, she went forth, not as she created, but as she was created.

Lalli became quiet, prompting Jessabelle to do the same. Lalli said, "Many times, things in our life don't go exactly as planned." Before Jessabelle knew it, Lalli was off on a short discourse. "Life is uncertainty. Our plans are only blueprints. In the building process, they often need modification. Never refute what is happening in the moment." Lalli ended with, "Remember, we're prepared for anything."

"Right, anything."

"But if you find yourself in a situation you can't handle, walk away. A hundred and forty-four pounds of gold is not worth sacrificing your life for."

A minute later a cluster of bright flashing lights reflected off the rearview mirror, piercing Jessabelle's pupils, puncturing her brain, sending her into slight shock. She blinked. Through half closed eyes, she inspected the beaming image further, revealing its source to be a bubble light on the dashboard of the plain white Chevy behind the truck.

"I think it's the police," Jessabelle said.

"Pull over," Lalli said. "See what the phantoms want."

'Phantoms' seemed an unusual term for the police, but Lalli's word choice would soon make sense to Jessabelle.

Jessabelle hit the brake, bringing the truck to a stop on the side of the road.

Uncle Trix appeared at Lalli's window wearing a stiff, dark navy-blue police uniform with a gold badge sewn on top of one of the shirt sleeves. "Get out of the car!" he demanded.

"First tell me," Lalli said, "what do you want?"

"I need to search this truck for marijuana."

"There is no marijuana in this car," Lalli said. "I've never used the stuff, preferring to get high on the bliss of the Self. Tell me what you really want. I will gladly give it to you."

"I know Shiva is in this truck."

"Shiva is in this truck, and not in it. He is in the world, and not in the world."

"Don't mess with me, Holy Woman. I know you got a solid gold statue in this truck." Uncle Trix jerked open the door on Lalli's side. He unholstered the high-caliber hand-gun on his belt.

Jessabelle gasped, the sharp edge of terror taut against her gut.

Uncle Trix pointed the gun at Lalli's head. "Get out," he said.

This was not part of the plan. No guns, they'd agreed. He'd promised.

"Do exactly what the man says," Lalli told Jessabelle. "I don't want you getting hurt." Before she stepped out of the truck, she squeezed Jessabelle's hand, a gesture meant, no doubt, to inject her with strength.

Uncle Trix hopped up, assuming Lalli's vacated seat. Wielding the gun toward the grassy shoulder of the road, he ordered Lalli, "Go sit on a carpet of grass and meditate, Holy Woman."

"What a good idea." Lalli walked to the place Uncle Trix indicated with the tip of his gun and seated herself there, crosslegged. She closed her eyes. Jessabelle read Jaya Shiva Om, Jaya Shiva Om, as it printed out on Lalli's silently moving lips.

Uncle Trix contorted his face in disgust as he turned back toward Jessabelle.

"You heard the woman," he hollered. "Do as I say. If you don't, I will blow your brain to pieces. Now get this truck moving. I got an antiquities dealer waiting for gold. If you try to jump out, I will kill your new friend. Got it?"

The thought of Uncle Trix shooting Lalli exploded in Jessabelle's gut like a poisoned meatball. It made her feel sick all over.

"A massive bloodsplotch would really mess up that white thingamajig she's wearing." Uncle Trix gave Jessabelle such a sinister smile, it made her blood blanch.

Would he really shoot Lalli?

Jessabelle wanted to believe this was just a show. But if all his maniacal talk, sinister smiles, and ominous expressions were merely part of a performance, he should be nominated for an Academy Award. His cold, desperate eyes pummeled her with the fear that he meant what he said. "This isn't what we agreed on."

"There's been a change of plans. Sorry if I forgot to tell you."

"I told you no guns. We agreed."

"Yeah, well, gunpowder is just what a man needs to control runaway slaves." He held the gun against her head. In this heat, it felt particularly cold against her ear. "Now let's go."

Jessabelle put the truck in gear, backed up, and hit the front of the Chevy. Uncle Trix jabbed the tip of the gun into her ear. "I swear, Jessie," he said. "I will shoot you."

"Can't you see? I didn't do it on purpose!"

Jessabelle put the truck in drive and hit the gas. The truck surged forward.

"Not too fast," Uncle Trix said. "I don't want to get stopped by the cops."

"You are the cops!" She took her foot off the gas, and the truck lost its speed. In her rearview mirror she could see Blondo, following in the Chevy.

"Funny. Now drive faster!" He pressed the gun harder into her ear. She squirmed, unsure if the fear of getting her brain blasted out made her do so, or the realization that she had spent the past three years of her life with a total lunatic. His life, her old life, seemed a crazy dream she wanted to get out of, alive.

A car passed in the other direction, and Uncle Trix lowered the gun so its tip jagged into her rib bone. He demanded that she turn right into an abandoned warehouse. At her questioning glance, he added, "Pit stop to be sure we have the gold, before going on."

The truck bumped across the warehouse parking lot (if a blanket of broken blacktop could be called a parking lot). He ordered her to park in the back, where she shut off the engine. "Now get out."

As much as she hated to, she obeyed him. He followed her out of the car with the gun trained on her head. They moved to the back of the truck.

Blondo emerged from the Chevy and came around to roll open the door to the truck bed.

"Whoa," Uncle Trix said, reeling back a step. "How many statues we got in there?" He gawked at an unidentified crate, and two more crates, the first marked "Party Supplies", the second "Ceramic Statue."

"Only one of gold."

"What the hell is in those other boxes?"

"I'll show you." Jessabelle climbed up onto the truck bed, approached the crate marked "Party Supplies," and pried off its top. A few spiral balloons sailed out. Jessabelle sent them out the back of the truck. They rose up into the sky. "On the way to dropping the statue, we were going to stop at the hospital to visit Bennie, the one she mowed down." She jabbed a thumb toward Blondo.

"How 'bout that one? You got a house in there?" Uncle Trix waved his gun toward the crate marked "Ceramic Statue," five-by-three-by-four-feet big, spacious enough to accommodate a 275-pound man with a thick-muscled physique, seated in lotus posture.

"Just a ceramic clunker," Jessabelle lied.

From the bottom of Hanuman's ass to the top of his skull

alone measured four feet. Throw in a pillow for him to sit on, and he hadn't fit in any of the ordinary crates lounging around the warehouse. Bhisma had risen at five that morning to custom-make that crate for his gigantic friend.

"Here's the statue," Jessabelle said, turning their attention from the "Ceramic Statue" box to what they desperately wanted. With her fingers, she jimmied off the front of the crate housing Shiva, exposing the golden god.

The sounds of "Ooo" and "Ahh" rose from the mouths of Uncle Trix and Blondo. While they admired the gold, Jessabelle hopped off the back of the truck and ventured out toward the street. Once out of sight, she'd make her phone call.

"Stop!" she heard. Jessabelle turned to see Uncle Trix pointing the gun at her head all over again. He clenched his teeth, narrowed his eyes, and glared at Jessabelle. "Where do you think you're going?"

"I gave you what you want so you'd leave my friends alone. Now I'm going back to Lalliville."

"Why do you want to go back there?"

"Meditation, truth, love."

Uncle Trix and Blondo chortled in sync with each other.

"Meditation, truth, and love won't buy anything."

"I guess the things I want are the things money can't buy. Lalli suggested I go for those, and all else will follow."

The sound of their mirth grew raucous, reminding Jessabelle of a pot banging on a kettle, perhaps because of the small engraved nameplates pinned on their breasts beneath brass badges. His read Officer Stewpot, hers Officer Kettledrum. Jessabelle wondered if the geniuses had been cooking something when they'd concocted those names.

"Hey, stupid," Uncle Trix said, after their hilarity died out, "do you remember Jim Jones?"

"Who?"

"Jim Jones. He was the founder of an agricultural commune in Guyana."

"So?"

"It ended when he persuaded his followers to perform a mass suicide."

She knew he wasn't just stating a fact. What he was really doing was accusing Jessabelle of getting sucked into something dangerous, and Lalli of plotting to murder everyone in Lalliville. "Lalliville isn't home to some crazy criminal cult leader," she said.

"Whatever you say. Now gimme the keys to the truck."

She slapped the keys in his hand.

"Now your phone."

She handed over her cell phone.

He jerked his chin to Blondo. "Tie her up."

"You can't be serious."

"Dead serious." Uncle Trix pressed the hammer of the gun with his thumb. "Do not try anything."

Blondo yanked Jessabelle's arms behind her back and bound them with rope. Then she demanded Jessabelle place her ankles together so she could tie them as well. Jessabelle put up no fight, just did as Blondo told her.

"Will you kill me?" she asked Uncle Trix.

"Haven't decided yet. You're good at faces and costumes. But now that we're retiring, we won't have much use for disguise anymore." He tipped his police hat. "All your talk of living in truth has made me kind of nervous. I mean, look at you, you're on duty, and you're standing there without any disguise. You might as well be naked. What happened to you in Lalliville?"

"I found my Self."

"Can't have your newfound self ratting us out. I think we're better off with you dead, and until then, real quiet."

Blondo slapped a piece of duct tape over Jessabelle's mouth.

Uncle Trix holstered his gun, threw Jessabelle over his shoulder, and carried her to the back of the box truck.

Jessabelle lay on the floor of the box truck, staring at the metal roof, replaying the last fifteen minutes in her mind. Had Uncle Trix really held a gun to her head while Blondo tied her up? The braid of rope cutting into her wrists and the strip of duct tape gluing her mouth shut told her it was true.

The box truck jolted over a bump, rattling her body.

Why couldn't she just have a normal life? An uncle who sent her fifty bucks every year for her birthday? Not one who killed her for however much money he planned to make off the statue.

She realized it was never really the money she wanted. Her deepest desire had always been truth and love. Having these seemed so natural. Why did it take all this artifice and pain just to have them?

Her life was so complicated. She couldn't fault Uncle Trix for that. She couldn't blame Mom and Pops, or even the Cozies. She blamed herself for thinking all along that the money would be her salvation. It wasn't. But could doing the right thing really rescue her from the abyss of wrong actions?

She had no regrets about her current position in life. She knew she'd done the right thing by ending her association with Uncle Trix. If by some strange stroke of fate, that parting of ways was destined to bring about her death, then so be it. Better to die at age twenty-three pushing upward to do the right thing than to spend eternity on this earth buried under wrong actions.

Something furry brown scuttled in the shadows. She flinched before realizing it was just a wolf spider taking refuge in a high corner. The wolf spider's eyes glowed like silvery blue-green dots, illumined by light seeping through the truck bed's fiberglass roof. Those eyes gave Jessabelle the uncanny feeling that the spider was staring at her in fear. No doubt the way things appeared to that spider—if it saw things the way people saw things—she was in deep shit.

"Despite the way things look," she inwardly assured the spider, "I am no longer afraid." She wasn't scared, because of her faith in the saints, in Lalli's wisdom, in that strong presence in the crate marked "Ceramic Statue." She heard Hanuman's steady breath, coming in and going out.

Impelled by her faith, she inhaled deeply through her nose and began moving by small degrees, contracting her body like an inchworm forced to lie on its side, gradually making her way to the handmade crate.

She head-butted the container three times, simultaneously humming the words "I need your help now" through taped-up lips. Then she rolled on her back and waited.

The crate's front panel cracked open. Hanuman emerged from the box. He untied her hands. With her freed hands, she extricated her feet and peeled the tape off her mouth.

Hanuman held out his cell phone, offering her its use. "No thanks," she said. "I've got one." Jessabelle rolled up her pant leg to find the second smartphone Lalli had suggested she wear, strapped beneath her jeans. She powered the phone on and dialed. On the other end, Lalli said she was in the back of a police car with Detective Douglas. She wanted to know if Jessabelle and Hanuman were okay.

"Yes," Jessabelle told her, "and we're on our way somewhere, although I don't know where."

"I do," Hanuman said, studying the GPS on his cell phone. "Wildflower Park."

"Wildflower Park," she repeated into the phone.

After she clicked off the phone, the truck stopped. Hanuman suggested they act as though nothing was up, at least for a few more minutes, giving Lalli time to arrive.

Following Hanuman's lead, Jessabelle wrapped the ropes around her ankles, but didn't tie them. She brought her arms behind her back, making it look like they were bound. Hanuman stuck the front of his crate back on, and then went around the back of it, squatting to conceal himself.

The door to the truck bed opened with the roll of metal, revealing Wrench. One of his arms hung over the handle of a pumpjack. He winked at Jessabelle. "Trix told me that after I move the statue, I can take you out into the woods. Won't be much of a fight this time, with you tied up the way you are."

Wrench hopped up inside the truck and flipped the switch that brought out the lift. He pushed the crate that held the golden Shiva out onto the platform, then lowered it to the ground.

"Who needs a pumpjack when we got three able bodies," Uncle Trix said. He nudged Blondo to come forward with him. "Wrench, Bernadette, you each take a corner. I'll take two."

They lifted the statue and carried it toward the open side door of a white Dodge van parked nearby.

Halfway to it, Blondo said, "Can we put this down a second so I can get a better grip? I'm afraid I'm gonna drop it."

They set it down. Jessabelle slipped off the ropes that bound her hands.

Hanuman flashed past her, right through the space where the statue had been. He leapt off the back of the truck, landed in the center of the statue's crate lid, and dropped to a crouching position. He swung his arm, connecting his right fist with Wrench's face, knocking him back. Instantly he whirled and his left wrist lashed the side of Uncle Trix's head. Uncle Trix went over. Hanuman sprang off the box and snatched the gun from Uncle Trix's holster. "Don't anybody move."

Hanuman ordered Jessabelle, "Scram! Go climb a tree."

Jessabelle skedaddled, scurrying off to find a tree she could climb. At the base of a big oak, selected for its choice knots and bark holes, she swung up into a bark hole and took hold of a knot, then ascended into the tree, climbing as high as a giraffe.

She positioned herself in a sturdy place, with her feet established on a large strong branch and fingers wrapped around a gnarly branch above for help maintaining her balance. A covering of leaves concealed her in the tree's canopy. She heard a birdsong, "Chippily chip chip chippio, chippily chip chip chippio." Following the sound, she saw a robin perched close by.

The sound of a wailing siren scared away the robin, scattering him and all his other winged friends in the vicinity. From Jessabelle's bird's-eye view, she spotted the police car, speeding through the park entrance. The black and white Taurus braked in the parking lot, kicking up a storm of gravel dust. Lalli and Detective Douglas emerged from the police car, followed by two policemen, dressed like Uncle Trix and Blondo.

"My comrades in law enforcement," Uncle Trix shouted toward the men in blue. "Thank God you're here. My partner and I are being held hostage by a lunatic."

The policemen drew their guns, moving in on Hanuman, who kept the trio at bay with Uncle Trix's gun. The police aimed their guns at Hanuman.

Hanuman indicated Uncle Trix, who lumbered to his feet. "This is the guy who tried choking the girl," he told Detective Douglas. "Check out his shoes."

Jessabelle grinned as the detective took note of Uncle Trix's Italian footwear.

"He's lying," Uncle Trix claimed. "My partner and I—" he waved a finger between him and Blondo, "we got a call about a robbery in progress. When we got here, this ape was stealing this statue. We tried stopping him, but he got my gun."

From her lookout point, everything below seemed so small. Standing there with the top of his uniform covered in dust, trying to dodge being caught red-handed stealing the statue, Uncle Trix embodied the shape and sound of the average criminal weasel. But judging by the way the police kept their guns leveled on Hanuman, they believed the sneak. Jessabelle shook her head in disbelief.

Lalli stepped forward, identified Wrench and Blondo as the two trespassers in Lalliville, "the ones who accosted me and hit Bennie with a truck." She used a tone compassionate and firm, bordering on polite. Her manner remained unchanged, even after Wrench had called her a holyrolling, lying bitch, a spasm that raised the detective's eyebrows and made Uncle Trix cringe.

"Who's he?" Detective Douglas asked Uncle Trix.

"A known felon. We were transporting him to prison. Sorry for his manners. He's a little touched in the head."

Detective Douglas directed the policemen to lower their guns.

"Is that your car?" the detective asked, motioning toward the van.

Uncle Trix confirmed with a nod. "Our undercover police van."

The detective sallied over behind the van, rummaging in the inside pocket of his navy suit jacket for his pad and pen. He jotted down the van's plate number, tore the sheet from the book, and handed it off to one of the policemen. "Please run a check on this." The policeman went off to the police car.

Detective Douglas moved up beside Uncle Trix, studied everything about him, his face, his body, his clothes. "You resemble a civilian who came to Bank U.S.A. two days ago and withdrew some cash." After a moment, his gaze dropped to the badge on Uncle Trix's chest. "What precinct are you with?"

"Greenville."

"There's no such place in Florida."

"Almost every state has a Greenville."

"That's why you said 'Greenville,' right? Because almost every state has one, you figured it was a good guess?"

"I said Greenville, because that's where we're from. Greenville, Florida."

The detective snapped his fingers. "Oh yeah, you're right. I just remembered, there is a Greenville, Florida, but it's nowhere near here, and your badge doesn't say anything about Greenville. Where did you get your badge?"

"State issued, from when I started my job."

The cop returned from checking the van's license plates. Following a brief, low-voiced powwow, the detective turned toward Uncle Trix. "Looks like you'll be getting another state-issued uniform—an orange jumpsuit."

Detective Douglas ordered the police to arrest the three desperados on charges of possession of a stolen vehicle, trespassing, hit and run, impersonating police officers, grand theft of art, and attempted murder. As the officers were reciting the Miranda rights, the detective lifted the handcuffs inserted inside the waistband of his pants and swayed them in front of Uncle Trix. "These are for you," he said, snapping them on. "I see you forgot to bring your own."

Chapter 38

Two hours after the police placed Uncle Trix, Blondo, and Wrench in handcuffs and carted the trio off to jail, Lalli and Jessabelle entered Pine Grove Hospital. They'd just said goodbye to Hanuman, who'd been met out front by Bhisma. The two guys were now on their way to deliver the statue to its new home—Lalli was donating the treasure to the Museum of Indian Antiquities in Miami, which according to Lalli was just four hours away.

Jessabelle rolled the crate marked "Party Supplies" on a handcart along a corridor in the children's ward. A question moseyed out to the tip of her tongue, one so obvious she wondered why it had taken as long as it had to get there. On her next exhalation, the question emerged from her lips. "Why didn't Bennie ask Hanuman, and not me, to teach him how to fight?"

Jessabelle had seen the way Hanuman took down Uncle Trix and Wrench. Immense physical power coursed through that body of his. Next to him, she felt like a misty rain falling adjacent to a hurricane. They each had capacity—him enough to power a city, her a toaster. "Hanuman is much stronger than me," she added.

"And you're much stronger than Bennie. He got rid of his Troubles, didn't he?"

"Yeah, but he's also in the hospital right now. If Hanuman had taught him how to fight that might not be the case."

"Who can say? Life is perfect in ways we don't always see."

Jessabelle heard Bennie's voice. "My guru's throwing me a party," he was saying, "and I want to be with my friends."

A male voice, probably Bennie's doctor, said, "Before we can let you go, I have to be sure you're okay to go. Your friends will understand."

"I don't want to miss the party. I can leave with my mom and dad when they get here."

"You whacked your head pretty good."

"It was just a little bump. Now can I go when my mom and dad get here?"

"Is it your birthday?"

"No."

"When's your birthday?"

"May eleventh."

"Yes, and what's your phone number?"

Bennie recited a series of seven numbers.

"If it's not your birthday, then why is your guru throwing you a party?"

"Because I saved her life." Pause. "I'm serious. One day I saw two thugs harassing her. Strength I never knew I had suddenly rose up inside. I ran fast as I could, tripped over a branch, and fell on a rock. It stabbed my side. It really hurt.

Wanna see the bruise?"

"Yes."

When Lalli and Jessabelle entered, Bennie was sitting up in bed with a fat pillow behind his back. He held his hospital gown high, proudly displaying the bruise at the side of his stomach while the doctor examined it.

"Do you want to hear something else?" Bennie said. "Right in front of all these people, my guru said, with great strength that I saved her life." Bennie lit up the room with a thousand-watt smile when he saw Lalli. "You're here!"

Jessabelle parked the crate in the middle of the room. Bennie gave her a questioning look. "Who are—" He glanced down at her tennis shoes. "Oh, it's you. Who are you supposed to be today?"

"Myself."

Bennie laughed as if she'd just told him a joke. Lalli told Bennie, "We brought something for you."

"For me?"

Jessabelle urged off the crate's lid. Balloons streamed out. Jessabelle caught a few and tied their strings to the silver rail of Bennie's bed.

"Wait until my mom and dad see."

"Wait until your mom and dad see what?" came a man's voice from the door.

"The balloons, Dad and Mom. Look at all the balloons!"

Jessabelle turned, her eyes landing on Bennie's mom and dad. Something about them hit her. Mom, Pops.

Everything went quiet except the sound of Jessabelle's heart. Its beat drummed through her ears. Blood rushed through her temples. *Mom? Pops?*

It could not be them. How could it be? How long had Jessabelle searched for Mom and Pops? Two years. And now Mom and Pops were here. Impossible.

Bennie's mom stepped into the room. "Looks like Bennie's

party has moved here." Bennie's mom greeted Lalli; his dad did the same. Lalli called them Lakshmi and Dharma.

Mom's voice, the trilling sound of it. Jessabelle hadn't heard it in a long time, but it was so familiar. And the way she moved, lighter and leaner now. Streaks of dyed blonde hair dipped around her face. Doing hard time must have been soft on her. And Pops. She'd never realized how short he was.

No. It couldn't be Mom and Pops. What would they be doing here with names like Lakshmi and Dharma, and Bennie calling them Mom and Dad?

"I have somebody I want you to meet," Lalli said to them.

Bennie's mom and dad approached Jessabelle. "Yes," Bennie's mom said. "Who are you?"

"Just something the cat brought in," Lalli said. She took a moment to laugh at her own joke.

"Yes, and what is her name?"

"I'll let her tell you," Lalli said.

Bennie's mom extended a hand. Jessabelle reached out to shake that hand, noticing how her own hand trembled. Bennie's mom held Jessabelle's hand as if she didn't want to let go. Bennie's mom studied Jessabelle's fingers, wrist, and arm as if it were her drawing assignment. Soon she held both of Jessabelle's hands in her own. "Have we met?"

Jessabelle tried to say, I'm Jessabelle, but her mouth and throat were so dry, she couldn't get her tongue working. It came out all wrong, more like a long "I" sound.

Startled, Bennie's mom passed her eyes up to Jessabelle's face. "You look like my long-lost daughter."

Can't you see I am? she wanted to say, but she couldn't talk. Jessabelle's knees turned to dough.

Bennie's mom let go of Jessabelle's hand and walked over to the side of Bennie's bed, holding her tin of cookies. She kissed Bennie on the forehead.

Jessabelle sucked in a breath of air, steadying herself, and moved to the edge of Bennie's hospital bed.

"We brought," Bennie's mom said, but her voice shook, and so did the tin she held in her hand. It rattled with whatever was inside. The tin slipped from her grasp and clattered to the floor. She came out from the side of the bed, rushed to Jessabelle, and gripped Jessabelle's shoulder. "You are her," she said.

"I am," Jessabelle said, and the two embraced.

"Is it really you?" Pops said.

"It's me," Jessabelle said, and he threw his arms around her. In his arms, her whole body went soft.

In their eight-year absence, Jessabelle had hoped and dreamed about seeing Mom and Pops, but never thought it could really happen. She often believed Mom and Pops were gone for good.

"When I came here to see one of my children," Mom exclaimed, "I never dreamed there'd be two."

"Life is abundant," Pops said.

"Time out," Bennie said forming a T with his hands. "Jessabelle? I thought your name was Isa?"

"It was, and now it's Jessabelle."

"Isa is really Jessabelle? What the heck is going on here?"

"This is your sister," Pops said, "Jessabelle."

"C'mon. First, you're Ganesh. Then you're Isa. And now you're Jessabelle? Are you sure there's not something behind Jessabelle?"

"There is, and it's called the Self."

"We tried to find you," Mom said.

"I tried to find you too."

"We called the Cozies, and went to their house. Those awful people told us you ran away. We trailed you to Creativo."

"So glad you got in there," Pops interjected, smiling.

His smile faded when Mom said, "Then we found out you dropped out. We traced you to the Wally's in Rolling Rivers, Washington, only to find out you quit, and then nothing. No person and no agency could tell us anything about you. Where have you been hiding?"

"With Uncle Trix," Jessabelle said.

"You've been with your uncle?"

Jessabelle nodded.

"That explains everything."

Mom proceeded to tell Jessabelle the story of how she was able to keep Bennie in prison with her. When he turned one, some people came to give Lalli's teachings. She started to meditate with Bennie on her lap and it transformed her whole life. When she was released from prison, she came to Lalliville, asked Lalli for a new name. She identified with that name more and more, became totally clean, started a legitimate profession. "Felt like one miracle after another, and just when I thought I couldn't hold anymore, you're here."

"It's so good to see you again, Mom and Pops," Jessabelle said.

"We've got new names."

"I just heard. Lakshmi and Dharma. Those spiritual names?"

"Our legal ones now. But you can still call us Mom and Pops."

Jessabelle swallowed, loss and resentment washed away, melted into the aura of love that always pervaded the atmosphere around Lalli. The removal of Mom and Pops from her life and subsequent placement with the Cozies had embittered her for so long, she'd forgotten what it was like not to carry that bitterness, until now.

"I think I like this face better than Isa's," Bennie said. "You're kind of pretty."

Everybody laughed.

Chapter 39

Jessabelle sat in Pierre's office, gazing out the window, steadying her eyes on the morning sun, its blaze surging on the horizon. The sun was so bright, Pierre's news so dark. "The committee has decided to give you three days to finish the project in the shed. And then you must leave."

The chance to complete what she and Bennie had started made her happy, but the words "You must leave" coalesced into an invisible twelve-inch butcher knife driven straight through her chest and heart, slicing out the other side of her body. She actually jerked back, as if she'd been hit by something.

She'd found paradise and was now getting thrown out for bad behavior. She begged and pleaded with Pierre, saying, "Please let me stay longer. I'll clean another moldy shed or scrub dirty toilets. Anything!"

"I'm sorry," he said, shaking his head. "I really am."

She left Pierre's office and rushed around, until she found Lalli exiting her house, a mala in hand. Jessabelle begged Lalli, "Please talk them into letting me stay longer, at least until summer's end."

"I don't run Lalliville," Lalli said. "I give teachings."

"But everybody loves you. Surely you have some sway over them."

"Why do you want to stay?"

"Because I love it here."

"You can always apply again," Lalli said. "Come back after you finish art college."

Jessabelle's opportunity to finish art college had come by way of Mom and Pops. As it turned out, in the time since they'd gotten out of prison, Mom and Pops had launched and grown a successful online booking business for hotels, airlines, and cruise ships. When she'd told them she'd been kicked out of art college for not paying her bill, Pops told her they'd bankroll the completion of her formal art education.

"I can come back to Lalliville?" she asked Lalli.

"Yes, of course."

Until that moment Jessabelle had operated under the mistaken impression that returning to art college precluded her from coming back to Lalliville. The possibility of having both, finishing her education and one day spending more time in Lalliville, lifted her spirits. Still, the thought of being away from Lalli while she finished art college made her sad.

As if Lalli could read Jessabelle's thought and feeling, she said, "Makes no difference whether you're here or there." She took hold of Jessabelle's hand. "We are not separate." Tears streamed down Jessabelle's face. "Walk with me." Lalli tugged her by the hand. "When you come again," Lalli said, as they moved along Devotion, "stay a while, if you'd like. Maybe for a year or two."

Jessabelle nodded.

"I'd like your help in developing the Lalliville theater program to dramatize teaching stories."

Jessabelle sniffled. "Really?"

"With the addition of your skills," Lalli elaborated, "our characters will be vivid, ones that will live on in the memory."

"Have no fear," Jessabelle promised through tears, "if it's vivid characters you want, it's vivid characters you'll get."

Jessabelle was still crying when she and Lalli parted ways in front of the administration building, where Lalli said she was going for a meeting. Lalli hugged her. Remembering that she and Lalli were one, Jessabelle smiled. The smile was in her heart, really, with rays so bright, it lit up her face.

In the time ahead, it seemed this smile wanted to stay, make its home within her, be there no matter what.

On the day Jessabelle left Lalliville, she packed her bags, then carried them down Strength and out onto Liberation. Heading toward the step van, she set her bags outside the education building and went toward the door.

Inside, she left her shoes in the shoeroom and entered the multipurpose room. She walked up to Lalli's chair and kneeled before it. Then she bowed in reverence to love and gratitude, Lalleshwari and Shiva, and the great power in the moon and teardrops.

At the step van, Bennie waited along with Vishva, Johann, and Chet, who all came to say goodbye. Jessabelle set her bags inside the step van, then hugged Vishva, who said, "Remember, your satisfaction lies within."

Hearing it, Johann said, "Remember, for next year's talent show, you promised Chet and me help with our costumes."

Chet remained quiet. After he and Jessabelle embraced, she glanced around for Doc, but didn't see him.

Moments later, she watched the front gate of Lalliville disappear in the step van's rearview mirror. She was leaving without the statue. But what she was driving away with seemed so much greater than what she'd come for. For one, she had her brother with her, and they were headed to Mom and Pops' house.

The fact she'd visited Lalliville made her feel as if she'd achieved something. She knew it may not seem like an accomplishment to some. With 209 people residing in Lalliville, along with visitors who came and went, she obviously wasn't the only one to make the journey to Awakening. Yet she now considered it to be one of her greatest accomplishments.

She and Uncle Trix had turned off Route 54 and traveled down an ordinary road to get to Lalliville. Yet, in arriving at this place, she felt as if she'd traveled through miles and miles of deep inner space. In that great expanse, sublime understanding had opened before her, and she'd found her own highest ambition: to become one with consciousness. She'd taken one step closer to the truth, discovered her own Self, and in making this discovery, become more of herself. And who was herself? Not Jessabelle. Not a makeup effects artist, but love, consciousness.

Just saying those words to herself—love, consciousness—put a smile on her face.

When she and Bennie arrived home, she couldn't help but smile. Their house was on the same lake as Doc's. Mom gave Jessabelle a second-story room in the back, from where she internalized the reflection of the moon on the lake in the evenings before she went to bed. In the mornings she ate breakfast with her family.

She'd been accepted back into art college with special expedited enrollment. To bide her time until school started, she was working on some effects she'd promised Bennie. Come Halloween, he wanted the ability to transform himself into the Free & Blissful Yogi. Two feet shorter and eighty pounds lighter, Bennie wouldn't make a believable Free & Blissful Yogi, but no doubt he'd have fun telling everybody he was.

Jessabelle completed step one of her Bennie project, making a mold of Bennie's face and head. About the time she made this terracotta duplicate, Doc's parents announced they planned on throwing a Fourth of July party, inviting Jessabelle's family. Jessabelle wanted to attend, but after all that had happened between her and Doc, decided against it. Bennie, Mom, and Pops went while she stayed home, happily working on the second step in the creation of Bennie's Halloween costume.

In a small upstairs guestroom, she had set the copy of Bennie's head on her rotating sculpture stand, atop a three-door bedside table with silver leaf finish. Jessabelle had dragged the table into the center of the room and covered it in plastic, along with the rest of the fancy furniture and carpet. The speakers of a cranked-up CD player blasted a recording of Om Namo Bhagavate Shivanandaya, with Lalli and a group of musicians singing, something Jessabelle had picked up in the bookstore before she left Lalliville.

Jessabelle covered the face of Bennie's double with lumps of red-orange clay. Using a portrait photo of the Free & Blissful Yogi for reference, she shaped those lumps into the Free & Blissful Yogi's mouth, nose, cheeks, eyelids, brow—Bennie's new features.

Drawing on her knowledge of facial anatomy, combined with her design intuition and what she observed in the photo, she carved wrinkles on the forehead, lines around the eyes, and grooves near the nose and mouth. With sculpting tool in hand, a sharp-pointed chisel, she dappled the sculpture with characteristics of human skin, bringing it to life, detail by detail, forming the clay into an image of the face it would ultimately become, as worn by Bennie.

When she finished etching lines in the face, Jessabelle paused from her work, turning the sculpture on its stand, one way and then the other, ensuring symmetry on both sides of the face. A slow, cautious creature movement drifting through the door caught her attention. What she saw when she glanced up was so unexpected, she almost screamed. She moved her hands to rub her eyes, and then remembered the clay sullying her fingers.

Was it a ghost? The blue jeans and short-sleeved orange cotton T-shirt seemed about as real as clothes could get.

Doc.

Her heart fluttered. She turned the music down, leaving a dab of clay on the volume control. "What're you doing here?"

"Inviting you to the party."

Would a ghost say something like that? "Inviting me to the party?" she repeated, just to make sure she'd heard correctly. She really hoped this wasn't her eyes and ears playing tricks.

"Yeah," Doc said. "I noticed you weren't there. Do you want to come with me?"

"When?"

"Now."

The nerve he had, popping up like this, thinking she'd drop everything to run next door to the party. She wanted to tell him no, it was too short notice. She didn't have enough time to prepare. She had other big, more important plans, like creating the Free & Blissful Yogi. Then he looked at her with those eyes of his, like pools of sunlight that made her want to dive inside him, and she said, "I'd love to."

"Fuzz has gotten big. You may not even recognize him anymore."

"I can't wait to see him." She wondered if Doc had forgiven her. That thought pumped nervous energy into her system. She didn't want to hope for too much out of fear she could be wrong. "I can't leave until I finish what I'm doing," she said.

"Of course."

"Shall I just meet you over there?"

"I'll wait," he said. "I can help while I do."

Jessabelle put Doc to work making whisker follicles. While he pricked holes along the jawline, using the coarser stylus in a set of sewing needles, Jessabelle added pores, using the finer needles.

"How did you get in here, anyway?"

"I knocked, but there was no answer. I heard the music."

"So you broke in, eh?"

"You broke into my house, right?" He said it with a smile. "Now we're even."

"Touché."

When they finished the pores and hair follicles, Jessabelle turned the sculpture stand this way and that. She looked at the Free & Blissful Yogi's face from all angles, adding a few more pores here, or another line there. When she was satisfied it was a finished sculpture, a sculpture from which she'd make a mold, a mold she'd use to cast a foam latex face, a face ready to be tinted, painted, and glued over Bennie's own face, she said, "Okay." Then she cleaned up, changed into a turquoise sundress, and met Doc downstairs. At the door, his palm met hers. He laced his fingers through hers and pulled her out the door. "We can go through the woods. It'll give us a chance to talk before we get to the party."

On their way through the woods, Doc said, "I have a present for you."

"A present for me? The last time I saw you, you hated me."

"I didn't hate you."

"Could have fooled me," she said. "You never came to say

goodbye."

"I was confused."

He halted beside a large pine. Facing her, he reached into his pocket, producing a small box that he passed to her. The edges of her eyes grew warm; tears stung, forming in their corners. With the back of her index finger, she wiped the tears.

Sudden alarm spread over his face. "Are you okay?"

She nodded and looked down at the small box in her hand.

"Go ahead. Open it."

She did, and stared at what was inside—a japa necklace.

"I hope you like it. It's from our Shiva."

She slipped the japa beads around her neck. "I love it," she murmured. She could no longer contain the tears. They poured out her eyes. But it didn't matter; she wore no makeup to mess up.

He admitted it was Vishva's idea. Jessabelle recalled the vow she had made in Vishva's presence. In situations that tempted her to be dishonest, Jessabelle would remember Shiva, and that satisfaction lies within.

Jessabelle dabbed at her eyes with the sleeve of her shirt. "The last time I saw you, you didn't want to talk to me. What's different?"

"Me. I used to think me and people who broke the law were two different entities. Now I know that's not true, because I feel really close to you. I can't stop thinking about you no matter how hard I try. Can you forgive me for being so stubborn?

She nodded, blubbering through tears, "I already have."

"I can see that someone would only go to the lengths you have gone to hide your true self out of great pain. I admit that I admire your courage and ingenuity in overcoming your abusive background through creativity."

A man like Doc, honest and clean, was here telling her he admired her, and she wasn't wearing a mask or 3-D prostethic makeup. It was her he appreciated, not Isa Newton or some other figment of her.

"I'm awed by your talent and want to work with you when you get out of art school. I have ideas to help kids and animals in need of prosthetics, but I need your inventiveness and design skills to accomplish them. What do you say?"

"Yes, Yes, and Yes!"

He took her in his arms, gently squeezed her against his chest. "I love you, Jessabelle." He gazed deeply into her eyes, and she into his, as if they could see to the core of each other.

"I love you too."

He kissed her, and she kissed him from the bottom of her soul.

After a time, they started walking again. The outline of his house came into focus. She remembered the first time she'd come to the mansion-in-the-round, how intimidating it had looked. How it had changed. How she had changed. She'd left this place as a thief and intruder, and was returning as an invited guest. She was no longer afraid.

For so long, she'd worried about people knowing who she really was. Now everybody knew who she really was, and it was okay. Jessabelle realized the dream had come to pass—the nakedness, the judges. It was not a punishment but an end to her negative behavior, a chance to start again. Lalliville had brought her life as a thief and a liar to an end, and given her this new beginning.

Jessabelle saw dark shapes moving slowly near the edge of the forest, as if those inky outlines were searching for something. Squinting for a better look, she thought they were sheep. About the time she opened her mouth to say, "I didn't know your family owned sheep," she saw the swish of a tail.

Not a short, wooly tail, but a long, thin tail. A head went up, ears stood at attention; a pig's snout sniffed the air.

At the edge of the clearing near Doc's house, Jessabelle counted seven boar in all. "You see," she whispered.

"Wow!" he whispered back. As Doc and Jessabelle observed the animals, a small one moved, a little shy, a little nervous, drawing near to them. It stopped, gazing at them through small eyes. "I was born here," Doc said in a hushed tone, "and never saw any wild boars. Seeing them now feels like a privilege."

Privilege seemed a good word, a symbol of her existence, the life she was charmed with. Jessabelle felt so lucky, lucky to see the boars, lucky all around. She had everything she needed. She lived in a nice house with a good family. She had a good friend beside her, seven more before her. In the fall she was going back to art college and right at this moment, a feast awaited her. Gourmet veggie burgers topped with cheese and black beans, she'd heard, along with potato salad, a vegetable kabob, corn on the cob, and chocolate layer cake for dessert. She didn't have a pink Corvette or a large screen TV, but she'd never wanted either of those things.

She felt like the luckiest woman on Earth. Lucky to have met Doc. Lucky to have found Mom and Pops and Bennie. Lucky to have slipped out of Uncle Trix's iron grip.

Gratitude filled Jessabelle, for all the things she had received from her visit to Lalliville, including the thing she probably needed the most, which was a new set of eyes. This gift had shifted her consciousness to a whole new level of awareness, changing her vision of the world. She'd come to see Shiva's love shining from under the surface of so many shapes. She felt it as humanity in the moon, grandeur in trees, beauty in flowers, and love in people. She perceived its essence in her own form.

This love was wisdom. It was power moving like one big

current under the surface of the world. Finding it made the whole world come alive. From the depth of her gratitude for this new life came the words, "Thank you," whispered on the air to the people she met in Lalliville. For it was through Lalli and the others that Jessabelle came to experience Shiva's love...to be aware of it in all things.

Fingering her japa necklace, silently, joyfully repeating Jaya Shiva Om, she wrapped her free arm around Doc's waist and drew him forward into their future. "Let's go."